FEW SLEPT THAT NIGHT—either on the island or in Fort Jefferson—and the full moon gave the illusion that it was not truly night. The shadows of patrolling sentries oozed across the mulled dust; sick men moaned, Joe Hunter raved in delirium, children whispered in dreams. Anne sat under the canvas of their lean-to with Annilea pressed to her chest and Rabbie's head in her lap; the moon-white faces of Johnny and Isaac lay beside her. She tried to picture the Indian attack, and what she would do.

Shoot them, Annie? Shoot the children? Jamie and Marybett, and Andrew? A pistol to your own head would be easy compared to that. How could you kill them if any chance remained of their living? Hadn't Esther survived capture? But Meshach had wanted her, loved her. The Chicasaw women love torture. What if I don't kill them and have to sit bound, watching them be burned bit by bit? Hear them screaming for death when I can't help them?

Dizziness spun her head again. She moaned aloud and rocked Annilea. This time she could not hesitate. She had to decide so she would be ready. Sweat rolled down her sides. Play it through, Annie, imagine every detail, every feeling you'll have. By the time the moon rolled to the peak of the sky, she knew she would not kill them. She would send them out on the north side to tumble into the ravine. Maybe they could hide, build a raft . . . She laid Rabbie's head next to Bird's, snuggled Annilea close to Andrew, then paced the enclosure until the sky stole the light from the moon.

Up from Mayfield Creek warriors burst with howls and shots . . .

God's Country

Martha Barron Barrett

BANTAM BOOKS

TORONTO · NEW YORK · LONDON · SYDNEY · AUCKLAND

GOD'S COUNTRY
A Bantam Book / February 1987

ISBN 0-553-26278-5

Published simultaneously in the United States and Canada

Bantam Books are published by Bantam Books, Inc. Its trademark,
consisting of the words "Bantam Books" and the portrayal of a
rooster, is Registered in U.S. Patent and Trademark Office and in
other countries. Marca Registrada. Bantam Books, Inc., 666 Fifth
Avenue, New York, New York 10103.

PRINTED IN THE UNITED STATES OF AMERICA

O   0 9 8 7 6 5 4 3 2 1

*Dedicated with Love and Respect
To the memory of my parents:
Margaret Smith Barron
Robert Chapin Barron*

Author's Note

I was about fifteen when I discovered a thin, tattered booklet titled *Annals of the Robert Aiken Family*. In no hurry to proceed with my assigned task of cleaning the bookcase, I flipped the dusty pages, then stopped. *An Interesting Narrative by Anne MacMeans Jamison*. Intrigued by the price (three cents per copy) and the place and date (Pittsburgh, July 23, 1824), I read on: "This is to inform all who are desirous to know what hath befallen me, and my family, and the causes leading thereto as briefly as I can. Sometime in the month of May in the year 1778 . . ."

The story was brief—thirty-five hundred words—and spell-binding. Hurriedly I scanned the genealogy section: Mac-Means—Aiken—Smith—Barron. Unbelievable! This woman, this hero of the Revolutionary War, was my own great-great-great-great-grandmother.

Thirty years later, I searched for a way to share the story of this founding mother of America. How did a Scot-Irish woman of the mid-1700s live, think, and love? I traveled to southwestern Scotland and Killyleagh, Northern Ireland; took the subway from my home to the libraries of Philadelphia; wandered the countryside of Octoraro Creek; and crossed—for probably the hundredth time—the Allegheny Mountains to Pittsburgh, where I had spent my childhood. Fort Pitt, more libraries, explorations up and down the Allegheny River, the Monongahela, the Youghiogheny, and finally by canoe down the Ohio and the Mississippi.

On July 3, 1979, almost two hundred years to the day after my long-ago grandmother arrived with George Rogers Clark to build Fort Jefferson at the confluence of the two great rivers, my son and I paddled past those iron red bluffs.

God's Country is a novel with Anne MacMeans as a fictional character. However, what happens to her on the rivers is true—every detail of her narrative checks with historical records—and entries described herein as writings in her *Commonplace Book* are her own words. But lest her descendants rail that she might not have been an indentured servant,

vii

that she might never have been tempted by lust, that
. . . that . . . that . . . let me state that I have exercised a
novelist's prerogative and given her a life that might have
been.

  God's Country is both the truth and the imagined truth of a
courageous woman's story.

Martha Barron Barrett
Portsmouth, N.H.
March 1986

The land was ours before we were the land's.
She was our land more than a hundred years
Before we were her people. She was ours
In Massachusetts, in Virginia,
But we were England's, still colonials,
Possessing what we still were unpossessed by,
Possessed by what we now no more possessed.
Something we were withholding made us weak
Until we found out that it was ourselves
We were withholding from our land of living,
And forthwith found salvation in surrender.
Such as we were we gave ourselves outright
(The deed of gift was many deeds of war)
To the land vaguely realizing westward,
But still unstoried, artless, unenchanced,
Such as she was, as she would become.

Robert Frost, *The Gift Outright*

Denture Lass

Eastern Pennsylvania, 1752–59

Chapter One

For the six weeks she was at sea, Anne Aiken MacKnight had imagined sailing into the port of Philadelphia with what folks called "the free winds of America" billowing the great canvas squares of the brig *Eagle Wing*, snapping her pennants and making her taut rigging sing. The dock and street would be full of people cheering the brave adventurers of the Atlantic. She told herself, Just as you come down the gang-away board, Annie, the cannon of the city will roar and the pipers will skirl their pipes and the minister will ask you home for salmon and a night's sleep in his bonnie house.

Her daydream ended, in silent, muddy New Castle on the Delaware River. Some passengers, hugged and kissed by waiting kin, rattled away in flatbed wagons; the English convicts, chains swaying, disappeared south to a town called Baltimore; Anne and the other bonded Scot-Irish found themselves crammed into a small boat and rowed upriver. Bewildered, Anne huddled in the bow. Surely America held better than this.

At midnight Philadelphia proclaimed itself in shouts from a darkened shore, blocks of grey shrouded with drizzle, a wharf, a flight of steps, a mucky street. A narrow prison yard stretched down the middle of the road; a brick courthouse with a bell tower sat at one end, stocks and pillory at the other. When the log gate of the yard shut behind the milling immigrants, Anne, clutching her kettle, spied straw gleaming crisp and dry from under a canvas canopy. Grabbing an armful of the best, she nested like a small mouse against the wall.

The loud toll of the bell woke her, and before she had collected her senses, she became part of the herd shuffling to the public wharf. The auctioneer cried out, "Bonds servants for sale!" A crowd gathered, and one by one the folk from Ulster disappeared down the streets and behind the doors of Philadelphia. When Anne's turn came, a woman shouted, "What are you selling—fleas?"

The people laughed and did not bid. Anne rocked with shame. She wanted to cry out, "Don't see me! Don't see me!" as she had in childhood games, but there was no hiding from

3

eyes squinting at her as though she were a runty beast at market in Downpatrick. When all the others had been sold, the auctioneer tried again, but the same rough voice cried out, "Shame on you, mister. That one couldn't lift a feather duster."

Back in the prison yard, Anne hunkered alone inside the peeled log fence and dug her nails into the wood as rain and tears ran down her cheeks. "They just don't know. They don't know who I am. That my father was Bartholomew Black MacKnight, ruling elder of Killyleagh kirk and subsheriff of County Down. That my mother was an Aiken from Galloway across the Irish Sea in Scotland. That her mother was a Watt, that—"

"What are thee saying, child?"

A woman held out a bowl of fish stew, and Anne took it in both hands. White fingers reached out to touch her hair. "The raindrops have given thee a crown of red diamonds, child."

Anne drew back her head and looked down her freckled cheeks. "It's Anne Aiken MacKnight you be addressing, and I'm no child but a woman of near thirteen." She raised her thin shoulders. "And I dinna care for your pity. Those folks on the dock were saps. Tomorrow someone will come and see I'm a lass of wit and gumption." She spooned the stew down her throat. "But I do thank you for the broth."

"Are there hard times in Ireland?"

Anne looked over the rim of the bowl. "Aye. The Laird Hamilton drove us off our land. He doubled the rent and because of the drought my pappie could not pay. He forced us onto the road with all the other drifting folk."

The woman watched her eat, then asked, "Had thee no friends?"

"Ooo aye, but my pappie dragged us over the length and breadth of Ulster, showing off our rags and skinny arms and saying that's what came of being ruled by an English king."

"Where did you sleep?"

"In ditches."

"What did you eat?"

"My minnie had her jug. I stole from the fields."

"Didn't you get caught?"

"Aye. But I lay with them and they let me go." The woman's eyes bugged. Anne licked her bowl. "Of course, there was an end to it all."

"What happened?"

Anne took the time to wipe her face with the frayed hem of her grease-green dress, then settled on her haunches. "One morning I was coming back with an apronful of almost-ripe

4

potatoes and when I got to the lip of the ditch I saw a man standing over my mother. The shape of him—rather like the far end of a fiddle—began to look familiar, and I saw it was the Reverend Bruce of Killyleagh. I rushed down thinking the troubles were over and we could go home—it had been two years now. But he said no, it was bad news he brought. The night before, my pappie had gotten extra loud—he was a booming big man, shouting treason and all—and when he left the public house, someone laid a stave alongside his head. He'd bled to death in the street with nobody daring to help him."

"Poor thing! What did thee do?"

"I remember rolling on the earth, and filling my mouth with it, wailing like a banshee. By then folks were up moving about and the sun was a round of pale cheese above the fog. I looked in my minnie's watery face and said very clear, 'I'm going to America.' I knew the brig *Eagle Wing* was loading up in Belfast Harbor."

"Was your mother sold off with the others this morning?" the woman asked.

"No, she dinna come. She said the Irish Sea had been her undoing and the ocean would surely get me, being half Aiken like I am. I told her it wouldn't and I was setting my sights on a husband with four hundred acres of good, deep land. The Reverend Bruce butted in snorting, 'Fairy tales! America's a howling wilderness lippin' full of wolves.' 'Put your own nose back on your own face where it belongs,' I snipped, and Minnie laughed. She gave me the kettleful of potatoes I'd dug, and on the top she tucked in Grannie Watt's wedding shoes that she'd never worn. See?" Anne held up a pair of stiff leather shoes. "I've not had them on, either. They pinch. Maybe on my wedding day."

"You're truly alone, child? You left your mother?"

"Ooo aye, it was sad. All about us men and women were climbing out on the road, babes in their arms, bundles on their shoulders. I wanted to take Hugh, my brother of eight with me, but Minnie wouldn't let him go. He'd always been her pet, you see. Sickly he was. So my minnie and I sat rocking and keening, holding each other. She wrapped her own long, gray plaiden about me, and the sun sucked the dew from it, making white steam. I picked up the kettle and climbed up out of the ditch to the Belfast Road. My Minnie was singing, 'Teribus y teri odin, sons of heros slain at Fodden . . .'"

The woman shook her head in wonder. "You have a marvelous gift for tale-telling, child. Then what did you do?"

"I'd listened sharp to the talk in the ditches and I knew just how getting to America was done. You presented yourself to a ship captain and he took you over the ocean. Once landed some kind soul would take a liking to you and pay the captain your passage money. You'd live with them for a while doing mending or some such, and then they'd give you new clothes and a list to choose a husband from. I found the captain, all right, but all he did was laugh, saying no one would ever buy a serving lass as scarecrow as me. He said when he sailed it would be with a ship full of fine, fat folk who'd bring a fair price in Philadelphia."

"So what did you do?"

"Every morning I'd present myself and he'd throw me off. At night I'd come back to sleep among the packing crates and steal my breakfast from the galley. Finally he made ready to sail. I courtsied extra low that morning. 'Bonnie day to you, sir,' I said. 'Fair wind for America.' He looked at me, shook his head and ordered the mate to stuff me in the hold. And that's how I came to America." Anne rose and gave the women a pert little nod. "Well, missus, will you be taking me home now?"

The woman paled and was moving toward the gate before she had fully gained her feet. "No, oh, no. You're confused, child. It's my Christian duty to come to the yard with food. But—"

Anne lowered her head and advanced on the woman. "You mean I wasted my breath on you? Used up my strength spinning my tale for gossip's sake?" The woman stammered; Anne spun on her heel saying, "I have no need for the likes of you."

At midday the sky lightened and Anne climbed to the top of the fence. Carts laden with bales of tobacco and skins, barrels of flour and whale oil, rumcasks, cordwood, black-skinned people, and kegs of molasses rumbled by. Gentry in chairs rode down the long, tree-lined drive to the big house of the Penns across the road, and Anne wondered if that was the best Americans could do by way of a castle. The clouds lowered, rain fell; she crawled under the canvas and sat all day besieged by horse flies, pigs who rooted under the fence, stones lobbed in by boys in the street, and men who peered between the palings. At twilight a shipload of men, women, and children barely alive from four months at sea straggled into the yard and sank groaning onto the straw.

At nine in the morning the auction bell rang again, but only a few people gathered. "No sense," one passerby said, "all there is today is one flea and a parcel of scarecrows." A merchant wanted a tutor, but he chose a boy instead of Anne— although she screamed out that she could both read and write Latin and do sums in her head quicker than he could say them. Soon even the idlers had shivered off to the taverns; the auctioneer slouched, tapping his stick against his toe. As though on cue, a carriage approached, a gentleman in broadcloth climbed down, dickered, and bought the lot, Anne included.

When packhorses had been loaded with supplies and the assorted sixteen souls lined up, a young man walked from one to the other, looping a thick rope around their necks. Anne ducked, kicked, and ran, but the man in broadcloth caught her and carried her screaming back to the line. "Truss this one up good, John," he said to the youth. "She's wild Irish for sure."

The driver cracked his whip and they were off, slogging down Chestnut Street while English Philadelphians shook their heads. "More Ulstermen for the frontier, God help the Indians." "I say God help anyone who gets in the way of those savage Irish." "I tell thee, they'll overrun the Commonwealth if they keep coming." "Agreed. If we don't stop the landing of them, some fine day they'll have us all singing psalms and damning the king."

A smith stopped pumping his bellows to call, "You expect to sell that crowbait to the Deutschmen, boy? They'll die on you before you get them across the Schuylkill."

The young driver laughed and patted the kegs on one packhorse. "I expect this whiskey will carry them farther than that."

"How far?"

"Octoraro. Been nobody out there selling since last spring. If they don't want them, I'll go north to the Dutch in Hickory Town."

"Well, at harvest time farmers'll buy anybody—after they bargin you to death. I don't know who squeezes a penny more, a Scot or a Deutsche. How come they look so poorly?"

"Four months at sea."

"Christ, soul driver, do you really expect them to last fifty miles?"

The driver nodded, then shouted at his charges, who hunkered, resting in the road. On legs still unaccustomed to land, they staggered on, while chambermaids in brick houses laughed out of second-story windows, and children threw

7

rotten apples from the orchards. When anyone fell, the whole line jerked to a stop, and the pox-faced youth cracked his whip and cursed, but when a small girl slipped from her mother's arms and lay in the mire, the driver cheerily swung the girl through the air, chucking her under the chin as he tied her on the sheepskin that covered the kegs. Anne watched with narrowed eyes; in the past two years she had come to read men well. Maybe he had to swagger to keep the convicts from bolting, maybe underneath he was pure mush.

A mile or so later when she asked for whisky to relieve the cramping in her stomach, he snarled, "No, no whisky. I can't understand a word you say."

She doubled her arms against her middle and cold sweat wet her brow. Maybe there's something wrong with me inside. I must be past the age for beginning my monthlies. Maybe what I did lying with men was a sin and God is punishing me with terrible cramps. But He made men and women this way, he must have known what would happen.

Town houses gave way to woods. Anne heard talk of a river ahead. Maybe the driver would take off the rope for the crossing; her neck was already raw. Fifty miles, the smitty had said—that must be clear across America. She wondered if she'd know a howlin' wilderness when she saw one. And what about wolves?

At the crossing the rope did come off, and the whiskey jug was passed from mouth to mouth. It almost jarred her eyeballs out of her head, but it soothed her stomach and kept her from worrying overmuch about the flat-bottomed ferry as it spun across the wide, black Schuylkill River.

On the other side a deadly thick silence closed about them. They waded Cobs Creek, the cold water circling their waists; then a tangled primal forest squeezed close like a living hand. The big girl in front of Anne began to bob and sway, muttering German rhymes.

Anne clamped her jaw to hold her terror in check. Had she died and gone to hell? The smitty had called the youth a "soul driver," and around the next bend could be fire and brimstone, snakes and thieves and adulterous women writhing in a heap. Thunder rolled like footsteps across the sky. "Satan's coming!" she screamed. She tugged on the rope. "Pappie! Help me, help me! Pappie!"

The whip cracked. "Keep walking! Stay in line. I'll beat you bloody if you stop!"

On one side the forest fell away. Dead trees rose from sullen pools; the crooked arms and gnarled fingers clutched at the gray, decaying belly of the sky. Huge, stiff black birds with yellow talons, hunched wings, and naked heads sat on their limbs. *"Hechs!"* the German girl cried, and the creatures' wings came unhinged like prehistoric hands, blackness and crackling feathers filled the air. The people staggered forward, arms over their heads. The bony hands of the woman behind Anne clutched her shoulders. Lurching forward, Anne clasped the round, firm flesh of the German girl. Each supporting the other, they stumbled on through the blinding rain.

Forty miles away, in Octoraro, seventeen-year-old Jim Glenn squeezed his prancing filly between his knees and called, "Hey, Luke! Come see what my pappie gave me for my birthday. I've named her Bonnie."

Luke's little sister squirted out through a rack of half-dried deer skins that hung beside the ragged cabin. "Lookee, Jimmie!" she squealed, holding up a tiny bobcat. The half-broken filly reared; Jim slid off her rump and grabbed for her bridle. Luke, his face squashed like it had been caught between two logs, scowled in envy at Jim, then whirled on his sister. "Get that varmit out of here, you muttonhead!"

She backed away, slipped on a mound of fresh cow dung, and went down in a tangle of skirts and bobcat. Luke grabbed the kitten and held it high by the scruff of its neck. "He's got one broken leg, might as well have two."

The heel of Jim's hand hit Luke's arm. "Stow it, Luke." He was startled that his voice sounded as deep as his father's. Luke dropped the cat and curled his dangling hands into fists. Jim backed toward his horse, then hesitated. He knew he couldn't beat Luke, but seventeen was too old to run away. This time his voice squeaked, but he got the words out. "Wait till I tie the filly, Luke."

Luke's first blow caught Jim in the stomach, but instead of doubling up, he flung himself forward. To his amazement he found himself astride Luke, pummeling his face with the heels of his hands. The older boy twisted away, Jim lunged on his back; they wrestled and rolled down the creekbank. Jim's legs became tangled in vines and instantly Luke was on top, holding Jim's ears and banging his skull against the muddy earth.

Then Luke, a blurry, wavy figure, stood over him panting, wiping blood from his face with the back of his hand. "Mess with me again, Jim Glenn, and I'll fix you for good." His bare feet punched holes in the mud as he strode up the slope and into the cabin.

Jim eased himself to his feet, gritting his teeth against the pain in his ribs. Luke's sister peered at him over the bobcat's ears. "There's blood on the back of your head, Jimmie."

Resisting the urge to probe his muddy hair, Jim shrugged and said, "The kitten all right?"

"Oh, yes! See—he's fine. But Luke's all bloody."

A smile of pride tugging at the corners of his mouth, Jim slowly climbed through the underbrush to where Bonnie stood. If only Willie could have seen me, he thought. He grazed his jaw with his knuckles, pretending the hand was his brother's. He could hear him say, "My wee chin-chopper did himself proud."

At midafternoon the soul driver halted his prisoners in a small meadowland. "Gather round," he said, "and listen to me good. I'll take the rope off your necks so's the women can boil meat and the men can gather kindling and boughs for beds. I'll do that if I can trust you not to go running away and get yourselves killed in these woods." He stood with his legs spread, his knuckles on his hips, and the whip curled in his right hand. The eyes of the men darted to the forest wall and back to his glowering, boyish face. "You listening?" he barked. They nodded, and raindrops spilled off the ends of their beards.

He described the thwunk of a scalp being pulled off a living head, the screams of a woman with burning splinters thrust into her nipples, the sight of a man the Indians had taken four days to kill. He told of snakes that squeeze, owls that pluck out sleeping eyes, wolves that wait for a man to stumble, and panthers with claws ready to rip open a human face. He finished by saying, "If you run off, that's how you'll die. If you're lucky, it'll be quick."

He paused and leaned toward the pale men and women. "But if you stay close by the camp, in a week or two you'll have your feet under an Irishman's table that's loaded with pumpkins, turkey, journeycake, raisin pudding, bear meat, and roasting ears." While he named the foods he slipped the rope from their necks.

Anne sat staring into the flames of the biggest fire she'd ever seen. Her stomach growled with hunger. If all those foods the driver named tasted no better than the crumbly yellow bread and bear meat that they had had for supper, she'd stay small as a flea forever. She wished she had some ale, or even some of that jolting corn whiskey. That would kill her hunger and cramps. She glanced at the driver sprawled under a half roof of tree boughs on the other side of the creek, then turned to the big round-faced boy who sat next to her. "I canna ken what the driver was saying about sitting at an Irishman's table, Jake. I'd best go and ask him."

The driver smiled when he heard her question. "Papist Irish? I've never laid eyes on one of them. I meant the Presbyterian Ulstermen in Octoraro."

"And if they don't want me?" she asked.

"Well, then some Dutchman will. They got the best farms in Pennsylvania and they don't bother nobody, either. Just keep their hands on the plow and their eyes on their oxen's arse. They'll work you hard, but you'll eat well." The young man pushed back his hat, uncovering brown curls; his eyes were warm and friendly. "No need for you to squat there in the rain while we talk. Come around to this side of the fire. And bring the whiskey jug with you. Person needs a little warming up on a night like this. Clears the vapors outta the blood."

Anne cocked her head. She hadn't figured on him wanting to lie with her; everyone at the other fire could see them plain as day, and she surely didn't want to go into those woods with him. Visions of masked animals, poison-spraying animals, animals full of needles loomed large as cows in her mind. She hesitated with her hand halfway to the whiskey.

"Don't be scairt, gal. I've got no mind to romp with you. I just want to jaw awhile. A man gets lonely in this business. The only people I have for company hate me worse than a polecat."

Anne crawled into the sweet-smelling circle of warmth. The driver dipped a piece of corn bread in bear broth and handed it to her. "Name's John Cooperson. You see, I don't hate indents. You're how I make my money. Dandiest-paying job I know."

Anne sucked the warm bread. "They give you silver for selling us folk?"

"Yep. I get half the profit I make on each of you. The man who bought you off the captain gets the rest. When I get twenty pounds laid by, Mr. Carpenter's going to let me board with him and read law."

"Read law?"

"Study books so I can be a lawyer." Anne frowned. "Lawyers are gentlemen that help people with property lines and such. Not a surveyor who lays them out, but a man who helps with the quarreling."

"Aye. Blood feuds."

11

"No, word feuds. See, even with all this land in America, there's going to be a heap of fighting over it. You'll see it come. Among Indians, Pennsylvanians, Marylanders, and Virginians. Oh, there'll be lots of trouble, and lawyers will be busy in America for a long, long time." Anne yawned. "Are you looking for a husband, gal?"

Anne sat up straight. "You offering?"

"No. I got a gal in Philadelphia willing to wait while I'm with Mr. Carpenter. I was just thinking that a husband would pay off your denture and you'd be free."

"Free? Out of the griddle and into the fire. No, Mr. Cooperson, I will not buckle till I find me a fine crofter with four hundred acres of his own." She snapped shut her jaw and lifted her chin.

John smiled. "I do believe you'll catch one." He passed her the whiskey jug and rambled on about Philadelphia gossip, the Penns, the Assembly. Anne lay back on the springy branches, the whisky trailing fire to her stomach, her skin steaming under her drying clothes. The rain pattered on the leaves of the lean-to; the edges of the wet logs hissed and spat; John's voice droned, and Anne slept.

It rained for a solid week. The dentures—except for Anne, who slept every night under John Cooperson's lean-to—were never dry. They coughed, John gave them whiskey, they coughed more, he gave them more. Two men were sold in Chester; the rest plodded west over gentle hills, through the swamps and swirling river of the Brandywine Valley and onto a deeply worn Indian trail. At Octoraro Creek they turned north and on the afternoon of the eighth day forded that swollen stream. In the midst of the crossing a frail and fevered woman flung herself face down into the rushing tan water. Her husband lunged after her and sank over his head; he was rescued, but it was dusk before the woman's body was found.

Anne curled against the warmth of John's brotherly back, grinding her teeth against the calls of the water kelpies, the spirits that drown travelers. When he asked her what the trouble was, she mumbled that women with Aiken blood were prone to tossing themselves in water to drown. "Creeks, oceans, water buckets. Whatever comes to hand."

In the morning the trail was a long cavern of mouse-grey fog, but Anne's feet hopped in excitement—today was the day. The day she would meet her new family.

Jim's filly danced through the church grove of red sugar maples. All the folk of Middle Octoraro—a half-dozen families

12

with eight or ten children apiece—were gathered; an auction was a social occasion. Jim flushed under the stares of the women in skirts of butternut, blue, or red; he imagined they eyed him as the heir of Matthew Glenn, a prospective bridegroom for their daughters. Children whooped and dashed through the leaves; a girl called, "Look, Louisa, look who's comin' on a spankin' red mare!" Jim's fair cheeks burned and he reined toward the men and boys clustered about the preacher's split-log stall; some wore Ulster breeks, most linsey-woolsey from their women's looms; the jug was out, the voices loud and merry.

Jim sat on his filly at the edge of the circle, staring at the festering cut his fist had left on Luke Cameron's chin.

Sam Brady hollered to him, "You're wise to stay on your horse, laddie. Louisa Vance's got her eyes out for you."

"Yeah," Luke said with a growl, "now that he's got his brother Willie out of the way he's got a clear field with the girls."

Some men sucked in a gasp; others didn't breathe; Matt's face turned gray. Luke's father, Jesse, was the only one who moved; his blow left Luke sprawled on the ground. "Sorry, Matt," Jesse mumbled. "I whup him regular, but he only seems to get meaner."

Jim drove his knees into Bonnie's side, but when the woods closed around the trail, the horse slowed to a walk and Louisa Vance's white throat filled Jim's mind. What would it be like to put his lips on hers? Not in some kissing game, but standing alone in the shadows with her . . . But what did he do then? Where did he put his hands?

By the time Jim reached the top of the ridge his body was prickly, randy with the smell of his own and the filly's sweat. Far away a horse nickered. The indents! He turned Bonnie to one side of the trail; a new feeling tightened his stomach.

All morning Anne had been squinting up into the glare of the fog; when it burned off she would see how America looked without mists and rain. It happened like the sudden blare of a trumpet and stopped her dead in her tracks; the packhorse ran into her back, and the woman in front of her yelled, "Hey!"

"Merciful sakes alive!" Anne shouted. "Cast up your eyes everybody! Up!"

The leaves were not green nor dead brown, but dazzling flames of yellow, red, and orange leaping against the blueing sky.

"How did God do it?" Anne cried. "How did he paint them all? It would take a thousand brownies a thousand years." She whirled on John Cooperson. "Be it done with fire?"

John slipped the rope from her neck. "Run ahead to the top of the ridge, gal, and look out across the valley. You'll see a sight that'll make you forget Scotland or Ireland or anyplace other than America. I don't pretend to know how God manages these colors, but it's plain that he's been getting this land ready for company-coming. And I reckon we folk are it."

Anne hurried through the crease in the steep hills, and when she came to the rough path that led to the ridgetop, she hitched up her skirts and began to sing. She sang about King William of Orange. "Come King William's royal call to his golden standard flaunting by the Boyne . . ."

At the top Bonnie stripped pea vines while Jim wondered about the two new faces which might be at his table for midday meal, two strangers who, according to Luke, might have come out of Newgate Prison in London. He tried his feet out of the stirrups, then in, finally crossing one leg over his horse's poll. Heaven forbid the driver should see him as a gaping backwoods boy; for added nonchalance he chewed a leaf stem.

He imagined the indents, all whey-faced and full of fever and vermin from the ship, crawling on their hands and knees up the trail, which was nothing but a dry creekbed full of stones and boulders. Maybe the women and girls would be crying, perhaps the boys, too. And the men would be mouthing foul curses while the driver whipped them.

The filly's head came up and her ears shot forward. Jim jammed his feet back in the stirrups. A stone cracked and rang as it bounced from rock to rock. They were coming! At least one of them must be almost up the hill. He thought he heard a voice but he wasn't sure. A bird? No, a girl's voice singing off-key.

"Whiles the crown dropped from his head. Up Orange, and up Orange . . ." Anne rounded the bend, raised her face, and saw him. "And huzzah!" she cried.

Chapter Two

Anne's feet, tough as the stones she trod on, slowed and stopped. Her ankles, scratched and scabbed, stuck below her green skirt; her shift sagged beneath the hollows of her collarbones; her breath came in little pants, and a crown of

14

orange leaves tilted on her curls. Shading her eyes, she squinted into the shadows where Jim Glenn sat on his horse. "Be you an Indian?" she called.

Jim nudged Bonnie into the path; sunlight blazed on his blondness, whiteness, the curried sheen of his horse.

Anne gasped, wondering if her mind had gone to mush. How should she address this gleaming apparition? "Be you Jesus? The son of an English laird?"

She sighed with relief when he shook his head—Lord Hamilton had been plenty enough for one lifetime. He could be something cooked up by the pope or the devil to tempt her, but she couldn't think of a way to put that into a question. Of course, this was America, and things went differently here. She studied him, working up from the strange skins on his feet to the stubborn cleft of his chin; his mouth was kind, and his eyes had a bit of wonder in them. "Could it be," she asked, "that you're from Octoraro? Son of a crofter there?"

Jim straightened his back. "Aye, the Glenn farm." Bonnie trembled as the girl approached and Jim spoke gruffly. "I suppose you're one of the indents."

Ignoring the intended insult, the small, untidy girl came on murmuring soft Scot words; the filly stood, then nickering, nuzzled her neck. Anne's green eyes rose in a hypnotic stare. "How many acres has your pappie got?"

"Four hundred."

The girl exploded like a tree struck by lightning. Her cap flew off, her curls and skirts bounced. "I won! I won-over all! Four hundred acres! See! Minnie, see!"

Jim, leaning his weight on the neck of his skittering filly, wondered if he was going daft. Grannie MacIllwain had told him of leprechauns, but she hadn't said they came life-sized.

Anne twirled on her toes and bubbled. "Is your pappie needing a lass to work?"

"Yes," he said. Then, feeling as though he'd just given his whole life away, he yelled, "I mean no! No! Besides, my mam does the choosing of house girls. And she'd never pick a skinny goose-cap like you. Why aren't you chained up with the others?"

Anne stopped dancing and blew air from her puffed, flushed cheeks. "Mr. Cooperson took a liking to me." She stretched her arms out straight from her shoulders and slowly turned around. "I'm a wee bit thready, but I'll fatten fine." Her shift hung low, exposing a crescent of freckled breast. To Jim's horror his mouth began to water, and lowering his hands over the lump in his crotch, he said thinly, "You got a drawstring for that garment? If you went down there like that . . ." He swallowed. "My mam . . . all the women in the valley are . . . well, they're strict about, ah, girls your size. . . . I mean, you're not being spoken for and all, and—"

Anne laughed as she peered down at her chest. "I'm fond of the freckles myself. And," she said, looking where he held his hands, "you have more to hide than me."

Jim almost fell off his horse.

Anne bent to scratch her foot, and her breasts hung like twin, peaked muffins against her rakelike ribs. Jim yanked loose the stickpin that held his stock. "Here! Make yourself decent."

"Ooo aye," Anne said, straightening up, "that'll fix me fine. Fasten it in the back. I have my minnie's plaiden on the packhorse that I can drape over my shoulders. I'll look like a lady, you'll see." She backed against his calf and lifted her tangled mass of hair. "Don't be skerrie, Jock. I'll meet you at milking time to give it back." Twisting her neck, she gave him a wink.

Jim jabbed the pin down through the bunched cloth straight on into his thumb. He swore.

Anne giggled, then chanted, "Pricked with a pin earns you a kiss, jabbed with a needle no longer a Miss."

Jim drove the pin on into her flesh; she whirled.

"I'm sorry," he mumbled. "I don't know what made me do that." The stormy darkness of her eyes drew sweat to his lip.

"I'll forgive you, m'laird, since you were doing me a good turn." Red circles of anger stamped her white cheeks. "But I'll have you know I'm not a lass you can bully about."

He stared, unable even to blink. Horses' hooves clattered on the trail. Anne patted his moccasin. "Now, laddie, tell me your name so I'll know who's to buy me."

"Glenn."

"North Irish?"

"Aye."

"Presbyterian?" Her face edged from winter into spring.

"From tap to toe, as they say. The Glenns of Paisley crossed to Glenariff, Ireland, fleeing John Graham of Claverhouse."

Her eyes blazed like summer suns. "Followers of Richard Cameron?"

He nodded. "True Covenanters."

16

"Ooo m'laird," she said, "we have them licked. I myself—"

Before she could say more, the filly backed and squealed as the file of immigrants—a dozen weatherworn nubs with a rope sagging from neck to neck—came around the bend.

"Take a breathin'," John Cooperson called, "but don't touch the hemp. I didn't bring you all this way to lose you now." His voice was brassy, the way it had been in Philadelphia.

"Do you have to do that?" Jim blurted. "Tie them by the neck like animals?"

John stiffened. "I'd trust an animal more than some of these humans. You're lookin' at the tailings of Newgate Prison, sonny."

He bore down hard on the 'sonny,' and a hot flush crept up Jim's neck. The driver couldn't be much older than he.

John stroked the coils of his whip. "The English are running a sewer line to America. See the little man with the stubby beard? He'd blubber to you that all he did was take a gentlemen's gloves from his carriage. He did that, all right, but in place of the gloves he left the man's wife all cut up in pieces. Go ahead and smile, Octoraro laddie, but that's the truth and that's murder, and who knows when he'll do it again. Just swallowing Pennsylvania air don't cure a man of his evil blood."

Goose bumps roughened Jim's forearms. "Are they all convicts?"

"Only four of the men. The others are alright. Jake Denner, the fat one, is the best of the lot. One of the women's a whore."

"Which one—" Jim began.

"Is the whore? The pretty one. I put her first in line. She waggles her arse, and the men follow." John winked. "Maybe your pappie will buy her for you to practice on."

Jim's try at a manly laugh made Anne wary. Two men joking about women was, she knew from experience, a risky situation. She began to back off, slowly edging toward her place at the end of the line. She didn't make it. John snatched her arm and pushed her in front of him. "Or maybe you fancy this little one. Name's Anne. Scrawny, but under the blanket you don't notice much." Anne was about to yell, "You never touched me!" but, hoping the moment would pass, she bit her tongue.

To show the boy on the fancy horse that Anne was his property, John poked her in the rear with the whip butt. Anne doubled her fist and whaled it against his cheek. John raised the whip, but before he could draw back his arm, Anne crowded him, growling, "Ca' cannie, mannie. Go easy. I'm no

17

beastie to be whipped." John's knuckles whitened, but he didn't swing. Anne shoved her face in his. "No man can take me over, if I don't want to be took. It doesn't matter whether his breeches be up or down, whether he has a whip or a slippery tongue. I do the choosing, John Cooperson."

"You Jezebel! After all I've done for you."

Anne didn't flinch. "Lay that whip on me"—her eyes flickered to Jim as she spoke—"and my new master here, Mr. Glenn, will lay it on you twelve minus one." Jim opened his mouth, but Anne's words shut it again. "And if he is not man enough, I'm certain his pappie is."

Jim couldn't understand how things had turned out like this. Why was he going to have to fight a man with a whip for a snip of a dirty girl who was more devil than human? He opened his mouth and again that surprising man's voice came from his throat. "What the girl says is right, mister." He banged his heels on Bonnie's sides; she wheeled, splattering mud from her hooves, and pounded down the ridge trail.

Rebekah and Matthew Glenn had settled themselves on the high seat of their wagon, the only wheeled vehicle in the church grove, to wait for the dentures to appear. No roads connected the valley farms of the Camerons, MacClymonds, Glenns, Vances, Bradys, and Dickies. In winter they traveled in sleighs, in summer in sledges that slid on runners over the grass, but this place of worship was on Glenn land, and Matthew had leveled a road to the spot so his aged father could ride on a spring seat to do his preaching. Reverend Glenn had been dead ten years, but Matthew had kept up the road, declaiming, "Before you know it we'll be calling my youngest the Reverand James and he'll be filling this pulpit."

Matthew, ruling elder of the church and the most prosperous man in the valley, tended his fences—and saw that others minded theirs, too. Whiskey barrels branded "Matt: Glenn" were prized in the taverns of New Castle, Chester, and Philadelphia; his paddock was enclosed, his animals sheltered, and his new house filled with oak and cherry furniture finely turned by his own hand. His two oldest sons were pioneering beyond the Allegheny Mountains, and either Jim or Willie had been expected to go abroad to a Scottish university—until the accident. Three daughters lay in the cemetery, but two had lived: Bess, his firstborn, esteemed as the widow of the Reverend Blackwood of Philadelphia and now back home keeping school for the valley children, and Dora, a hard-driving maiden of twenty-five.

Rebekah Glenn's stiff white cap rose no higher than her husband's shoulder, and in contrast to his broad, bearded face, hers was pinched and filled with little cares. His hands lay strong and freckled on his knees, hers were tightly clasped about the Bible from which she constantly quoted. Idleness, dreaminess—of which her oldest daughter, Bess, had a touch—was a sin that made Rebekah flap in a frenzy, but although her tongue snapped and drove, she also loved—except in February, when the melancholies of the MacIllwain's turned her inward. She raised her puckered face to her husband. "Do you think I was too hard on the girls setting them to shucking corn on auction day?" Matt shook his head and patted her hand.

Jim Glenn had not ridden from the ridge pell-mell into the grove, but rather had let Bonnie browse her way across the meadowland while he pondered going home with a pretended bellyache, leaving the selling of Anne in the hands of God. The sight, however, of Luke picnicking with Louisa set him trotting toward the grove.

Loosening the mare's girth strap, Jim leaned against her flank and avoided his parents' eyes by watching John Cooperson herd the indents to the broad sycamore stump. He chewed on his lip as the women climbed up: the pretty buxom one, the little girl and her sick mother, the hefty German, and Anne.

John quickly began his business by pulling the pretty girl to the front of the stump. "Smile," he hissed. Arms rigid by her sides, she stretched her lips back from her teeth in a ghastly grin. John looked at his slate. "Name's Tine Plum. Twenty years old. And forgive me, ladies, but I'm dutybound to read out the record, and I always conduct my business honorably. Served one year in Newgate for soliciting gentlemen. Four-year denture. A bargain at fifteen pounds, and we'll up her service from four to seven years."

Tine Plum yowled, "No! I served my time in the foulest prison in the world. I've laid for 70 days chained hip to haunch in the bowels of a ship. I won't be sold like a whore by an English boy who gives away three more years of my life with no more thought than he'd give to kicking a dog." She crumpled to her knees. "Have mercy, good folk. I've harmed no one."

John assumed a preacher's pose. "Don't weep, gal. These Presbyterians know that God tempers justice with mercy."

Anne found herself wondering, might she herself be called a

19

whore? Hadn't she spread her legs in exchange for a bowl of broth and a piece of bread?

Matthew Glenn's voice rolled over the grove. "Sin is sin. It is not for man to forgive the harlot, only Jesus can do that. Put her down, driver. We'll have no whores in this valley."

Tine Plum rolled from the stump into the soggy leaves. Disgusted, Anne raised her chin. I can't be a whore—they have no pride. I'm a child of the Covenant! Anne Aiken MacKnight! She jiggled her shoulders and lifted her nose; that sniveling English bundle of rags had no connection to her.

"Kathleen Adams." The soul driver pointed to the little girl whom he had plucked from the muck that first day. The child smiled shyly from under her brushed blond hair; death streaked the mother's cheeks. "Five years old. The woman, Eleanor, is twenty-nine. Belfast folk. Both have had the pox. Girl, eight pounds, dentured till twenty-one. Mother twelve pounds, four years. Husband's over there. We'll get to him later. Take the mother and girl both for eighteen pounds. Be a shame to break 'em up."

Eleanor Adams swayed, and John quickly sat her down with one hand and with the other grabbed the arm of the German girl. "This here's Rita Englerot. Fifteen. Rest of her family was sold off in Philadelphia. Five-year denture. Fifteen pounds. Good, strong girl in her best years. Peasant stock." He lifted her arms and pressed the firm curves with his thumbs; Rita began to hum.

Sam Brady blared, "Where did you get such a mixed bunch, Cooperson? Been buying up the leavings of the Baltimore auctions?"

Before John could answer, Anne called out, "Who do you think you're calling leavings, mister? Maybe your own head has been too long in the leavings of the ale barrel!"

John hustled her forward, snarling out of the corner of his mouth, "Keep that up and you'll never be sold." He smiled at his customers. "This little snippet's listed as Anne, folks."

"My name," Anne sang out, "is MacKnight. As good a name as any what's here." Her wild red curls quivered, her greasy skirt shimmered; she resembled a rooster ready to fight.

John Cooperson's eyes stopped on Jim, then moved on. "There's a young man here," John called, "who claims this wench, Anne, is his. Let him start the bidding at fifteen pounds for a denture of seven years." Jim froze solid as a washbucket in January. "He's wearing a white shirt and new walnut-brown britches. In fact, he may be too big for them."

Men snorted, girls laughed, and a boy yelled, "If he's on a red mare his name's Jim Glenn."

Heads swung to Jim, then to his mother who shrilled, "Get yourself down off the horse, James."

Jim did, and although he came nowhere near matching the six-foot frame of his father, he topped his mother by a head and a half. Rebekah angled her chin upward and spoke loud enough for everyone in the grove to hear. "Now, what's all this about?"

Jim dug the toe of his moccasin into the mud and mumbled, "The driver was ready to whip her. I stopped him by saying we'd buy her."

"Humph. I full well understand his craving to whip her. Never saw a body more in need of it." She rose on her toes. "As for you, young man, you lied. You do not have fifteen pounds."

When Jim muttered that he didn't see anything so bad about lying to a nasty soul-driver, Rebekah's tiny hand smacked his cheek. "Lying to a man lower than you makes him higher than you. Whatever Mr. Cooperson might be, he's got you by the tail feathers now."

She paused for breath, and John called, "Hey, boy, come out from behind those skirts and pay for this wench. Or won't your mam let you play with gals yet?"

A nightmare of laughter rolled around Jim, and his father's fist jabbed his back. "You sing out loud and clear that you lied. Offer yourself for church discipline Thursday evening."

Jim astonished himself. Instead of nodding, "Aye, Father," he asked, "Why don't you just buy her? She'd work faster and eat less than the fat Dutch one. I'm sure Mam would bridle her tongue. Then"—he almost smiled—"I wouldn't have lied."

Jim turned to his mother. "Your cooking would fatten her up so the bones of her ribs don't stick through her skin like—" He shut his mouth quickly, but it was too late—his mother's eyes had bored into his thoughts. He turned to signal Anne that the jig was up, and his jaw dropped. She was smiling! "Judas priest," he muttered, "she's daft for sure."

Cheerily Anne tapped John's shoulder. "Read this out," she commanded.

Faces swiveled from Jim to Anne then back again. Jim wished the earth would swallow him. No, swallow Anne MacKnight. The whole mess was her fault. To be dressed down by his mother in front of everyone like he was still wet behind the ears . . . and there stood Luke and Louisa Vance snickering at him. Well, he was through. He was getting out.

They could sell her to an Indian trader, for all he cared. He inched back beside Bonnie and bumped into the iron arm of his father. Trapped. He was trapped.

Agony curled his toes. He cursed Anne's tongue, the smirk on her face, the fact that his stickpin held up her shift, then to his horror, found himself imagining her throat, her white freckled skin rising to mellow nipples. . . . He pulled his tingling fingers into fists. She's a devil! A devil sent to tempt me.

Anne thrust a paper into the driver's hands, and after scanning it, he read loud and clear: "'The bearer, Anne Aiken MacKnight, has designed to go to Pennsylvania and America. These are therefore to testify she leaves without scandal, having lived in Killyleagh, County Down, Ireland, soberly and inoffensively, and may be admitted to Church privileges. Given this day, August 1, 1753, by James Wallace Bruce, Presbyterian minister of the synod of Ulster.'" Anne jauntily waved her fingertips at Jim. "'Postscript: Her grandfather, James Bartholomew Black in noble service to King William of Orange did, against the forces of the Catholic James, hold his place on the wall at London-Derry 104 days.'"

Rebekah Glenn was off like a shot toward the stump, calling, "Of course, any of us would be proud to have a daughter of Londonderry in our homes, but it so happens my son spoke for her first. He must have known she was one of us." Taking a firm grip on Anne's wrist, she cried for Matthew to bring the purse, then said, "Now, Mr. Cooperson, you can go on with your selling of the others. I'll give you hard coin for this lass."

"But we bid, ma'am. We bid on the girl. Fifteen pounds is the starting price."

"I'm giving you ten, which is twice what she's worth. But there'll be no bidding. This lass is a daughter of Londonderry."

"And," Anne added, "my mother was a Watt. Granddaughter of Jamie Watt, taken at Bothwell Brig. My great-great-grandfather was Dr. Thomas MacKnight of Glasgow, who—"

Anne's green eyes twinkled and she would have gone on, but Rebekah reached up, saying, "Aye, the blood of martyrs flows in your veins." Anne's leap almost knocked Rebekah over, but the little woman held her tight, saying, "God has brought you to us, Anne MacKnight."

Anne peeked past Rebekah's spotless white cap at Jim. "Aye," she said, "I believe He did."

Jim Glenn, however, galloped the half mile home feeling the breath of Satan, not God, hot on his neck.

Anne woke at midafternoon. She had no idea where she was. Motionless, she waited while her mind searched for her body along the roadsides of County Down, in the hold of the *Eagle Wing*, and in John Cooperson's lean-to. But those places were hard, and where she lay now, softness billowed right over her head. Could she be an angel resting on a cloud? She squirmed, testing to see if her shoulders had wings. The Glenns! She was in Mr. and Mrs. Glenn's bed. "Where I have no business being," she whipered, "if they catch me . . ."

Poking aside the feather ticking she found sunbeams and silence, nothing more. She sighed. The bread pudding and cream stomachache that had driven her to this refuge was gone; she snuggled deeper. You deserve the rest, Anne. It's a harrowing day you've had.

First there had been the broken stick that had whapped Mister Glenn on the back of the neck as they drove home from the auction: She had jumped off the back of the jouncing wagon, exclaiming that her arse was getting stuck full of splinters, and Jake, stuffed with his own importance at having been bought before any of the other men, had snickered when Mrs. Glenn snapped, "Watch your language, Miss Snippit!" The stick with which Anne had clouted Jake was rotten, and the broken end of it had whistled through the air, almost knocking Mister Glenn from his perch. That had brought on her first switching.

Second, she had told Mrs. Glenn that her new split-log floor should be taken up quick before everybody got their feet as full of splinters as her own arse was. That earned her a swat with the stirring spoon. Third had been her refusal to go to the wash-up tub. "Soap is hard on things, ma'am. It weakens the fibers of cloth and makes my fingertips look like rotten onions." Mrs. Glenn had whirled, snapping, "'Wash you, make you clean. Isaiah 1:16.'" Anne had rapped back, "'Dirt bodes luck. Scot proverb.'" Mrs. Glenn's hard fingers had pushed her out the door. Anne had came back muttering, "It's sinful to waste soap and water on a lass like me who falls in the creek so regular."

The worst of it had come just as they sat down to dinner. The hard-grained sister Dora had growled, "You're having the scogie-lass at the table?" and Anne had gone for her head like a crazed cat. That fracas had ended with Mr. Glenn excusing Dora from eating at all and setting Anne in the inglenook of the chimney with orders to eat every bite in her trencher while reciting "Blessed are the meek" between mouthfuls.

Anne sucked on a corner of the ticking. No wonder I got a bellyache and had to take to bed. At least I bit my tongue before asking where their brother Willie is—that might have landed me upside down in the spring. A sudden rustling startled Anne to her feet, causing the slack bed ropes to sag and plunge her into a sea of smothering down from which she howled, "Who's there?"

A calm voice replied, "Just me. Bess."

Anne's head popped up. "You scared me half to death!"

"I didn't think anything frightened you, Anne MacKnight."

Anne cocked her head. Bess's words sounded like clear water sliding over smooth stones; her skin was cream, her hair butter, her breasts . . . "How do you get that line between your titties?"

Bess rose briskly. "Come along. We're to do the Sabbath cooking before supper."

Anne trailed the stately woman into the hearth room. "I'm not much of a hand at cooking."

Bess handed her a chopping knife. "At least you can whack up turnips. Didn't you help your mother?"

"Ha! My minnie—" she stopped. "I much preferred riding with my pappie on business."

"Did you have schooling?"

"Ooo aye. The minister's wife got upset about how I was being reared, and it was either a case of being her scogie-lass, scrubbing pots and carrying slops, or going to school." Anne tossed her head. "I can read Latin."

Bess nodded. "The turnips need more than one whack, Annie. We're not feeding horses."

"It must be the lacing on your vest that holds your titties so high. I wonder if I—"

"Dear"—Bess rested her wrists on the table— "some matters are fit for conversation, some are not. What would you feel like if Jim suddenly appeared in the door?"

"Oh . . ." Anne shrugged.

Bess hugged Anne's bony shoulders. "I want you to be one of the family. And your manners will have to be mended before that can happen."

The warmth of Bess's body and words clogged Anne's throat, and the woman and girl chopped and grated, boned and cored, baked and boiled with only Bess's humming to keep them company.

When all the pots were simmering, Anne said, "Jim told me

you're a widow. Is it all right to wonder out loud how old you were when you married?"

Bess smiled, and the crystal blue glow of her eyes stopped Anne's heart. "Twenty when I married the Reverend Blackwood and went off to Philadelphia."

"As a minister's wife you must have lived in a bonnie big house."

Bess shook her head. "Hinting about how well-to-do folks might be is not appropriate either, Annie. But yes, a fine house. On Chestnut Street. It's closed now, with all the furniture sitting just as it was the day he died. A two-story brick with room—"

"For a dozen children," Anne blurted.

Bess walked out through the door.

When she came back Anne was struggling to roll out the cracker dough. Bess slipped her arms over her shoulders and took the rolling pin. "Put your hands over mine, child. Lightly. There. Feel how it's done?"

Anne twisted so she could look up into Bess's face. "I'm sorry. That was a terrible thing to say. Children dying is something no one wants to be reminded of." She poked the dough. "I'm not sure you'll be able to fix me up to be one of the family."

Bess sighed. "The Reverend Blackwood and I never had any children. He was older than I and . . . Well, anyway, we didn't, and in eight years he was dead. I came back here and started the school." Bess pushed the round cutter through the thin dough. "Sometimes God denies us the thing we want too badly."

Anne bit her tongue on the question of why she didn't marry again.

Bess laid the crackers on the griddle. "Check the apples, Annie, and if they're baked we'll sneak ourselves a snack."

They sat on the stoop of the new room Matt was building Bess for her teaching, and Anne moaned with pleasure as she scooped the cinnamon sweetness into her mouth. Gray geese patrolled the pigs, who rooted for acorns under the oak tree; blue autumn haze smudged the color of the hills and the yellow tops of the great sycamores by the stream. "I love this place," Bess said. "Do you?"

Anne tilted sideways until their bare arms touched. "Aye." Including you and your brother.

"Was Ireland much different?"

"Ooo aye. There was the frowning castle of the Hamiltons on the hill, a church at the end of the lane where sometimes on orders of the king chains bound shut the doors, houses pressing close, stone walls running everywhere, making things small. And it was never quiet like this. There was always bells ringing, saying, 'Do this. Do that,' and women quarreling at the well or whispering behind their hands about your mother. This time of day the men would be coming from the fields in a long line of bent backs. There was none of the feeling of—of ease that's here."

"Ease?"

"Ho! Anne MacKnight!" Matthew strode up the path from the whiskey sheds that lay around the bend of the stream. "Bring the milking buckets and I'll introduce you to Bawsie, Kye, and Prick-Me-Dainty."

The brown cows, steaming in the twilight, watched Anne approach the paddock; Kye and Bawsie resumed grinding their cuds with a wait-and-see look, but Prick-Me-Dainty bawled her doubts across the valley.

"You'll have a time with that one, lassie," Matthew said. "Let me see your hands. Ooch, it's been a while since you've milked. Maybe you'd better call Jake—"

"I'll do just fine, m'laird. I milked fifteen a day in Killyleagh."

Matthew patted her palms. "You don't have to put on with me, Anne. I've heard the tales of drought out of County Down."

Anne swaggered her shoulders. "Do you think I'm a lump of your pumpkin? I'm Anne Aiken MacKnight! I can read Latin. I can—" Her glance hit on his stallion and she tossed her red head. "I've ridden horses in the market races at Downpatrick that would leave that tumble-turd stud of your's wheezing in their dust."

"Someday," Matthew said, "I'll let Lucifer knock the bragging Irish from your lips." Anne stuck out her tongue as he walked away.

When Bawsie was dry, Anne went inside the old one-room house-turned-barn and forced her cramped fingers to strip Kye's teats. Dusk settled down, the milk foamed white, cats bumped her thighs, and a calf bawled against her shoulder. The smell of years of human cooking mingling with straw and dung made Anne imagine herself in Killyleagh. There, that shadow in the doorway must be Pappie coming home. No, it was Jim Glenn, with his hands rolled tight and his face a blend of come-and-go.

"You've been spying on me, James."

"Just watching."

"'Tisn't fitting."

He folded his arms and spread his feet. "Why not? You're just a denture to my family. I can do what I want about you." Anne stared, barely believing her ears. "You rattled me good this morning, but I'm over that now." Anne said nothing, and his voice rose. "You're sold Irish. Probably can't even read. Mam says you'll buckle with Jake come spring, if not before."

"Jake! You're daft!" Why had Mrs. Glenn said that?

"And I'm not going to kiss you. You think I'm stuck on you, but I'm not."

"I don't care."

"Yes, you do."

"Bragger!"

"Better that than a skinny scogie-lass with loose teeth."

Her hands rushed to her face, and sudden tears poured through her fingers.

"I'm sorry. I—I didn't think you ever cried."

"I don't!"

He spread his hands. "What—"

"What makes you think I'm crying over you?" Anne spun on her stool and grabbed the cow's teats again. "It so happens I've got a fierce cramp in my hand. That's all."

He touched her shoulder. "Let me finish Kye. She's always hard at the end. I can—"

Anne climbed on her high horse. "No, m'laird. Milking's an Irish denture's job." She readied more words to throw at his back as he left, but he didn't move. His breath grew quick. "I've come for my pin. It belonged to my grandfather the minister."

"It's down my back where you put it."

"Here?"

"Aye."

"It seems to be stuck."

She felt her shift sag. "You got it." His palms were clammy on her shoulders; he pushed his lips awkwardly against her hair. He straightened and she felt his member hard against her back. "You can touch me if you want," she said. He fled.

"Tomorrow!" she called after him.

Kye, her breath sweet with wild marsh hay, licked her arm. Anne told herself that the feathery laughter from the loft was a waking owl's wings, or brownie voices in her head. Of course it was not. It was Willie Glenn.

* * *

Throughout the fall months, bits of Willie's story came to Anne's ears. His parents had thought of him as the last child in a family of five—Bess, Zac, Tommy, Dora, and now William, with the faraway blue eyes and black hair of the MacIllwains. The youngster worked his heart out to earn his father's praise until—at about thirteen—he turned moody and took to spending most of his time alone the woods; he refused to go to Edinburgh or Boston to study for the ministry. After Zac and Tommy left for the West, he thanked his father politely for offering him a full partnership in both the farm and the whiskey business, then drove him to fist-waving despair by leaving the plow standing while he carried a nest of blind mice to safety, or the scythe rusting in the hayfield while he trailed a buck to the banks of the Susquehanna, or an empty place at the supper table while he romped with the dentured girls of the Germans and the maidens of the Indian camps.

By the age of twenty Willie Glenn was known far and wide as the best woodsman, best hunter, and best horseman; even virgin Scot-Irish girls waited in out-of-the-way places, hoping that the lanky lad with the raven on his shoulder and the eyes of deep blue would happen along. Then came the accident. After that the name of Willie Glenn was only whispered.

No one ever explained the accident to Anne, and she never saw Willie's face—only a blur of black and white as he snatched back from the loft window or hatchway—but she grew accustomed to feeling his eyes on her back, and his spying added excitement to the chaste kisses of Jim's God-fearing lips. His mocking laugh or melancholy Scot songs often kept her company as she milked alone by lanternlight, and she wondered if he were daft. But Anne, remembering the mad of County Down locked in stalls like raving beasts and the cripples' hands that reached from the shadows of Belfast streets, curbed her curiosity to peep into the loft. She wanted no ugliness to mar her days of rising warm to the smell of buttered porridge and her nights of lying down with Bess's smiling face beside her. She kept Willie a fiction like the brownie Aiken Drum—until New Year's Eve.

Rebekah had cracked about the house for two days, supervising the scrubbing and bleaching of the long plank table and wooden floor, the shining of the pewter pieces, the pounding of soot from the linen hanging that hid the feather bed from the big hearth room. Last year with Matt ailing from the miseries and game scarce, Rebekah had let it be known that visitors, after their ritual first step across the threshold, would be served their gill of whiskey in the yard. This year was different.

All day a boar had roasted over a pit fire in a warm December drizzle; the house glowed with an extravaganza of candlelight that flickered off rafters and windows hung with herbs, dried fruit, and boughs of evergreen and bittersweet that Anne and Bess had brought from the forest. Ho and Clara MacClymonds, whose farm lay over the hill to the south, arrived with their handsome son, Roger, then came the huge Brady clan from across the creek; the Vances, who lived five miles to the north, and their neighbors the Dickies came together in a enormous harvest sledge pulled by six oxen; the Camerons had not been invited. By dusk the smells of the hearth applewood fire, steaming toddy and pies, pork wafting in through the open doorway, and the sound of laughter and songs from Bess's fiddle, snapped the air with such excitement that Anne thought some folks might fly right out of their skins.

Sam Brady raised his noggin. "Here's to 1753 and may Lady Luck smile on thee!" Led by the fiddle, the voices, heavy with drink and brouge, shouted the song of King William of Orange. Anne, her shape now more that of a lithe, long-legged colt than a peeled-down twig, watched both the biscuits and Jim, bobbing and grinning in the midst of a bevy of females. Anne's jealousy, especially of Louisa Vance, might have run amuck if Roger, a sophomore at Harvard, had not been sitting behind her, surreptitiously rubbing her calf with his knee.

Ooo Annie, she reminded herself, how different it is from last year, when Pappie was parading us shivering in our rags up and down the Belfast streets and shouting like an Old Testament prophet, "Cast your eyes upon us and know what the English law has wrought!"

Shrugging her shoulders to rid them of ghosts, she wriggled into the goodness of the room; Roger, misunderstanding, began to stroke her moons. He'll be under my skirt in a minute, she thought, but before she found the will to move, the room fell silent. It was as though a minister had lifted his arms for prayer. Those sitting rose to gaze at the doorway.

A young man, tall and lean with ebony hair and beard, lounged against the barked log door frame; candlelight lit his sardonic half smile and the soft white curve of his cheeks, but shadows hid his eyes. He wore a ruffled stock and a black linen coat and folded his arms with casual grace.

"William." Matthew spoke as though by the force of one word he could restore his son to his world.

Willie nodded. "Evening, Father. I've come to drink your health. Everyone's health."

The neighbors, catching the bitter-whiskey tone, stirred nervously and pulled back into the room, trapping Anne on the stool where she had climbed.

"You look real nice, Willie," Clara MacClymonds boomed. A shudder passed from shoulder to shoulder, and Anne wondered why. He did look nice, his hair and beard were combed, his shirt clean. He's not mad, Anne decided, just given to drink to hide his shyness—like Minnie was, probably has make-believe friends, too.

Rebekah snatched her husband's full dinner bowl and shoved it at Willie. "Welcome, son."

Willie took the bowl. "Still offering the teat, eh, Mam?"

The guests took another step back, leaving a circle of bare floor around the Glenns and their son. Anne gasped. Willie wore a skirt! His head turned. "Oh, dearie me, I've gone and upset our Erin lassie. We've never met, you see. The introductions were overlooked." He bowed. "The name is William MacIllwain Glenn."

Anne curtsied. "Mr. Glenn."

"Mister? Canna you see I wear a skirt?" His curled lips mimicked her Scots. "'Tis one of Bessie's best. Do you not think the blue sets off my eyes just grand?"

"I . . ." She looked at Matthew.

He spoke in words of hammered iron. "Mind your manners, William. This is still my house and you my son."

"Your son?" he barked. "I wasn't good enough for you even when I was whole. No one's good enough for you, Lord Matthew."

Before Matthew could reach Willie, Rebekah's arms circled him. Willie grinned. "You just muckle in, Mam, while I eat your vittles. That'll make me seem more like the babe you loved."

Like a stunned black fly, Rebekah clung to her son while Bess grabbed her fiddle, and people, bowing their heads over their bowls, shifted their feet. When Willie had carefully licked his fingers, he called out for his brother to bring a stool. "And bring the red-haired lass, too. I want to show her my bonnie leg."

Someone whispered, "He's mad." Another replied, "I always said he had MacIllwain eyes and you know what that means."

Clutching Jim's shoulder, Willie hopped up on the stool and lifted his skirt to his knee. His right leg, white as a snake's belly, was bare except for a shoe; he swung his thigh, and the calf and foot jerked, like a puppet's limb. "See!" Willie cried. "You don't have to wonder what it looks like anymore. Wouldn't you agree it's a fine braw leg?" He searched the faces of his neighbors. "Right, Bo Dickie?" One by one he called out their names, and they bit their lips and looked to Matthew, who stood clenching and unclenching his fists while Rebekah clung to him as she had to Willie.

Willie grasped the dangling shoe and shoved his slack, hairless calf in Anne's face. "I can see how you're dying to crawl between the skins with this brawny leg of mine. Don't it put my brother Jim's to shame?"

Matthew hurled himself past Anne; his shoulder hit Willie's stomach. Like a sack of meal, he hung his son across his back and carried him into the night. Willie raised his head in a wolf howl and Rebekah hurried to shut the door, but Anne was out, her feet sliding on the glaze of muck that lay over the frozen ground. She followed, watching Matthew grunt and strain as he stuffed the limp, drunk Willie up into the barn loft, and secured the hatch door by tying the rope around a peg.

She backed into the barn's shadow. Moon-bright clouds lit the tears on Matthew's face as he passed by; sobs from the loft beat cold in her chest. She saw Jim coming and reached for his hand; instead he held her and spoke with anger. "Pappie had no right to treat him like that. Willie didn't hurt anybody. Not really. Himself maybe, but . . ." His hand closed on the back of Anne's head. "I understand now what Willie meant. Pappie never treated him like he had the right to be himself. He couldn't let Willie be different. Especially after Zac and Tommy left. Willie had to be just the person Pappie wanted him to be. Even after the accident—"

"What happened? What was the accident?"

Jim steered her into the barn, where they huddled close in the hay while he talked. "Both Pappie and Willie took sick last winter. Pappie's rheumatism crippled him up, and Willie had pneumonia. That left the hunting to me. I hardly ever got so much as a hare. It was an awful time. Every noon there was nothing in the stew but turnips. I . . . Anyway, it was our first winter in the big house and the floor hadn't been laid and the logs sweated from the heat of the fire. It poured rain all the time. No wonder folks were sick.

"When the warm days that April borrows from June came around, Willie said he smelled deer in the meadow, and we went off to get one. They caught our scent and drifted into the woods. Willie and I split up to circle a glade where a doe stood with her fawn. I was lying with my musket barrel on a log

31

waiting for the doe to turn when my flint slipped out. It fell in the wet leaves, and I couldn't find it. By the time I dug another one out of my pouch, my hands were shaking. Just as I jammed it in, I heard Willie's shot." His voice broke. "I fired without ever looking up."

Jim held his face in his hands. "Willie had run into the clearing to catch the fawn, and my ball hit his knee." He rubbed his cheeks with the back of his hands. "We took him all the way to Baltimore in a dugout canoe. The surgeon wanted to cut off his leg and fit him with a wooden one, but Pappie said no, that our bodies are temples of the Lord and his son would go to heaven whole. Mam stayed there with Willie until the danger of infection was past, and when they came back, Willie was cheerful and determined to make the best of it." Jim shuddered. "But the pain was awful, and worse yet, he couldn't roam the woods. He was like a trapped wild thing and finally he took to hiding in the loft swilling whiskey during the day and riding out on Lucifer or Bonnie at night."

"It's a wonder he hasn't hung himself."

"Every morning when I come to the barn I expect it. Oh, God . . . Anne . . ."

She held him. "Doesn't anyone talk to him?"

"If anyone so much as pokes his head above the hatchway he growls like a beast. We just slide up a trencher of food and leave."

"Maybe if I—"

"No, Anne. There's something strange in the way he watches you. Please leave him be."

Anne was about to argue, but Jim brushed his lips across her forehead and over her eyelids. In all their kissing times she had never felt him tremble like this. The boundaries of herself dissolved. Marry me, Jim, marry me quick. Aloud she said, "I'll be fourteen next September."

Chapter Three

In ten days Jim was gone. The Glenns had decided he should begin his studies in Philadelphia immediately; Ben Franklin's college was not Edinburgh University, but it would do. So Jim and Anne kissed farewell in the big hollow sycamore tree by the creek and Anne, realizing that his nose-in-the-air manner was just varnish covering his fear of leaving, apologized for saying at dinner that he'd make a pompous arse of a minister. He held her tight, whispering he'd love her forever and that they'd marry when he returned.

After Jim left it was Bess who petted Anne when Matt or Rebekah had taken a switch to her "stubborn, willful Irish hide" and who encouraged her dreams of marrying Jim, saying she hoped one day there would be a dozen of their children running like lambs over the fields of the Glenn farm. When they were not laboring together, dyeing and spinning, pickling and tanning, baking and churning, Bess taught Anne to form neat letters using a crow's quill dipped in blackberry ink and to soothe her impatience by composing long letters to Jim. "Waiting for what you want is a large slice of life, Annie. An important part of growing up."

Twice during January, storms from the south and west collided in blizzards that made sawing hay from the frozen stack, or fetching water or wood challenges in fortitude and courage. With the February thaw came fogs and fevers; warm air sucked the snowbanks into clouds that rode the hilltops; smoke stayed clogged in the chimney. The whole Glenn household came down with the shakes and the sweats—except Jake, who writhed with the dumb ague. As a last resort to break his fever, they carried him outside to the washbench, poured near-boiling water over him, then let the March winds whip about his nakedness. It did no good. Jake, the strong, young ox, was dead by sundown.

No sooner were they done burying Jake—they were so weak it took three days to dig the grave—than Bess got word that old Mrs. Blackwood was ill in Christiana over near the Delaware, and Bess left to tend her. Furious at this second desertion, Anne grabbed a pile of fleece, a lantern, and moved to the barn loft—Willie now lived in a hut he had built on the hill above the house—and there she sulked with only swallows for company.

Summer, hot and dry, edged out spring; the land parched and the valley folk crushed empty heads of grain in their hands and trod barren blossoms underfoot. By autumn the sun had seared the meadows to a crackling brown and the air was hazed with the acrid smell of fires; the people, like the harvest, were sparse and brittle. Anne, hardened as a cracked and stony creekbed, worked late and slept dreamless, her only softness coming when she shared tales with Willie, whose mind no longer raged but rested simple as a child's. Matthew roared about like a mountain fire; Dora merged with the meanness of the land and smirked when the spring went dry and Anne had to lug buckets from the stream; Rebekah's tongue whipped through her sonless home.

On the first day of November Matthew, who was hauling winter logs with the help of Sam Brady's twins, stopped short when he felt a drop of water on his cheek. Telling the boys to leave the wood by the house and the oxen unyoked in the barn, he strode across the log bridge into the field, where huge wafer flakes of snow wet the earth, then crept white up the green blades of rye. He stood, boots, shoulders, eyebrows soaked, both arms raised in joyful prayer when a voice hailed him from the road.

"Reverend MacMillan!" Matthew shouted back. "Did you bring this glorious gift from the Almighty?"

"That I can't claim, Mr. Glenn, but I do bring a letter from your son in Philadelphia," The clergyman waved his saddle pouch in the air. Although Myles MacMillan now held a high position in the Philadelphia synod, he escaped whenever he could to ride his old circuit again.

The family was assembled and the letter read aloud. When Matthew said, "That's all of it," Anne bounded to her feet and switched across the floor, her curls bounding like the tails of angry red squirrels. She ran through the snow-blurred dusk and climbed the pegs to the loft. It was empty. No Willie waited for his evening tale of Aiken Drum or the mermaid of Barnhourie. "Willie! Willie!" She banged her fist on the floor. "Why aren't you here when I want you to be?" Grabbing Willie's whiskey jug from the corner, she flounced up the hill, pausing where the white-faced, nightcapped gravestones nestled in the hollow; she had never been to Willie's hut and didn't want to go there now. Brushing clear a spot on the Reverend Glenn's slab, she sat down on her folded apron and drank. Snow fell on the sheepskin fastened across her shoulders; twilight settled as though her mother had pulled the woolen bed-curtains in the stone cottage in Killyleagh.

Minnie. The gloaming-blue flakes conjured her mother crooning her melancholies by the ashes, and Anne sighed, remembering her scorn, her certainty that she would escape that fate, and now . . . She drank again. Five more years of a drudging denture while Jim sipped tea in Philadelphia drawing rooms with long-toothed gentry. And what if he never came back? Who would she marry then? Who could ever take Jim Glenn's place?

By the time the air was dark and the snow fields light, she had studied every man and boy in the valley as a possible husband and rejected each one. "Better wear no shooen at all," her mother had said, "than ones that dinna fit."

Tipsily Anne packed the empty wide-mouthed jug with snow, stuck in stalks of wild oats, and set it in front of Jake's rough stone. Perhaps this winter I will die, she thought, and in the spring Jim will climb the hill and find my grave. He'll cry and beat the earth, wailing, "Too late! I came for my Annie-luv too late!"

She turned and saw a gray phantom steed rushing through the snow; the forest trees became the spires of Philadelphia. In a flurry of flakes a carriage of brass and wood rolled to a stop, and out stepped Jim in his fine black suit, his blond hair thick in a ribboned queue. He kissed the hand of a lady in satin upon whose ivory cheeks the snowflakes turned to diamonds. "Annette, my love," he breathed. "Dear James," she said with a sigh.

"He's mine!" Anne cried. "You're a simp, a whimpering sop of nothing." She raised her calloused hands. "You can't lift a kettle or hold a horse. You can't jolly a man in the hay. Your babes will be weak and blue."

Her tears were wild, her jaw square as she whirled on Jim. "And you—you can go straight to hell!" She stumbled between the rattling ghosts of corn, on to the top of the hill, and down the path to Willie's dark hut. She threw herself into the emptiness, onto the skins laid by the banked fire pit. I'll run to Bess in Christiana, live in Philadelphia with sweeping silk skirts of my own, show Jim Glenn that . . . She banged her forehead against the furs until sleep came.

Anne was picking greens along the paddock fence when Jim, bent and staggering, appeared. She grasped the rails to keep from falling. Rebekah cried out and darted muddy from the garden to catch him; from all directions the family flocked like herding dogs around a sheep. Anne came slower, dazed and wondering. She stared at the nuzzling crowd tucking their feverish pride and joy under quilts and rugs before the fire. Anne, she murmured to herself, you have no rights. You're not his mother or sister or anything at all.

She meandered, head down, toward the barn. But one day you'll be his wife and then . . . Her chin came up. He's home! Jim's home! She skipped, then ran. She whistled for

Bonnie and threw her arms around her neck. "He's home!" He's home!" She raced through the paddock, scattering sheep and geese; the bull strained at the end of his tether; Shep, the border collie, raced by her side. Jim! Jim! Jim!

That evening she moved into the loft of the house and pulled her mattress beside a big knothole through which she could look down on Jim's firelit face. At first she was put off by the leaness of his jaw and cheeks, the weary older look of his eyes, but seeing the familiar pouty curve of his lips, the cleft of his chin, and the broad flatness of his brow, she collapsed with a whoosing sigh. He had come back.

For ten days Jim shivered with exhaustion and fever while his mother fed him warm nettle tea and rubbed his chest with tallow. Above him lay Anne, listening to his tales of Philadelphia—and how he came to leave it. On a blustery night in February he had stood flushed with love in the Arnolds' drawing room as Annette moved about on the arm of her newly arrived cousin, a captain in the British army. Her petticoats swept across the polished floor, her fingers drummed on his arm. "This is my fiancé, Captain Winslow Arnold. And this, dear Winslow, is our family's pet Westerner, James Glenn."

Jim stood dumb as an oak.

"How did you tame him?" Winslow asked.

"Changed his animal skins for broadcloth."

"Is it true"—the ruddy face peered into Jim's—"that you colonials carry scalping knives to use on the Indians?"

Jim stared at Annette. Her eyes above the haughty smirk of her mouth glittered. Pet Westerner. Pet. Tame. He rested his hand on his hip, where his hunting knife always hung. "Captain, I'd sooner walk among Indians than the scum that hides in the alleys of your cities."

Winslow's hand went to his sword hilt. "But gentlemen are always prepared."

Jim pushed aside his coat. "Maybe you'd like to take a closer look at a scalping knife."

Annette trilled, "Mama! They're going to fight!"

Jim walked out. He marched through the windy streets to his rooms and packed his trunk. It had been a hard, wet journey home.

Anne nursed her anger beyond the wall of hovering backs that wiped his face with warm cloths, told him gossip to make him smile, shushed anyone who spoke when his eyes were closed. Once as Anne passed by, Jim reached out for her hand.

She paused. Anne, if you take it you're done for. Once you touch him you won't be able to stop. You'll just throw youself on his bed. Dora's toe tapped. Anne wheeled on her heel, saying, "Best you get your sickie's arm back under the covers before his blue blood takes on another chill." She strutted out like a banty rooster and loosed her devils by hurling stones against the barn, against the faces of Dora, of Annette, and— "God forgive me," she muttered—of Jim.

The family circle kept Anne blocked out until on a morning bright with the gold and purple of dandelions and violets, he stepped from the door and lowered himself onto the bench beside her. She kept her eyes on the goose feathers she was stuffing into a new red comforter until he said, "Hello, Anne." Then she looked up. His smile turned her body to jelly, and her "Good morning" was merely a gurgle.

He rubbed his upper lip. "Do I need a shave?"

She laughed, thinking, there he is, there's my Jim. "Aye," she said, "and I need some summer freckles."

"You look just fine."

"How do you mean 'fine'?"

"Well, just," he shrugged, "fine."

Panic chilled and froze her love. She was the denture lass, just a denture he'd kissed in the sycamore tree. She was a throwaway nothing, just someone he'd practiced on, played with. Now at nineteen he could look back on that foolishness and laugh. She could almost hear him saying, "But you didn't take it seriously, did you, Annie? You didn't really believe I'd marry you, did you? Great governors! You mean you waited for me!" She burned with shame.

He touched her hand. "Look. Look what Shep's pup is doing."

Eyes dancing, soft ears perked, the black and white border collie was luring a knobby-kneed lamb away from its shaggy, grass-tearing mother. The ewe ignored the two young ones until they stood nose-to-nose, then she lowered her head and charged. The pup tripped on her oversized paws and tumbled down the bank onto the freshly raked dirt of the graden. Dora flew out the doorway, screeching and flapping her apron, causing the frantic puppy to get wound in the linen lining strings. Dora slid howling down the slope and Anne yelled, "Skedaddle, dog! She'll put you in the sauce to boil!"

The puppy hightailed it toward the barn with Dora after her, and Jim, his eyes moist with laughing, said, "To think what I missed by being in Philadelphia. It's good to be home." Anne studied his face again. What was he saying? What did he mean? "Aren't you glad I'm home, Anne?"

Glad? Glad was what friends were. What she felt for him had nothing to do with a word like that. If he loved her he'd feel the same. He'd know that his coming home meant . . . She couldn't even think of a word big enough for it.

"Anne, are you angry with me?"

"Yes." There, she felt better. It was he she was angry with, not herself. She waited for him to say, "I'm sorry I dallied with Annette while you were here being true to me," but he didn't. He started off on a tale of his hardships getting home as though it were she who should feel sorry for him. As though he were showing her that her anger was petty and childish next to the great things he had suffered. She was to be the puppy who when her master comes home flips on her back and waves her paws in the air.

"Aren't you making that a bit fat?"

Anne looked down at the comforter; she had stuffed in feathers so furiously that it looked like Clara MacClymond's great rear. She stood up. "I have to go to Mrs. MacClymond's now. It's my day to help out there."

"Oh. I forgot to tell you. Mam sent her word that you wouldn't be over anymore. She says she needs you here this summer."

Anne choked. "Needs me here! You mean now that the little prince is home, the serving girl has to stay close to wait on him instead of earning a few pennies on her own!"

"What's wrong with you, Anne?"

"I hate you! That's what wrong with me. I hate you!" She marched off, dragging the comforter behind her.

By afternoon Jim was doing barn chores; the next day he helped his mother plant peas, and on the sabbath he rode Bonnie to church. "The prodigal son!" Sam Brady shouted and Anne muttered, "Aye. Kill another fatted calf." Jim's deep blush when Louisa took his hand and batted her brown-cow eyes was the last straw for Anne; she switched down the grassy track for home, and no one even seemed to notice.

The next morning, Matt and Jim set off plow the bottom field.

"Anne," Rebekah ordered, "finish up quick and get to skinning those rabbits Willie left out on the shed roof. The men will need a hot stew in the field."

Anne's eyes followed Jim out the door—the swing of his shoulders, the set of his britches over his buttocks. Aye, she thought, I'll take him a hot meal in the field. Aye, I surely will.

Jim whistled softly as he yoked the two white oxen, then together he and Matt guided the bumping plowshare down past the garden and over the rough plank bridge. Each grasped a handle holding the blade to a straight first furrow, but after that Jim worked alone—back and forth across the waves of walnut brown, sweating, singing, pausing to smile at the pup who chased the settling birds.

Anne seated herself away from the eyes of the house in the tiny shade of the sycamore's pods and rehearsed her plan. While Jim ate she would be gay and coy, then she would press her thigh against his, loosen the string of her shift, and run her fingers along his cheek. She grinned. Then, Annie, when you got him panting and pleading for more than kissing and hugging, pick up the crock and say, "Well, laddie, I have to go now."

But her plan collapsed. Without a glance at her, Jim hunkered by the stew crock and ravenously stripped the meat from the bones. He cleaned the pot with a slab of bread, wiped his hands on a clump of grass, and asked, "Will you be my wife now, Anne? I'm done with the city and school."

She sat stunned, relieved but cheated. She wanted to start all over, do it her way, have him whisper those words as she had dreamed it for a year—him bending above her, the stars on his shoulders. Instead he was cradling the puppy, crooning into her white ruff.

She snatched the empty crock and stomped off to the stream.

Kneeling on the bridge, she watched the water flow into the earthen pot and tried to slow her angry breath. Her fists longed to smash something, hit someone. She wanted to hurt him, take revenge. But how? The mirror of the stream reflected his shadow, the crowns of the trees, the billowy clouds—and then Jim's head above hers.

He had come, he had come to her. Anne's shoulders sighed and slumped, but a demon took her tongue. "About your proposal of marriage . . ." Head cocked, she looked up at him and said, "Well . . . I'll think on it, laddie," and turned away.

Jim's shadow stiffened. "Aren't we the grand lady."

Touch me. Kneel beside me and run your hand across my hair, down my back. Please, Jim, please. He did not move. She raised the crock and poured out the water, smashing the shadows. "Somewhere I got the feeling you preferred grand ladies to dentures."

"Don't mock me, Anne. I suffered."

"You suffered! And what do you think I did for a solid year while you were playing Bonnie Prince James in Philadelphia? I was toting out the slops and night pots while your tight-arsed sister tapped her toe and glowered and thought up new chores to crack my back and wear down my fingers. I'm only fourteen and worn to a frazzle! You suffered? Hoot!"

But when she heard him shout, "Gee! Gee-up!" to the oxen in the field, fear jolted her to her feet.

She grabbed the tail of his shirt and babbled, in anger finally screaming, "And I didn't have anybody to talk to! No one but poor simple Willie." The plowshare caught on a root and while Jim flailed away at it with his hatchet, Anne beat on his back with her words. "I'm no simpleton, James Glenn. I know Matthew's been nettling you about settling down and getting some sons to run the farm. Don't shake your head. I heard him with my own ears." Jim sat down and dug about in the earth, searching for the root; Anne bent over him. "After making such a goose of yourself in Philadelphia, I can see your wanting to play it safe. I can see you thinking, 'Well, I'll take no chances this time, I'll just wed with old Annie. She's close at hand. Since I can't have Annette, I'll chose a healthy sow to bear my brats.'"

Jim looked up, and bright circles of pink mottled his cheeks. "I said that? You're daft."

Anne stuck out her knob of a chin. "It's what you thought. It's in your mind now. 'Ole Annie can just slide onto my mattress and be my wee wifie. My life won't have to change one hair.'"

"Anne, stop—"

"And if you had the gumption, you'd ride over to the Vances and propose properly to Louisa. But"—she tossed her head—"it was easier just to ask the dentured lass when she brought you out your dinner."

Jim rose slowly, his eyes fixed on her face. "Much obliged for the thought. Maybe that's just what I'll do." His broad, dirt-caked hands grasped the plow; he barked at the oxen and moved down the furrow, without looking back. I'll wager Mistress Anne's manners would be improved the next time I ask her to be my wife, he thought.

That evening Mr. Vance offered Jim his own chair and a gill of his best white whiskey. Jim stretched his legs toward the hearth, conscious of how his calf muscles bulged under the tight white hose and how the fine linen hugged his thighs. Mrs. Vance plied him with cheese, warm bread, and spring lamb cracking on the spit. Grown-ups and children hung on

40

his tales of Philadelphia, of the spring blizzard that had struck while he made his way home. While the others ooed and ahhed, Louisa skipped off and returned wearing a chemise that barely covered her nipples. The children were shooed to the loft, and on his way to bed Mr. Vance paused and asked, "What are your plans now, son?"

Jim almost answered, "Fondling your daughter's teats, sir," but he managed to clear the whiskey from his tongue enough to reply, "Farming and raising a family."

Gib Vance smiled, winked, and shook Jim's hand. "You don't need luck, son, and you know you have my blessing."

A warning buzzed in Jim's mind, but before he could pin it down, the sight of Louisa's bosum as she knelt by the fire swarmed all over his brain. She placed a warm cup of whiskey in his hand, pressing the heavy flesh of her breast on his knee. Sweat trickling down his chest, he leaned back and shut his eyes. You see, Anne MacKnight, I don't need your sharp tongue goading me. Other women know how to treat a man with respect.

"They're gone," Louisa whispered. Jim stared at her mouth, wondering why she sounded hoarse.

And furthermore, Miss MacKnight, they invite a man to kiss them and, he thought as he slid from the chair to the bearskin, maybe much more than that.

His mind shut down and his body, guided by liquor, lust, and heat wasted no time in gaining its objective. Jim found his member poised at her opening. Startled, he hesitated.

Louisa shoved her hips up. "Now. Do it now."

Jim struggled to stop. He was a child on a sled rushing down a steep hill and at the bottom was a pond, black, cold, and deep. He flung out his arms, his mittens slid over the crust of the snow. Nothing. There was nothing to grab. He cried out.

"Don't be afraid, Jim . . . you're not taking a virgin."

He clutched her words in his fist and held on. "Who?"

"Luke"

The sled spun in a circle and stopped. Jim reeled to his feet. Luke. The face leered at him. He wanted to pound it. Again and again. He moved, and his britches caught about his knees. He turned his back and pulled them up. Louisa called. Her thighs squirmed. Longing wet Jim's mouth, but the look on her face dried it. Cold eyes, tight lips, almost as if . . . His head ached. He stumbled for the door.

* * *

Matt poked his head through the hatchway of the barn loft. "Have a good night, James?" He grinned and winked.

The midmorning sun hurt Jim's eyes, his brain and tongue wore fur coats. He spoke without moving. "Where's Anne? She's late with the milking."

"Oh, Dora did it hours ago. Anne took a fancy to the moonlight last evening and now she's shivering in her bed with a cup of dandelion tea."

"The moonlight?"

"Aye. Seems she slept the night in the hollow sycamore." Jim groaned and covered his face. "When's the wedding, son?"

Jim worked his shoulders and rubbed the back of his neck. "We haven't set a date, but it will be soon." He stopped in the middle of a yawn. How did his father know? Had Anne told him last night? He raised himself on his elbow. "How did you find out?"

Matt laughed. "Gib Vance was here at sunup with the news. Seems he and Abigail have been hoping for this since you were a pup."

Jim sat up; the blood drained from his head. "Pappie, they've got it all wrong. Nothing happened last night. Nothing. I may have kissed her overlong, but"— he swayed and dropped his head—"I swear I said nothing of marriage. Nothing."

Matt's eyes narrowed to hard slits under the bristles of his eyebrows. "Gib said it was settled before he went to bed. And Louisa confirmed it this morning. I'm glad you've chosen one of our people. She of fine stock on both sides of the family."

"But . . . but I—"

"Gib's asked that you live with them the first year so that Louisa can help her mother with her new babe when it comes. I agreed. Seems to me Abigail's a mite old for birthing, but . . ." His voice trailed on over Jim, who had laid back down on the straw, his hands over his face.

"Gib and I figured a week Friday would be fine for the wedding. Best to work it in between planting and hoeing. He's telling Louisa. Reverend MacMillan will be up that week examining for communion, so it all fits nicely. Well, enough time spent gabbing. I'll need your help with the harrowing as soon as you feel fit to move." Matt disappeared, then his head popped up again. "Your mother's pleased."

Jim's skull, his whole body throbbed with the weight and clang of the iron harrow; he wanted to scream and run away, but Matt Glenn, the oxen, and the earth held him fast. At last the dinner horn blew and after the meal when the house had emptied out, he climbed the pegs and stuck his head into the dim loft. Before his eyes could adjust, Anne sang out, "I'm glad you finally found a woman willing to kiss your pompous arse."

Jim rocked backward, and the plea he had readied shriveled and died on his tongue. He bowed his head for a moment. Then slowly, without a word, he withdrew.

As wedding preparations churned about him, his lips remained silent, his eyes a stubborn, prideful blue. Like a child who has threatened to run away from home, he waited to be rescued from his wedding day by a word from God or Anne. Neither spoke.

Anne knew what he did not—that his father and mother were propelled on their furious course, at least in part, by the fear that he would choose her. If she challenged the wedding plans they would openly denounce her as an unfit wife and catalog her sins, and this she could not bear. So she kept silent, forcing herself to believe that Jim had lain with Louisa and that Matt and Rebekah were merely doing their Christian duty in seeing them wed. Everything turned inward; her sniffles settled in her chest, her fever rose, her mind grew dull.

On Jim's wedding day Anne lay alone in the loft, suffocated by fluid in her lungs and sorrow in her heart. She was surprised when she did not die.

Chapter Four

When Bess returned from Christiana and word came that after a fortnight at the Vances Jim had joined the army going West, Anne's illness dwindled and color returned to her world.

Gibson Vance had stormed into the barnyard, shouting the news of Jim's departure. "Why should he care about that wilderness when there's crops to be planted here? What does it matter if the French hold the land beyond the Alleghenies? What good will the Ohio River ever do me? What—"

Matt interrupted to say mildly that Jim was no doubt just taking the chance to visit his brothers Zac and Tommy, whom he had not seen for seven years.

"And I suppose he plans on returning from his little holiday about the time his year with me is up."

Matt stroked his beard. "I thought it was Abigail's giving birth without Louisa in the house that concerned you. Or were you just angling to get a year's work out of my son? You know, Gibson, it's usually the woman's father who gives the dowry. Not the other way around."

Chins jutted, words grew harsh, and the two men parted in anger.

Anne was jubilant as she snuggled next to Bess that night. "Now I don't have to toss and turn thinking of him in bed with that wet-eyed cow."

"Aren't you worried about him going into danger?"

"Oh, I don't think he would have gone if there had been any chance of him getting hurt. Jim's too careful for that."

Bess lay very still. "You say you love him?"

"Ooo aye."

"Bring the Bible. There's something in Corinthians I think you ought to memorize and include with your prayers every night."

When Bess blew out the candle, Anne recited the words into the darkness. "Love suffereth long, and is kind; love envieth not; love vaunteth not itself, is not puffed up, Doth not behave itself unseemly, seeketh not its own, is not easily provoked, thinketh no evil. Rejoiceth not in iniquity, but rejoiceth in the truth; Beareth all things, believeth all things, hopeth all things, endureth all things. Love never faileth."

After a long silence Anne said softly, "That's how I feel about you. Why is it so different with Jim? Why did I . . ." She choked and hiccuped into the pillow.

Bess put her arm under her head. "Because you are fourteen and Jim is nineteen. You are just finding out who you are, and you fight to protect that fledging self. You both used love as a weapon. It's different with me because I'm older and settled into who I am. You and Jim have to grow up."

Anne's head reared off Bess' arm. "But I am. I—"

"I don't mean the kind of grown up you thought you were when you were stealing potatoes to feed your mother and little brother. That was an animal clawing for survival. I mean growing up inside. Those verses go on, you know. 'When I was a child, I spoke as a child, I understood as a child, I thought as a child; but when I became a woman, I put away childish things.' The most dangerous living thing is a child's mind in an adult body."

Anne sniffed and pressed her forehead against Bess's shoulder. "I'll try."

* * *

The big blond woman with the gentle full face and the coltish, apricot-haired girl stayed close as two peas in a pod, side by side planting and fleecing, picking and drying, dyeing and dipping, gathering and stitching, cooking, and scrubbing clothes in the bubbling stream. Matt's arthritic joints had collapsed under the strain of a full load of work, and Dora had at last gotten her wish to work in the fields; one was barely cut before she was behind the plow herself, preparing it for winter planting.

The first letter from Jim arrived in September.

I've had my bellyful of soldiering and have parted company with the army. There was more fighting between the militia and the regulars, and the Indians who moved in and ate up all our stores, than between us and the French. You will hear charges of murder against a Virginian named Washington, who took command after our colonel died. It's true we did follow the Seneca Half King and at dawn ambush a party of French led by Joseph de Villiers. We shot him along with all but a few of his men, whom we made prisoners. A sorry busness, shooting humans in their blankets. After doing that we should have known de Villiers' brother Louis would take revenge and built ourselves a fortification, but Colonel Washington ordered us to keep on road-building toward Fort Duquesne. We got surprised, retreated to a meadow, and had to fight protected only by shallow ditches and a circle of upright saplings. Some of the men were drunk and it rained all day; we were up to our knees in water and wounded when Washington surrendered that night.

The French let us keep our baggage so I lit out for Gist's Plantation a few miles up the road where Zac and Tommy's place is. I should say "was." The French had burned it and a hired Indian had run off with Tommy's two-year-old daughter Esther. (His wife had died birthing her.) We are preparing to go into the Ohio country to get her back. Zac is a huge man and very skilled in tracking and fighting; Tommy is his shadow and together they make a powerful team. (Tommy is still simple and quiet so Zac does the thinking for them both.) They send their love to you, Mam.

A friend who is with me is heading East to catch up

45

with the army who high-tailed it for Fort Cumberland, so I'll send this letter with him. Don't worry if you don't hear for a while because Zac says there's nobody but Indians where we are going.

This land is beautiful and Zac is determined that it should be taken from the French, although they have built a very strong fort at the junction of the rivers. Of course, even if we get it from them the Ohio Company and the Virginia gentry will try to gobble it up. This Washington's already got thousands and thousands of acres in his name.

Please read this letter to Louisa.

Your loving son and brother, James Alexander Glenn

For days after the letter came, Anne sulked and slapped about the schoolroom she was helping Bess ready for the fall term. Bess ignored her mood until Anne dropped a pile of slates, breaking two. "What is the matter with you, child?"

"Jim. He's off having a good time, and I'm stuck here—"

Bess seized her shoulders and shook them. "Haven't you learned anything about love yet? Is it only words you're repeating every night? Love means thinking about the other person, not yourself. Do you realize how unhappy he is? He shot and crippled his brother. He didn't finish his studies for the ministry. He allowed his father to bully him into marrying a woman he didn't care for. He had to leave the home he loves. His army has been defeated and now he's going off into Indian country to help his brothers and perhaps get killed. And because he's a good God-fearing person he's taken all these things to heart. Don't you think he's praying every day for God to forgive him and call him to his life's work?"

Anne's chin dropped on her chest. "I don't see why God can't call women, too."

"He does. Clear as a bell he called me to teaching."

"I haven't heard any bells." One corner of her pouty lips twitched in a smile.

Bess rocked her in her arms. "Annie, fifteen is not very old." She kissed her curls. "And while you're waiting for your special call, God did give us a description of what a woman should be."

"What?"

"'Strength and honor are her clothing, and she shall rejoice in time to come. She openeth her mouth with wisdom, and in her tongue is the law of kindness. She looketh well to the ways

46

of her household, and eateth not the bread of idleness. Her children rise up, and call her blessed; her husband also, and he praiseth her."

"Well, if Jim were my husband—"

"Anne, you must realize that can never be."

"Louisa might die."

"Anne MacKnight! Don't ever wish a thing like that!"

Anne sighed, and her shoulder blades stuck out like wings as she slouched to the window. "I'm not doing too good on growing up, am I?"

"Now, now. Wallowing in self-pity won't help matters at all. I know you haven't had things easy, but just remember, neither has Jim. In fact, I don't know anybody who has."

Anne turned, a deep frown cutting between her red-gold brows. "How . . . how did you stay so kind and good?"

"God is our refuge and our strength. No one can do it without God."

"He never speaks to me."

"Maybe you're not listening."

When Bess had suggested to the family that Anne be her assistant that fall, they had cocked their heads and looked skeptical. Anne had rolled her eyes, looked woebegone, and said that standing whacking away at meat and turnips overtired her and surely milking out in the damp autumn air would bring on a relapse of her pneumonia. The suggestion that she sew brought true horror. "The strain on my eyes would affect my brain, which is already weak from my sickness." So Bess got her way and Anne's Killyleagh schooling was put to the test.

Anne was blessed with a marvelous memory. She could hear a passage of Shakespeare twice and have it memorized, she could do the same for a column of figures, and she could remember exactly where each child was in his or her lessons. However, Bess's efforts to translate this ability into writing failed miserably. Anne saw no sense in laboring with quill and ink when words rolled so effortlessly from her tongue. Her familiarity with Latin was limited to perhaps a dozen words.

Every morning at first cock crow Anne would dart from the bed they shared in the schoolroom, shovel the ashes from the back log, add fresh shavings and sticks, and pull the crane that held the kettle of water out over the flames. Then she would snuggle back under the downy comfort with two steaming mugs of English tea, her throat full of love, while the music of Bess's voice—the words were irrelevant—filled her ears.

One dark February morning, after Rebekah and Matthew had driven off to the MacClymonds, Bess paced silently from stone chimney to south windows, to the shelves filled with a hundred books from the Reverend Glenn's Belfast parsonage, to the doorway into the hearth room of the house, back and forth.

"I feel company coming," she said suddenly. "My nose has been itching ever since I woke up."

Anne rubbed her own small freckled one. "Mine, too. Do you suppose old Mrs. Vance is bounding over the hills to rave about you teaching her grandchildren tales of William Shakespeare, that ungodly Englishman?" When Bess didn't laugh but gloomily replied, "She's not the only one who would condemn me from straying from the Bible and the *Book of Martyrs*," Anne posed and cried, "'And all our yesterdays have but lighted fools the way to dusty death. Out, out brief candle!'"

Bess laughed then, but even after seventeen pupils, most of them Bradys, had arrived, she kept doing nervous things: jabbing her finger with a quill, spilling a pot of ink on the floor, staring out at the hushed lavender world and thickening clouds. At noon she took *Hamlet* from the shelf; the children tiptoed to hang their empty leather lunch buckets over the pegs that held their coats; the mad prince stalked the dim room.

The sudden sound of boots and a booming, "Anybody home?" from the hearth room lifted every rear right off the benches.

"It's Reverend MacMillan!" Bess's hands flew over her face. "We're not prepared!"

"Bah," Anne said, "he's only a preacher."

Bess whirled on her snapping, "And also the overseer of education for the synod of Philadelphia." She frantically stuffed *Hamlet* back into the bookcase and ordered the children to tidy the room.

The door opened; the children rose. "Good afternoon, Reverend MacMillan," they chanted as the big man in black broadcloth strode in. He had holier-than-thou pouches at the corners of his mouth, and eyes sharpened to pencil points from years of piercing their way into people's souls. Before greeting anyone he stooped to pick up some bits of chalk that had fallen on the floor; Bess templed her fingers over her mouth and shut her eyes.

He greeted the children formally, shaking hands, asking names and ages and questions about their families. Sniffing out sin, Anne thought, and tried to make her eyes blank, to hide her reoccuring visions of Louisa Vance lost in the woods, captured by Indians, eaten by a bear, or drowned in the creek.

Reverend MacMillan, however, didn't even look at her but turned to Bess and asked, "How much longer on her denture?"

"Four years. She's fifteen."

"She's growing. Her future should be thought of. For a lass blooming like this, nineteen will be too late to make plans for a wedding."

He raised one eyebrow in a smirky adult way and Anne's cheeks flamed, but before she could get a word out of her mouth, Bess said, "Be seated, children. Now what would you like to hear them recite, Reverend MacMillan? We—"

The minister nodded at Tod, who jumped to his feet. "Master Vance, what were you doing when I walked in?"

"Picking up, sir," Tod smiled. "Making the room neat for you. Sorry we missed the chalk."

"Don't be glib, young man. What lesson were you on?"

Anne jerked the minister's black sleeve. "History, sir," she lied.

"Then why," he said slowly, "didn't Master Vance tell me that?"

"He's slow." Anne tapped her forehead. It's not too far from the truth, Annie, he is a Vance. "Got kicked in the head by a horse when he was just a wee tyke."

Tod crossed his eyes and grinned foolishly.

Reverend MacMillan bent down until his eyes were level with Anne's. "I have a feeling that the devil wouldn't even have to turn sideways to walk into the cracks in your soul."

The corners of Anne's mouth stiffened, the veins in her temples pounded, unforgivable words swooped out of her brain, and she locked her teeth to keep from uttering them.

"Myles—Reverend—please—" Bess stammered.

Anne whirled and flinging out her long legs, thudded across the floor. Only Bess's cry of "Shut the door quietly, Anne!" prevented her from giving it one mighty slam. She hunched on the chimney stool, her chin in her hands. Well, Annie, you've done it again. This time you've got a minister of God on your neck. She stared into the orange and white embers without moving.

The door opened; Dora and a blash of cold air swept into the room. The heavy work of the fields had broadened her shoulders and thinned her face and hips. "Where's dinner?" she demanded as she slung her bullwhip over the peg by the door.

Anne glowered. "In the kettle."

"Why isn't the table laid?" Dora yanked the sheepskin from her shoulders and bits of straw as yellow as her hair flew into the air. Grabbing a bowl she filled it with broth, and slurped as she spoke. "Time you did a little honest work for the amount of food you pack away."

"I took on scutching the flax, didn't I?"

"Well, you won't have to do that anymore."

Anne sat still as a rock. If I don't do the flax, who will? Has Dora hired somebody new? Has she had someone bring a denture from Philadelphia?

Dora took a piece of gristle from her mouth and tossed it toward the fire.

Anne rose, stretched, and keeping one eye on Dora said, "Guess I'll do a little scutchin' one last time, anyway. Keeps me limber."

"There's no need," Dora snapped. Anne kept on toward the door. "Sit down, Anne MacKnight."

Anne whirled, hands on her hips. "Sounds like you're trying to keep me out of the barn. Maybe there's something there you think I shouldn't see." Dora bit her lip as Anne tied Matt's old sheepskin over her shoulders. "What's in the barn, Dora Glenn?"

"None of your business!"

"Have you found a new denture to work to death?" Dora didn't move. "Are you too cheap to pay the hired men what they'll ask come spring, so you—" She paled, her voice rasped. "No, not even you would do that. Or would you?"

Dora's back stayed stiff as an oak as Anne banged out the door.

In five minutes she was back, snow flecking her cap, her face set in cold Scot fury. She punched the door shut with her rear and bellowed. "Slaves!"

"There's nothing wrong with it!"

"They're slaves!" Anne raised her arms like a wrathful preacher. "Black men with their feet in shackles and their wrists in chains! Slaves! How in God's name—"

Reflected candle flames burned in Dora's eyes. "As I recall you were bought off the block, Anne MacKnight."

Anne's head whipped back with the slap of the words, then thrust forward to the end of her neck. "Maybe that's how I know it's wrong. If you'd worn a rope around your neck, Dora Glenn—"

50

"Good Christian people see nothing wrong—"

"And for their blindness they'll burn in hell! And Mr. Glenn will say the same!"

Dora leaped to her feet. "Don't you talk about my pappie! You have no right! You're nothing but Irish scum, while he—"

Anne's hand cracked across Dora's cheek.

"Get out of my house."

Anne trembled, but when the door of the schoolroom opened the Reverend MacMillan bellowed, "What are you women yattering about?" she tossed a triumphant glance at the bewildered Dora and shouted, "Sin! There's sin in this house!"

"Where?" The minister looked around as though it might be lurking in the chimney corner or the water barrel.

Bess, peeking over his shoulder, called, "Whatever it is, Annie, please don't say it in front of the children."

"In the barn!" Anne flung up one thin, freckled arm. "And it's a sin that everyone should see!" She rolled her eyes heavenward, and then as Dora sped out the door Anne shouted, "See how the devil flees before the light!"

Pandemonium filled the hearth room. Children pushed, the minister and Bess argued about whether to go to the barn or not, Anne preached from the tabletop about the wages of evil, and Rebekah came in from the cold. The Reverend MacMillan won the argument, and everyone "for the good of their souls" bundled themselves against the wind and filed through the doorway. Anne led, her black shawltips whipping like raven wings, her chin as high as her grandfather's at Londonderry. Reverend MacMillan and Rebekah followed her, and the big boys crowded behind, hiding their unease in nudges and loud guffaws. The girls trudged silently, shoulders hunched against the sudden chill; Bess, brow furrowed, trailed the crowd.

Inside the barn, Anne held the lantern high and saw the hatch door of the loft hanging down. "Gone!" she shouted. "Again the devil flees before the light!" She dove back through the gawking children, crying, "To the malt house!" Like a loose-jointed hound running a fox to the ground, she led the bundled figures past the house, along the old track by the corn cribs, and around the bend. The whiskey sheds loomed dark against the whipping trees.

"There!" Anne cried. "There stands sin!"

Reverend MacMillan shouted, "Halt!" and Dora crowded two men of color behind her. "Stand aside, Dora Glenn!"

An old black man stood like a post, his wide nostrils flaring against his scarred cheeks; a chain held his hands in front of his belly, and one end ran to his ankle irons. A taffy-colored boy, shivering with cold, put his arms around his woolly head and danced on his cloth-wrapped feet. Bess turned her back and covered her ears against the sound of the clanking metal.

The group surged behind the Reverend MacMillan as he advanced, crying in full pulpit voice, "Woman, what have you done?"

Dora gathered herself into two tight fists and a stony face. "Bought help for the farm. Try running four hundred acres with convicts, vagabonds, and boys with no pride in their work."

Hard snow drove across the empty fields; the children squinted against the sting; Reverend MacMillan hunched his shoulders and shifted his weight. Anne jutted her face into the wind. "You can't buy people, Dora. You can't buy human beings and keep them like oxen to do your work. They're men!"

"And you tell us, Anne MacKnight," Dora said with a rasp, "just how you get men to do your bidding. You were in the hay with my brother Jim before—"

Anne sprang for Dora's head, but Rebekah wedged herself between them, shouting, "'He that is without sin among you, let him first cast a stone at her.' John 7:8!" She glared at everyone. "I'll not judge what Dora's done. She's shouldered the burden for us all." Her tiny, gray-skirted body walked down the track, back the way they had come, her feet firm on the crusted roughness.

Reverend MacMillan cleared his throat. "Dora, take those poor shivering creatures back to the barn." When they, too, had disappeared into the blur of snow, he raised his face in prayer. "Lord, we will rest in your judgment and mercy. Command the consciences of us all. Thy will be done. Amen."

Anne spoke before the white wind had grabbed the "amen" from the minister's mouth. "I don't need a preacher to speak to God for me. I'm an Aiken and a MacKnight, and I'll tinker with my own soul, thank you. Right is right, and I won't stay for one minute in a place that has slaves on it."

Bess stepped beside her and took her arm. "Come, Annie." Anne balked, thinking Bess was trying to hustle her off, and her jaw dropped when Bess added, "We'll get packed up so we can sleigh out of here soon as the snow lays."

The tall woman turned to the minister, and her voice was cool as the wind. "If you wish, you may ride with us to Philadelphia."

"Philadelphia?" Both Anne and Reverend MacMillan gawked.

"Yes. I've had it in my mind for some time to go back." Bess put her arm around Anne's waist. "The house on Chestnut Street has been empty and needs looking after."

"You're doing this to protect that lass!" Reverend MacMillan roared. "You'll uproot yourself, dote on her, and mark my words all you'll get for your trouble is a twitch of her backside and a 'Fair thee well'!"

"I guess that will be up to God, won't it, Myles?" Turning and holding Anne close against her shoulder, Bess started down the white, rutted road.

Chapter Five

Hugh MacKnight had watched with round-eyed awe as his sister climbed from the ditch by the Belfast Road. "She's up and done it!"

"Niver mind, laddie." The Reverend Bruce fluffed his hair. "You and your mither will be ma charges noo."

For a year Hugh took advantage of Mrs. Bruce's puddings and biscuits thick with butter and the minister's library of books. His impish freckled face, azure eyes, and fire-gold curls won smiles from all who saw him. When his mother slipped away with the pox, the minister received many offers "to care for the winsome orphan laddie."

The childless man bristled at these suggestions and began calling Hugh "ma son," which caused the wary twelve-year-old to lay plans for his escape. One morning he raised innocent eyes above his porridge bowl. "I've heard the Reverend Bangor is heading up his flock to sail to America. I guess I'll be going along."

When Hugh appeared in the hearth room to ask Mrs. Bruce for a basket for a long sea voyage, she wailed, but he replied, "Anne is my sister and you have no legal right to keep me from her." He knew this was true from the books he had read.

Reverend Bruce, realizing he was cornered, put on a cheery face. "I've been waiting to tell you, laddie. Ma cousin Joseph Cannon is sailing on the *Eagle Wing* in a fortnight. He'll pay your passage in exchange for you serving him on the voyage and deliver you to the Second Presbyterian Church of Philadelphia, where the name of James Bruce is respected." He puffed his chest and hung his thumbs in his waistcoat pockets. "And if you don't die of consumption before seventeen, I expect you'll amount to something. I trust you'll remember ma kindness then."

Hugh bowed as he said, "Your servant, sir."

Hugh had half expected Anne to meet him on the dock, and he certainly was shocked to find that no one in either the First or Second Presbyterian Church had ever heard of her. He had better luck on the public wharf, where John Cooperson, now an auctioneer, threw back his head and said with a laugh, "Who could forget a wench like that? I sold her off to the Glenns of Octoraro."

Hugh chose the wrong wagon in which to hitch a ride west and woke the next morning to find himself working as a farmhand in Darby.

By changing horses twice, the sleigh holding Bess, Anne, Reverend MacMillan, and Ho MacClymonds reached the inn in Chester just as lowering clouds began sifting snowy bits of themselves into the twilight. Clara MacClymonds, having seen that it would cause Rebekah Glenn distress—theirs was the eternal feuding friendship of isolated neighbors—had bullied Ho into making the trip.

Anne and Bess hunched on creepie stools by the fire with bowls of rabbit stew warming their laps and cold-cramped stomachs. Ho, his nose as blue as the evening snow, stomped in from the stable and after him came Myles MacMillan, his face blessedly free of the constipated squint he had worn all afternoon. Anne stripped the damp wool stockings from her white feet and wiggled them in front of the blaze. A small purr whirred in her throat. Annie, you lead a charmed life. Going back to the city where you were so disgraced to live in a fine house with fine furniture with the most beautiful, kindest lady to care for you. Perhaps destiny is etching the frosty pane of your life with the gold of the rising sun. . . .

The stout innkeeper sloshed hot rum into wooden mugs, and the men, standing with shivering backsides to the fire, passed the time of day. When the second round had been poured, the host cleared his throat. "I've got a sick lad here, Reverend."

The men rocked on their steaming wet shoes and finished discussing the possibility of a heavy storm from the south before Myles asked, "Is he dying?"

"Don't know for sure. He's been in bed most of the week. Coughing and all. Missus says he's consumptive."

The minister pulled the only rocker onto the hearthstones and sat with his big hands cupping his mug.

"Want to see him?" the innkeeper prodded. "He's one of your flock. The missus found a church letter on him."

The minister sighed. "In the morning."

The innkeeper rubbed his chin. "There's a matter of a week's board. See, he just appeared one morning after some travelers had left. Usually I throw them stowaway boys right out on their ear, but the missus took a fancy to him. You know how women are over a likely child. But considering my wife's time nursing him and the vittles—"

"Fetch him!" Reverend MacMillan roared. "One thing I will not do is climb into a cold loft and get pneumonia myself!"

The innkeeper's burly legs soon reappeared on the narrow stairs followed by spindly ones in coarse stockings. A pale, freckled face peered under the rafters.

Anne shrieked, snatched the boy off the stairs and twirled him about. "I knew, Hughie. I knew you'd come."

"Mother died."

Anne's bare feet slowed, then picked up the pace faster than before. "Never mind, Hughie, we've got us a wonderful new mother."

Their entrance into Philadelphia was not, however, the triumphant affair Anne and Hugh had planned while waiting out the winter storm and the biting cold that followed. Gripped by winter fevers, they didn't even raise their heads from the floor of the sleigh but merely muttered from time to time, "How much farther?" Mr. MacClymonds wheezed out answers, but Bess was beyond talking at all—the crossing of the Schuylkill had done her in. The poleman had been half drunk, the wind high, and the water black and racing. Horses, sleigh, and people had bulged against the rope sides of the raft, tilting first one way and then another.

Anne had begun screaming, "They're calling me! The kelpies! Don't let the water kelpies get me!" Then in midriver, suddenly realizing that Hugh was twelve, almost to the age when their mother had tossed herself into the Irish Sea, she dragged him down under the furs, shouting, "Somebody sing! Somebody sing to keep the sprites from getting Hugh!" Reverend MacMillan burst into the Fifty-fourth Psalm, "Save me, O God, by thy name, and judge me by my strength," and somehow the crossing was effected.

Hugh, his blue-green eyes slick with fever, coughed and could not stop; Anne held him tightly and bargained with God. If I concede, Lord, that it is you and not luck or sprites or brownies and such that have the say in how things go in this world, I'll expect you to let Hughie live. She pulled down the covers and looked straight up to heaven. I'll even try to control my own pride in such matters.

The arch of the trees above them had been replaced by plumes of smoke that bumped the low, gray clouds; sleigh bells jangled, soft hooves thudded past. Anne gasped—how many chimneys are there? A hundred? A thousand?

Reverend MacMillan shouted, "Mr. John Morton!"

Bess cried, "Cousin John!"

Bit rings clicked, leather squeaked, a horse breathed frost into the air above the children. "I got your note from Chester, cousin. The house is dusted and aired and I've had fires going in every room for two days. Welcome!"

John's huge face resembled a serving platter set with two saucers of china blue, his smile was half a noggin rim, and bowls of cherries filled his cheeks. The horse slobbered, and Anne ducked under the robe. So that was Cousin John. Her head popped up when she heard him say, "Well, I could use a lass with a quick memory in my shop to keep books. I've opened a furniture business on Second Street just around the corner from your place. If you send the boy to the Academy she should have some sort of a trade besides housemaid to fall back on. Let me know if you decide on it."

Anne peeped out at the big man. Me keep books! Merciful heavens!

April, Hugh, Anne, and Philadelphia became entwined— from the King Street wharves west to the greening meadows along Eighth Street, from South Street eight blocks north to Vine, the city of the Penns belonged to the laughing girl and the pixie boy.

They poked in shops and alleys, ate pastries off trays and

56

oysters from barrels; they eavesdropped on Quaker meetings and British soldiers lolling by tavern doors. They watched mechanics—blacksmiths and coopers, tinsmiths and silversmiths, wheelwrights and joiners—at their work. They counted the wagons on Market Street—how many of skins and tobacco, of cordwood, of barrels of whiskey, flour, and whale oil—and the unloading of crates of cloth, casks of rum and molasses, crowds of soldiers, dentures, and slaves. They scurried like water rats along the docks, and when the cryer sang out the name of a new ship, they ran to the top of Society Hill and watched her come like a queen out of a picture book, flying the flag of Boston, Providence, Portsmouth, New York, Charleston, Havana, Portugal, or the bold, proud Union Jack. Hugh dreamed of being a sailor in the rigging, Anne of being a captain's wife standing by the rail in billowing skirts, hugging ten children under her arms.

They crept into Christ Church and saw the implements of the devil: kneeling benches, a pipe organ, a gold cross, and even a black-skirted rector. Hugh wanted to sneak into the Popish chapel on Fourth Street, too, but Anne drew the line at that. "The tinkle of one Mass bell would plunge our souls into their purgatory for a thousand years." But when players came to town they watched, although they knew the sin of it rivaled seeking pleasure on the Sabbath or taking the name of God in vain.

The two places avoided were the Market Street prison, with its pillory, stocks, and dunking stool, and the public dock, with its auctions of dentures. One afternoon, however, Anne stopped dead by the steps to the wharf. Seizing Hugh's arm, she dragged him down toward the young man with brown curls. "John Cooperson," she said in wonder. A tall woman whose body resembled two boxes—a rectangular one on top and a square one on the bottom stood alone beside John. "Poor thing," Anne murmured. "Just like I was, she's the leavings of the barrel."

A man called, "Take her arms out from under her shawl, mister! We're not buying a pig in a poke!"

The woman had only one hand. Mister Cooperson bravely waved her empty arm in the air and yelled over the hoots, "There ain't nothin' she can't do with this stump! She'll get you more work done in a day than any two flighty young things with four hands between them. Now, what am I bid?"

People made a show of turning their backs and walking away. The veins beating white in her temples, Anne rubbed

Bess's marketing list off the slate with the side of her fist and wrote out an I Owe You. She passed it up to John Cooperson. How do I know you're good for the money?"

"Can't you read?" Anne snapped. "It's signed by the Reverend Blackwood's widow." Turning, she took a step toward the silent, hard-faced woman. "You'll be coming with us."

John's ale-hazed eyes widened. "You're Anne MacKnight! I sold you off in Octoraro. What are you doing here?"

"I live in the big brick house on the corner of Chestnut and Second. The two-story one where a gardener takes care of the flowers and grass."

He laughed. "You gilpy! You always were a sassy one! I'll be there first thing in the morning for my money."

Anne's back shivered as the woman's hard soles thudded on the dock behind her. Anne MacKnight, you've done a large thing. How do you know she won't run away? Won't pull a dagger from her skirt and do you in right in the muck of King Street?

The soft flesh of the woman's stump tapped her shoulder, and Anne jumped a foot. The wooden jaw moved. Her voice was gravelly, as though it hadn't been used for a long, long time. "My name is Mrs. Held. I'm obliged to you for taking me on. In London my husband was a butcher. Mean as gristle. I up and told him one day I was leaving. He cut off my left hand. On the block with his meat cleaver. Next time I went without telling him." She rolled up the sleeves of her dress and took the market basket. "And here I be."

Bess was on her knees polishing the hearthstones with cream. Mrs. Held repeated the words "Here I be," added "ma'am," and knelt beside her. While Anne and Hugh babbled explanations to the dumbstruck Bess, Mrs. Held, with the rag wrapped around her stump, finished the hearth and rose and clomped through the house, collecting clothes from every peg. She dumped them in the tub, and uttering the single word "wash," disappeared through the door.

Mrs. Held, like an ancient, hoary tree—although Bess thought her no more than twenty-five—had an immediate and profound effect on the household. Hugh and Anne kept their distance, and if her black eyes turned toward them they ducked out of whatever door was handy; Bess worked side by side with her until she twisted her back in a fall over a cat on the stairs. After that Mrs. Held took over all but the cooking and sewing. The cat she strangled as a sign of her devotion to her mistress.

While Bess sat stiff by the front window with flannel-wrapped bricks down the back of her dress and while Mrs. Held's brogans tyrannized the rest of the house, Anne and Hugh began a carefully planned second delving through the city. This time they not only looked but also asked the smith why he was adding copper to silver, the sailor how the horn pipe worked, the workmen how they would hoist the huge new bell into the State House belfry. The fatal question "Mister, why did you choose that horse to bet on?" was overheard by Joseph Cannon, now an elder in the church. He grabbed their ears and marched them home where Bess, despite the pain in her back, scrubbed their faces, necks, and arms up to the elbow with strong lye soap while muttering, "Gambling, idleness, ostentatious display, drunkenness, loose-moraled women. Now rinse yourselves in the rain barrel and march upstairs to bed."

Anne eavesdropped on the hearth room conference of Bess, Reverend MacMillan and John Morton then reported to Hugh. "They say our willful temperaments are to be curbed immediately—yours by the Academy on Fourth Street, and mine by bookkeeping for Mr. Morton."

"The wages of sin," Hugh said and dramatically thrust his hand from the bed covers. "Luck to you, Annie. Ouch! You don't have to hold on so hard. Why be upset? We saw most everything."

Reverend MacMillan passing through the hall below shouted, "I thought Widow Blackwood told you 'No talking'! Get into your beds. You are both to be called on the stroke of five tomorrow." The front door slammed behind him.

Hugh pulled back the bedclothes. "Get in." Anne did.

"Maybe," Anne whispered, "you ought to be a minister, Hugh. Bess has her heart set on it, and after all, she's paying to raise you."

"Well, there's nothing wrong with having doubts. And I'll bet Jesus had them when he was my age, but because He was the Son of God he had no choice." Hugh paused. "School, Annie. A real school. Masters who can speak Greek and Latin . . ." He squeezed her wrist. "I'll tell you everything in the evenings. Don't be sad. I'm going to live right here in this house for the rest of my life. It'll be you who leaves to go off and marry."

"Who said I'd marry?"

"That Jim Glenn you moon over is not the only man in the world."

Anne's cheeks puffed. "That's because you've never seen him. Besides, more likely you'll be moving a wife in here."

59

"No. It would be a sin for me to marry and leave a flock of orphans."

Anne banged his leg. "Don't talk about dying like that!"

"Shhhh. You'll have Bess climbing the stairs with a switch. Or worse yet, Mrs. Held and her evil eye." Anne squirmed out of the blankets; Hugh grabbed the back of her nightgown. "You're mad at me."

"It's not that," Anne sniffed.

"Look, even if you marry, we could all live here. I could be another father to your children."

"In a week, Hugh MacKnight, you won't even know I'm alive."

"Annie, I swear—"

Bess's foot hit the bottom step, and Anne lunged for her bed.

John Morton had had the huge bellows and forge hauled out of an old farriers' shop; a window cut beside the big sliding doors; and deep, clean straw laid over the earthen floor. Although charcoal and horse smells still clung to the beams, nose level was sharp with lumber and wood shavings. A huge plank carpenter's table stretched from the front door to the back like a flat open mouth filled with the teeth of vices and clamps. Over the giant mouth hung a dozen chisels and gouges, hammers, adzes, a drawknife, shavers, hewing hatchet, mallet, open saws and frames saws, augers and bits, and planes and rabbets for every curve and shape. Enough tools, Bess remarked, to build the city of Philadelphia twice over.

Anne's stool and slant-topped table stood by the window in the best light, and for the first two mornings Mr. Morton was constantly beside her explaining this and that about columns, entries, and letters to be written. She had no trouble doing the figures in her head, but the letters she pretended to blot and then took home to Bess, who patiently drilled her on writing clear sentences in a round hand. Anne argued against using big words that were so much harder to spell, but Bess convinced her that the Academy would indeed take Hugh away unless she kept him on with her education. For the sake of Hugh's companionship Anne was willing to do anything—even write like the gentry.

Talk of war rolled from the tongues of everyone who came into the shop. That first small battle on the muddy Great Meadows just south of Gist's plantation had spread worldwide, but who would rule North America remained at the heart of the conflict. The French claimed that all the land west of the Allegheny Mountains belonged to them, and as Jim had predicted, charged Colonel George Washington with murder. The great British general, Braddock, assembled two thousand soldiers and with red coats gleaming marched on Fort Duquesne.

Bess, in agreement with social custom, had had a balcony, an awkward elbow jutting from under Hugh's bedroom window, built onto the house.

Every evening after a bread and milk supper Bess, Hugh, Anne, and Mrs. Held changed into clean clothes, and clutching sewing or whittling, crawled out the second-story window. Chairs and stools were arranged so that Bess looked uptown, Mrs. Held downtown, and Hugh and Anne—who endlessly whittled new handles for everything rather than sew—kept an eye on the street below. Twenty thousand souls now inhabited the city, and it appeared as though they all strolled the streets, handkerchiefs brushing away mosquitoes and flies, voices raised in debate over rumors that Braddock had been defeated and the whole of Pennsylvania lay open to the savagery of the Indians and the army of France. Occasionally Bess allowed Hugh and Anne to join the walkers, but they went so burdened with instructions as to how little ladies and gentlemen behave that it was less taxing just to sit.

Anne, careless of how deeply her knife peeled splits for a new broom, stared into the dust-drifted road, playing out a drama in her head: Louis de Villiers, le Grand Sieur de Jumonville and older brother to the dead Joseph, comes riding a big black stallion down Chestnut Street, his buttons and epaulettes catching the evening sun. Behind him come rows of blue marching men, their boots stirring up great yellow clouds. He raises his white gloved hand: a sergeant cries, "Halt!" Louis walks his horse to the balcony and bows over Bess's hand, murmuring, "Your brothers were brave in battle. It is unfortunate they chose the wrong side. Has the auld alliance of Scotland and France come to mean nothing?" Then he turns, sees her, and—

"Cutting those a mite thick, girl," Mrs. Held said with a rasp.

Anne raised her head but her eyes never reached Mrs. Held's face. It was not the imaginary French commandant who sat on a dusty red mare a mere yard from her, but a husky blond youth with eyes the color of an unclouded sky.

Jim had come back.

Anne sat as rigid as death while his jaw, no longer softened by boyish curves, moved with the message he brought: Four

61

hundred British regulars and militia dead, four hundred more wounded. Sixty-eight of eighty-six officers killed or incapacitated. Braddock dead. No regrouping of the retreating forces at Fort Cumberland, just a mad scramble east.

"Zac? Tommy?" Bess breathed.

"Not hurt. We were all to the north, scouting the Allegheny River for possible French reinforcements. We came back to report and . . ." He put one hand over his eyes and reached for the railing with the other. "Sister," he said softly, "I'm falling asleep."

The next morning, Anne leaned on a clothes post behind the house.

Annie dear, you're suffocating already. How are you going to get through the morning? And what is going to happen when he walks in the shop or you come home and see him sitting at the table, the sun shining on his hair? Maybe I'll faint. Just faint away. I really don't think I can stand it. She raised her eyes. God, if you want me to behave like a Christian lady, you'll have to figure out something on your own, because this poor weak flesh is not up to it. She took two steps and stopped dead. And if he once touches me . . . if just once the tips of his fingers . . . She shut her eyes and swayed. In that case, Lord, I'm warning you, no power on earth or fear of eternal damnation can keep me from falling straight into his arms.

She sat on her stool; any figures she wrote came from fingers that were not hers. And when Jim did appear at the door she laid her head on her desk and cried.

Jim's fingers, the warmth of his palm caressed her hair— "Annie, Annie." With a cry and a rush she flattened her cheek against his chest, and his arms circled her like an iron hoop.

Above the roaring of her blood she heard Mr. Morton shout; Jim let her go. Her forehead fell back on the open ledger, her fists pounded the wooden desk. Cries pierced and echoed in her brain. I can't bear it! I can't, I can't! He's mine, he's mine! She couldn't breathe, the blood drained from her head. Then all was still.

Mr. Morton held a cup to her lips. She dripped with sweat and tears. The figure of Jim stood dim in the corner, his hands clenched behind his back. She slumped. I can't, I can't. Dear God, it's too hard.

An image of Bess entered her mind, and her voice sliced the grayness. He's a married man, Annie. And any move you make will disgrace you both, drive you apart so you will never lay eyes on him again. The pain is a woman's cross you'll have to

62

bear. He loves you. Let that be enough. It is more than many ever know.

Anne ran her tongue over her lips. "I'm all right now. The strain . . ."

Mr. Morton's hand awkwardly rubbed her back. "Of course, lass, of course. This business of war . . ." He shook his large, oval head.

Jim had stepped into the yellow blare of the morning sun. She nodded. I love you. I love you beyond anything in the world. His lips formed a small, tight smile. And you love me. But for now we must let it be. Keep it our secret, Jim.

John Morton gave Anne's shoulder a final pat. "What do you say, Jim, to coffee at the Merchant's?" Jim wiped the heels of his hands across his cheeks and nodded. "A lot of folks—important folks—are going to be interested in what you saw in the West."

They left; Anne sat alone, eyes staring but not seeing. The sounds of feet and hooves and wheels were muffled by dust that lay thick as powder in a rifle pan; sun motes danced like sparks. At the boom of the courthouse clock she clapped her hands to her ears. Bess was right. He could have been killed. He could be lying dead out there instead of drinking coffee a few yards down the road. She shuddered. Aye, Annie, now you see. Now you see that love is caring more about him than yourself. He's alive. He's still in this world. That's what matters. Love beareth all things, believeth all things, hopeth all things, endureth all things.

Minutes after Jim and Mr. Morton returned three men, one broad, one lean, one stubby, presented themselves in the bright doorway like silhouettes from a Mother Goose rhyme. The lean one spoke. "We're here to see the young man in from the West. John, I believe you know Mr. Franklin, and this is Mr. Galloway, the Speaker of our Assembly."

In contrast to Franklin's plain, owlish look, Galloway wore an emerald coat of stiff brocade with sleeves wide enough to hide a piglet in each one; the girth of his paunch was cumbered in silk, and lace spilled down his front; his wig was tight with freshy ironed curls, and he posed with two fingers pressed against his powdered, jowly cheek.

John Morton introduced Jim, hands were shaken, then the three men flipped their coattails and perched on the window seat with their canes held between their spread knees. Galloway rapped the tip of his against the hard earth floor and squeezed words out through his arrogant nose. "I am given to understand, young man, that you have had some, ah, experience with the unfortunate situation in the West."

"Aye," Jim said, his back stiff.

"It is imperative, my man, that you tell us at once all that you know." Galloway flopped his hankerchief toward Jim. "Come on, man. You were there, weren't you? Speak up. There's got to be more to this story than some savages behind trees with bows and arrows. I smell a whiff of cowardice. Desertion of Braddock by his officers, perhaps? This Colonel Washington surrendered once before under most peculiar circumstances."

Jim's lips moved an inch apart, then snapped shut again. Anne drifted through the shadows until she stood behind him.

Galloway stood and shook his cane. "I didn't bring myself out in this heat to be gaped at by a backwoods Scot-Irish boy who's incapable of uttering one word of the king's English." He waved a ringed finger at Anne. "Have that wench there fetch me some water and I'll be on my way."

Anne leaped forward, thrusting her face into the fat powdered one. "You've never met me, Mr. Galloway, but I drank in the tales of your family's tyranny with my mother's milk." Her hair came undone and tumbled down her back. "My long-ago grandmother, widow of Jamie Watt taken at Bothwell Brig and shipped in chains to Barbados never to be heard of again, once rose on her toes at the feast of Michealmas where the old Earl of Galloway was strolling among his starving serfs, puffed up with himself that he was roasting two ox to give them their first taste of meat in six months or more, and he made the mistake of shoving a noggin in the face of Grannie Watt of Glenturk, and crying, 'Crone, get me fresh ale.' Well, sir, she did what no one in all the land had ever done before, she rose up on her toes and spit in his eye."

As Anne leaned forward, Jim's fist closed around Galloway's raised cane forcing him back down on the window seat. "I'll give you one chance to phrase your question to me like any civilized Christian gentleman in America should."

"Chair!" Galloway screamed. "Someone get me my chair!" Jim stepped to one side, and the Speaker strutted like a routed goose out through the doorway.

Issac Pemberton, the Quaker leader, sighed. "Deliver America from the conscience of the Covenanter." He put his hand on Jim's arm and looked at Anne. "Old grudges must be buried in the ground of the old country, not in our heads. This is neither Scotland nor Ireland"—he glanced at Jim's wide fists, and the purple trough on his forehead left by an Indian war club—" nor the frontier. America can survive only through compromise. Each man must recognize that there are many paths that lead to the same end."

Jim swallowed hard. "What end, Mr. Pemberton?"

"Liberty. Liberty for all."

Franklin raised his scraggly head, innocently sniffed the air, then spoke. "I do believe the Widow Robert is lifting the quail from the pot at the Indian Queen. Can't you smell it, Issac? What do you say, Mr. Glenn, and you too, John, to a dram of good whisky, a fat quail, and a pile of biscuits light as air?" He flicked the folds of his cravat under his double chin and rose. "It has been my experience that politics taken straight are liable to stick in a man's craw, but given the proper acompaniment"—he kissed his fingertips—"*Voilà!* They slide down slick as a whistle."

Jim blushed. "I have no coat."

Franklin touched his homespun shirt. "No matter, son. With shoulders as young and broad as these"— he winked at Anne— "you can go anywhere. And the sooner you passionate Scot-Irish learn that politics is not what you say but how you say it, the better it will be for all of us." He cocked his hat. "Politics is an art."

"And no one, Benjamin," Pemberton said, "practices it better than thou."

A special session of the Assembly was called to deal with the threat from the French armies to the west, and Jim Glenn was asked to address it. John Morton gave him a quick course in Pennsylvania politics. Thirty-six legislators—elected by the propertied citizens of Philadelphia, Bucks, Chester, and the surrounding eastern counties—met every fall in the State House on Chestnut Street. The average voters' concerns were the condition of the roads, the laxness of the town watch, and control of young men who rode their horses pell-mell down crowded streets. They had for years assumed that as long as they cast their votes for those who did not represent the Crown, the larger issues of commerce, taxes, and war would be decided in favor of the common man. This was no longer true. An aristocratic circle composed of the Penns, whose need to protect their huge holdings from taxes allied them with the British Crown, of prosperous Quaker merchants, and of pacifist Germans now controlled the Assembly and passed legislation in their own interests. Fear of the populous, ambitious, politically skilled Presbyterian community had tightened the circle, and they fought to exclude them by keeping the counties beyond Chester disenfranchised and voters in the habit of casting ballots for men endorsed by them.

The defeat of Braddock, however, had convinced men like Franklin, Pemberton, and Galloway that the Scots and Scot-Irish must be temporarily granted some power until the French and Indians ceased to pose a threat to their city.

While Cousin John educated Jim in the foxy ways of politicians, the Reverend MacMillan undertook to sharpen his speaking skills. He found his task an easy one. Having spent all his formative years under the same roof as his silver-tongued grandfather, Jim seemed simply to tap a spot in his brain, and words with the iron of Moses, the song of David, and the pith of Jesus rolled forth. When Myles MacMillan found he could not improve Jim's speech or the mightly cadence of his delivery, he slumped into his chair, muttering, "When the church lost you, Jim, it lost a giant. I hope someday you reconsider."

Jim's face closed. "I'm a farmer, sir. With a wife to support."

The elegant brick entrance hall of the State House glowed gold with light. Hugh called from where the great bell sat on its timbers, Anne lifted her skirts and petticoats high and ran across the grass. "Hugh, it's huge! They'll never get it up there." They circled, reading the inscription: Proclaim liberty throughout all the land unto all the inhabitants thereof. Leviticus. 25:10.

Anne nodded gravely. "That's what Mr. Pemberton said. Liberty for all." A tingle of pride straightened her spine. "And that's what Pappie used to shout. If only he had come here instead of—"

Hugh slipped his hand in hers. "But we did, Sissie."

Inside the State House brother and sister stood like Hansel and Gretel before the gingerbread house, too awed to do more than nibble at this and that with their eyes: ceilings twenty feet tall, carved wainscoting, polished floors, paintings, mirrors, liveried servants serving breakfast drams of rum, glittering men and women reaching out, saying, "Mr. Glenn, Widow Blackwood, Miss MacKnight, Master MacKnight. Charmed."

Anne's cheeks flamed and she desperately tried to make her

body conform to smooth curtsies. It's a blessed thing, Annie, that Bess didn't give in and let you dress the way you wanted to. When Anne had first seen the shimmering gray silk purchased for her new dress, she had mumbled, "Do you really think gray is my color? Doesn't it seem a bit drab?"

Bess had dropped her hands in her lap. "If there is one thing we are going to be in midst of that assembly of gentrified English peacocks, it is respectable. Gray is respectable. It does something to tame the wildness of your looks."

"Just because the English have boring skin and hair and eyes that all blend into looking like a piece of a road, why should we try to ape them? Now with my hair and eyes a bright emerald green—"

Anne sank with relief into a seat in the back of the Assembly room between Bess and Hugh. However, a glimpse of Jim chewing on his knuckle tied her stomach in knots again and she whispered, "Please, God, don't let him be so nervous he loses his place."

The long prayer ended; Speaker Galloway rose from his desk on the dais and called out Jim's name. Anne sat dry-mouthed and dumb as a stone, but Jim rose, tugged down his coat sleeves, and with the rolling stride of a backwoodsman, walked to the front.

On the dias he turned and planted his heels as though confronting a walleyed, balking horse; the papers shook in his hand, the lapels of his new coat curled, and his voice halted and squeaked like a wooden wheel. Anne died a thousand deaths until he cleared his throat and the word "thirdly" thundered rich and deep. His cleft chin jutted above his plain white stock, and his azure eyes seemed to suck thoughts from other men's faces, forging those ideas into words that ran from his tongue as smoothly as sleigh runners across packed snow. He rolled his notes in his farmer's fist, raised it, shook it as he spoke of the battle and Braddock's falling and Colonel Washington's efforts to rally the panicked troops.

Bess beamed; Hugh sat entranced; Anne gaped at this stranger who instead of fearing the gentry confronted them as though the black robe of Geneva fell from his wide shoulders and the righteousness of John Knox—who had made even the Queen of Scots weep—commanded his tongue. He's a king, Annie, no doubt about it. He's king of all these wigged men sitting with their hosed legs kitty-cornered under their desks. They should see him sweaty, shouting to his oxen, "Ho! Ho!"

Heads swiveled. Anne jerked in fright. Had she spoken out

loud? No, it was something Jim was saying . . . he was speaking of her! She leaned forward, cocking her head, her curls trailing down her cheeks.

"By the age of twelve she had seen more of the tyranny of men than I trust I shall see in a lifetime. She watched soldiers take her schoolmaster through the gates of Hamilton Castle and emerge with his limbs soft from broken bones. She wandered homeless when her father was turned off his land—the land his family had farmed for five generations. Think on it, gentlemen, five generations. Then the Lord Hamilton snaps his fingers and this man, Bartholomew Black MacKnight, elder of his church, subsheriff of County Down, is deposed, left to wander a vagrant of the road. Sleeping with his family in roadside ditches, sending his small daughter to slink through the mists of the Irish morning to steal potatoes. Why, gentlemen? How could this horrible thing happen?"

Anne wiggled her bottom in satisfaction. You say it as well as me, Jimmie.

Jim leaned forward, his face fierce, and each word shot out like a ball from a musket. "Because Bartholomew Black MacKnight did not own the land he worked." Silence. "Englishmen, Scotsmen, Irishmen may cry 'Liberty!,' may shed their blood for liberty, but I say to you"—his words thundered and echoed about the chamber—" there is no liberty without land! If gentry, not the common man, holds title to that land, only they have liberty.

"If we allow this land to become one of lords and serfs, we will have failed our forefathers, we will have failed God, we will have failed ourselves. For it is ourselves, gentlemen, to whom we must give to this land of living."

"Hear! Hear!"

Jim flushed and rose on his toes. "The two most powerful kings in the world are fighting over the land beyond the Allegheny Mountains. And well they might—it is rich beyond measure. We as British subjects will fight the French, but victory will only bring others scheming to be lords of those forests and rivers. Virginia planters. Traders. Indian chiefs. Aristocrats of Philadelphia."

Jim's lower lip crept forward. Ooo aye, Anne thought, they're in for it now.

"But there are others who also dream of this verdant land. Others who do not lust for tens, hundreds of thousands of acres but just enough for crop, orchard, and woodlot. They live in the glens and slopes of those western mountains. Their cabins are crude, their women go barefoot, often their children are

68

hungry. 'Dirty Ulstermen', they're called. And when they get scalped, nobody cares."

He paced, and his plowman's fist struck the rail. "Well, gentlemen, you'd better care. You'd better hope that it's those hardworking, God-fearing pioneers who settle that land. You'd better hope it's them who ride the back of the Ohio River west to the Mississippi. You'd better hope that they keep on pushing and fighting for land of their own, because if they don't—if the French and Indians wipe them out—you will see a West carved into kingdoms of speculators, see feudalism clamp its black maw over God's Country.

"But I say, gentlemen, if we today have the courage to do the hard things that must be done to secure freedom in that land"—he brushed back, as though by accident, the lock of hair that hid the scar of the Shawnee war club—"if we dare to risk now for future good, we will indeed glorify our lives and our God by securing true liberty throughout the land and for all its inhabitants. Gentlemen, our consciences demand that we do no less!"

Assemblymen rose, and over their applause Jim shouted, "I propose that this assembly have placed before it a motion to vote funds for the building and garrisoning—with our own Pennsylvania militia—a string of forts along the Blue Ridge Mountains!"

Canes thumped. Voices cried, "Hear! Hear!"

Galloway's high heels clicked to the front of the dais. "Mr. Glenn, am I to understand you do not favor another British expedition?"

"You understand wrongly, Mr. Speaker." Jim did not even glance at the dandified man. "I do favor another British expedition. But we must remember that if their army fights our war for us, they will present us with the bill—in taxes. The London treasury has a bottom, and their citizens will insist that we bear the burden of our battles. The greater the costs of the British army here, the more taxes you will see. Who taxes this commonwealth and whose army marches across it determine who rules it. I prefer the rule of the men in this room, my neighbors, to that of a Parliament thirty-five hundred miles away. What we do not decide here will be decided for us there."

He stepped from the dais, and his "Thank you, gentlemen" echoed in silence.

Benjamin Franklin rose and stood quietly by his desk, frowning, pulling at the flesh of his chin. When every head had turned to him, he spoke as though thinking out loud. "For a long time we have squabbled in this chamber over whether the Penns' lands are subject to taxation. I suggest we close that Pandora's box for the moment and return to it when this emergency is past. I move that we accept the proprietor's offer of a gift of five thousand pounds while reserving our opinion that they are not above taxation. And I further move that sixty thousand pounds be appropriated to be used for the defense of the western citizens of this commonwealth, that defense to take the form of fortifications—manned by our militia. Pennsylvania men."

Issac Pemberton, on his feet before Franklin had finished, said, "Mr. Speaker, I regret that my faith does not permit me to second what appears to be a necessary motion, but I am sure others not so bound will act in our mutual interest."

The motion did carry and the gavel rapped. Anne and Hugh scurried to the entrance hall.

As Anne hesitated Jim's voice fell on the back of her neck. "Were you proud of me, Annie?"

She shut her eyes and turned, and sure enough, when she opened them there was his face all fair and pink and stuffed with love. "Aye," she said. "I was fairly overcome—the way you made the land come to life . . ." Her breath gave out.

He smiled. "I borrowed a long cloak. If you like, we could drape it over both our backs and walk home. Who needs a carriage?"

Her mouth opened wide and her laugh was full. "Wait. My new shoes." She held his arm while she removed them, then lifted her skirts. He dropped the cloak over their heads and they ran out, boots and bare toes scuffing the puddles.

Chapter Six

Jim left for Octoraro in the morning. Two days later he turned Bonnie north at the church grove, away from his parents' farm, and handed himself over to Gib Vance's harvest and Louisa's bed. Both father and daughter greeted him with stiff necks, anxious to extract an extra pound of flesh for his waywardness. He bore the long days of work, the long nights of Louisa's seductive thrustings for a child by locking himself in memories of Anne. Others mistakenly thought that the war, the horrors he had seen in the West, made him withdraw, but in truth he lived with the tilt of Anne's head, the ring of her laugh, the freckles that danced on the white of her chest, the long-legged bounce of her hips as she walked, the bold love in her eyes for him. Sometimes his scythe stopped in midswing, sometimes he turned from Louisa in bed and said, "I have to milk now. Tonight we'll . . ." His voice would fade, and her nails would slide off the leather of his britches, leaving rough, tan streaks that even the dust of flailed grain would not erase.

He remained at the Vances' through hog butchering, then announced that he and Roger MacClymonds were off on a winter hunt that would take them to the far side of the Susquehanna, maybe beyond. To cure Louisa's unstoppable tears, he promised to return before New Year's Day.

In mid-November Anne returned from Christiana where she, already immune to the pox, had kept house for a MacIllwain family going through inoculation. Her first glimpse of the narrow brick house on Chestnut Street filled her with foreboding; inside she found Hugh on a pallet by the hearth, his muddy eyes sunken in the snow white of his cheeks, his breath quick and rancid; Bess said it was the tenth day of his illness. A sudden spasm of coughing left his bedclothes and chin flecked with blood, and Anne fled from the crumpled, weepy face Bess raised to her.

Upstairs she knelt beside her bed, her voice strangled with dread. "Not Hugh. Not Hugh. Dear God, not Hugh. Anyone but Hugh."

Bess brought broth, but Anne crawled between the autumn-damp sheets and turned her face to the wall. All night she bargained with God. She promised Him anything in return for Hugh's life; she renounced every sinful, selfish thought she had ever had and swore that each day of her life from then on would be an accounting of good—she would be good enough for herself and Hugh. "Even Jim," she said when she woke to the too-silent house. She repeated it so God would be sure to know that she meant it. "I will give up Jim if you let Hugh live."

Anne crept past Bess snoring in her bed, around Mrs. Held asleep in the rocker, her wooden jaw hanging on her chest, and crouched staring at the humped pallet until certain he still breathed. "All right, God. Whatever you say."

She heard a voice. Build up the fire. She did. Wipe the

blood from his lips. She did. Say, "Thank you, God," five times. She did. Hang the kettle of broth on the crane without making a sound. She did. Did he stir? Did his eyelids under his blond brows flutter? Watch him—watch him. She did.

The voice dictated her every move. If she disobeyed and Hugh died . . . The thought was unbearable.

Time became skewed—sometimes minutes were days, whole nights of sleep the wink of an eye. Ritual filled her with tiptoeing fear. When the voice declared, Seven spoons of soup, no more, no less, she obeyed. When it whispered, The tip of the ear of a black cat might help, she clipped one. Read to him, his mind is going. She read until her throat ached and she coughed and felt tight in her own chest. Maybe they would die together. She and Hugh. She saw their coffins side by side. Our Father, Who art in Heaven, hallowed be thy name . . .

"Annie." She listened, but no orders followed. "Annie." She turned toward the pallet. Hugh's lips moved. It was Hugh, Hugh who spoke! "Annie, please don't stop reading," he said. She reached for the Bible. "In the beginning was the Word and the Word was with God and the Word was God. In Him was life; and the life was the light of men." Her voice trembled.

Hugh smiled. Anne leaned closer. There were flecks of green sun in his eyes. Thank you, God. Thank you, thank you. Then she slumped and cried.

They studied together all winter, every book on history, theology, and mathematics that he would have read if he had gone across the river to the college in Princeton, New Jersey.

In March Hugh weakened again, but by May he was walking to the top of Society Hill; in June Anne returned to John Morton's shop and Hugh, reveling in his new strength, split roof shingles for him with a mallet and froe; a month later, Reverend MacMillan asked him to ride the summer circuit. Anne balked, unwilling to let him go, but Hugh bounced with excitement, leaping in the air and clicking his heels.

"He's only asking so you'll be persuaded to go into the ministry," she said sourly.

"Well, maybe I will."

"I can't imagine anything worse than spending two months with that black-backed crow."

Hugh folded his neatly muscled body onto the stoop; his voice squeaked and slipped as he reached for a man's tone. "But Annie, I have to think of how I'll make my living. You'll marry and—"

"Never! Never!" She pounded her foot on the cobblestones. "I'm done with that forever!"

Hugh leaned back and looked up at her. "Well, if you grow much taller you'll be a giantess and no man will want to live with you anyway."

She swung her fist, he ducked and laughed, and she chased him clear to the end of the public dock, where she boxed his ears and called him a runt.

After Hugh left, Anne sulked. Bess asked if she wanted to go to Octoraro to escape the heat; she thought of Lucifer and the rolling hills and the cool springhouse with its crocks of butter and milk, and she almost said yes. Then she imagined Dora and the sound of her boots and Jim and Louisa living as man and wife just five miles away—facing them every Sabbath. "No!" she shouted. "No. We left because of the slaves and they're still there, aren't they?"

Bess shrugged. "I haven't heard of their being sold. And I doubt if they will be until Jim comes home."

"Why hasn't he . . ." She stopped and turned away. Bess didn't answer. Anne never thought of Jim in a concrete way, as a separate person married to Louisa Vance; Jim Glenn lived inside her, entwined with her deep self; nothing he or she ever did would change that feeling of being together.

Business in the shop was brisk; the Indians, who had come close enough to lift scalps within sight of the Christ Church steeple, had been driven back and the forts built; immigrants—all needing chairs and dressers and bedposts—arrived by ship and cart and foot every day. Anne felt easy now with most of Mr. Morton's old customers, and although ladies with big hats and arched voices still set her teeth on edge, she leaned forward when the men talked politics. She had been in the State House—an invited guest!—seen the important men, and heard Jim Glenn's speech; she had read Aristotle and Plato with Hugh, she was educated; she imagined herself a Boston lady where, she'd heard, women talked politics over their tea.

Robert Bailey was one of the men who wandered into the shop almost every day. He leaned his hips against a barrel and talked of this and that while John drilled and varnished. Sometimes when Anne knew he wasn't looking she would cup her chin in her hands and study him.

She had no curiosity about the boys Bess dragged to her side after Sabbath church, but Mr. Bailey was a man—a prosperous, respected merchant, owner of a fine estate on outer Chestnut Street, and often she led Cousin John into conversation about him. A second son, he had come to the colonies in '41 with fifty pounds to his name. Ten years later he possessed a half share or more in a dozen coastal ships, two newly built schooners for Caribbean trade, a beautiful wife, and three sons. He apparently held the world in his hands until Martha Bailey took leave of her senses at Mrs. Chew's annual first of May tea party. For years she had been homesick for England; now he took her there behind a locked cabin door. And returned alone. When he commissioned a statue of her and placed it in his garden, friends sighed, saying it was a blessing she was out of her misery and he was free to marry and give his boys a mother. Bess had clucked about widows and spinsters throwing themselves in his path, but Anne knew their efforts were in vain. Once, with John Morton and John Cooperson in the shop, she had heard him with her own ears say, "No, John, the only things I care for, aside from the business, are my sons, my garden, and racing my horses." After he left, Cooperson had snorted and said, "Add to that a jaunt now and again to the fleshpots of the Caribbean." Anne had pondered the possibilities behind that statement for days.

Having received a long oval mirror framed in walnut from Cousin John as an early seventeenth-birthday present, Anne was newly and vitally interested in the human body. Although Mrs. Held warned of the devil stealing her soul, and Bess, citing Scripture against the sin of vanity, said never to look in a mirror longer than to check for a dragging hem or hairs that had strayed out of her cap, Anne ventured farther and farther into the wonders of admiring herself. At first she inspected her face for imperfections—none appeared except perhaps her mouth was a trifle too large and her ears too small—but one night she had peeled away all her garments and stood, arms at her sides, staring: freckled breasts, belly and thighs curving around her bones like beaten egg whites flecked with cinnamon, a triangle of red-gold hair shining like a lighted lantern. Ooo Annie, she thought, you should not be doing this.

Afterward she had felt the weight of her sin every time she looked at her nakedness, but since stopping was impossible, she rationalized. After all, Annie, how can God expect you, a bonded Scot-Irish orphan, to be more perfect than Eve, whom He Himself took from Adam's rib?

It amused her to discover that when she began studying Mr. Bailey with new found imaginings about naked bodies, he dropped his eyes and turned away. Once when Mr. Morton was not in the shop she tested her power by flashing him the smile she had practiced in her mirror—lips pressed together, corners turned up, green eyes dancing above her high cheekbones. Mr. Bailey had actually paled before it.

The sun blistered the city. John Morton's moon face waned in the heat until one day he yanked his apron over his head. "It's too hot for any man or beast to work. Go home, Annie, and find a cool spot if you can. Come back when it's cool tonight if you want to." Unbeknownst to Bess, Anne spent the rest of the afternoon in a tub of water in the shed, reading a novel. After supper, clad in her old shift she padded to the shop. Opening both the back and front doors to entice the faint river breeze inside, she began sweeping.

Second Street lay shuttered and still, puffy with dirt; a yellow haze sickened the sky. Sounds drifted from Chestnut Street: children playing hide-and-seek, the occasional muffled clop of a horse's hooves, or laughter from the balconies. Into the drowsiness burst an open carriage of gay young ladies.

Anne pulled a stool into the doorway and wiped her damp face with a corner of her sleeve. Now, Annie, would you really want to be heading off for the Thursday Night Assembly? Dancing the minuet and playing cards and dropping your hankie on some fool's buckled shoes? She shut her eyes. No, I'd rather be in Octoraro at threshing time. With long tables of food set under the trees, fiddles warming up as the stars begin to come, Jim, his hair dripping from a dip in the trough, taking my hand and— Stop it, Annie, you promised God you wouldn't.

Gloaming descended and the mosquitoes swarmed; Anne rubbed tallow on her arms, laid a handkerchief over her face, and leaned her head back against the doorframe. The breeze died and the heat pressed down; Anne dozed, and into her sleeping came the sensation of being watched.

She rose and stepped into the shop. Her hands had already gripped the door to slide it shut when a man's figure stepped from the light into the dimness beside her. She whirled to run, but his arms clasped her from behind and his lips pressed her neck. "Anne, Anne."

Mr. Bailey! Her mind spun, her arms hung by her sides as he turned her and kissed the tip of her chin, her mouth. She had never been held so tightly or kissed so long, never felt a man's tongue caress hers. He released her and she almost fell, but he did not steady her or even speak; he simply disappeared out the door. Anne held her face in her hands, tasting him on her lips. Mr. Bailey. Robert Bailey.

She bolted the door, felt her way across the dark shop and out the back. When plowmen had seized her in the fields of County Down, they had not kissed her like that. No, their mouths had lunged for her breasts, and the weight of their bodies had forced her onto the ground. This kiss had been different and Mr. Bailey had whispered, "Anne, Anne," with such . . . love? Her head snapped up. Had she been Called? Called to be Mrs. Robert Bailey?

That night she dreamed of a forest by a river. Strangers told her to be calm, that there was no danger, but she ran, searching up and down the high riverbanks, calling for someone whose name she did not know. There were children crying.

She woke to a world without color, a solemn, dove-gray place. Frightened, she tried to doze off, to finish the dream so it would not come again, but the cat leaped from the sill and padded across her coverless body. A shriek of dawn hit the mirror, flushing the room with pink light. She jerked upright. Annie, Mr. Bailey—Robert—kissed you. You've been Called—to riches! Your life has begun!

She took special care dressing and in spite of the summer sunlight that streamed through the shop window, sat prim and cool on her stool; she had laid aside her cap, and her hair flickered with copper. She expected that Mr. Bailey would come early to catch Cousin John alone; he would speak to him as he would to her father. She played out the scene of his asking for her hand; and when John's back was turned, practiced how she would tilt her head as she said yes.

The tower clock bonged another half hour. Where was he?

A shadow fell across the door. Anne half rose, but it was only John Cooperson.

He perched on a keg of nails, the smell of his ale breath filling the shop. "River's damn low," he said. "Both the *John Bailey* and the *David Bailey* hoisted anchor yestereve." He spat out the door. "With the water they draw they'll be lucky to get out—damn channels so silted up."

"Did Robert sail with them?"

Cooperson laughed. "Surely did. Probably figured the Caribbean couldn't be any hotter than Philadelphia."

That night Anne sat naked on the foot of her bed, staring into her mirror. Her shoulders slumped in the heat; so did her mind. Her reflection looked pasty and ugly. She pulled on her worn cotton shift and stepped to the mirror. The edge of a huge yellow moon peeped over her shoulder and lit the room with magic; she fluffed her hair. "Don't you realize, Robert, that it is impolite to keep a lady waiting? She may get angry and leave you."

                                    * * *

Three weeks later the crier shouted, "The *John Bailey's* made port! Molasses and lumber and . . ." The Bailey carriage, with all three sons on the box, dashed down Second Street. Annie clung to her stool, thinking, he'll go straight home. Tomorrow he will come and . . . Again she pictured him and Cousin John talking while she sat waiting, but now the scene no longer pleased her. She would not sit like a piece of furniture about to be bought.

The next day dawned crystal clear, with a spanking wind out of the north, a whiff of autumn to come. Anne leaped from bed, sure that the good weather was God's approval of her plan. Blue linen, white lamb's-wool shawl about her shoulders, a hasty mouthful of porridge. When the clock banged nine she spoke. "Mr. Morton," Too loud, too heavy. She pitched her voice higher and recited the words she had practiced. "Mr. Morton, we have a smidgen of bills that could go out today, and it's such grand weather I thought I might take them myself and save you the cost of hiring a boy."

John Morton didn't answer, but his large freckled arm, busy sanding a tabletop, slowed, speeded up, then slowed again. "Whose?"

"Whose? Oh, yes." She shuffled bills, cleared her throat, and said, "The Plumstead Warehouse on King Street, the Chews on Vine, the MacDowells on Fifth, and . . . there's was one more . . ." Say it! Her face flamed. "The Baileys on Chestnut."

Mr. Morton rubbed the sander across his own flat cheek; bits of sawdust furred his chin. "It's a long walk to the Baileys."

He knew! "But the air's so fresh . . ."

"All right," he said and turned his back; the sander whoosed across the wood.

No, Annie, he doesn't know. He's letting you go. Get up. Get out.

She crossed the street, then muttered a prayer to the steeple of Christ Church blazing against the sapphire sky. King Street, where the brick warehouses shoved their overhangs against the loading wharves, was a bare-chested, rum-sweating world of shouts and grunts and curses. Holding herself very tight so no man would think her slack or loose, and with her bonnet providing blinders against their nods and winks and muffling their whistles and hellos, Anne moved with her eyes fixed on the Plumsteads' sign.

Inside the warehouse she held her breath against the gagging odor of whale oil; once back on the street, the bales of tobacco, hemp, and tanned hides smelled almost sweet. See, Annie, you're handling things just fine.

She stayed on King Street until Vine, then turned the corner into the stillness of dusty trees and droopy, tail-swishing horses, frame houses with shuttered faces, and gardens turning yellow. A servant bustled from a door, a basket on her arm—as mistress of the Bailey house Anne would send her cook to market early while the greens still were fresh. A lady, her hair piled high, stepped into a sedan chair—as Mrs. Bailey, she would . . . What did ladies do all day? Dress up and pay calls? Ugh.

The Chews' dogs lunged and barked at her; the butler extended a tray for the bill. I don't want to live with a butler Anne thought, even Mrs. Held would be better than one of them.

On Fourth Street she quickened her pace. The British soldiers lolling in front of the Cross Keys Tavern must be avoided, the jostling students outside the Academy must be ignored, the Popish chapel hurried past . . . Horace Jones leaped into her path. Full of excitement, he waved a pickle at her.

"Miss MacKnight!" The pickle, fresh from a vendor's barrel, dripped juice into the dust. "May I walk with you?"

"It depends, Mr. Jones, on what you intend to do with that."

He looked from her to the pickle in bewilderment, then bit off one half and offered her the other. She shook her head and laughed, pushing his hand away. He took that as a friendly sign and fell into step beside her. Crunching and slurping and swallowing, he said, "Mama wants to know when you're coming to tea. Widow Blackwood promised her you would."

Annoyed, Anne walked faster and Horace galumphed along.

"I am about to make my fortune, Miss MacKnight. My uncle is organizing a party to round up wild horses and cattle in New Jersey and ship them off to the islands to sell as meat."

Horace Jones on a horse with a wild cow charging him? No, Horace Jones balancing tea in his mother's parlor, maybe taking old ladies for a drive . . .

Horace peered around her bonnet. "Are you laughing at me? Well, you shouldn't. Uncle is having a Pennsylvania rifle made for me."

"You won't be able to lift it." She bit her tongue. Here she was, scared of soldiers and the rough men on King street, yet sneering at Horace because he was gentle. She turned up Spruce Street. Where did Mr. Bailey fit? She began putting him in different scenes, trying to figure out how he really acted, not just the way she pretended he did in her daydreams. As she cut across the ruts of Fifth Street her palms began to sweat—she didn't know Mr. Bailey at all.

She left the timid Horace on the MacDowell's porch drinking cider and hurried on past the State House where the boardwalk ended in sullen dust. What if Mister Bailey lunched at eleven? What if he napped after eating? Last night it had all seemed so clear: Instead of waiting for Mr. Bailey to come to the shop, she would go to him where he could kiss her again, say he loved her, and ask her to be his wife. She mopped her face. Bess is right, the reading of novels has softened my brain. In front of her the Bailey house rose like a mountain: square brick turrets at each corner, a dozen pillars supporting a second-story porch, windows as tall as those in the State House.

"Ooo aye, 'tis the bonnie queen herself come to grace the hoose o' Robert Bailey." A gangly gardener with tight gray curls clicked his pruning shears.

Anne gulped. "I've come to see Mr. Bailey on business. I—"

He winked. "Come. We'll seek him oot o' his hidin's."

They ambled up the walk, he gabbing, Anne gawking at the house. On the porch a woman rose with her mending; a needle bobbed from the corner of her mouth, and her words rode right over the man's. "I be Sarah Jamison, lass, and I'm wed to that dandy there." Anne looked around, puzzled. The woman laughed, and her belly bounced. "Him. The one who's been gabbing your lug off."

She muckled up close to the other side of Anne and the three of them started around the house, Mrs. Jamison bragging about the handsome son they'd left in Scotland and Mr. Jamison adding with a wink that he'd need a wife when he got to America.

Mr. Bailey rose from when he knelt planting tulip bulbs. His shirt was streaked with dirt, his calves bare, and his toes curled into the soil. Anne bobbed a foolish little curtsy. Either this man had never kissed her, or all the novels she'd read had been wrong. He was just Mr. Bailey with the friendly brown eyes, a man who came into the shop to talk to Cousin John. No "tide of passion rose in his face," no "masterful hand" was laid on her arm. He simply sent the Jamisons off to prepare lunch for them all.

Anne reached in her pouch. "I've brought Mr. Morton's bill."

"And your own, I presume." Robert took the paper.

She was undone—fallen to staves like a bushel basket left out over the winter, spread flat, helpless to gather herself together. Robert had turned so that she could not read his face.

"Come," he said. "I'll show you my garden."

Her suddenly docile feet followed him. He named flowers and shrubs, and explained the giant sundial of marigolds. "Now there, see how the shadow is almost touching the bronze ones? Look sharp and you'll find they make a XII for noontime. Campbell Jamison's a genius. We're creating a garden as fine as my father's." He smiled proudly.

Anne thought of the days she and Hugh had rooted in the cold winter earth hoping for a forgotten turnip or two for the kettle.

They stopped by the fish pond and her feelings went topsy-turvy—the statue of his wife was not a large, green-streaked bronze edifice but rather a nymph of black marble kneeling beside the water with arms reaching upward, exposing perfect satin breasts.

"My wife," he said.

"Yes."

"Do you find it beautiful? The artist . . ."

Anne didn't hear. Artist. So this was art. Now she understood. Art was something made by human hands that rivaled God's creation. God had made Mrs. Bailey's body, but the artist had captured it in a way even more lovely. Well, God was in the hands that made it. But was He? Had He spoken to the man with a chisel as He had to Matthew, Mark, Luke . . . Bess said all beauty belongs to God. All truth. But . . .

Mr. Bailey's hand closed around hers. She yelped and drew back, then blushed and stammered. "I—I—I—"

"Never mind," he said and walked to a grape arbor, where he plucked a giant purple bunch and handed it to her. "Eat. You must be hungry."

She ate; she stuffed grapes in her mouth, swallowed seeds and sour skins. Had he been about to propose marriage? Her mind roiled in shame. She'd acted like a child. All her worst fears about herself had come true. She was a sow's ear and would be one forever. He wouldn't want her now. No one would. Fool. She crunched and ground the seeds between her teeth. Fool!

A handbell rang and Mrs. Jamison called, "Hew-whoooo! Lunch!"

Anne followed Mr. Bailey's back, trying to get the words "I can't stay" past her teeth. She entered the French doors still mute.

She had been in houses like this one before only in make-believe. As a novel heroine she had swept in and out of dining rooms with burgundy velvet at the windows, panels of oak covering the walls, sideboards bright with silver, crystal set on a stiff linen cloth. Now she was just Annie and it was a nightmare. Only Mrs. Jamison's coming and going, the swaying of her great breasts and hips kept her from disgracing the MacKnight name further by jumping from her chair and racing out the door like a daft backwoods clod.

Soup, cheese, cold grouse, bread pudding with cream. Anne tasted nothing, heard nothing of what Mr. Bailey said. Mrs. Jamison served coffee and port, and the door swung shut behind her. Silence pressed, deadly as the eye of a storm. Anne's small spoon clattered in her saucer; she dared not touch the fragile goblet. Was it over? Could she be excused now?

"Anne, please look at me." She squinted, but he stayed a wavy meld of browns, not earth browns, but polished ones, hard and shiny like mahogany. "Anne, I apologize for what I said about you presenting your bill. I have behaved badly. That night before I sailed, that night in Mr. Morton's shop . . ."

Bread pudding leaped in Anne's stomach, started up her throat. She swallowed and didn't move.

". . . at fourteen you were a wild creature coming out of the forest. I watched you grow and lose your fears, become beautiful . . ."

He rose and started toward her. Faint! If she could only faint!

His hand pulled her head against his shirtfront; his heart thumped in her ear.

". . . for the past year I've known that . . . that there is no one in the world I want more for my wife."

She clamped her jaws.

"But I already have a wife."

Good. He has a wife. I can go home. But his hand—his hand was stroking her cheek!

"I wanted people to believe she is dead." He took a breath and let it out. "Because it is easier than the truth. She's in England in my father's house. Locked in the back room. Mad.

His cheek was resting on the top of her head; his fingers were burning small holes in her arm. "I never should have kissed you. I should not be touching you now. Anne, Anne . . ."

His face was beside hers. His mouth . . . "She may live as long as I. Maybe longer. Anne, I love you."

Love. Love doth not behave itself unseemly, seeketh not its own . . . Love never faileth . . . But when that which is perfect is come . . . Jim, Jim. Did she push him? Cry out? She didn't know, but when she opened her eyes, Robert Bailey was by the French doors, his fist beating a tattoo on the wall.

"For Christ's sake, Anne!" he cried. "Say something!"

If she were in a novel she would say, "I'll wait for you, Robert," but she was Anne MacKnight, so she sat silent, her hands, folded, while God gathered up the staves of her self and bound them tightly with hoops of ash. She stood up.

"Anne?" His voice was pebbly now, and his fingers pulled the ruffles below his coat sleeves.

"I must go, Mr. Bailey. I'm late for dinner."

He followed her into the hall and handed her her shawl and bonnet. She wished she were old enough to say something to ease the twisted sadness in his face, something that would let him know that she understood, that it was all right. But if she tried he might touch her and . . . and the staves would come undone.

"My carriage," he said. "I'll—"

"No!" She burst out of the door.

Mr. Jamison drove her to town and to her horror followed her into the house. She fled upstairs to her bed. "That nosey old busybody! Who does he think he is? Lies! He'll tell her lies!"

However, by the time she heard him bid Bess good-day, she had to acknowledge the truth in her bones: Mr. Bailey's kiss in the shop had been prompted by lust and was in no way an offer of marriage. His use of the word "wife" today had been a ploy so that he might have his way with her. Around the edges of her thinking boomed the voice of the Reverend MacMillan. Had she led him on? Had she given him reason to believe that . . . She jumped up. I am not a whore! I'm not!

She did not hear Bess's tread on the stairs, and by the time she glimpsed her shadow coming around the end of Hugh's bed she had had time to do no more than rub her cheeks on her sleeve. The stern look on Bess's face melted into a moan, and she cradled Anne in her arms. "How could you know. How could you be expected to know?"

Within the week a hired wagon had been loaded, Mrs. Held given her freedom and a bondwoman's due of two sets of clothes and five pounds, instructions left for Hugh to go straight on to the college at Princeton, and Anne and Bess were on the road for Octoraro.

Chapter Seven

The valley people did not seem surprised to see the Glenns' eldest daughter and the denture lass she had taken as her child.

It was the same at the farm—kisses, hugs, no questions. Bess barely had her bonnet off before she was set to making gravy, Anne to washing a tub of beans. At the blast of the dinner horn the two hired hands and the slaves addressed as Mr. Black and Mr. Brown trooped in, glanced at the new women, then bent to their food. Dora stiffly embraced Bess, nodded at Anne ladling cider, said, "Certainly can use some more hands around here," and heaped her plate with biscuits and beans. Matt beamed at Bess from the foot of the table, and Rebekah sat pertly at the head; ten- and eleven-year-old Cissy and Cindy Brady, on loan to Rebekah as house help, completed the table.

The harvest consumed them all, and Bess's trunk remained unpacked until the end of September; by then Anne had stirred Robert's kiss into stews, kneaded it into bread, husked it with corn, and dried it with pumpkins until it had become part of once-upon-a-time. The crib was fat with hard yellow corn, the barn with the last of the dry, sweet hay, the root cellar with two tons of potatoes, turnips, and squashes, the barrels with cider, the rafters with honey fruit and hanks of yarn dyed goldenrod, blackberry, and sumac. Anne and Bess, stunned by the sudden hush, sat limp-handed, staring while the song of the cicadas reached its furious peak.

Bess roused herself to send out word that school would commence in a week, but Anne prowled the far edge of summer, restless, not knowing what she sought. She climbed to the top of the sycamore and saw nothing that was new; she dunked her woman's body in the beaver pond, bled, and felt no calmer; she walked to the MacClymonds—found Roger had gone to sea—came back, and considered she had been nowhere. Each day she wandered farther.

The first time Anne stood, her shadow blending with the

forest, looking down the slope to the Vances' house, she called herself daft and quickly strode home. Her next trip was more deliberate: She lured Lucifer to the pasture beyond the knoll, tied a lead rope on his halter, mounted, and rode the long way around through the woods. Leaving the stallion tied in a thicket, she crept through the tall grass to the lip of the meadow. Sheaves of flax had been hung on the fence above the barn, and Jim, bare except for his britches—the unbuttoned bottoms of which rode over his kneecaps as he swung the heavy-jointed stick—flailed the sun-burnished stalks. Dust dulled his skin, the rooster comb of hair between his nipples, the ridges of his belly. Anne lay without breathing; the rhythmic rise and fall of Jim's wrists, his little grunts, stiffened her crotch against the ground. She gripped the grass, sawing the edges of it into her fingers while half her mind screamed, He's mine! and the other half, He's not!

The blatt of the dinner horn straightened him, and staring at the place where she hid, he mopped his face with the back of his arm. She pressed the earth, and her lips moved against the heat of it. Annie, you shouldn't be here. You promised God. Maybe Hugh will die. Annie, Annie, what are you doing? She waited for Jim's shadow to fall over her. It didn't. She raised her head; he was gone.

She became obsessed. Again and again she returned to the Vances and came home feeling empty, her next trip already plotted. She knew no peace. Her mind, her movements grew cunning as a cat's; she could freeze for an hour if need be, move through a weed patch without a ripple, see by starlight. She did not name what she craved, what she went for, what she returned without.

On a day when the sun flamed brass in a colbalt sky, Jim came from the barn, a leather seed pouch across his naked chest, his butternut britches flopping. Whistling the mornful lullaby "Balow My Babe," he climbed to the high north field, entered the rows of dun, dead corn, and broadcast rye between the stalks. Anne circled through the woods, then stepped into a world apart, an oven of heat trapped in the still air between the ground and frayed, bent tassels. Jim's shoulders and arms rasped and rustled the split dry leaves; his whistle, clear, piercing, solitary, traveled up one row and down the next. He turned at the far end and started down the furrow next to the one where she waited. Closer. Louder. His yellow hair flashed, sweat gleamed on his chest.

Berserk explosions of color, snatches of pictures, overpowering smells blew words from Anne's mind—she became the cat she had mimicked, dumb with only a body to speak, with only the moment to comprehend. The scraping, crackling stopped.

Jim had paused, his hand in the seed bag on his haunch. Her muscles coiled. He pushed aside the dry stalks.

"Anne!"

The silence shimmered. A dog barked once, far away; crows cawed above the woods. Anne swayed, her tongue lay flat and still; she raised her hand toward him, grasped the paper leaves, stepped closer.

He pulled back. "Anne . . . No . . ."

Her eyes stared; her toes crept through the dust, between the stalks; her fingers touched the sun-flecked skin of his shoulder, the tufted hair of his chest. She had a sense of coming home.

"Anne." Sweat threaded his dusty cheeks. "Don't. Please don't."

Thick odors of flesh, earth, autumn sealed her against him.

"I'm married!"

Her hand followed the tail of his hair into the trough of his back, down the hard plate of his hipbone, then, pressing flat, drew him.

"No, Anne. What if . . . No, we can't. A child. You might get with child!" His breath was hot and smelled of his name; she smiled, and her tongue, curling, growing broad, slowly licked his lips.

He raised his chin, and as the cry "God!" rose in his throat, she slid down his body until she knelt in the dust; her face pressed between his thighs. She caressed the flesh where his britches hung low, kneaded the soft beginning of his hips.

"Our Father," Jim panted, "who art in heaven . . ."

Anne turned her face from side to side; cat noises sang behind her teeth. His muscles twitched, his member moved. One of her arms circled his buttocks, one hand worked at his buttons.

He twisted, she clung. Words ripped from his ribs. "Leave me alone! For God's sake, leave me alone! Louisa's with child!" He pushed on her head; she jammed her face into the wetness of his belly, sucked on his skin.

"You're the devil!" His howl sliced her skull.

Something inside her broke. Her arms loosened, her face grew cool. Her hips rested back on her heels. Her eyes focused on the dust that clung to the hairs of his calves while her lips formed the words, "I want your child. I want your child," but there was no sound.

"We'd be damned. Don't you see, Anne? Adultery would damn us!"

Her head hung heavy. She could not raise it. She rubbed the top of his britches between her fingers. He stepped back. Her hand fell.

She never looked up as she rose. She never looked back as she walked away along the furrow. She never saw Jim lying face down, the hard, shiny rye seeds spilling about him, his fist pounding the earth.

"If Jim doesn't come," pouted Cindy Brady—she and her sister had elected to stay at the Glenns instead of returning to their own household, which now numbered twenty—"I'm taking my present for him to the Vances right after dinner." She crossed her thin arms and looked defiantly at Rebekah.

"Me, too," Cissy said loudly. "It's New Year's Day. A special New Year's day because—"

"Don't be saucy." Rebekah spoke quickly, but her voice dragged.

"Louisa's afraid to let him out of her sight," Dora muttered.

Rebekah sighed and turned away to offer the Reverend MacMillan, who stood shifting uneasily in his fine city clothes, more cider; Cindy raised her voice. "Everybody in the whole valley was here last night but him. I hate Louisa."

"I do, too." Cissy copied her sister's crossed-arm stance. "Besides, if he doesn't come soon he'll miss—"

"Enough!" Matthew roared. "Didn't your parents teach you girls to ever shut up? I suppose you get it from your father. Sam's mouth is always open."

Dora straightened her shoulders. "They're right, Pappie. Jim should have come. We haven't seen his face for months."

Matthew's fist hit the table. "He has his reasons for staying away, and we should all pray to God that today is not the day he changes his mind."

Everyone looked at their shoes, and Rebekah, using the same dead tone, ordered the children to their chores. Matt and Myles, alone by the hearth, fidgeted uncomfortably. The minister cleared his throat in a blustering way, but his voice was timid. "Is there more to this business, Matt, than just losing a son to his bride's family?"

Matthew filled the minister's cup but avoided his eyes.

86

"Louisa's not carrying her babe well. She's stayed right at home, and Jim's stayed with her."

"But to ride five miles to see his family—"

"Gib works him hard."

"Matt . . . May I speak as your pastor, Matt?" The older man folded his lips and nodded. "There's trouble between you and Jim?"

Matt knuckled his forehead. "It's hard to talk about, Myles."

"Has it got something to do with what's happening today? In Philadelphia, when Jim was there, there was some talk about Anne MacKnight and he. Matt, is your conscience clear?" He paused. Matthew groaned and tugged at his hair. "Did you force Jim to marry against his will?"

"For his own good I—"

Cindy's head darted in the doorway. "He's coming!" she shrieked. "Jim's coming, and he's got a pack of presents!" She grabbed her gift of candy and ran out crying, "Here, Jimmie, here!"

A minute later Jim, the girls dancing around him, stood in the doorway; his eyes warily searched the corners of the room, widening at the sight of the minister. His mother tugged him in and smothered him with kisses; his father pressed a new long rifle into his hands, and everyone formed a grinning, bobbing circle as his blunt, dirt-stained finger traced the silver-etched plate of the gun. "Are you going to cry, Jimmie?" Cindy shrilled. He blinked and shook his head, then opened his sack of gifts.

Rebekah buzzed about him like a mosquito, constantly landing pecks on his cheek. "Great graminey, but it will be good when you come home, son. When is it Louisa's due? Mid-April? So by the first of June, young man, I'm setting your place at the table." She rapped his shoulder. "Now, don't go pale on me. I intend to be sweet as pie to your wife."

"Let's eat," Jim blurted. "I had no breakfast." He put an arm around his mother. "Just saving up for your cooking, Mam. Should I lift the bird?"

"Wait!" Her little hand flew to her mouth. "You see . . . Jim . . ." Everyone stood stock still, waiting for Rebekah to say it. Jim's lips hung loose as he looked from one to the other. "Jim. Dear. I don't know how . . ."

Cindy danced in. "They were just coming!" She squeezed herself in front of Jim, took his hands, and locked them under her chin. "You'll see. It's a surprise. Just watch."

Slowly, silently, Anne entered the room. She wore her blue

linen and winter white shawl; a lace cap clamped her curls. Pain bleached her face of freckles, flattened her eyes. Jim, hypnotized by the green pulse beating at her temple, never saw his brother, washed and combed and clad in a ruffled shirt, until the Brady twins set him on the bench in front of the Reverend MacMillan. Anne moved so that her hand rested on Willie's shoulder.

"We are gathered here together in the sight of God and these witnesses . . ." Matthew's iron fingers shackled Jim's arm. "You cannot stop it. She carries his child." Jim stood blind, deaf, and dumb.

Anne did not know he was there. The buttons on the minister's vest bounced before her eyes, and nausea induced by the odor of roasting goose threatened to seep between her clenched teeth. Annie, you'll never last through it. Fat dripped on the logs, and saliva filled the back of her throat.

Reverend MacMillan glanced at her, cut his sentence short, and leaned forward. "William MacIllwain Glenn, will you have this woman, Anne, for your wife?"

Anne took Willie's hand in hers, rubbing it with her fingertips. His faraway blue eyes looked up at her. "It's all right, Willie. Just nod." He did, and Anne pushed back a lock of his black hair. A son of his will be a handsome thing. And a Glenn.

When Reverend MacMillan asked, "Anne Aiken Mac-Knight, will you take this man, Willie, as your wedded husband?" she did not answer because she was back in September, walking from the Vances' cornfield, wandering through the lank-leafed woods until she found herself by Willie's hut, dark among the trees; her mind crying, Jim! Jim! while her feet walked through the door, her arms embraced Willie, and her hands helped his to slide the shift from her shoulders.

"Miss MacKnight?" Reverend MacMillan looked as though he were about to shake her. He really doesn't like me, she thought. She clasped Bess's arm tightly and said, "I, Anne Aiken MacKnight, do take this man . . ."

Jim had gone. They heard first his boots, then Bonnie's hooves crack across the frozen snow.

Anne and Jim did not meet again until April—in the pelting rain in the Vances' mucky dooryard. Two Brady boys helped Anne out of the oxsledge and onto the planks laid across the mud to the house. Head down, body unwieldy, legs cramped, she moved cautiously; Jim's arm reached out to steady her.

They squeezed inside—into the darkness, into the stench of wet wool and manure-caked boots. Matt as ruling elder led the service: "We'll begin by singing the Twenty-third Psalm." Anne leaned against the log door. "The Lord is my shepherd . . ." Only a few voices finished; the room had become stuffed with silent Scot weeping. Anne could see a corner of the coffin—a bit of pillow and blond hair. Matt's hand, big, calm as God's, rested on the edge of the pit-sawed planks. "Let us pray," he said.

"Dear Lord, Father of all, accept this young woman and her babe into your kingdom. Comfort Jim, her husband of so short a time, her mother, Abigail, and her father, Gibson, who have suffered such a grievous loss." He raised his eyes to the smoke-stained beams. "It is difficult, Lord, always to discern your purpose. Sometimes we mortals find your wisdom hard to accept." His sigh echoed in many chests. "'Now we see through a glass darkly, but then face to face.' 'In my Father's house are many mansions; if it were not so I would have told you.' Reach down, Jehovah, into this house of sorrow . . ."

Abigail Vance, her own babe held tightly to her cheek, sank into her rocker; Anne saw Louisa's face and gasped. Smooth, young, golden. Beautiful. Dead. Dead. "'The Lord giveth, the Lord taketh away . . .'" It could be you, Annie. In two months you might be lying in a coffin with words being said over you. The people shifted, and Anne could see the infant in the crook of Louisa's arm. Jim's son. The newborn face so incredibly tiny under a mat of black hair. The child in Anne's belly woke and kicked; looking down, she could see the folds of her dress move. No, this one will live. No babe this strong could die. ". . . and give you peace, both now and forever. Amen."

The mallet thudded on the pegs that sealed the lid; the candles played on Jim's twisted face. He's blaming himself, Anne thought. He's blaming himself for marrying where he didn't love. Blaming his lust, his pride. Jim. Jim. If I could hold you, comfort you. She shut her eyes, her mind reciting, ". . . and have not love I am nothing." Boots shuffled, people drew apart, wiping their tears, covering their heads. Anne drifted forward. Just to touch his hand, let him know . . .

Matthew Glenn stepped in front of Anne and put his arm around Jim. "Come home with us, son." Jim shook his head, the marks of his teeth blood bright on his lip. "I can't. I owe the Vances a life. Two lives." Matthew's shoulders slumped; he clapped his hat on his head. "I suppose you must follow your conscience. But when the debt's paid, come home. Your mam and I . . . We need you."

Jim, startled by the plea, blushed and cautiously touched his father's sleeve. "It's not only that . . . I—"

Gib Vance pushed Jim aside, crowded him against the wall as he grasped the head of the coffin. "We're ready now, Matt."

Ho MacClymonds pointed to the roof, where the rain drummed in furious gusts. "Shouldn't we bide a wee, Gib?"

"Why? It ain't never going to stop raining for me, Ho. Not for me it ain't. Never. Come on, Matt, let's get this done."

Six men grunted as they lifted the coffin, and the women and children crowded into the corners as the pallbearers maneuvered through the doorway and out into the lashing wetness. Jim followed; his boots made sucking, gaping holes in the mud; his hands flopped at his sides. The others, clumped in twos and threes, sank like cinders into the gray sheets of water. Anne turned from the door. She and Grannie Brady were the only ones left to tend the bed full of wide-eyed children. The old woman said, "No sense, Anne MacKnight Glenn, burying the dead in your own head. Give Matt and Rebekah the grandchild they deserve." She cackled. "You're carrying high, under your heart. It'll be a son."

"I know," Anne said.

The child, a boy, came two weeks later and lived only a few hours. Anne's sadness was tempered with relief—she wanted no ties to Willie now. Matthew and Rebekah, tight-faced, spoke of God's will; Willie frowned, trying hard to grasp what had occurred; only Bess grieved, and she carried the grief like a stone in her chest. Anne stayed in the hut at the top of the hill; she cleared land and made a garden; she roamed the woods for herbs and berries; she broke two yearlings to the saddle.

Hugh came for a visit but stayed only three days. Bewildered at the circumstances of his sister, embarrassed by Bess's defense of her expense in schooling him, and unnerved by Cindy and Cissy's attempts to have him bare himself to them in the barn, he hid in the schoolroom, reading the Reverend Glenn's books. When Dora dragged him forth for chores, he turned sullen, resisting the rough hardiness of the men with his arms folded across his narrow chest; at meals he insulted Rebekah and Bess by merely nibbling at the heaps of food set before him. Anne, remembering that this was how he had acted in their father's presence, took him aside, telling him he was fifteen now and should put away childish behavior; he growled, "Nobody at Princeton seemed to take me for a child."

The next morning he appeared at her hut with his knapsack on his back, saying he didn't suppose he'd have any trouble picking up a ride on a wagon heading for Philadelphia. She nodded then walked beside him down the hill, along the stream, and up the knoll, all the time groping for words to make things right between them. At last she simply blurted, "What's wrong?"

He scuffed the thick grass of the track as he walked. "You're so different. You live in a shanty, you're married to a half-witted man, you tromp through manure in your bare feet. How could you change so much? How could—"

She picked up a stone and hurled it as far as she could. "You're different, too."

"Am I?" He looked pleased.

"And it's not all to the good." She tossed another stone, hitting a tree dead center. "You used to think whatever I did was just fine. Now you're so stuffy and critical."

"Annie, it's like I don't even know you!"

She let the rock she held in her hand drop. "I don't either."

They said nothing more except "Godspeed" when they hugged and parted at the church grove.

Anne walked back slowly, the long grass tangling in her toes, the sun baking her bonnetless head. It's true, Hugh. I don't know what's happened to me. I wish I could be happy the way I was with you and Bess in Philadelphia. It's like I've fallen into the bay and am bobbing helpless on the tide. I don't like it, but there's nothing I can do about it except see what happens next. She stopped suddenly, plucked a stem of oats, and chewed on it. I guess that's what I get for growing up. She wrapped the stem around her tongue. You've hit on it, Annie. That's what it is. You've grown up in a way he hasn't yet. Give him a few years. He'll catch up. Then he'll know what it's like to want somebody all his own. Aye—she tossed the frayed grass away—in a few years we'll see eye to eye again. She lifted her skirts and paddled about in the stream.

Willie was gone much of the summer. Sometimes reason briefly lit his eyes and he talked so he could be understood, but as autumn neared, the light went out and his awake mind became no different than his dreaming one. When the wild geese sailed in giant V's across the clouds, Willie lay down on top of Anne. She struggled but he gripped her neck as though she were a small bird he meant to kill, so she lay still, praying his seed would go astray. Three times he mounted her, then rose, clothed himself, tied his belongings in a sheepskin, and hobbled out into the wind. Anne cleansed herself with vinegar and drank a purging tea. The next day she moved down to the schoolroom with Bess.

No matter how hard Anne struggled to recapture her old feeling of contentment, the center of her remained restless, flowing with the pull of the moon. In name she was Mrs. Glenn, wife of the son Matthew had named his heir, but her place in the family hierarchy ranked only slightly above where she had been before. Anne knew it would have been different if the babe had lived, but she felt no regret; she could not imagine herself caring for Willie's child. Why Annie, she'd mutter, you're nothing but a loose-legged filly yourself.

As spring warmed the land Anne moved back to Willie's hut and the presence of Jim became constant. He sat by her as she ate, lay with her at night, talked as she spun, walked with his arm around her.

Abigail Vance set oatmeal in front of Jim and lightly touched his shoulder. "It was a year ago today that God took our Louisa." Jim tucked his cleft chin against his neck and spooned the brown and cream and honey gold into his mouth. He stood in the dooryard sun wiping his bowl with a square of cold corn bread, then gathered his belongings, whistled for Bonnie, saddled her, and waved good-bye.

Anne trudged down to milk the cows, lug the buckets to the springhouse, turn the cheeses, fill the souring pans, slop the sow, and then warm her dewy feet in the ashes while she ate her porridge. She told Bess she guessed she'd be gathering greens instead of helping in the schoolroom. Taking a gunny sack from the shed, she trotted down the slope to the track beside the stream. The sun warmed her back as her knife sliced tender dandelion shoots from their roots; she hummed snatches of a Scottish love song.

Jim traveled the spine of the ridge above Octoraro Creek, admiring the mint-green trees waving against sheep-gray clouds, and whistling softly to his mare.

Anne wandered, stooping here and there; at the crossing she turned from the track and climbed the hill beside the gurgling creek.

Bonnie, sensing home, broke into a gallop, halting only on the crest of the knoll where, nostrils flaring, she announced herself to the farm below with a ringing neigh. Lucifer's shrill answering whinny set the rooster crowing from the dung heap and the collies racing from the barn. Anne froze, like the oxen who paused midstream to raise their dripping jaws and stare.

Jim dismounted as Lucifer soared over the fence, and he pulled the saddle from Bonnie's steaming back and the bridle from her head. Whacking her rump, he called, "She's coming, Lucifer!" Then as the horses ran side by side, black and red against the green, he hunkered, chewing a sprig of sweet new grass. I'm home, he thought. It's been so long it's a wonder I don't have a beard like Methuselah. Jim saw himself as a child solemnly peeling bark from the sycamore trees; as a chunky boy struggling up the path from the spring, sloshing water from the heavy buckets; and then taller, with a musket, proudly following Willie's moccasins . . .

With a rush the dogs were on him, pushing him down, licking his chin; he hugged their squirming, loving bodies, then panting, "Enough!" got to his feet. The Glenn women and the schoolchildren were gathered like a gaggle of geese by the door, shading their eyes, searching for the one who had ridden the red mare home. Not seeing the sheen of Anne's copper hair, Jim's eyes skipped from the shadows of the barn and sheds to the swollen stream to the doorway of the stone springhouse. Where is she?

Anne moved with the wind that rippled the grass, but when Jim turned and saw her, she stopped. All the wonderings of what she would do, what she would say, disappeared—he was not Jesus, nor a laird's son, nor Louisa Vance's husband, he was her Jim standing with his farmer's boots dug into the soil. She cocked her head and called, "Have you seen any ripe strawberries in your travels, Mr. Glenn?"

His body spread in laughter. "Oh, I've missed you, Annie."

She walked closer. "You're all right now?"

"Aye," he said. "Older."

She nodded. "Me, too."

"I'm sorry about the child."

She nodded again. "It's all right."

"You've worried about me?"

"Some."

"Do you . . . see Willie? I have to know."

"No, not like that. He wintered with the Indians. Sometimes he comes now and sits for a few hours and I tell him a tale. That's all. There won't be any more babies." April clouds—some white, some gray—spun above them. The dogs had fetched Bess and Rebekah and were hurrying them across the creek. "Will you wait for me, Jim?"

He turned in surprise, almost touching her arm. "What?"

"Wait till Willie's gone for good."

"Gone?"

"He'll go with the Delawares again in the fall. Down the river to hunt the Chesapeake marshes. He seems happy with them. One day he'll not come back."

"But Anne, we have to get this straight so that—"

"Shush." She pressed a finger to her lips. "When the time's right, we'll know. Till then it should be our secret."

"Know? How will we know? I don't understand what you're talking about."

Rebekah cried, "Jim! Jim!" and Anne said, "Ask God. I think He knows."

Throughout the summer, autumn, and winter, Anne and Jim never exchanged a touch, word, or glance beyond the ties of brother and sister; their passion, like the water backed behind the dam the beavers built, lay cool and deep, content to wait. It was enough to be near, to see, to talk, to not risk losing what they had by wanting more. "You've learned," Bess said to Anne.

"Aye. 'Love beareth all things.'"

Jim took on the role of son and heir: clearing new land, building boats to carry whiskey barrels down Octoraro Creek, the Susquehanna River, Chesapeake Bay to Baltimore, fencing more pasture, drawing plans for a big new barn. Summer evenings he squatted with his father beside the smudge fire in the barnyard, in winter huddled with him in the light of the Betty lamp, planning a plantation it would take half a lifetime to build. "The slaves?" Anne asked him. "In time they will be freed," he said, "but I hope they will stay. Mr. Brown is a very smart farmer." Dora hovered, part woman of the house, part man of the fields, her eyes watching, her toe tapping.

Jim was elected an elder of the church and met every second Thursday with the new minister to discuss the morality of God's elect. Occasionally they discovered sin—most often, fornication—and solemnly marched off in a body to confront the offenders or their parents. While Jim bound himself to form and structure, Willie slipped loose; Anne was not exactly sure when he physically left, she knew only that now it was his spirit who visited.

March winds pruned the deadwood from the orchard trees, April rains swelled their knobby buds, May sun sucked them into blossoms. Jim, hewing logs in the shade of their dizzying sweetness, paused, leaned his broad ax against a half-squared timber, pulled on his shirt, and went up the hill.

He found Anne sitting on the straw mattress she had dragged outside to air, her hands working a niddy noddy, spinning wool into thread. He sat down beside her. "Have you seen the foal today?"

"Aye. He's a wonder."

"The best of both his mother and father."

"Aye." They looked here and there, anywhere but at each other.

A breeze brought the scent of blossoms; birds twittered. The silence lengthened, gathered a voice of its own. Jim shouted, "What should we name him?"

She spoke to her hands. "I thought maybe Cinder. His coat has some of Bonnie's flame under Lucifer's black."

"He's yours."

Her mouth flashed with joy; their faces turned, eyes caught—green, blue, the waters so long dammed, riffled, peaked, roiled; leaning, they held themselves on the crest, on the edge of spilling over.

Anne placed her fingers on his lips. "Wait."

"Why?"

She drew back, breaking the spell, forcing them both to breathe again. "Willie will be gone for good soon. Roger MacClymonds says the Delawares made him a medicine man, a priest."

"A priest?"

"Because he's mad. No, I hate that word. Because he has a different way of looking at things, they think he is in touch with spirits. Maybe he is."

"How does Roger know all this?"

"He's been trading with the Indians."

Jim rose to his knees. "You saw him? You saw Roger MacClymonds? When?"

Anne chuckled in what Bess called her "all-knowing" laugh. "Aha! The green-eyed monster's got you."

He nodded. "True. You. You're the green-eyed monster that's got me." His hand hovered over hers. "You do love me, Annie."

"There's never been another. Never will be. It's like . . . well, this sounds silly, but it's like with Hugh. Because he's my brother, because I've always known him, I could never get mad and stay mad, never stop loving him. We couldn't see eye to eye when he was here last summer, but that doesn't change things. Even when you were married to Louisa, I never felt any different about you, you were still inside me. Maybe because you caught me young, right off the boat, so to speak. All I've learned about love has been with you." She paused and played with the knobby wool. "There's been lots of bumps, but this last year has been smooth, and I don't want to spoil it by rushing in when we might still hurt Willie. He may not understand a lot, but he'd know if we'd been together. He feels things."

Jim locked his fingers in hers. "We'll wait until he comes to get the last of his gear." An understanding, clearer than words, passed from palm to palm.

The breached dam of Anne and Jim's emotions could not be restored. Trickles, gushes, floods of longing swept them toward each other, spilled over into blushes, trembling fingers, breathy voices; each wore a lighted mask of beauty in the other's eyes. When they sat at midday dinner their knees almost touched, when they passed in doorways their hips and thighs brushed, clinging for an instant. Their senses swam in imaginary acts of love until their chests groaned for even one youthful kiss in the hollow sycamore. They paced, dashed springwater over themselves, waited . . . waited . . .

In the fields corn plants, bursting from their withered kernels, reached white fingers down for food, green heads up for light; they sprouted, waving arms and stretched their tassels toward the summer sky; inside the layered husks the baby ears grew fat and milky with the heat of noon, and their silk flowed long and ripe. Harvest time; Willie came with two Delaware women and took the last of his belongings.

They met under the arch of the milky way in a field of newmown hay. "Willie's gone?" Jim asked.

"Aye. He came yesterday. He took everything—his traps, even the blanket off the bed, and from the way he said goodbye, I know he won't be back." She moved close to Jim and tucked her hands into his.

He pulled back and paced stiff-legged. "Anne, there are things I must say first."

She gritted her teeth. "Words have always wronged us, Jim. It's time we listened more to our bodies and less to our minds."

"I have to explain. Men are different from women. They can't just act on feelings. They need to know that what they do is right with God."

Anne sighed but she held her tongue, telling herself, He's nervous, Annie. Talking will give him courage.

"I used to think you were sent from the devil, Anne. From the minute I laid eyes on you, I thought that. I blamed my own passions on you. I tried to escape you. But now I know that I can't because—" he touched her shoulder carefully—"because it was God drawing me to you."

Anne turned her face away, muffling the squawk in her throat. It can't be me, it has to be God. Jim rambled on about lust and pride. Aye, keep talking, Jim, and you'll drive me away again. I don't need to bear the burden of your guilt. "It's all my fault," he said. Anne's brain screamed, The world doesn't revolve around you, James Glenn! There's me and Willie and Louisa. We're people, too, not just shadows God's placed in your life!

She flounced off and cooled her anger, hunkered on a rock, listening to the far-off sound of a fiddle and the nearby rustlings of field mice as they scurried about in the luminous straw. Jim came and stood behind her. "I've made us a dry nest of hay in a hollow."

She reached for his hand. "Sit by me. Closer. Now, don't say one word." The presence of his body, still, warm, and hard, gradually brought tenderness, then love for the whole of him just as he was, then longing. She handed him Willie's wedding ring. "We'll say the vows, and you put it on my finger."

"The Bible calls it levirate."

Anne bit her lip. "We don't need a name for what we do, Jim."

"But—"

"Hush, mannie! For God's sake and ours, hush." She clasped her hands about his neck and placed her mouth on his. "Now say, 'I, James Alexander Glenn, do take thee . . .'"

They repeated the vows, and he lifted her up in his arms. She nestled her head in the hollow of his shoulder, squirmed her hips against the bump of his belly. The woman and child in her became one, and when the smell of summer straw and Jim's skin closed about her, the circle was complete. Whole. At last. Dear God, at last. Anne melted like custard set by the fire and flowed inside his body. There was no chill, no dew, no other.

Jim was reluctant to make love to Anne in the place she had shared with Willie, but the rawness of November drove them from their beds of crackling leaves and meadow hay onto the skins piled about the hut's firepit. Anne enjoyed the coziness, but Jim was ill-at-ease, listening for footsteps, shying away from lying naked in her arms. On the first warm day in March Jim begged Anne to go out into the woods with him.

"You must be daft," she said. "There's not a dry spot in the whole of the commonwealth."

He returned to his whittling, savagely slicing long shavings from a hickory haft; Anne whacked at a turnip with a hatchet. As she crawled after a white quarter that had spun across the earth floor, she said, "It's time we had a child."

Jim's knife skittered off the ax haft; he sucked his cut finger and said from the corner of his mouth, "But you're still Willie's wife!"

"So who's to know the babe is yours?"

"It might resemble me a bit."

"Then folks would say it looks like Matthew." She knelt beside him on the fire-warmed furs and breathed against his neck.

"Stop it, Annie. You know what that does to me."

She chuckled. "Aye. I do."

He pulled away. "Pappie will be done fixing the crib door and need me to help him hang it."

"Excuses. You think your pappie's going to come looking for you here? He's never come near this hill since Willie built the hut six years ago. What he wants to ignore he doesn't look at." She kissed his ear. "Now, take off your clothes."

"All of them?"

"Aye."

"Why?"

"Because I'm tired of always hiding and hurrying."

"But Annie—" He flushed.

"Hush. Your worrying will be the death of us both. And Jimmie, don't pull out."

"Don't pull out! But then—"

"Aye," Anne said nodding. "That's the point of it. Remember?"

He pouted for a minute, then said, "You first."

Anne smiled, and he touched the freckles that swept from her nose and across her eyelids; she unlaced her bodice, and his fingers followed the flecks of brown down her white breasts. She stepped out of her skirt, and below her shift the fine gold hairs of her legs glowed in the firelight. Jim reached for her and she backed away, curling her toes into the soft skins. "Now, now, laddie, don't be impatient," she said with a laugh, but her own face was round with excitement. She stood, grasped the hem of her shift, and raised it over her head.

Jim moaned as he laid his hands on her thighs and turned her. She flexed the muscles of her legs against his hands. "Off with your clothes, mannie."

He did not move but murmured, "It looks like the grass on the knoll in fall, blond and curly and soft."

Anne bent, her breasts falling against his hair, took his shirt in her hands, and pulled it off. "Now your britches."

"Aye," he said, "my britches," and buried his face in the white of her stomach.

Sweaty, panting, Jim arched his back as his seed shot into Anne's womb. "God! God!" he shouted, collapsing across her, and Anne cradled his head in her arms, murmuring, "My own, my own. Forever and ever."

She faded, then opened her eyes to see him naked beside her, his member sprawled across his groin. Her hand crept down to press its sponginess; it swelled, moved, rose. Jim, blushing, laughing, tried to stop her, then lay back, delight rippling his face. Leaning down, Anne touched the wet tip with her lips. Jim gasped, reached for her, and their bodies, suddenly frantic with an unknown passion, tangled—slippery, groaning, shoving. Anne's thighs enveloped his face, her hands worked, her mouth opened—

She looked up.

The bulk of Matthew Glenn blotted out the sunlight.

Twilight stole the earth's color; Jim returned from his parents' house. He sat on the skins, his shoulders bowed, his voice old. "They knew all the time, Annie. About us. From the time we first kissed in the barn, they knew." He rubbed his eyes with his sleeve. "It wasn't God or my pride that kept me denying my need for you, it was them. Why couldn't I see that was why they sent me to Philadelphia, pushed me into marriage with Louisa? Blind, blind, blind fool."

Anne crept from a dark corner, and he pulled her head

against his chest, her fingers dug into his arm. "They made it very plain," he said, "that you must go. As long as Pappie didn't see us, didn't have to confront what he knew . . ." He let out his breath, "Mam says Mrs. MacClymond's sister in Philadelphia is looking for help. She's got a dozen little ones." His voice was empty. "If there's a child—a child of ours—you must promise it to them as soon as it's weaned."

Anne's thoughts froze like a white hare against the winter snow. "What will you do?"

"I don't know!" he shouted. "I don't know!" He rushed past the deerskin hanging, out into the night.

The March winds sang against the corners of the hut, the tree limbs whetted each other like knives on stones. Minutes, hours, passed; then out of the whipping blackness came Willie's phantom. Anne did not move; she was not surprised. "Hello, Willie."

He walked upright across the floor and sat down next to her. Was there a glimpse of William MacIllwain Glenn in the faraway depths of his eyes? She took the apparition's hand, but it was a stranger's, not her Willie's, and she slid it gently back on his knee.

The wind rushed in and Jim stood in the doorway, moon shadow branches dancing on his face. "I've been calling for Willie," he said. He let the flap fall and stepped to the fire. "I want to tell you what I should have told you years ago." Jim's low voice blended with, entered the magic. "I loved you, Willie. More than anyone else in the world, I loved you. And then I shot you. I've never been sure it was an accident, Willie. I was jealous . . . of the way they loved you . . . Mam and Pappie . . ." Hair wild with wind and rain, Jim hunkered by the pit. "I'll never know if I . . ." Willie's shadow self put his arm around Jim's shoulder, and Anne could hear his whisper, "My wee chin-chopper. My brother Jimmie."

"And now, Willie, I'm taking your wife."

Anne held her breath. Taking his wife?

"And if there is a son, I'll name him for you."

The gray of Willie's hand moved along Jim's jaw, and Anne said, "He knows. He understands. It's all right."

Wind tore away the deerskin and howled through the room, scudding dry leaves across the floor, blasting a whirlwind of sparks from the fire. "Good-bye, Willie," Anne said softly. "God willing, you'll be content in your new life."

The two were left alone. Jim took kindling sticks and wedged a blanket across the doorway, blocking the wind; he squatted again. His face was scratched and welted by branches and bushes, his hands hung square and tired between his muddy knees. Anne saw him without his farm, his four hundred acres, just plain as he was. "I can be ready to go by first light," she said. There would be another farm someday, somewhere.

"As Willie's wife you have your rights here. If you want to fight—"

"No, Jim, it's you I want."

He nodded, heavily, slowly, and reached in his pouch for his lead and bullet mold. "Aye. Well, there's things to be done then." He turned. "Do you favor heading east or west?"

Together. They were going together. She wondered that she could speak at all. "West."

He chipped lead into the mold and shoved it into the ash to melt. "I thought you would."

High, wind-carved clouds crowded the east with creamy gold as Anne shouldered her blanket knapsack and picked up the Killyleagh kettle full of cracked corn and salted pork; Jim took up his long rifle and led the way down the hill.

Matt stood by the hearth. "You go with that woman and you go without my blessing or any of my goods!"

"Matt, you can't!" Rebekah's voice was shrill. "He's your son! Your own flesh!"

"He'll take nothing of mine to make his sin easy."

"I've worked for you for years!" Jim cried. "Don't I deserve something for that?"

"You've done nothing more than any son would do. If you stay, the farm and everything on it is yours. I will deed it to you today as soon as that whore—that creature of Sodom—is gone. You may run it as you please. It will be yourse—lock, stock, and barrel."

Anne reached the doorway as Rebekah placed her hands on Jim's shoulders and said, "You don't know any trade but farming, son. You'd live in sin and poverty. Let her go—it would be best for both of you. In this world and the next. Besides, your pappie and I need you here to care for us. We have no son but you. 'Honor thy father and thy mother that . . .'"

Jim winced, bowed his head; his mother's voice ran on. "This is your home. We are your kin. All you feel now is your passion—and guilt. But in a few months, a year . . . Can't you see that even she would be better starting over in

101

Philadelphia? She's tough. She'll snare herself some well-to-do city man in a twinkling."

Bess sat with the steam of her porridge rising in her eyes.

Matthew's face in the watery morning light was lined and tired, but as Jim's shoulders shrank under his mother's tiny hands, he straightened his. "God allows each man his choice according to his conscience, but my conscience will not bear your sin. If you leave with your brother's wife, I will disown you as my son."

Jim swayed. They ask too much, Anne thought. Her mind had already turned to go when she heard Jim's voice. "I'm sorry that's how you see it, Pappie." His chin trembled, but it was high. "I can't compromise my conscience, either. In God's eyes Anne is my wife." He bent and kissed his mother's forehead. "I'll always"—his voice broke and his head fell against her shoulder—"let you know where I am." She ground the fabric of his shirt between her teeth.

Bess placed her broad Glenn hands on the table and pushed until the bulk of her stood upright. "Wait, Jim."

Matt grabbed her arm. "Bessie, sit down."

Bess didn't seem to notice; she stared at Anne, who had stepped inside. Bess! Bess! I may never see you again.

Although it was only a hand Bess extended, Anne felt her love rush across the room and fold her as tightly as Jim's mother clung to him. She shut her eyes and leaned against the warmth of it.

Bess, her eyes never leaving Anne's face, undid her father's fingers from her arm and backed toward the door of the schoolroom. "Wait. Wait just a minute." She disappeared.

Rebekah let go of Jim and rushed after her. "What are you doing?"

The answer, muffled by thick log walls, eddied about the room. "I'm going with them."

Matt crashed down into his chair. A leg sprang from its socket, and he slid from the tilted seat onto the floor. Bowing his head, he rapped his brow against the edge of the table. "Why, God? Why do you take my children? What have I done?"

Rebekah darted from son to husband, touching first one and then the other. When Bess appeared with a small trunk, she included her in her flutterings. "Where will you go? Where will you go?"

Jim lifted the trunk from Bess's hands. "West to Zac and Tommy."

Rebekah cried, "So far!"

Jim turned at the door. "I'm taking Bonnie and Cinder, Pappie."

Bess kissed her mother. "I'll write."

"I'll never see my children again! I'll be dead—"

Matt rose slowly, spoke sonorously. "Remember your dignity, Rebekah," and he stood with his arm around her.

Jim strode ahead; Anne clung to Bess as they crossed the rutted muck of the dooryard.

Jim whistled, and Bonnie, dozing under the sycamores with Lucifer and Cinder, raised her head; then, tail and mane flashing red in the slant of morning, she cantered across the stream and exuberantly cleared the paddock fence.

Dora emerged from the shadow of the barn, but her shouted question died when she saw the trunk Jim carried; with grunts of "Ho!" and "Haw!" she yoked the oxen. Bess, sidesaddle on Bonnie, and Jim and Anne, walking hand in hand while Cinder nosed their backs, disappeared over the knoll.

Restless Years

Fort Pitt and Philadelphia, 1759–70

Chapter Eight

In 1758, the year before Jim, Bess, and Anne—always introduced simply as Mrs. Glenn—had left Octoraro Valley, the British General John Forbes had cut a new road across the mountains of Pennsylvania. The names of the places it connected ran like a song from east to west: Susquehanna River, Piedmont Plateau, Carlisle, Allegheny Front, Blue Hill, Kittanny Mountain, Fort Loundon, Fort Littleton, Tuscarora Mountain, Sideling Hill, Bedford, Ligonier, and the armies' goal—the French fort at the confluence of the Allegheny and Monongahela rivers. Although an impetuous major named Grant had led a disastrous early raid in which the Indians allies of the French had slaughtered his Highland regiment, the main force under Forbes had walked into the deserted, smoldering remains of Fort Duquesne unopposed. One of the first acts of Colonel Bouquet, a forceful officer of Swiss descent who had assumed command from the dying Forbes, was to order the Indians to bring in their white captives; thousands came, Esther Glenn among them.

Construction began on the largest British fort in North America—to be named for William Pitt, the statesman, "the organizer of victory." George Crogan, appointed British deputy to the Indian tribes, leased some of his sixteen hundred acres to farmers charged with supplying the new fort. Zac and Tommy Glenn—who had traveled with Crogan in their attempts to locate Tommy's daughter, stolen by the Indians in '54—received two hundred acres on the Allegheny River between Crogan's trading post and the new fort. Official British policy stated that to keep the Indians quiet, no new settlers were to be permitted across the mountains, but Jim pulled strings both in Philadelphia and Pittsburgh and by fall had secured the necessary permit to join his brothers; the little group linked up with a trader's pack train heading west along the new road.

Bess, as though her true journey were through inner rather than outer space, rode or walked in the splendid autumn weather with a pilgrim's pensive serenity. Anne, all skips and bounces and claps of her hands, told tales of trips with her pappie beside the Strangford Lough, south to the Mourne Mountains, and north to the fells and rills of the nine glens of Antrim. "I guess," she'd say over and over, her face beaming, "I'm happiest when I'm a Scot gangin' body," adding quickly, "but going alongside people I love is the best of it." Bussing both Jim's and Bess's cheeks, she'd rush off ahead, swinging down the road paved with leaves of scarlet, gold, and orange, jumping dry gullies, singing off-key as she stooped to pick bright weeds.

Jim would smile at Anne's blitheness and his member stir, longing for the bed of boughs they would share that night; then, catching Bess's eyes twinkling at him, he would cool his body by riding the quarter mile back to the packtrain to check on their goods. Bess had gotten an excellent price on the sale of her Philadelphia house, and ten sturdy mules lugged all the essentials and some of the luxuries necessary for a house and farm. Four oxen, loaded with crated geese and piglets, three ewes and a ram, a milk cow, a new Shep that herded anything that moved, and Cinder, now a graceful yearling, completed the Glenns' entourage. Jim, once out of sight of Anne, turned his thoughts to farming: he'd build away from Zac and Tommy, create a new Glenn farm finer than his father's, big enough for all his sons and daughters. Bitterness left him—God had Called.

Stormy weather, after a month of dry, blue skies, halted the packtrain outside Fort Bedford, forcing the Glenns to put up at a house with the drivers and drifters who had attached themselves to the convoy. Anne drew back from the men's open stares, but it wasn't until she went into the fort that she knew fear, for although she walked very strictly, her steps small, her cloak clutched across her breasts, and the edges of her bonnet far before her face, the eyes of the militiamen seared her skin. Hastily returning to the inn, she found lined up before Jim, farmers, woodsmen, and trappers coughing and spitting and waiting to find out which woman—the old gentled one or the filly—was his and if they could bargain for the other.

Jim gave the owner of the house hard coin for the use of his own room, and Bess and Anne found themselves locked there with a lunch of broth.

At Ligonier the Glenns made their own camp far from the fort, and Jim, determined to find a way to his brothers' land without having to go near Pittsburgh, as the new town was called, questioned the traders. They shrugged, saying that as far as they knew all travel to Crogan's post was done by canoe from the fort. On the morning of the day they were to arrive, Jim was off searching for a possible Indian trail to use as a shortcut when a cry came from the lead scout: "Soldiers! An escort from the fort's coming!"

Anne along with the others cheered, "Hip, hip, hooray!" as His Majesty's American Regiment, neat toys in red coats with royal blue trim, topped the hill; the music of drum and fife sparked the air. Then the soldiers broke ranks, grinning and shoving traders clustered around them, but their startled second glances and slack-jawed stares were directed at Anne. She turned and gazed into the woods, pretending to watch black squirrels stuff their cheeks with acorns.

Above the babble a voice shouted, "There he is!"

Anne kept her head bowed.

"Yep. See there, on that big stump." "My gawd, but ain't he a huge 'un!" "I figured he'd show up. He don't miss anything that's going on for a hundred miles around." "That's cuz he's more panther than human." "And a bear when he's in his cups." "I'll grant you his fighting side, but there's no man I'd trust farther—except with my woman—than Zac Glenn."

Anne turned. A man, his silhouetted shoulders starred by the slanting autumn sun, his coonskin cap a crown, his long rifle a scepter, stood on a tree stump partway up the rise. The hairs on the back of Anne's neck prickled.

With a screech Bess broke from her side and rushed at the figure; he, moving too quickly for the eye to follow, cocked and leveled his gun at her. "Zac! It's me! Bess!"

Leaping from the stump, he caught her, swung her in the air, and jigged with her flying from his arms as though she were little Rebekah, not his tall, hefty sister. Anne clutched at a low bough and hung on; no imaginings had prepared her for this. Bess called for her to come, and she walked very slowly past the clumps of narrow-eyed men, then up the slope. Zac's arms dropped from Bess's back. "My God!"

A tingling so tight that it raised the top of Anne's scalp off her skull allowed the sun to beat on her brains and turn them to mush. Before her stood all the power of Matthew Glenn in a body as hairy, black and bold as her father's.

Bess reached for her wrist. "This is Zac. Our brother Zac. Give him a kiss." Bess was hysterical with excitement.

Anne pecked the brown cheek above the wiry beard, then stepped swiftly back.

"My God," he breathed, and his buckskin leggings quivered over his thighs. "My God."

She raised a shield of words: "I'm your brother's wife."

"Jimmie's wife?" His eyes left her to scan the faces of the militiamen and traders. "I hope he's grown big and willing to fight." His tongue wiped the corners of his mouth.

Anne's scalp peeled away, down the back of her head to her neck. Bess's grip was firm. "Jim won't let anything happen to her."

Zac's glazed eyes undressed Anne, then he took off his cap and shook his tangled head. "Nothin', nothin' like you has ever come across the mountains before. Nothin' even close." He wiped his lips with the back of his hand, murmuring, "Woman, woman, Jesus God . . ."

Jim shouted, ran panting down the road, and the brothers thumped each other's backs. "Come to farm with us, Jimmie?"

Jim grinned. "Yep. I did."

"Bring seed? Ours ain't worth diddly-squat."

"I brought a lot of everything." Zac raised a bristly, questioning eyebrow, and Jim stiffened. "Bess has been very generous with the Reverend Blackwood's inheritance. She outfitted us."

"Bess? What about Pappie?"

"Have you got a place for us?" Bess said quickly. "I mean, just for a while. We'll be building."

Zac shifted his feet. "Tommy's married up again. Rhoda. Decent woman, just a bit sickly. She came west with her brother, who'd joined up with Forbes. She did washing and such for the men. No whore, mind you. No whore. They got a one-room cabin about a mile from me."

Jim asked, "Do we have to go into the fort to get there?"

Zac pointed. "Indian trail here that cuts across. Six miles. Little rough. You got stock? Mare looks in good shape." Bonnie stood beside Jim with her head high, nostrils quivering, haunch muscles rippling silk in the morning light. Zac's black, bold eyes took his measure of the mare, then seemed to suck up Anne, squeezing her against his chest.

Jim dropped his arm from Zac's shoulder.

Fear pressed Anne's belly on her bladder; if they fought, Zac would win; she spread her legs and peed where she stood, hoping the stamping of Bonnie and Cinder would hide the sound of the splatter.

"But what about you?" Bess crowded Zac. "You live alone?"

"I live with a woman and some young 'uns."

"Yours?"

He shrugged. "Some are, I guess."

Bess's mouth rounded with shock. "You've taken a squaw into your house?"

"She's white. Whiter than Anne here—she ain't got freckles." He laughed.

"But—are you married to her?"

Zac laid his rifle over the crook of his arm. "Nope."

"Has she got a husband someplace?"

"She may. We never talked about it. We don't pry at each other."

Bess shook her head in bewilderment. "What's her name?"

"Tine."

Wind rattled in Anne's throat. She heard the voice of Matthew Glenn: Put her down, driver. We'll have no whores in this valley. "Tine Plum?" she squeaked.

Zac squinted at her. "Aye. That's what she called herself when she came West with Braddock. It's Tine Howser now. Did you know her somewhere?"

Two red spots appeared on Jim's cheeks, and Anne drew herself up very tall. "I'll not stay in the house of a London whore."

Zac bit his lip, letting his anger come and go. "That's up to you, Sis. Tine and I, we suit each other."

Even Zac winced at the squalling, smelly blackness that rushed out of his cabin door. Then roaring, "Tine! Get your arse outa bed!," he kicked furs and tools, garbage and children out of the way. Jim, Anne, and Bess huddled just inside the door as Tine stumbled toward them, the smell of her breath preceding her by half a room. Bess circled out of her path, peering into the pale, ferret faces of the children. "Which one's Esther? I thought you wrote she was staying with you, Zac."

"She's supposed to be," Tine said in her singsong whine. "I done my duty by fetching her here when Rhoda took to her bed again." Her stringy fingers were busy with the knots in her hair. "It's not my fault she's always running off."

"Woman," Zac growled, "put on some clothes that folks can't see through. And go tell Tommy that Bess and Jim and"—his cheeks puffed red as he glanced at Anne—"his new sister have come on from Octoraro."

Tine pouted. "Why didn't you tell me they was expected?" She sidled up to Jim and bobbed a curtsy. "Pleased to meet ya, Mr. Glenn. Sorry ya caught me short fur company." Backside to Bess, she hissed in Jim's ear, "Now, don't go blaming me fur Esther's not talking. She was queer that way when the Indians brought her in. It ain't none of my fault. I been kind as anything to her. Ain't I, Zac?"

Frowns narrowed Bess's face. "The child can't talk at all?"

"Not can't, Bess, won't," Zac said. "I don't understand it." Zac rubbed the heel of his hand on his brow, like a boy with hurt feelings. "I don't think she knows who Tommy is, and I don't think she cares. She's dim to everything except what she's doing right at the moment. Sometimes I think she's sleepwalking and one morning she'll wake up and be all right."

"Does she try to run off?"

"No. When she's alone she's happy as can be. Sometimes I even come on her singing some song of the Iroquois."

Bess patted her own hand as though consoling or convincing herself. "She had only four years with you and six with the Indians. Was she bright as a babe?"

"Bright! I'd taught her her letters already and she talked just like a grown person. Tommy and me was both her mother and father. And pretty! Lord, there never was one prettier. Still isn't."

Tine fingered the ribbons on Anne's bonnet, but no glint of recognition entered Tine's red-rimmed eyes. Anne backed out the door away from Tine's rancid smell but found the yard air just as foul: Skins dried on racks, dogs leaped and snapped at freshly gutted deer, two filthy children rolled in the muck, biting and scratching each other. Zac yelled at Tine, "Go fetch Tommy!"

After the mules were unpacked, watered, and tethered, the animals belled, and human bellies warmed with cornbread and whiskey, Zac led them off through a field of sunburned grass. They found Esther kneeling on a stone in the middle of a stream, and they hunkered behind a broad chestnut tree in order not to startle her. Anne blinked, peered, blinked again. Esther was no human; she was a wood's fairy clothed in doeskins bright with beads that clung to her childish back and buttocks, a nymph with braids of white gold, honey cheeks, and blue eyes that darted with the fish shadows in the pool.

"Don't she look nice?" Zac whispered. "I made her outfit."

Esther's arm flashed in and out of the water, and a trout flopped on the bank. Her laugh rippled like autumn wind, a magic coming and going known only by its passing. Anne expected her to disappear in a puff of brownie dust, but she stayed, kneeling, humming, watching for another fish. Anne edged toward her. How does a person catch the wind?

"Come, Annie," Jim called. "We're going now."

"No," Anne said and she stayed and built a lean-to among the eastward-spreading shadows.

Tommy came, calling her name from far away, and she instantly loved this gentle white ox of a man who carried embers for her fire. Silently they sipped tea, ate apples, and an ill-shaped cheese sent by Rhoda. "She's terrible shy, Rhoda is." His slow voice matched his fair, boyish face. "When Zac came across the field with Jim and Bess she took the babe and hid out in the woods." Frown lines worried his brow. "Bess wants to stay with us."

Anne thought of Bess taking charge, making over the cabin and their habits to her liking. "Maybe just until Rhoda feels better. Tell me about Esther."

Tommy spread his big hands. "Me and Zac came with Gist. Hired Indians to help clear, and two stayed on. Just boys. We called them Shadrach and Meshach. Meshach"—he chuckled—"did a lot of the taking care of Esther. Farming was too hard. She liked being with him. He called her Child-of-the-Morning-Sky." He nodded. "It was a good name for a fair Glenn."

His mind drifted off, and Anne had to call him back to his story. "The day the Frenchies burned us out, he and Shadrach came back with a lot of braves. The others held us while Meshach carried Esther off. They gave him a"—he unfolded one, two, three fingers—"day head start. We never picked up his trail."

"How did you get her back?"

"Meshach died. Shadrach brought her into a big parley Crogan had. He was afraid to keep her. They're all afraid of Colonel Bouquet."

Tommy left; the waning sun slid down the creviced bark of the chestnut trees. Anne sang her mother's lullaby, hoping that maybe Esther had learned it as a child. "Balow my babe, lie still and sleep. It grieves me sair to see thee weep. . . ."

Purple clouds rose up to swallow the sun, the day colors faded, and deer tiptoed to the pool to drink. How would you feel, Annie, if you had been carried off to live among savages? Maybe you would have stopped talking, too. Maybe this Meshach forced her into his bed, did vile things to her. Maybe she was passed around among a whole lodgeful of them. Or maybe—she sat up straight—maybe she misses them! Maybe she's grieving for Meshach and her life there.

The yellow fire dwindled; Esther, a slight gray-white mound, sat—as though dropped by the dying wind—at the corner of the lean-to. Be still, Annie. Don't get panicky. Follow your plan. Reach for your sack and take out a cake of pemmican. Nibble it slowly. Now take another cake and lay it there so she can reach it. Don't stare at her. Don't say anything yet.

Anne finished the cake before she realized it had been badly oversalted, and she cursed Tine Howser's carelessness.

Esther's hand moved toward the other cake. I ought to tell her. I ought to warn her about the salt. She opened her mouth, but unable to think of any words or gestures that would not frighten the girl, she simply held her breath.

Esther took one bite, then another. "Agggggh!" She spat out the cake and ran for the stream. The sound of her splashing and sucking the water made Anne's mouth pucker and her mind fumble. Then Esther swayed back through the musky air of the park, and kneeling and nodding, held the front of her shirt up in a bowlful of water. Slowly Anne lowered her face, slurped in the cool liquid, and sighed, "Whewie!" Esther's laugh breezed through her hair.

Anne scraped her tongue against her teeth and tried some of the Delaware words she had leaned from Willie. "Greetings, Child-of-the-Morning-Sky."

Esther's face quivered, and the water ran out of her shirt. Leaning forward, she sniffed Anne's hands and the base of her throat, her hair, and her mouth. She patted her cheeks with quick, soft strokes, then plumped them as one would a pillow. She did not speak.

"Esther." Quietly. Slowly. "Child-of-the-Morning-Sky-Esther. My name is Sister Anne." She thought for a minute, trying to remember Willie's Delaware name for her. Ah! Running Torch. She touched her chest. "My name is Running-Torch-Anne." She smiled.

The blue of Esther's eyes did not flicker or deepen, no soul entered. Anne repeated the words. Nothing changed.

"Will you be my friend? My Jo?" Anne asked as she fingered the tips of Esther's grease-tipped braids. "I've never had a girl friend—or a sister. That's it—we could be sisters. We almost are, anyway." Esther rocked, and Anne rocked with her. They slept curled together under stitched rabbit skins.

When the tree trunks steamed in the morning sun, Esther, with whoops of laughter, tore down the lean-to. By nightfall a snug bark lodge as big as Zac's cabin stood by the banks of the stream, and by the time the first snow whitened their world, the ridgepole sagged with smoked trout and squirrel, dried pumpkin and corn; firewood filled in one wall, baskets of nuts and meal another.

114

Time dissolved into pale, pink dawns, days of twilight, long nights of stars. Anne wrote Hugh that her life was as simple and silent as that of a a cloistered nun.

Chapter Nine

Jim laid out Glenturk—the name had sprung from Anne's childhood memories—like a shiny doorplate with its shaft braced against the green Allegheny. The house, facing west toward the river, stood where the keyhole would be, and the fields and woodlands spread like a knob around it. The bottom lands—which had provided the great timbers for the house— were planted with flax and oats, and on the slight rise between the grassy track and the house were saplings of cherry, plum, and pear. Anne's garden arched behind the house, peas and beans delicate against the dark of the wild laurel thickets that rimmed it. The rough, tumbled land to the south had been left in wood, except for the bared knoll of unstumped cornland, but on the north side, in a natural meadow fenced only by the lure of sweet grass and Shep's staring eyes, the Glenns' cattle, sheep, and horses browsed.

A gullied creek meandered through this loaning, lost itself in the thickets behind the garden, and then reemerged to form a washing pool, a moat between the dooryard and the south woods, a shallow ford across the track, and before it joined the river, another pool for soaking flax. A spring partway up the south ridge was used for drinking water and to cool the butter and cheese.

Zac had suggested clearing the trees back to the spring, saying that standing they offered too tempting a cover for thieving Indians, but Jim said they'd be gone for firewood soon enough. The trees would stay.

The two-story house stood honest and sturdy as Jim himself; every log was squared and chinked, every window fixed with both blinds and shutters that could be opened to the sun and breeze or locked against the winter storms; every clapboard shingle of the roof was straight and tight, and every brick of the two wide-end chimneys added firmness and grace to the whole. A ragtag shed holding tools and harness and sheltering the root hole ran off one end, but that would be dismantled

115

when the barn was built. Crogan's Hall two miles up the track to the north was a pretentious vanity; Zac and Tommy's cabins a mile over the ridge to the south were hardscrabble poor; but Glenturk fitted the land and spoke of people come to stay.

If Jim missed his parents and the Glenn farm, it never showed. He worked from dawn to dusk—and sometimes beyond, when the moon was up—but thanks to Bess he had the money to hire help.

Esther still looked at the world from her own silent corner, but she took being part of the new household seriously; she learned the art of making butter and cheese and doing plain weaving and even how to print out her full name—Esther Rebekah Glenn. Anne left the house to her and Bess and rode the land on the fleet, strong-muscled Cinder. Although Jim wouldn't allow her to do heavy work, "We must think of the babes to come," he'd say—she drove oxen, broadcast seed, turned and stacked hay, and followed Jim wherever he went—except to Fort Pitt. Her one trip there had caused a brawl.

When there were purchases to be made Anne rode to George Crogan's trading post, enjoyed the dickering and bartering, but left in a hurry when any rough strangers appeared. It surprised her that a chance meeting on the road frightened her more if the man were white. Jim said, "It should. A white man will rape." "Ooo aye, and an Indian will just scalp me." "Only in war," was his reply.

Jim often urged her to carry a pistol, but she said she preferred the speed of Cinder's legs. She had never hunted with Jim, or ever raised a rifle in a hog or turkey shoot as Dora and Missus Brady had claiming that "I'd do more damage to my own feet and fingers than anything I ever aimed at." Jim, however, seldom went anywhere without his rifle; he said it was in case he sighted game, but Anne thought there was more to it than that. Rumors of Indian uprisings could always be heard at Crogan's.

During the first year Anne had written faithfully to Hugh, but his replies had been so sporadic and filled with sly references to Dr. Smith's wife and pompous praise for the profession of medicine that Anne gave up and started a commonplace book instead. Bess defended Hugh by saying that politics and society always would be of more interest to him than soil and stock. Anne's reply of "Nothing elegant ever happens here" changed in January of 1763, when an invitation to attend a fancy dress ball at Crogan's Hall arrived. Word had come from the East that a peace treaty between Britain and

France had been signed, making the entire mainland of America east of the Mississippi River—except for New Orleans, which the French were ceding to Spain—British territory. The French would retain the rich sugar islands in the West Indies.

The news called for a celebration and Mr. Crogan had leaped to it, inviting folks from as far away as Ligonier and Fort Bedford. At first Anne declared she would not celebrate anything remotely pleasing to an English King, more particularly when it was being held in the house of a Dublin Irishman—she held her father's belief that South Irish blood, except for the pure Norman strain, had been hopelessly corrupted by Spaniards, English Cromwellians, and peasant Irish with pretty blue eyes and Papist souls.

Jim, to whom good relations with his neighbors were important, reminded her of the advice Mr. Pemberton had given them in the shop in Philadelphia. "Leave the old quarrels buried in the old soil, Annie. Pitt will see that the colonies get a fair shake in the House of Commons."

Anne snapped her jaw and twitched her hips. "It's empire they are interested in, not us."

In the end the whole family, except Esther, went and the evening would have been a great success if some of the ladies, envious of Anne's slender waist and nimble feet, had not made remarks about her childless state within Bess's hearing. She, who knew from experience the cruelty of such words snapped, "Put your noses back on your Bedford faces and hoe your own rows." Anne, a little wobbly and loose with rum, noticed the sharp-edged women circling her sister-in-law and dove into their midst with a cry that brought Zac to her side and the women's husbands to theirs; only Crogan's authority prevented a melee.

The winter sky was white with morning before Jim and Anne arrived at Glenturk and dropped into bed; Anne pulled the cold sheets around her chin and asked, "Do men taunt you about not having children?"

For a split second his warm skin drew away; then he hugged her tightly. "There's plenty of time."

"But you need sons to help with the work. Even now you'd be forty before one was full grown. Do you suppose there's something wrong with me?"

"Why would you think that? You've gotten with child before. No, Annie, there's nothing wrong."

"And you got Louisa that way. So—"

117

This time he did move away and lay very still. Finally she put her head on his chest and twirled the hairs between her fingers. "What's wrong, Jimmie?"

A harsh swallow rippled his throat. "I don't think that was my child."

She rose on her elbow; his face resembled grainy snow hardened by wind. "What?"

"I was very careful with Louisa. I didn't want a child. Oh, it might have happened—she was very insistent sometimes, but"—he took a deep breath—"I think the child was Luke's."

"Luke's! God! Jim . . ." She jammed her cheek against his jaw. "No . . . how . . ."

"That was part of my awful guilt when she died." His breath blew cold around her ear. "I don't know. Maybe it wasn't Luke's at all, but I wouldn't have blamed her if she had gone to him. Anne, I tortured that poor woman . . ."

She had stopped listening, staring instead at the beams emerging from the gray of the room. Louisa, too. Both of us. Her head began to ache.

". . . so you see, there may be something wrong with me. That may be the reason—"

She spoke against his lips. "Hush. Hush, Jimmie. God will give us children when He sees fit. Besides"—she reared back, and her smile was wide—"it's sort of fun not having any little ones around interrupting our lives just yet." She spread herself on top of him. "Make love to me, Jim." Luke. My God. Luke and Louisa . . . and me and Willie. She squirmed under the covers until her head curled on his belly. "I love you more than anything in the world. More than children, than Glenturk, than . . . anything."

Rhoda's confinement time neared; Anne and Bess suggested that she and Tommy and the two little girls move into the big house. Pale with fright, Rhoda refused, but when a blizzard threatened, Tommy simply picked her up, carried her the mile to the house, then went back for the toddlers and the livestock. "She ain't going to die like Esther's mother," he said, the lines in his forehead slashing deep. "Women need women for birthing."

Anne didn't mind bedding with Jim by the kitchen hearth, where the smell of the porridge slow cooking and the seep from the cider barrels flavored her dreams, but the idea of lying down when Zac was visiting made her skin prickle. Although he acted the gentleman to her face, she feared he undressed her as soon as her back was turned. One night, feeling particularly grumpy, she bellowed, "Zac Glenn, why don't you go home so decent folks can get some sleep?"

Zac laughed. "It's cold out there. I was hoping to bed here for the night."

Jim tipped his tongue with iron. "There's a mattress upstairs next to Bess and Esther's. You're welcome to it."

"Maybe later." Zac spoke to Jim respectfully, but when he turned to Anne, he teased. "Sis here's going to tell us a story now. I don't want to be sent to bed and miss it."

"A story! Aren't you a little big for that, Zac Glenn?"

"I don't mean the kind you tell Esther, I mean a real story. I'm sure you could spin a fine fierce yarn. This family's in need of a storyteller who doesn't attach a moral and Bible verse to everything. Jim's fine on Sabbaths, but"— Anne's eyes shied away from his—"how about something out of the old country?"

Esther appeared out of nowhere and settled at Anne's feet; Bess climbed down the ladder, saying, "I wasn't asleep. What are you going to tell?" Jim nodded encouragement, and Tommy smiled expectantly as their whittling knives lay idle in their hands.

Anne was embarrassed, tonguetied—her tell stories to the Glenns? Only the oldest and wisest were storytellers. But she didn't say no, and while the wind whined in the eaves, Bess set mugs of cider on the hearth to warm, Zac added a log to the fire, stools and rockers were hunched closer. Just like, Anne thought, in Scotland when Minnie was a girl and her family spent the winter nights circling the fire pit, their backs making a wall against the cold while Grannie Watt told tales of the killin' times when John Graham of Claverhouse hounded the Covenenters like rabbits in a hayfield. She swallowed her fear. "All right. I'll recite my mother's story the way she used to tell it to Hugh and me." She shifted on her stool and with one hand resting on Esther's hair began:

"My thirteenth summer had crisped into autumn and there I was sitting on the crown of the Moorhead of Glenturk, amusing the cows with tales of the brownies. All unknowing, I was that below, on the Wigton Road that wound beside the River Cree, galloped the horse of Bartholomew Black Mac-Knight." Anne felt her mother come and sit inside her body, giving her tongue a life and will outside its own. "Swift as the wind he rode with the point of his iron-gray beard jutting over his pony's ears like the prow of a lang syne Viking ship come to pillage and rape the land of the Scots. While I plumped white clouds with my dreams of my Rabbie-luv, that man with the sword and pistol rode down the lane to my mother's door, the hooves of his pony sucking the coarse bog-land of our croft.

"He shouted down his bare cheeks at my mother, who wrung her hands in fear of what news this man on a horse might bring. 'Be ye Martha Watt, wife of Adam Aiken, granddaughter of the learned Thomas Watt of Glasgow?'

"'Aye,' she said, gaining courage, 'and cousin to the family of Richard Cameron, bravest of Scots since Robert the Bruce.'

"'And you have a daughter Mary?'

"'Aye.'

"'Ready to wed?'

"'Only thirteen . . .'

"'Ready to breed, I'll wager. I am Bartholomew Black MacKnight, son of the Blacks of County Down and the MacKnights of Galloway, and I have need of a wife. Here is my offer.'"

"But let me tell you first of the days before the coming of Bartholomew Black MacKnight. How it was with me as a child in that bit of the Scottish Lowland hard by the Irish Sea. The year of my birth was 1722, and to my wee wondering eyes the ends of the world were the heathered skirts of Mount Crainsmoor of Fleet and the silver shine of the Solway Firth. Little did I know then the shore that Fate would carry me to.

"Thistle and stone and yellow ben-weed; porridge and kail and Bawsie's warm milk; the lilt of my bonnie mother's songs, and the feel of my pappie's broad shoulders riding me pick-a-back down the lane. That was the whole of it when I was a lassiekins, but then came the starvin' times. I was but five when my father, the proud, lean Adam Aiken, took his staff and a sack of oats and left our hungry house to be a summer soldier for the king of France.

"Ever after my mother and brothers tended our poor stony land, earth so coarse that it took eight oxen to drag the plow. Land not divided by fields, but by rigs and furrows chosen by lot at the whim of the laird, the earl of Galloway. Where out of each harvest of poor spindly grain the laird's men cut the best third for the manor barns. Ooo aye, it was a bitter cup we drank in Glenturk. But I was wee and the sun was free and the water cool on my paidling toes. And I lay on the hill with the grazing Galloway cows and watched the clouds with my laddie-luv. His name was Rabbie Jamison and folk said we were like two peas in a pod—blond and curly, pink and plump, for the cowherder lives on the fat of the milk. Ooo how I loved my Rabbie, my lang syne Rabbie-luv.

"Come winter when from the Irish Sea the westlins blashed across the moors, whistling through the chinks in our house of stones, ruffling the steamy hide of our Bawsie, we Aikens turned our backs and circled close about the fire of peat. Minnie would have a babe at her breast, Pappie would be rubbing the stumps of fingers lost to the English in battle, and I would crowd my brother's hunkered knee and sway with the words of Grannie Watt. My grannie's face hung like a frostbit apple left on an empty tree, and her tales were like the smell of her hair when she bent and burned it in the fire—shrill and pinching and full of death.

"The Watts, the Aikens, and all our kin were covenanting folk who would swear no oath to any king, and Grannie's stories were all of the killin' times, of outlawed preachers holding conventicles in secret glens and of the English devil John Graham of Claverhouse and his hired bullies from the Highlands who hunted down our people like rabbits in the field. My grannie's husband, the braw and golden Jamie Watt, was taken at Bothwell Brig and shipped in irons to Barbados, leaving nothing of himself but the babe in her womb. Grannie's father was Thomas Watt, the great scholar of Glasgow who died in the cold prison yard of Greyfriars below the castle of Edinburgh. Her brother, who rode with Cousin Richard Cameron shouting treason at King James, had his head stuck on a pike on London Bridge. Do you wonder that my poor grannie was daft?

"But make no mistake, Grannie Watt had her ways of taking revenge. I saw it happen once at Michaelmas as I sat on my pappie's shoulders in the market square of Minnogaff. From the brig end of Dumfries to the braes of Glen App, folk had gathered about the oxen roasting over the fiery pits, and the earl of Galloway was strutting skeigh and haughty, loving himself for being so kind as to give his tenants their only taste of meat in half a year. He made the mistake of insulting Grannie Watt, and up she raised on her toes and spit in his face. The earl of Galloway swelled like a cock rooster with flaming comb and flaring ruff, but Grannie Watt stood her ground and dared him to run her through with his sword, saying that the English Saxon devils had already murdered the best of Scotland and she'd be happy to be sent on her way to heaven to join them. Sputtering and clutching his wig, he walked away, and the smirks of the Scots followed him down the streets of Minnogaff beside the River Cree.

"Everly after I gazed at my grannie with awe and wondered

at the fierceness of her spirit. When I drifted in the lilt of her tales as I lay with my Bawsie warm in the straw, I would see myself doing brave deeds, maybe drowning at the stake like Margarett Willson, refusing to say 'God save the king' even as the wild rushing tide of the Solway rose about my chin.

"But in truth I was dreamy and shy, a fey bairn who spent my days in my hidlins on the lea instead of romping and playing games with the other lads and lassies. Only in my head could I be brave. I ducked in the bracken when others came by. Ooo there's no point in plowing under the pain of my life, I may as well say it out. There was a ditty the children sang about Mooling Martha Aiken, who was my mother, and I knew the words were true. Coarse men who lived about us remembered the blythe, bonnie lass she had been and how she had married a man from away instead of one of themselves. So in dusty summer twilights, as she trudged weary from the fields, they would pin her on their lust, filling the womb that belonged to the absent soldier, Adam Aiken, with the seed of men of Glenturk. My wee brothers did not know who their fathers were, and the village made a game of guessing.

"Grown people spoke of the starvin' times as being the cause of stilling my tongue, but I knew it was not so—it was the shame of my mother. Ooo I talked with my pappie when he sat idle in winter, sang lullabies to my wee brothers, and mimicked the way of human folk while the fairies laughed. And, of course, there was my Rabbie-luv, who was saving up silver, fees from his work at Gray Abbey, and as soon as he had enough laid by for a cow we'd be wed. But we did not know that Bartholomew Black MacKnight would come from across the Irish Sea riding up the Wigtown Road and calling my mother out of her house.

"I never knew how they bargained. Maybe she went down on the straw for him. He was a man of enormous lusts. Subsheriff of County Down, ruling elder of Killyleagh Kirk, thrice widowed by women who flailed his flax, birthed his children, wove his cloth, and pitched into an early grave. Ooo and I never knew how my minnie felt as she filled the small black kettle with oats, handed me her wedding shoes, and told me to be a good wife to Bartholomew Black MacKnight. I never saw her, or Grannie, or my pappie with his stumpy hand and his war-twisted legs again. I walked in the pony's dust down the Wigtown Road to the sea, and when I looked up at the Moorhead of Glenturk there stood Rabbie Jamieson, my laddie-luv, with the sun a crown of gold on his head. It hurt so much I couldn't wave.

"The sloop sailed out of Wigtown Bay, across the Irish Sea, and I watched the hills of Scotland dwindle while the gray-green of Ireland grew. The Bay of Larne became a mouth, the cliffs of Ballygalley teeth all ready to snap, the river a throat down which I would slide, down into the belly of Bartholomew's land. I knew what I had to do. Up over the side I eased myself and lay me down on the beckoning breast of shade and sapphire. I sank, and as my head was filling with dying, the wee folk welcomed me and made the dark change into light. But the devil snatched me back. Rough hands clutched and dug, dragged my sodden body up over the gunnel rail, and I retched on the winking black of Bartholomew's boots. Spurning the ship captain's offer of a cat-o-nine-tails, my husband—God forgive me, I can barely tell it—hung me over his knees and bared by buttocks to the breeze. The sailors cried aloud, and the whacking of Bartholomew's hand gave rhythm to their panting jeers.

"Ooo for the rest of my life I wished I had drowned. Indeed, I lived as though I had, as though I lay pressed on the bottom of the sea, the weight of it roaring in my ears, the dark of it fogging my mind. All the world was wavy, and my mouth filled up with water when I spoke. But my comfort was the wee folk who stayed on to live in my head, and oft we were merry together. They filled my cradle with one of their own—a lassie with hair of red and eyes of green and a spirit of let-me-be. I named her Annie Aiken MacKnight, and ooo what a child she was."

Anne stopped abruptly. She didn't know when her mother had left her, how long she had been speaking with her own mind. She saw the others working to get back into their skins, back into the hearth room of Glenturk on the far side of the mountains of America.

"It's a long way you've taken us, Annie," Jim said.

Zac rubbed the beard on his chin. "Magic. You've got the magic, Sis." He squinted at her in a new way, not seeking her flesh but giving respect. "I never heard anyone spin a tale like you just did. You got all the truth in, not just what people did, but how they were inside."

Bess stood fluffing her skirts. "Aye, it's the only way to keep the English from gobbling history up and spewing it out in books with themselves the heroes."

Anne stroked Esther's head. "They'll do it here if we don't watch out. They'll put us down as savage Ulstermen, and that will be that."

Tommy sat slack-jawed, staring at Anne, trying to make out what was here and now and what was long ago. Rhoda touched his knee. "It's time, Tommy. It's coming." Her breath was fast with fear. The next morning, Tommy's first son lay in the cradle.

A spring unlike any before thundered through the valley of the three rivers: Earthquakes opened yawning holes, floodwaters ripped and slashed. The Glenns built a ramp to their second story, and there they and their animals huddled, filling the air with prayers, lowing, whinnying, bleating until the swirling brown waters ebbed. For a month everything they touched was coated with mud—dishes, beds, stored roots, sheeps' wool, tools—and Jim wondered if the earth would ever dry enough to plant. By mid-May, however, normalcy had been restored, and a family dinner was planned for the twenty-eighth to celebrate Esther's twelfth birthday. Bess, worn out with preparations, collapsed under the chestnut tree that grew by the front of the house, and she dozed away the afternoon with Tommy's infant in her lap.

Anne was tired, too; she had spent the day helping Esther dress the loom with long warp-threads and begin a new piece of linsey-woolsey. The warmth of the second-floor room, the heavy thwack-thwack of the batten, the dust motes dancing among the taut threads, and the sun shining ginger gold on the swift and spools and temples that Jim had so patiently carved had had a hypnotizing effect on them both.

"Why don't you get dressed, Esther? And see if there are any strawberries in the meadow. We've done enough for now."

She watched Esther's new red birthday dress bob over the north meadow and sighed. It would be nice to be a lass of twelve again and have only berrying on my mind. Or—she nodded at the shower-shiny forms of Bonnie and Cinder standing head to tail and swishing flies from each other—a denture lass ready to risk a switching for a gallop along the trail. Weaving is a boring thing. Moving to the front window, she saw that Bess had the plank table set in the grass before the house, the white tablecloth spread over it and held with stones against the breeze. Ah, Annie, you have a few minutes yet. You can cut the turnips small and they'll cook quick. She sniffed. And the rabbits are stewing fine. Sit down and rest your weary bones. All this working will make you old before your time. Yawning, she rested her elbows on the sunny south windowsill. Far up the ridge Jim's back, pure bleached white except for the brown slash of his apple-seed pouch and the yellow queue of his hair, zigzagged up the weed-choked track; he paused every few steps to bend and shove a seed into the earth. He'll have every acre in apple trees before he's done, she thought. Trying to outdo his pappie's whiskey business with cider. Well, why not? It'll bring a better price than corn.

She laid her head on her arms; the young May breeze ruffled her hair. Maybe that means he's stopped worrying about this place being just a lease. The prickles and doubts that always assailed her whenever she heard—or even thought—the word "lease" she smothered by saying aloud, "But Mr. Crogan is not the Laird Hamilton. Land is just a business to him. He'll sell to us when the price is right."

Snuggling her face into the warm crock of her arm, she allowed her mind to rise on the odor of damp earth and growing things and float over Glenturk. Peace filled her bones. She slept lightly, her eyelids flickering at each intrusion—Bess's choppy snores, the clunk of a cowbell, a snatch of song from Esther, the rasp of a crow, a distant shot. She dreamed, becoming one with what she knew and did not know . . . what could not be and yet was.

To everything there is a season and a time to every purpose under heaven. A time to be born and a time to die.

Jim Glenn fell slowly, soundless as the puff of powder smoke that rose above the trees. Apple seeds spilled from his pouch, blood from his back.

A time to plant and a time to pluck up that which is planted.

Jim raised himself to his hands and knees, trying to stand, calling, "Anne! Anne!" But the grass of the road claimed him again and he lay, stretching his fingers toward his rifle.

A time to kill . . .

He rolled on his back, and half sitting, poured powder into the pan. Feet thudded on the track. Moccasins lifting, running, calf muscles bunched, straining. Jim raised his head and saw the painted black chests, the war clubs, the hatchets. He reached for his knife. The bodies were slender, the faces young. They're lads, Jim thought, just lads. He raised his knife. "Anne! Run! Run! God!"

Anne opened her eyes. A time to weep and a time to laugh; a time to mourn and a time to dance. "Jim? Jim! Where are you, Jim?"

The braves were too eager; their first blows missed. Jim rolled away in the high weeds. He caught the arm of one and wrestled him down; his blood stained the green grass red. Another arm rose, and a tomahawk slicked between Jim's shoulders.

A time to get and a time to lose.

Anne jumped to her feet, staring wildly, seeing only the dream.

"Run, Anne, run!" Brown fingers twisted his yellow hair. A knife circled his scalp.

A time to love and a time to hate.

Anne clutched the sill, screaming, "Bess! The shutters! Close the shutters!"

Tomahawks and knives carved their boyish triumph, their new manhood on Jim's flesh, his beating heart. Anne. Anne. A time to die.

Chapter Ten

Leaning out the window, Anne flipped down the clasp that held the thick square shutter and yanked the thong. The woods, the track over the knoll, the running braves disappeared. The next shutter hid the chestnut tree and the sliding river, the last the garden, the thickets, the light. Anne stood blind, and a voice—hers?—called, "Bess! I put a wedge under the door! Take it out!"

Her naked feet curved around the hard ladder rungs . . . one step, two, three. Her eyes peered below the rafters. Where was Bess? What was that smell? The rabbits! They've boiled dry. What will we serve? The pickling barrel's empty. . . . Her foot hung suspended between the rungs; nothing stirred in the room below. A long rectangle of light from the open doorway lay across the floor.

A shadow appeared, crept along the sunlit boards—feather . . . topknot . . . head and neck . . . shoulders . . . tomahawk. The head waved like a snake's, back and forth—searching. Every muscle in Anne's body jammed and locked. A moccasin slid over the sill. Silhouetted shoulders slithered across the room. The shadow head reached the bottom of the ladder and started up, the black outline waving in and out over the rungs.

A nightmare stuffed her throat; she could not scream. Her

fingers white as bone gripped the wooden ladder sides. I'm going to die, I'm going to die. The shadow reached her toes.

In the dark behind the door an edge of metal flashed. "Aaaaaaaaaaaaah!"

The Indian—blown, it seemed, by that strange and savage cry—hurtled, face frozen in amazement, palms outstretched, across the room; the blade of a broad ax protruded from his spine. Bess rushed from behind the door and wrestled the ax from his flesh. The brave thrashed, shuddered, died.

Bess knelt, pushing on his hips, his legs, trying to move him out of the doorway. The whites of her eyes and broad teeth flashed at Anne. "Help me!"

Anne's feet moved downward, touched the floor. The neck was half severed; blood pumped from inside the swollen, peeled skin. Her toes slipped in the thick wetness. Hog butchering, she thought.

Bess pushed on the door, but the legs slid, wedging against the table leg.

Anne grabbed the man's arm—the flesh was still alive. Gagging, she pulled; his shoulder moved, but his head did not. A spurt of bright, bubbly blood splattered her face. Bile rose swiftly, and she retched on the smooth, brown back.

Bess's fingers grasped her shoulders, lifted her, wrapped her arms around the baby. "They're coming! Run! Into the woods! Run!"

She jumped over the legs into the sunlight and scrambled for the corner of the house. Her head snapped back as an arm hit her windpipe. A fist wrenched her jaw, forcing her head back against a man's bare shoulder. The fist uncurled and became a hand that covered her mouth and nose, then moved on to grasp her hair, jerk it high over her head; the pull on the nape of her neck brought tears to her eyes. She dug at the arm with her nails.

Another set of hands dove into her breasts, prying at the baby. A boy, red claw marks across his cheeks, panted sourness in her face. She twisted and threw herself backward. The man behind her staggered off-balance; then his chest hardened against her back.

The boy, his black eyes dancing with glee, grasped the baby's blanket and yanked. Anne lunged forward, and the point of the scalping knife slid hot from her temple down her cheek, her neck.

"Aaaaaaaaaaaaaah!" Bess's warrior cry and the sound of her ax splitting bone were one.

The Indian fell backward, dragging Anne with him, and the baby slipped from her grasp. She shoved at the man's heavy arm that pinned her across his gurgling chest. Bess hauled and tugged to free her ax.

Twisting her shoulders, Anne raised her head. The painted boy had stripped the blanket from Wee Tom, and the infant howled as the air hit his pink, creased skin. He dangled head down from the brown hand that circled his chubby legs; the Indian poked his tiny penis and laughed.

Once, twice he swung Wee Tom around his head; the third time the small skull struck the corner of the house. The crying stopped.

Anne sank back as though her own brains clung to the splinters of the logs. Bess heaved frantically and spilled over backward, the ax in her hand. Under Anne the man's throat rattled and his arm slipped from her chest, his fingers from her hair. She rolled away and lay in a ball in the weeds.

Wee Tom was dead and . . . someone else . . . She curled tighter, her arms over head. Maybe if she stayed very still she would die, too. Bess shouted "Run!" in her ear, pulled her arms loose, and slapped her face. "Run! Go!"

The boy's eyes watched them as he fumbled at Wee Tom's smashed scalp with his knife; then a sudden spurt of whoops from the road made him turn his head.

Anne ran. Around the corner of the house, toward the thickets, trampling pea plants into the earth, leaking urine on her thighs, blood on her neck.

No hands caught her, no bullet thudded into her back, no war yell circled her head. She dropped on her knees and crawled into the laurel, then on her belly wormed across the stinking mold while the branches dug at her back and head. On and on into the scratching darkness until she felt her heart burst. Then she lay still, waiting to die.

Pain returned, then consciousness. You're alive, Annie. God spared you. Why? I wanted to die! She couldn't remember the reason, but she knew it was true. She willed the white of her dreams to come, to wrap her, hide her away, but her mind would not let go. Think! Think, Annie! You can't just lie here.

Blood from her banging heart forced her brain to reason: All right. Let's see: I left a trail a child could follow from the house. Probably haven't crawled more than twenty, maybe forty yards. Haven't even reached the stream. How many Indians had been on the ridge road? No! I was asleep! I didn't see anything! Nothing! She buried her head in the leaves until the black and blood left her brain and her breathing slowed. Easy, Annie. Forget the ridge road. You know two Indians are dead, but the ones who whooped will be at the house looking for booty and scalps. Then where will they go? To Zac and Tommy's? The brothers were burning slash; she had seen their smutty fires that morning.

Her mind wandered off; she dragged it back. But would the Indians go even closer to the fort? How had they dared to come this near? A chill tightened her spine. Maybe there were other bands . . . maybe . . . Could it be the war that traders at Crogan's had sworn was coming? Maybe there were hundreds of them and . . . maybe thousands. Maybe they would all die anyway.

The stiff laurel leaves rustled. They're coming! They're coming! Her head roared with the sound, and fear dripped from her mouth as she drove her elbows into the ground and pushed against the trunks with her feet. The noises came from here, then there; the pink buds swayed to the left, then right. Faster! Faster! Her dress was seized, lifted. A silent nightmare scream ripped her throat.

A catbird shrieked.

She collapsed. The back of her dress ripped away from a branch. Catbirds! Catbirds driving me from their nest. Stupid! Stupid! Tears of anger squeezed from her eyes. How can you be so stupid? She raised herself on her forearms. Bess. Where was Bess? She pictured her in the yard, the bloody ax in her hand. Where would she go? To Zac's. Of course. She'd run to warn Zac and Tommy. She'd run through the washing pool and up the wood's path past the spring. Fool! She banged her fist on the rotting muck. And here you are, stuck in the middle of a thicket! You don't deserve to live!

She wiggled to the stream. Gnarled and twisted branches hung low, but she slipped under them and into the chilling water. Zac. Zac will save me. And she knew that Jim could not, but she buried the knowing in blackness. Nothing can hurt Zac. She crawled across slippery, bruising rocks, through numbing water; boughs snagged her hair, bringing mews of pain from her mouth. Swirls of red—her hand and knee-prints—floated before her.

Sunlight, sudden and blinding, glared off the water. One hand, one knee, the other hand, the other knee, up the muddy bank and along the squishy path. Odd noises filled her head, and she dropped to her belly and squirmed over roots and stones. Her head poked through the weeds.

The house! Merciful God, I'm back at the house! She bowed her head on her sticky hands. I'm too stupid to live. I turned the wrong way. Her brow fell into the prickles. Far off—to the south—rife shots drummed the air. Zac. Tommy. Dead. Everyone . . . her head hurt . . . everyone would be dead. Everyone—Esther! I forgot about Esther!

She dragged herself to her feet. I'll find Esther. We'll be together. Smoke poured from the wide chinks of the shed. The tools inside, sledges and hay rakes, shovels and scythes, roared as they burned. She saw Jim's hands creased with soil, gold with hair, curling around the wooden hafts . . . . Walking wet, slouched and slow, uncaring if she were seen or not, Anne circled the garden. Thwack-thwack. She stopped. From the upstairs window came the rhythmatic beat of the loom. Thwack-thwack.

"Bess!" She hurried through the trampled pea vines. "Bess! Is that you, Bess?" The noise stopped, but no face appeared.

She hoisted herself in the back window. The man's body had been dragged out, and the floor was puddled and streaked with browning crimson. The smell of burned rabbits was sickening. Through the open front doorway she could see all their pewter, crockery, blankets, clothes piled on the plank table. Under it lay the two dead Indians, and from the limb of the tree hung Shep and two lambs, their throats slit. The shed flames crackled, licking, burning yellow in her skull. She started up the ladder. The loom resumed its heavy click-thwack-thwack.

Her head rose above the floorboards. Sunbeams twinkled through the lines of thread. On the stool sat Esther. Esther. Humming and weaving.

As Anne approached, Esther pointed to the rows she had woven; her round cheeks shone, then fell as she saw Anne's face. Her finger traced the knifemark; she turned over her hands and kissed the hurt palms. "And look!" Anne raised her skirt and showed her tattered knees. Esther hugged her and gradually the heat of her breasts warmed Anne's heart, sending tingles of feeling to her fingers and toes and brain.

She glanced out the open windows; the road and fields were empty. "Come, Esther. We have to get away. Quickly. They'll come back."

Esther followed Anne down the ladder, but in the dooryard she pulled away. Freeing the tablecloth, she carefully wrapped wee Tom's remains in it.

"Esther! Come on! Hurry!"

But the girl moved slowly, peering into the faces of the dead Indians and stroking Shep's black hair.

Anne grabbed her shoulders and her voice ran wild. "Please! Don't you understand? Bad men! We have to hide! Hide, Esther! Hide!"

The round, flat blue eyes blinked; she shook her head.

"Indians!" Anne screamed in her face. "Indians!" She pointed to the swaddled body. "They killed wee Tom!"

Esther tucked the bundle up under her arm and began to run—not for the ridge woods, but straight for the road.

"No!" Anne ran after her. "No! Hide! Esther—"

Esther did not stop. Quick and white her feet flashed below her skirt. Across the road and onto the hard dike between the flax and bleaching field she sped. Anne ran after her, crying, crouching to ease the stitch in her side and to keep from falling as her skirt, heavy with water, dragged between her legs. Esther flew, a redbird freed from a cage, on feet that skimmed the ground while her head was borne aloft by a stream of white-gold hair.

Annie, you'll never catch her. God! Please, God, stop her! Stop her!

Esther paused for an instant on the high riverbank, then disappeared. Anne stumbled and almost fell. The current would take her, swirl her away. Red floating on wavy green water, her hair spreading behind . . .

The lip of the bank trembled under Anne's feet; the floods had chewed at the old riversides, moving them back and back, then finally receded, leaving a concave arch—almost a tunnel—behind. Yards of mud and uprooted trees stretched between Anne and the water, but Esther was not in sight. Anne shaded her eyes against the glare of the sun-dipped waves, but no red dress popped up. She imagined Esther a water sprite swimming among the fish and the dusky currents, like Mary Aiken in the Irish Sea. Anne looked for a way down the bank to join them.

"Pssssssssst!"

Anne jumped back, expecting a snake at her feet. The noise came again and she kneeled, peering over and under the thin edge of the bank. Esther sat in a cave between the roots of a giant oak. She smiled and beckoned. Anne looked behind her. The dike was covered with matted, trampled grass—no footprints there. Leading across the dooryard? Perhaps, but they would be hard to find among the jumble of hooves and boots and sledge tracks printed there since the morning rain. Anne lowered herself onto the roots, then turned and straightened the grasses she had bent. Standing on tiptoes, she

131

squinted south—a dozen braves, rifles in their hands, trotted single file up the track. Anne ducked.

Anne and Esther sat, their spines curved against the damp mustard earth, the hum of the river in their ears, the glint of diamonds in their eyes. Through Anne's mind flitted tales of women who had smothered crying infants, choked whimpering toddlers while hiding from Indians. You won't have to do that, Annie. Wee Tom is dead, his blood soaking through the linen, and Esther won't talk at all so . . . She rubbed her fingers against her eyeballs. What am I thinking? Pray, Annie, pray. God is our refuge and strength, a very present help in trouble. Therefore we will not fear . . . there is a river whose streams whereof shall make glad the city of God. . . .

A twig snapped and her eyes burst open; then came the swish of grass, the rattle of leaves brushed by—was it the wind or a human hand? She tried to move, nothing happened; her body became a giant pounding heart. She gauged the distance to the river, marked a path through the crisscross of timber. The sun, rolling down the steep western slope of the sky, lost warmth, and her clammy legs began to twitch, rubbing linsey-woolsey across her raw knees. Setting her teeth against the pain, she fixed her eyes on the grasses above her head, waiting for them to bend—almost hoping they would so she could jump and run.

A hoot came from the north, one from the south, another from the road behind. They were closing in. Annie, it's time to take Esther and go drown yourselves. She grabbed Esther's wrist and half rose, but Esther pulled her back, stroking her cheek, humming a lullaby. Ravens rose screaming from the flax field, flapped like blacks haunts over the paling river. Indians must be on the dike. In a minute they'll be here on the edge. It's too late to run. Dear God, how it's going to hurt.

She pulled Esther's red dress up and bunched it in her lap; she grabbed her own ankles and pulled her heels back against her thighs. They could see nothing now unless they bent and peered under. Our father, Who art in heaven, hallowed be Thy name, Thy kingdom come, Thy will be done . . .

The earth trembled overhead and bits of dirt fell on her hair. Someone was standing up there . . . he might even fall through on top of them. . . . If I had a knife . . . Bess's ax. . . . Without moving her head, she slid her eyes toward Esther. She wore the blurred face of a lass dreaming away a May afternoon. Does she want to be found? Go back to Meshach's village? Were those dead men Ohio Iroquois? Someone she knew?

Grains of yellow soil rained on their knees. Anne looked up, waiting for the black topknot, the plucked scalp, the thin hooked nose to come over the edge. The grass moved. A man grunted. Brown legs came down, the toes of his moccasins rested on the root in front of her eyes. She breathed softly, through her nose; she didn't blink. The back of his heels were dry and grainy, his calves smooth and hard. He swung his leg idly back and forth, the edge of his moccasin brushed her shirt.

The foot stopped; the man shouted. The tip of a canoe appeared on the river. Esther's red dress! Slowly Anne twisted her body across her, her hodden gray across that splash of color. She stared at clay and fine root hairs and hurrying ants. How would she know if the canoe turned toward shore? When Esther waved? No, no, don't think like that!

The man halloed again. The bank shook; she heard feet shift on the root. She tightened her back into ridges so the knife wouldn't hurt so much. She hoped she would die before he yanked on her hair. Rustling, then silence. She turned a little—the legs were gone! She twisted farther—the river was empty. Where was he? She dropped her head on Esther's shoulder. Her arms came up, soothing, stroking. They waited.

"Auck, auck, auck." The ravens were settling in the flax again. Anne's body sagged, her head fell against the blood-stained bundle of wee Tom. They were gone. They hadn't found them. They were safe. She was going to live. No, maybe not. Already a dead place inside her was growing, spreading coldness.

Esther hummed and began to pick twigs and dirt from Anne's hair.

"No! No, don't. It hurts. My hair . . . it hurts so much."

Esther rocked her back and forth. "Poor Annie."

Anne dozed. "Poor Annie." The velvet voice of a mourning dove. Poor Annie.

Annie's eyes sprang open. Roots twisted like harpie arms above her head. Moonlight? No, the treetops and sky were locked in black. Dawn? Yes, steam rose from the river.

She lay very still, her tongue wiping the taste of smoke from her teeth. What woke me? A wet, cold nose touched her foot. She strangled the gasp in her throat. Sniffing and whiffing, the nose and whiskers moved up her leg. A humped back of glistening black fur cut by a broad white stripe loomed beside her hip. She shut her eyes. That's all you need, Annie. Skunk spray added to all these wound reports—throbs and pain, aches and stiffness—that are coming in from your toes to your tap. She let her head loll. Maybe she could still manage to die.

"Esther! Annie!" Deep and powerful, rolling to the river and back. Zac's voice.

Zac! Praise God! Zac's alive! And then she knew that Jim was not. A moan rattled her chest. The skunk's body stiffened. They stared into each other's eyes. Go away, please go away. Please. Her nose twitched, and she blocked a sneeze with a sudden "Chirk!" The skunk reared back, ready to whirl and spray.

Another voice called, far to the east, and another from the south. Soldiers. She fixed her eyes on the skunk's, staring him down, willing him away.

"Pssssssssssssst." Esther made the snake sound and the skunk backed away so quickly he lost his footing and rolled down the bank. Esther giggled.

Anne was already climbing the roots to the top.

Zac, Tommy, Esther, Anne, and the squad of soldiers reached the crest of Grant's Hill and paused with weariness. Fog lay in quilts along the rivers and spun in feathers through the waking town. The sky was dull, and the Union Jack hung like a bloody rag above the drummer boy. The tattoo began, and the soldiers double-timed down the hill. The commandant, Captain Eucyer, his white wig shining below his three-cornered hat, disappeared from the rampart, leaving a dark figure swathed in an English offier's coat. Bess!

The captain climbed on his wooden platform and barked the morning orders: Bring everyone in! Fire the houses! Red-coated soldiers rushed off to the town; one detail banged on doors and pointed to the fort, another carried rail fences to the south ramparts breached by floods; a third hacked away the bank of the Allegheny and let a brown tongue of water into the moat. The people stacked goods helter-skelter on tumbrel sledges, put straps over their shoulders and surged toward the ramp leading into the fort. Soldiers threw burning torches on the thatch or split shingles of the cabin roofs; the fog turned an ugly gray.

Zac and Tommy bent, picked up the ends of the tablecloth, and started down the slope into the shadows where the sun had not risen.

Bess swayed against the sodded parapet. Anne raised her

hand and Esther's. The English greatcoat fell from her shoulders, and in a moment she was on the parade ground, fighting her way through scarlet soldiers, leather-clad farmers, women wrapped in babies, pigs, dogs, and children.

They met on the edge of a field of new wheat. Zac's arms circled Bess; Tommy opened the bloody linen. At Bess's cry Anne whirled and looked. It was not wee Tom, it was a man. She should have known from the size and weight, but she had not. Tommy wiped blood from the broad white face with the edge of the dewy cloth, then placed it over the brow; he folded the square, farmer's hands over the chest. Anne, gray-faced, clad in mud and blood, tottered forward on bare feet. She knelt, still not knowing.

The sun, a pale and smoky sphere behind the haze, inched upward, grew warmer.

Anne traced the face with her fingers, her hand patted his cheek, she kissed him. He did not awaken. She bent again and spoke his name against his lips. He did not move. Bewildered, she looked up at the faces around her. Bess was crying.

"Jim? Jim?" He would come. He always had come. He had appeared on Bonnie beside the balcony in Philadelphia, he had ridden over the knoll as she gathered greens, he would come here. He was hers. He would come. He always came. Jim always came back. He was on top of the ridge and she called out "Be ye Jesus?" and he moved into the sunlight, shimmering in white and gold.

She touched the flesh again. He was not there. His body was here, but Jim was not. "What happened? Jim, where are you? Where did you go?" She raised her head. "Jim! Jim!" Her cry split the morning in two. "No! No! Not Jim! Not Jim!" She clutched his shoulders, shaking him. The cloth fell from his head. She screamed and rolled away into the wheat. She rubbed handfuls of dirt into her cheeks, tore at her hair. Jim, Jim, Jim. No, no, no. She shriveled into nothing.

Captain Eucyer tried to stop the funeral train from leaving the fort; hostile Indians already blocked Forbes Road, Braddocks Road, all the rivers. The rebellion of which the traders had warned had happened; the great Chief Pontiac had passed the war belt. No fort in the Northwest, from the mighty Michilimackinac on Lake Michigan to Fort Bedford, had been spared. Soldiers who had been promised safe conduct had been made prisoners, British officers roasted over slow fires and eaten still half alive.

"At any moment," Eucyer said, his hand tight on his pistol,

135

"they may attack the fort." But Bess faced him down, saying Jim Glenn would be buried on his land, war or no. Captain Eucyer studied her face, then Zac's and Tommy's. He spoke to his aide, ordering twenty soldiers as an escort and the schoolmaster to read the service; four black horses pulled the hay sledge that bore Jim's body.

Anne would not let anyone near her. She walked alone, close behind the coffin; occasionally she reached out and touched it, steadying it and herself. She wore the English greatcoat, for it was morning again and the rivers and valleys had not yet thrown off their bedcovers of fog—the dark blue tails of it dragged in the silver dew. Behind her strode Zac and Tommy, with Esther and Bess between them; soldiers boxed the procession.

The sun, a flat, wan circle, an open mouth in a sick yellow sky, breathed sorrow in their faces as they walked. Not until they reached the last ridge did its color deepen to pulsing orange, its glow squeeze vapor from their backs.

Anne began to shake when they reached the land of Glenturk: the hills of corn among the stumps, the green track sliding down between the river and the curve of forest that hid the house. Tommy moved to take her hand. When the sober woods gave way to tender green saplings, Bess cried, "Halt!" The horses blew and tossed their heads; Bess turned to Anne and asked, "Shall we earth him here among his apple trees?" Anne nodded, but her eyes were blank.

The soldiers, their muskets primed, formed a circle facing outward; Zac and Tommy took wooden shovels from the sledge and dug between the orchard rows. Anne sat apart, looking down to the bottom lands, where fog spun from the river and fields and melted away from the house, leaving chimney fangs in a white, empty mouth. Then a crazy bridgework of half-burned timbers emerged; part of the loom-room floor remained, black, swept bare by fire. Glenturk was dead. No geese guarded the dooryard, no sheep backs humped the meadow, no calves bawled or colts pranced stick-legged, glad with morning. No Shep. Gone. All gone. Soon the wildflowers, the bees, the songbirds that had followed Jim's ax would disappear and the forests would creep forward until Indian fires drove them back again in a stinking, smoldering death. The shovels scraped and Anne turned, puzzled. She saw the coffin. We're planting Jim.

An ensign and three soldiers returned from scavenging and laid what they had found on the sledge: table boards, crocks from the spring, the fireplace crane, the burned, smelly Killyleagh kettle; a gray kitten they handed to Esther. That was all. All. No coins from under the hearthstones. Nothing. Zac and Tommy climbed from the empty hole. Empty. Gone. Nothing. Where had Glenturk gone? Where had Jim gone? He had been right here yesterday, right here . . . where? Jim, where are you? What's separating us? It's so thin. Like a moment of time. You're there. I'm here. But I can't reach you. She waved her hand through the empty air.

Then out of the fog came Cinder. Trotting, head high, steps wary. Anne leaned forward on her hands. Bonnie? But no shape followed Cinder; he came alone, up the track, shying from the soldiers who reached for his halter, straight to Anne. Anne rose, would have leaped on his back and ridden away if Bess had not held her; she laid her face against his living flesh. "We've lost them, babe, we've lost them."

Zac and Tommy grunted as they lifted the coffin and set it beside the hole. Esther, the kitten tucked in the pouch of her skirt, laid a pattern of daisies over the rough saw marks of the coffin boards. Tommy straighted the seedlings that boots had bent; Zac stood beside Bess, fists tight, leather shirt caked with clay, cheeks angry red above the black of his beard. Sunlight trimmed the flax with gold, the river shimmered, somewhere a bird sang. Anne clung to Cinder.

The schoolmaster, a gangling boy with a freckled face that was at sixes and sevens with itself, hitched himself to the graveside. Bess, standing with one arm around Esther, motioned to Anne. Tommy knelt, his muddy hands curled on his thighs, tears running from the sun-squinted corners of his eyes. The schoolmaster's fingers rattled the pages of the Bible; he glanced nervously left and right over his shoulders and cleared his throat.

"We'll go to Hugh," Anne whispered to Cinder. "We'll go and find Hugh." She walked to the graveside and Cinder walked beside her, his muzzle on her cheek.

Zac growled at the schoolmaster and he began, "The Laird is m' shepard . . ." His voice squeaked and his cheeks turned red. ". . . he maketh me to lie doun in green pastures." His accent was Sam Brady's mimicking the talk of the Edinburgh streets. "Yea, though I walk through the valley o' the shadow o' death . . ."

The first breeze of day ruffled the boy's orange curls and filled the air with char and ash. ". . . and I shall dwell in the house o' the Laird fore'er."

Zac stirred restlessly and the boy tucked the Bible precariously under his arm, then struggled to read from an ink-blotched paper. "Let us noo praise famous men an' our fathers that begat us. There are those that ha'e left a name behind them to declare their praises. An' there are some which shall ha'e na memorial, who are perished as though they had nae been, and are become as though they had nae been born."

Anne's chest had shrunk; it would take no air.

"We shall remember James Alexander Glenn, grandson o' the Reverend Campbell Glenn, son o' Matthew Glenn and Rebekah MacIllwain, brother to Elizabeth, Zaccheus, Thomas, Dora, and William, beloved of Anne Aiken MacKnight Glenn. For James was a mon o' mercy and wi' his seed shall remain continuously a guid inheritance." Anne laid her arm across her belly. Could it be? Could a part of Jim still be alive there? Her teeth dug into her lip, willing it to be so. "His body is buried wi' faith and his name shall livith to a' generations. Amen."

"Amen, Jim," Tommy said loudly. His tears were a river now.

Zac brushed everyone aside and hunkered next to the coffin. "You were a good man, Jim Glenn. Too good, I guess." His words clicked, flint striking steel. "You did your best by every beastie and every man—white or red—who ever crossed your path. And for that you were shot in the back as you came from your planting to sit at your board with your family." His hands on the box became fists, his knuckles mountains of white in forests of curly black. "Aye, you came to the land in peace. And you made it grow. Gentled it with your plow. You . . ." He paused; his chest and arms swelled, and he lifted his head and shouted, "They'll pay!"

Bess laid a hand on his shoulder. "Zac," she said softly.

He rose like a thunderhead mounting the sky, a prophet of the Old Testament shaking his fist at heaven. "As God is my witness, I'll be your true brother! I'll avenge your death! For every slash of their knives one of those murderers will die!"

Bess's hands clutched his shirt. "Vengeance is mine, saith the Lord."

Zac's lips peeled back and his large teeth chomped. "I don't believe that."

She shook her head. "No matter, Zac. Jim did."

Zac whirled away and stood with his hands circling the poles of the harvest sledge.

The soldiers shifted, the schoolmaster shrugged and took a

step forward, but as Anne moved to the coffin, he stepped back again.

She stared as though she could see through the wood, see Jim lying there; then she curled beside the box as she always had curled beside his knees as he squatted on his heels eating the noon lunch she had brought him in the field. The tips of her fingers caressed the pine as though it were the linen britches that covered his living flesh. His voice flowed around her, talking of this and that, of how the oats was coming and if the cow had calved. Then he rose and brushed the crumbs from his shirt, saying, "Well, back to work, Annie. There's much to be done." The same words he said every day.

Anne's hair was knotted in wild rust curls and her face smashed with grief, but she raised her chin. "Aye, Jim. You go along. I'll be coming after a bit. No doubt I'm to stay here awhile and finish up." She smiled. "I'll know you're out there, stumping, plowing up a new field while I tend to the garden. I'll do my best, Jim."

She drew up her shoulders and sat ramrod straight. "And when you get done for the day and come to the house, call me. I'll be close by listening and I'll come running." She bent and kissed the boards. "But listen, Jim, if I'm delayed and you get lonesome waiting, just start in making me a rocking chair and have it sitting ready on the hearth next to yours." She could feel his hand in hers, and she raised it to her cheek. "So good, Jim. You were always so good."

She laid his hand back down. "Make the rocker of cherry, Jim. You always did your best with cherry wood."

She stood tilted and bowed. "I'll be along by and by."

Turning, she walked alone from the orchard and up the hill.

Chapter Eleven

The eighteen acres of Fort Pitt were enclosed by a triangle of earthen works that pointed like an arrowhead toward the Ohio River. The Allegheny and Monongahela formed natural water barriers on two sides, and the third was protected by a moat. The town of Pittsburgh, a scattering of crude log cabins and a few more substantial buildings, covered six acres, and on the other twelve stood the five-bastioned star of the fort itself, where a Roman legion would have felt at home. Its ramparts of earth, wood and brick—kilns had been built nearby—rose twenty feet high and were sixty feet wide; sodded parapets protected the soldiers who patroled them. Inside the rampart's thick walls were storerooms, a dungeon, and two magazines built to hold two thousand barrels of powder apiece; the barracks that surrounded the acre of open parade ground could house a thousand. In the summer of 1763 two hundred soldiers and three hundred settlers faced the fury of Pontiac's multitude.

Anne slept. She slept anywhere she could lie down. She would feel her body begin to fold and she would pitch forward onto whatever was handy—a pile of furs in the barracks cabin, a corner of shade by the parade ground, Esther's lean-to by the south bastion. It felt like dying, this sudden going down into blackness.

Day after day, a hot, greedy July sun sucked water from the rivers, dried the moat and the rain barrels, burned the faces of the soldiers on the ramparts, the children playing leapfrog in the dust; it cracked the earth, the wattle chimneys, the people's nerves. Hordes of writhing squirrels swarmed down the crusted riverbanks into the yellow water, while inside the walls, people slapped and cursed, battling clouds of flies by day, mosquitoes by night.

Anne's sleep became lighter and dreams more real than life. In terror she would start up from wherever she lay and pace the ramparts, counting steps until she no longer heard Jim's cry, heard the sound of steel shattering bone, saw the gray of wee Tom brain's against the corner of the house. Militia and soldiers watched her from their posts on top of the walls.

On the forty-eighth day of the siege, in the hours that followed Captain Eucyer's second parley with the Indians, Anne had trouble with the southwestern side. The sun, directly overhead, beat on her skull, uncovered except for a rag, and dizzied her. At the outer point, where the men stood above her shoulder to shoulder, she continually lost count by hurrying, but this, the fifth time around, she walked very slowly, setting one heel down at exactly the proper distance from the other toe. Often she stopped and looked back at the prints in the dust to see if they wavered; the white line of pain between her brows matched the white scar on her cheek.

A drum rolled; Captain Eucyer climbed to the platform above the parade ground; the people rushed like termites from a rotten log. Afraid of being trapped in their midst, Anne ran for Esther's lean-to.

Esther sat cross-legged, braiding loose threads from her tattered dress. Anne glared, wishing the whole thing would unravel. She hated the red of it, hated it. The day Esther had held the gray kitten limp in her lap after some boys had pulled its limbs out of their sockets, she had stood over her, screaming, "Kill it! Kill it! And burn that dress! Burn it!"

The heels and buttocks of men invaded the scanty shade of the lean-to, and Anne curled against the logs. She tried to breathe deeply, to ease the feeling of being held, being trapped, but even in her own skin she felt a prisoner: Flea bites circled her waist, mosquito bites dotted the inside of her arms and elbows; scabies had burrowed into her wrists; patches of eczema reddened her upper lip; a rash ran down her legs. At first she had feared the rash was measles, but one night as she lay wide-eyed, unable to sleep, she had seen how spiders lowered themselves on threads from the low rafters onto her bare calves.

Bit by bit she had burned off her hair so that if the Indians came they could not grab it and hurt her: the smell of the flaking ends kept the death of Glenturk in her nostrils. The infested, stinking crowd backed ever closer, and she clenched her hands in her lap so that she would not dig her fingernails into her scalp, her arms, her belly, her peeling ankles. She feared that once she started to scratch she would go daft and tear herself apart; already her fingers were bloody where her teeth had ripped at hangnails.

In dreams she searched for water; awake she imagined herself immersed in the river or in the firewater barrels, washing away the stench of bad food and latrine trenches, the foul dust that clung to the hairs of her legs and crotch.

From his high platform Captain Eucyer, splendid in red and white, shouted orders, putting the fort on full alert. This time the people did not murmur, "Bouquet will come," but shuffled away, burdened by the weight of the sun.

Well, Annie, now you really must get clean. Jim would be disappointed to see you looking like this. Tapping Esther's knee—Esther knew the ins and outs of everywhere—Anne told her she must get to the river. Esther frowned, and Anne made scrubbing movements with her hands. Nodding, smiling, Esther led her away.

The acre of parade ground, squared by barracks rooms and log walls, sat at the center of the fortification; beyond that were ditches, then the huge, star-shaped ramparts. The spring flood of the Monongahela had breached the south rampart—water had stood twenty feet deep on the parade ground—and the rubble of bricks, timbers, and earth had been left as it was, and a new palisade made from the rail fences of the town had been erected beyond it. Into this maze of caves and tunnels in the ruined rampart, Esther led Anne; some parts were dimly lit, others were black as pitch. The second time Anne barked her shins she tugged on Esther's hand—she must have misunderstood, we can't get to the river this way. "Esther—" Esther clamped a hand over her mouth and turned her head so she could see into the room beyond.

A naked man stood there. His side was to them, his head bowed, and he was rubbing his legs like a bather coming from the water; he had neither seen nor heard them. Light, filtered through the earthen roof, outlined his body as though it were a white crescent moon in the evening sky. His legs, long and slender, melded into his small, round buttocks without a crease; the arc of his chest was narrow, and curls tumbled from his head over his cheeks and neck. He stepped into his britches and straightened; his member hung long and soft; he tucked it gently down and did up his buttons.

Esther pushed Anne under a wedge of timbers and crawled in after her. In a moment the figure, whistling softly, passed them in the darkness and disappeared. They tiptoed into the room where he had been, and Esther took Anne's hand and plunged it into an old powder barrel. Water! She gurgled as Esther undid the lacing of her shift, held herself naked on the edge of the barrel, then slid thighs, hips, breasts, shoulders into the silky womb. "Ohhhhhhhhh." Her sigh encircled the room, the barrel, her cradled self.

Her toes and hands explored, but no dead creatures shared her tub, and she didn't care if the young man had; the water smelled only of wet earth and gunpowder. Probably, she thought, empty barrels had been stored here, and the flood had filled them. She dunked her face, her hair; she bounced, giggled, and splashed; the same noises came from Esther's barrel. Anne wished for soap, then laughed at her greediness. What did it matter? Her scalp tingled, her face smiled, her skin jumped with a thousand jolts of joy. She fumbled in the darkness for her grimy shift and hodden gray dress and scrubbed them against the staves. Die, fleas! Ants! Scabies! She rubbed harder. Die, you little white eggs!

When her clothes hung dripping over the edge of the barrel, Anne scrunched down until her chin was lapped by tepid waves. She dreamed of floating on a green leaf on a summer
142

river; the leaf grew until her whole naked self lay on it and she twirled across a reflected world of fluffy clouds and bottomless blue. Another body lay beside her . . . long, lean limbs . . . curly hair against her shoulder . . . sweet, white, clean. His hand closed on her shoulder, turned her over . . . his young chest lay across her breasts . . . they dipped and rocked, swirling round and round on their green leaf boat, his member smooth inside her. She moved back and forth in the water, pushing it between her thighs, against her nipples. . . . Ah, Annie, you'll die clean after all.

Anne had no intention of going to bed that night, not with the hordes of biting creatures that lay waiting in the straw. Besides, why sleep away her last night on earth? Instead of doggedly pacing she skipped, light-headed, giddy about the base of the ramparts. Looking up, she could see nothing but the tip of the thousand-foot-high Monongahela bluff and an arch of fading, heat-smeared sky. Perhaps, Annie, you could fly to the top. She leaned over to gaze into a water barrel—do you resemble an ant or a bird? The reflection startled her—sharp bones, hyacinth-colored skin, eyes with the green scrubbed out, hair a wispy halo. You look like nothing so much as death.

A fierce little spring uncoiled and thrilled within her. Death. A leaving. A saying good-bye to earth—she ran her hands down the sides of her breasts, waist, hips, thighs—her body. Ah, Anne MacKnight Glenn, you should not go out like a crawling ant; a soaring eagle is more your style. What can they do if they find you on the ramparts breaking curfew? Shoot you? Whip you? What does it matter when by noon everyone will most likely be dead?

The men on duty had clustered on the east side, watching Grant's Hill, the Allegheny, the place where the town had been, so when in the darkness between gloaming and moon-rise Anne stole up the ramp at the northern point, no one was there. She crossed the wall and peered out between the two parapets. Wonder of wonders! The world existed—north, east, south, west—jumbled hills with stars perched on their peaks, the great silver Ohio. Down—she could look down! Like a crazed cat she tried to climb higher, to the top of the sodded parapet, maybe onto that star. . . . But her toes kept sliding off the dusty grass, so she turned instead and leaned out over the edge. If the river had been below she surely would have jumped.

If you could fly, Annie, where would you go? Her mind skittered away from Glenturk and sped across the mountains and farms to Philadelphia. The high bank of the Allegheny

143

became the bank of the Delaware: Wharves stretched into the water, masts rose beside them. Out of the flat nothing of Pittsburgh rose the belfry of the State House, the steeple of Christ Church. The dry moat below became Chestnut Street; wagons loaded with cabbage and corn passed by, then carriages and small boys chasing a squealing pig. And there was Hugh! His bouncy strides bobbed his brassy curls, and his hands, so much like her own, jabbed the air with soaring gestures. She joined him, a girl in blue linen, skipping, waving at folks on their balconies—

"Anne Glenn."

She almost tumbled over the edge before her fingers dug far enough into the sod wall to stop her. She held her breath. Had someone really spoken? "Anne Glenn." Hamlet's ghost? She edged back and pressed herself flat against the wall.

"Come noo. I dinna mean to be scaring you." The voice was young, the accent familiar. She squinted into the darkness, and in the angle of the wall made out the shape of a hunched form with long white hands dangling over bent knees. "It's meself, Andrew MacMeans."

She frowned. Was she supposed to know him? "I don't seem to recall . . ." Her tone was as stiff as though she were trying to discourage Horace Jones from following her down Chestnut Street. There was no reply. Maybe she'd hurt his feelings. "Andrew MacMeans, you say?"

"Aye. You do smile at me noo and again. I be the lang lad with the red hair and the shackle-banes and ankles what shoot out of ma Edinburgh duddies. You ken me. I spoke the burying words o'er your husband."

Anne slumped in relief. "Oh." A boy, not a soldier. She was safe. "I'm glad it's you."

Andrew caught his breath in a little chirp of joy. "Truly? You are?"

"Do the soldiers know you're here?"

"Aye. I told ma cronie Billie to catch a smoke or two while I stood watch for him. I do be militia."

Anne couldn't think of anything to say. Of course he was militia. Twelve-year-old boys were militia. Captain Eucyer had organized everyone except the infants in their cradles.

"I helped to build the firewagon."

She chuckled. "Will it work if we need it?" It seemed odd to be holding a pleasant, matter-of-fact conversation with someone as though they had indeed met on Chestnut Street.

"Weel, maybe." He laughed. "Let's hope we will na be needing it. I thought the captain sounded dead convincing telling the savages that three armies be on the way. An' if that dinna carry the day, those blankets out of the smallpox hospital should."

Anne shook her head, then realized he couldn't see her. "My brother Zac says they'll attack at dawn."

"Nay into the cannon again?"

"No, he says they'll have a trick this time."

"I've heard it said Zac Glenn thinks like an Indian."

"He's studied their ways."

"I would na bother meself. You could hand them this country on a platter of silver for all of me."

"All of America?"

"Ooo na! Only westard of the mountains. I do na ken what good this place be to anyone. Like my mither used to say, 'when you shear a sow there's much cry and little wool.'"

Anne laughed. "You're not a farmer?"

"Never. I do na care for being dirty and wet."

"You sound like my brother in Philadelphia."

"Philadelphia? 'Tis likely you'll gang-away East then?" He seemed to be holding his breath waiting for her answer.

"Andrew MacMeans, are you daft?"

"Na."

"Then what are you talking of going for? Nobody is going anywhere. Except to heaven or hell."

"I'm nay full ready for heaven meself." He stood up, surprising Anne with his height.

"How long had you been here when you—before the funeral?"

"In this howling wilderness? A fortnight. Aye, I was scared right out of ma breeks. You noticed?"

"You did just fine."

Again that quick happy noise from his throat. He licked his finger and held it up. "Aye. A breeze. A canty one right off the Firth o' Forth."

Anne sniffed. "Dreamer. I can't even smell one." But what is unusual, Andrew MacMeans, is that I can't smell you. She sniffed again, just to make sure. No, none of the siege rankness clung to him, even though he stood so close his arm brushed hers.

"Well then, come doun to the moat with me. There's everly a river breeze there."

"The moat? You are daft."

"'Tis dry as a bane, Widow Glenn."

"I didn't mean that. It's dangerous."

145

"Hoot! I do it every night. Like a wee mousie I hug the rampart wall so the soldiers canna spy me, and I lug a pistol to deal with any stray savages."

"You talk big for a laddie."

There was a pause; his hurt weighted the silence. "You have called me daft, a dreamer, and a laddie. Have you any other choice names, Widow Glenn?"

"I'm sorry, Andrew." She put her hand on his arm; it was all bone. "I didn't mean to hurt your feelings. I'm snappish. No worse than anyone else, I guess, but oh, I don't know . . . Who knows? Nobody knows."

Gently he covered her hand with his. "We're all a bit out of the traces, Anne." She gulped, holding back an overflow of sadness, of loneliness; he dropped his arm loosely around her back. "We all be hurting bodies," he said, drawing her head into the hollow of his shoulder.

She sagged against him. She had not allowed herself to lean on anyone. Even she and Bess had locked themselves into their own private sorrow, avoiding the hug, the tears that might never stop.

"Ma pappie died yester-autumn," Andrew said, "and I still grieve for him. And my mither, too, and I was but a wee laddie when she went with the angels."

Humph. You never look like you're sad about anything, Andrew MacMeans. Every time I've seen you you're grinning, happy-go-lucky, freckles popping out all over your face. She moved away a step but Andrew put his hands flat against her shoulder blades, and the firmness of them pulled her close. The bottom of her belly turned soggy.

Again Andrew drew in his breath with that chirp of joy. Back off, Annie. Back off before he thinks . . .

"You smell like a flower all sweet and clean," he murmured. She didn't move. "So do you."

He spoke into her hair. "I walk the moat at night, then sleep in ma cave under the old ramparts by the river during the day. And when I wake, I bathe. There's some old barrels—"

Anne heard no more. She saw the slender white limbs, the dark curls, felt that white crescent moon holding her. She wanted to enter that water limbo, float off on that river of reflections . . . cool, drifting, quiet, clean . . .

"Come, Annie," he whispered. "Come doun to the moat and walk with me."

She knew what he hoped. Bare warp threads of death stretched before her eyes; Andrew's body, a satiny dogwood

146

shuttle, sang back and forth through them . . . weaving. Weaving what? New life? Life, not death?

"Have you kenned how I've watched you, Annie? For forty-eight days you have never left ma mind for one wee while." His lips were awkward in her hair and his palms wet. "You be all the woman I ever have dreamed of. Aye, and a dight more, if I'm not mistaken."

She took his hand and started down the ramp.

He had been right; the moat was pleasant and cool. It was Chestnut Street, and Andrew—Hugh?—held Anne's hand. When the moon rose he led her to a shadowed crevasse in the moat wall where they lay on the cool earth, lulled by the cool murmur of the Allegheny. Now that their feet were still, they heard little sounds—grunts and scrapings.

"Animals?" Andrew whispered.

"Aye. Sounds like foxes digging burrows. We'd better not talk, noise seems to carry." She laid her head back on his chest; his pounding heart muted but did not still the sounds. She shut her eyes, not wanting to hear anything, think about anything, be frightened of anything. "Andrew, I would like to know you."

His hands moved uncertainly but tenderly, his body trembled but did not hurry. He kissed and touched like a boy lost in wonder, and Anne laid her hands on his to guide him. Twice he spilled his seed on her thighs. What if he ran out? What if there was none to . . . "Please, Andrew," she whispered, "don't pull out." Her whole mind was dark except for that one point of light . . . fill me, fill me, fill me. She could pretend it was Jim's.

As the gray tailings of night dissolved into morning blue, she watched Andrew's face take shape. His nose and chin, even his cheeks and jaw were sharp, quick, and new. Nothing had yet taken its toll, dulled the glow of his eyes—Dresden in the light, bottle green in the shadows. She saw her own image mirrored in them, saw them widen with awe as he studied her face, heard him repeat her name over and over. "Luv for you is on me, Annie."

"Aye," she said.

"Is it Philadelphia you're wanting?"

"Aye."

"Will you gang with me as ma wife?"

She didn't answer.

He sat up and dangled his hands over his knees, twirling a twig round and round. The corner of his mouth trembled; she thought of Hugh. She wanted to cuddle his head on her breast, twist his curls, wanted to make him smile again, hear him say again, "Luv for you is on me, Annie," dissolve the stones piled in her heart, her belly, her head. She touched the back of his hand. "I'll speak to my family, Andrew."

Dawn splashed Grant's Hill with rose, and Andrew looked down, searching her face to find what lay behind her words. His brows and lashes were diamonds and sand. "Is it aye or nay that you're saying, luv?"

She turned away. Annie, what have you done? Marry? You can't marry this boy. Don't hurt him. He's so earnest. Give it some time—a week. Maybe today will be all that there is . . . She pinched her lip between her teeth.

He stroked her hair. "Do na fret yourself, lassie. We—"

Rifles cracked from the riverbank, whoops and shots answered from the ramparts. They fled—around the corner, along the edge of the shrunken Allegheny, back through Andrew's secret entrance—safe inside the ramparts.

Anne ran for her battle station by the barrels; she never even bade him good-bye.

The noises they had heard in the night and dismissed as burrowing animals had been human diggers, Delawares who had scraped foxlike holes in the bank of the Monongahela and now lay concealed, firing musket balls and arrows at everything that moved on the walls.

Thursday—Friday—Saturday—and into the Sabbath. Lacking dramatic charges or sorties, cannon fire or even much bloodletting, the battle took its toll of those within the fort through the monotonous whine and thud of bullets by day, the soundless light of fire arrows by night. Men's excited grins changed to haggard scowls; women's tempers and sometimes their minds snapped from sitting in dark, hot rooms with cranky children who quarreled, pulled on them, and then at night rose up from nightmares with howls of terror, believing themselves attacked by monster fireflies. Every afternoon the air quivered with thunderstorms that hid beyond the bluff; rain never fell.

Whenever Anne saw Andrew, who was in charge of taking powder and shot to the southwestern wall, she studied him. She stared at his peeling nose, flat hips, toes that wiggled through cuts he had made in his too-small boots, trying to see inside, learn who he was to himself and who he could be.

148

What she saw on Sabbath morning was a laughing boy, his stick legs striding up the ramp with reckless unconcern that a bullet hitting the powder keg he carried on his shoulder could blow them all to kingdom come. Full buckets in hand, she hurried after him. "Good morning, Andrew," she said quietly to his back.

He didn't turn, but his voice cracked in a sudden burst of love. "Annie, I canna stand much more. If you do na speak to your family soon, I'm going to ask your brother meself."

"No!"

"He do na scare me!"

"Ha! Zac Glenn scares everyone. A panther is not an everyday person."

"You scared to ask him?"

"Yes."

Andrew turned, his cheeks pink with the slap of her words. "You feel shame for who I be?"

"No. No." She spoke quickly, wishing he would walk on. She didn't want Zac—wherever he was—to see them talking. In the past two months he'd fought men merely for glancing in her direction. "I'll see to it. Truly. But he's a bit of a bear right now, having no sleep for four days and—"

"I have na slept too guid meself." He raised one sandy eyebrow.

Anne laughed. Andrew MacMeans was no puzzle, he wore no mask, his true self lived in his face.

"Boy!" Zac's voice roared from the rampart. "Stop your dithering and get up here with that powder."

They both jumped. Since when had Zac been assigned to this wall?

A chorus of voices joined Zac's, and Andrew, as he loped to the top of the ramp, made a joke of pretending to throw the keg at them.

Anne set her buckets on the edge of the rampart walkway, scurried back down to the barrels, and then, seeing others watching the wall, turned. Zac, his face black from the backfire of his rifle, held Andrew by the shirtfront while shouting about bad powder. Andrew swung at him, but Zac twirled him around, put a moccasin in his backside, and kicked him over the wall.

Andrew sprawled in the dust, clutching his ankle. Then, like a wounded, growling red terrier attacking a mountain cat, he hobbled back up the ramp and tackled Zac's legs. Zac didn't even stagger. He lifted Andrew by the collar, cuffed him about the head, and dropped him over the side again.

At noon Anne returned to the barracks room. Bess stood by the hearth, ladling out a sulfurous-smelling soup while Zac, stripped to his breechclout, sweat trickling through the black mask of his face, regaled the family with the tale of what he had done to the boy who had brought him bad powder. Rhoda, Tine, and the children shrieked with delight and egged him on to tell it again. This time Zac, enjoying himself immensely, picked up a child and tossed her across the room onto a pile of skins. "That's how the red-haired puppy flew, his arms and legs going all which ways. My God, what a swack he made hitting the dust. He—"

"Shut up!" Heads whirled toward Anne. "Shut your mouths. You sound like a pack of Girty's squaws!" They gawked and blinked. "What would Jim say? He would never even have kicked a dog the way Zac kicked Andrew."

Zac stepped toward her. "Andrew is it? Don't tell me you're sweet on that Scot birkie, Sis?"

"There's nothing wrong with him."

Zac snorted. "A lad that size should have his mother's milk out of his nose by now. He's a ninny."

"Does everyone have to be exactly like you to be any good?"

"And what's wrong with what I am? Show me a man west of the mountains that's better than me. I'm—"

"A bully!" Anne yelled. "An ignorant, bragging bully!"

Zac threw his bowl to the ground, and the soup splattered on his hairy legs. "Why are you getting your back up over a toothpick boy? Insulting your own brother?"

"Because I'm going to marry Andrew MacMeans!"

In the silence the noises of war seeped into the rank, dark room—rifles cracked, men cursed, a hurt child cried.

"You lie!" Zac roared.

Bess stared at her. "You really do know him? I mean—"

"Yes. He's good, Bess. He—he loves me. We're going to Philadelphia together if—" Anne didn't know who was speaking, who had taken control of her tongue, who stood in her skin.

Zac raised both fists in the air and shook them; the acrid odor of his armpits staggered her. "No sister of mine is going to run off with a fifteen-year-old, whey-faced creature who can't wipe his own arse."

Anne raised her chin. "He's almost sixteen."

Bess gasped and grabbed her shoulder. "So young, Annie?"

"It's not fittin'!" Zac shouted.

Bess's arm tightened around Anne as she faced Zac. "You're

a fine one to talk about what's fitting. I don't see any wedding ring on Tine Howser's finger."

"I feed her kids damn well."

"How do you know any of them are yours?"

Zac leaned forward, his beard almost touching Bess's brow. "She was carrying mine before the tree ever fell on Herr Herman Howser."

Anne yelled in his ear. "She's always been a whore, Zac! In London—"

"I know, I know," he said, baring his teeth, "I told you once and I'll tell you again. Tine and I suit each other." Anne wondered if there was more to the story of Zac's coming West than she had ever heard, but before she could speak, his breath covered her face. "And I've been more of a husband to her than that white-pawed puppy MacMeans ever could be to you. You'd starve with him."

Anne backed up, dragging Bess with her, and shouted, "A man doesn't need to fight and hunt to live! There are other ways!"

"Like what?"

Anne said the first thing that came into her head. "He fancies being a Philadelphia merchant."

Zac mimicked Andrew's breaking voice. "His pappie's going to buy him a couple of ships, I reckon."

"His pappie's dead." She couldn't think of anything—even a lie—to fill the silence.

"Ha!" Zac snorted in triumph.

Bess tightened her grip on Anne. "John Morton still holds money of mine. There's enough for a dower for Annie, if this Andrew's the one she wants."

Zac jerked away, spat, and ground it into the earth. "What's that puppy doing in Fort Pitt, anyway?"

"He signed on with Mr. Kenny," Anne said, "to teach his children and help out in the store."

"That prissy Quaker. They make a good pair."

"Zac," Bess cried, "do you have to be so mean about everything, so bitter? What—"

"Yes, goddamnit!" Zac shouted. "Yes, I have to be so mean!" He grabbed up a hatchet and drove it into the doorframe. A splinter flew back and cut the corner of his eye. "I hate them! Hate them! You didn't see what they did! What they did to Jim!" The hatchet slashed again and again into the post. "When I get out of here those murdering bastards will pay!" Blood vessels bulged across his muscles, blood and sweat sprinkled the floor.

Everyone pushed back against the walls except Tommy; he rubbed his hand over the splintered post. "Be damn lucky," he said slowly, "if the roof don't fall in on us tonight."

Zac, mouth twisted with tears, let his head fall on Tommy's freckled shoulder.

"Hey, Zac," Tommy said, "If Annie really wants the puppy, why don't we get him for her?"

Zac raised his face. "You mean dust him off and prop him up for the service? I think I busted his ankle, Tommy."

Tine Howser spoke from the corner. "That ain't the part that a bridegroom's got to worry about, Zac."

Zac guffawed, and the laughter spread from throat to throat until children who had no idea what was funny rolled on the floor in spasms. Bess grabbed Anne and shouted, "A wedding! We're going to have a marrying!"

Anne planted her feet. Had they all gone daft? "Not right away! Not right away!" No one seemed to hear.

Zac dodged for the door. I'll get the whelp, Annie. My Gawd, what a brother he'll make, huh, Tommy?"

Anne clutched at his hairy arm. "No, Zac! Wait a minute. I have to talk to him. Alone."

"I'm in the mood. Let's do it now."

Anne screamed, "No!" at the top of her voice, and Zac stopped. Bess moved to block the door. "She's right. You don't understand some things. Every lass has got a right to choose the day." She looked at Anne. "Time to get her gown ready and such."

Anne frowned. Why does Bess look so saggy and old? Is she thinking of Jim? Thinking that he and I never married properly and now . . . She jammed her knuckles into her forehead. What am I doing? Jim, what am I doing? This isn't me standing here talking of marrying.

"Bess's right!" Tine yelled. "Let the Indians stop shooting before this Andrew starts his." Her cackle drove Anne out into the withering heat, down to the dusty corral where Cinder, head low, ribs stark, came to lay his chin on her shoulder. Round tears rolled down her cheeks. Jim! Jim! Where are you?

Here, Annie, right here.

When she got over the fright of hearing his voice in her head they had a good, long talk.

On Monday the fort woke to silence. Men and women lifted their heads and strained their ears. Nothing. They ventured onto the parade ground, up the ramparts. The land was empty, so were the rivers; the Indians were gone. They waited. One hour, two hours, still nothing. The eerie silence held them as tightly as the sounds of battle had. First they spoke in whispers, then not at all.

Monday passed . . . Tuesday . . . Wednesday. The children did not play, but hunkered on their thin haunches, listening. Grown people slouched, knowing yet not knowing, the superstition—if a thing is spoken, it will come true—binding their tongues.

Simeon Eucyer sent for Captain Zaccheus Glenn, dismissed his aide, and barred the shutters. In the dripping darkness they talked. The braves, they said, had not gone to their villages in the West, they had gone East. Gone to ambush soldiers coming to relieve Fort Pitt, to massacre them in the forest the way they had the troops of Braddock eight years before. Catch them as they marched, terrorize them with fiendish howls, fire into their bright red coats while they kept their own brown nakedness behind brown trees. Surround them, scalp them, leave their bodies to feed the bears whose mothers had fed on Braddock's dead. Seal off Fort Pitt to starve in the winter snow.

The little Swiss commandant limped—he'd taken an arrow in the leg—to the window and opened the shutters. They watched the listless movements of the people, another child carried to the smallpox hospital, the soldiers sprawled dozing in the heat, the women slack-jawed, the militia sullen. Perhaps the Indians wouldn't have to wait for them to starve. If Turtle's Heart returned to parley and spread a hundred English scalps in the dust of the parade ground, apathy might well become despair. Simeon Eucyer told Zac that despairing armies always found a way to commit suicide: They might believe an offer of safe passage; they might mutiny, break open the stores, and die drunk; they might brawl, killing each other.

Zac roiled like the rainless thunderclouds piled to the east. "Then give us the order to go after them now!"

Eucyer sighed. "You, too. Don't you think Turtle's Heart has planted an ambush for us, too?" Turning, he called his aide to light pipes for them both. They puffed. "How's your family bearing up, Zaccheus?" His accent was German, his words sometimes French.

Zac chuckled. "My family ain't thinking about the Indians at all. They're getting ready for a wedding."

"Whose?"

"My brother's widow."

"Now?"

"Simeon, you know those things don't stop for war. I sometimes think wilderness folk have weddings just to take their minds off their troubles. Even the thought of a gathering makes them bubbly as toddlers. The idea of dancing, getting drunk, forgetting for a while—"

Eucyer yelped and whacked his captain's bare, hairy back. "Zac, my boy, that's it! That's it! Your sister is going to have a wedding! A wedding like this place has never seen! A full-dress honor guard. Pig and rum! High noon. Noon tomorrow. I'll do the service myself. Have her bring me a copy of what she wants said. Who's she marrying?"

"A laddie called Andrew MacMeans."

"Who? Oh, never mind. That's not important. Get moving, man. Spread the word. No, wait. I'll tell them myself. Lieutenant! Have the drummer sound assembly!"

A long column of red-coated soldiers marched over a ridge and down toward a silver stream. About them flitted dark shadows. Shots cracked from the trees; the soldiers returned the fire, moved forward. Smudges of white puffed all about them, the circle tightened. They fired and ran backward; some fell and lay like red rags.

"Fall back to the ridge!" The order echoed from mouth to mouth.

There, amid the bitter smoke, shrieks, and howls, the soldiers formed a hollow square. Some knelt and fired from a barricade of saddles and fallen trees, while in the center others tore flour bags from four hundred plunging horses' backs and built a wall about the wounded. Squads of men dashed against the enemy, but their bayonets found empty air, while the Indians' bullets found their mark. Colonel Henry Bouquet's horse died under him.

Night came—squads tried and failed to reach the stream; thirst became unbearable, sleep amid the periodic howls and flashes of powder impossible. Bouquet wrote in his dispatch book, "Sir, in case of another engagement tomorrow I fear insurmountable difficulties . . ."

Anne opened her eyes; her throat was scratched by screams. The bluff of the Monongahela smoked, and the sun rose like a huge ball of drying blood. She sat in her chair in the doorway; Zac crouched beside her. "You were dreaming, Sis. A bloody nightmare, I'd guess."

"Was there a battle?"

His lips brooded. "Maybe there was. Out there. In any case, don't speak about it. Enough people are close to panic. Just before sunup the sentries saw a Delaware walk the river, waving the scalp of Eucyer's last dispatch man. The captain's moved the wedding time up to ten o'clock."

"Zac, I don't think I can go through with it."

He rose. "You must." The cannon boomed reveille; Zac's "Be brave, Annie" joined its echoes. His huge, callus-thickened hand almost touched her hair. "Be brave for Jim."

People tumbled from their doors into the misty August morning. Bess, shaking the blue velvet Mrs. Kenny had brought for Anne to wear, called, "The wrinkles didn't all hang out. I'll steam it over a kettle and see what that will do." She disappeared. Anne rocked. Well, Jim . . . The nearness of him made her heart crack. Maybe by the end of the day I'll be with you. If not, I guess I'll be Andrew's wife. Jim took her hand and rocked with her. Anne sighed. It's a way to get to Hugh. Jim nodded. That seems to be the only important thing—to get to Hugh. The dust kicked up by hurrying feet filled her face, making her sneeze, and she rose quickly. Be brave, Annie.

Captain Eucyer shouted the new wedding time from the platform, joking that if they waited till noon the pig would be overdone and the rum too warm. Men caught his flippant spirit and boldly bathed in the river; women called out for bits of finery to borrow; children bobbed about the dozen fiddlers tuning up for the dancing. The orange sun heated the air to steam. Females dressed their hair, males shaved, Mr. Kenny sold the last of his wares at auction, fourteen pigs turned on the spit.

Neither Bess nor Anne spoke as Bess stitched the dress close to the frame of Anne's protruding bones, and if their eyes met, they turned away quickly, shuttering sadness, raising their chins for courage. By the time Bess finished, Anne itched with sweat. "Well"—she cleared her throat—"perhaps I'll just melt in the sun and not have to worry about being either dead or married."

"Oh, Annie, don't—"

"I'm sorry." She paced. The dress was short, and her moccasins showed beneath. "I'm beginning to understand why men like a battle. Like you with the ax. Whack—it's over one way or the other. Marrying seems like much the harder of the two." Bess stayed on her knees, her hands drooped on her lap. Anne bent and shouted, "Why don't you stop me?"

Bess whispered one word: "Zac."

The heated air pulsed with it; the tread of the soldiers' feet repeated it. Zac. Zac. Zac.

Anne slumped against the post splintered by Zac's hatchet. "Yes." She plucked a splinter and traced her scar. "You know me better than I do myself." Bess did not reply. "I may always regret Andrew MacMeans. But"— Anne picked up her skirts—"here I go off to sacrifice myself on the altar for the brave defenders of Fort Pitt." She laughed deep in her throat. "No, no, don't hug me, Bess. I'll go mushy and I couldn't stand tears on top of all this sweat. Hand me my charming cap of lace, and off we go."

Shiny-buttoned soldiers formed two lines, and Mr. Kenny and Andrew appeared at their head: Andrew in borrowed breeks of gray, a navy coat he could not fill, and stockinged feet blackened to look like boots. The resplendent little figure of Captain Eucyer approached in buttoned leggings of spotless white; breeches, waistcoat, lapels and cuffs of royal blue; coat of scarlet; cockade of black silk, and pistols of silver curved from his cummerbund. He handed his cane to Mr. Kenny, the best man, slapped Andrew on the back, and whispered a joke.

The fifes began to play as the Glenns assembled at the foot of the tunnel of brilliant, sun-drenched soldiers. Zac and Tommy, slick with washing, marched Bess in rusty black silk and Esther in borrowed doeskin down to the front and returned for Anne. She laid one white glove on Tommy's gold fist and the other on Zac's mat of black. Drums beat, fifes whistled, and off they went.

"I'd rather be wrestling a bear," Zac muttered to Tommy over Anne's head, then whispered in her ear, "I admire your spunk, Sis. You're out-Glenning the Glenns."

Andrew's blurred face sharpened into stark whiteness, and when Zac and Tommy's huge moccasins stopped beside his stockinged feet, he staggered against Mr. Kenny.

"You strong enough," Zac rumbled, "to hold up that Scot puppy, Kenny?"

"Shush, Zac!" Bess said with a hiss. "Don't you spoil Anne's day."

Captain Eucyer's gaze darted from the propped groom, to the giant sky-framed Glenn brothers, to Anne's wide-eyed sweat-prickled visage, and he immediately launched into the service.

"'The design of marriage is that fornication may be avoided, and as our race is more dignified than the lower creatures, so

156

then our passions should be regulated by reason and religion.'"

Anne felt like one of the pigs on the spit, and when he said, "'Secondly, it will be particularly binding upon you, sir, who is the head of the family, to maintain the authority that God hath given you,'" she snorted.

Andrew remained glassy-eyed and oblivious until the captain read, "'Lastly, it is incumbent upon you, madam, who is to be the wife, to acknowledge the authority of him who is to be your husband, and for this, you have the example of Sarah, who is commended for calling Abraham "Lord."'"

"Lord?" Andrew's mouth formed a stricken O.

Anne had to laugh, and when Captain Eucyer intoned, "'. . . but if you cannot gain your point by persuasion, it is fit and proper that you, madam, submit in matters in which conscience is not concerned,'" Zac said with a growl, "Aye, that's where you got him, Annie: conscience. That gives you the right to throw his duds in the street."

The captain, apparently afraid the service might disintegrate into a free-for-all, said quickly, "Do any here know any reason why Anne MacKnight Glenn and Andrew Magee MacMeans should not be wed?"

Anne heard the rustle of Bess's skirts behind her and hoped? feared? she would shout, "Yes! She is my brother William's wife!" But the question echoed twice more, with only the usual mutters and snickers for a response. The captain proceeded: Mr. Clapman will offer a prayer for the bride and groom."

The portly old gentleman gathered his wind and began.

Twenty five miles away, on the hill above Bushey Run, brown men dashed against the western side of the hollow square of soldiers where a thin red line fired, loaded, fired. At the base of the ridge, deep in the ravine that circled it, two pincers of bare white shoulders edged through the leaves, slowly advancing toward the massed Indians. The brown men, like a many-headed monster, roared and threw themselves against the barricade; the soldiers, also as one body, rose to meet them with bayonets.

Bare-chested, kilted, the men of the Black Watch Grenadiers scrambled up from the ravine. Those on the north side shrieked the ancient battle cry of their clans and charged the Indians' flank. The braves stood, faltered, regrouped, but as the Grenadiers rushed again, they fell back into the musket fire and steel of the second ambush. The gore-smeared Grenadiers killed and killed until the forest was silent.

"Widow Glenn," said Captain Eucyer, "what is your reply?"
She looked past the thin bridge of his nose into his troubled brown eyes. "Aye," she said. Then louder: "Aye!"
His small lips smiled. "Kiss your wife, young man."
"Noo?"
The captain nodded, and Andrew whooped with joy.

The siege ended with the Black Watch Grenadiers marching over Grant's Hill to the skirl of the pipes, while the defenders, smitten with the glory of it, stood on the ramparts like a woodcut from a history book. Anne and Bess waved their head rags; Zac and Tommy thumped each other's backsides and joined the thunderous hip, hip, hoorays for Colonel Henry Bouquet; only Esther turned away, to gaze at the Ohio flowing west. Mad joy and a hugging, singing fellowship lasted the morning, but by afternoon, drunkenness, disputes, and bare-chested wrestling rocked the dusty parade ground. Zac shook his tomahawk and shouted that he was off to carve up a dozen redskins, but Rhoda, who was pregnant again, mustered the spunk to wrap herself about Tommy and refuse to let him go. Tine wiggled up to the brawny knees and thighs of the Grenadiers, and Bess gave way to the pain in her back and lay rigid on her pallet.

Anne, filled with a single-minded terror of the fort—both what it had been and what it had become—would have left that very minute, but Andrew, hearing the soldiers' tales of the Indians' murderous devastation that stretched all the way to Carlisle, hesitated. Anne yelled and stomped her feet, saying that if he didn't make up his mind, she would go alone. When the ragtag line of refugees and walking wounded straggled up Grant's Hill under a guard of Royal Americans, Anne—with Cinder close behind her—and Andrew were with them. Esther had already departed—in the other direction; Bess, still immobile, told Anne that she would come as soon as she was able.

Stoney-eyed Anne hurried eastward—past smoldering mountain cabins and shallow graves desecrated by both animals and Indians, past burn-scarred women and dazed men and starving children. Past the Lancaster jail, where men from

Paxton had killed the dozen Indians sheltered there, past the army of frontiersmen marching on Philadelphia to protest the removal of those Paxton Boys to that city for their trial. Blind to suffering, blind to cries for justice, frenzied by weeks of delay—it was now February—Anne scrambled through a tunnel lit by a childhood vision of Philadelphia's spires and the house on Chestnut Street. She slept lightly, dreaming of wide-board floors gleaming in the morning sun, of Mrs. Held grinding coffee, of the comfort of warm quilts, of Hugh's bare toes emerging from his bed. Once awake she would thicken his thin boy's legs into men's thighs and calves; she would imagine his face, older and serious, ordering his carriage to some mansion on outer Market Street—a place like Robert Bailey's.

Chapter Twelve

Anne woke with the smell of books, dust, and unwashed cups clogging her head. The stuffiness ran into her nose, and she reached for a hankie but found no pocket, no skirt. She lay naked in the midst of a feather mattress, and Andrew was not beside her. Flat, cold winter light outlined staggering stacks of books, scattered clothes, a washstand, and a chair. On the chair hung the shirt she had worn for seven months, and she blew her nose in one corner of it. The close, damp room had given her a head cold; her back ached from having feathers, not ground beneath her; and the child within her kicked in anger.

Last night she and Andrew, after bedding Cinder in the stable of a sleep-rumpled Reverend MacMillan, had, following his directions, found Hugh at the top of a flight of narrow stairs, occupying two small rooms across from the courthouse. If he had still been the golden boy Anne remembered she could have dismissed the shock of his lodgings and hugged him with joyful abandon. But Hugh, at twenty, was a hollow-chested, unwashed, self-styled philosopher who, embarrassed by his sister's boy-husband, her condition, and their obvious poverty, resorted to expounding political theory.

Andrew and Anne had fallen asleep—she in the only bed, Andrew in a chair in the front room—listening to Hugh quote Aristotle, Montesquieu, Locke, Rosseau, and Cicero.

Anne raised her head from the pillow at the sound of voices in the front room. Had Hugh talked all night? Or was he just continuing his explanation of the concept of eternal community, of an enduring government of justice in which the people participated? Andrew's voice overrode Hugh's, asking if mice had gotten the last crumb of bread.

"But don't you see, Andrew? Don't you understand the importance of taking the opportunity of forming a pure, new government here in America?"

"No. When will the bakery be opening? When will the milk cart arrive?"

"Any minute. Look what is happening right now. There are the men from Lancaster—the so-called Paxton Boys—camped in Germantown, an angry rabble, a force of anarchy. Philadelphia has played the tyrant trying to drag men to the capital city for trial, just like the English have always dragged the Scots to trial in London. The Scots learned to take their armies with them, camp them in Scotland Yard, and demand justice or else. Is this what America is coming to?" His voice was shrill, urgent. "We must break the old habits, old patterns. What we need is a government where both sides, all sides, are participants, where compromise can be reached within the legislature. Full representation for everyone! It's the only way to keep the cannon out of the streets."

"Cannon?" Hugh had caught Andrew's attention. "Here? Will there be fighting? I'd heard Philadelphia was chock full of Quakers. And they don't fight."

"Ha! You should have seen them as soon as they knew that this time it was their scalps on the line. Silent meetings changed to musters. Suddenly guns were holy weapons. John Wharton will have them drilling down there in the square as soon as the frost is off the cobblestones."

Anne buried her head under the pillow. Fighting here, too? Killing in the streets of Philadelphia? Dear God . . .

"Will you fight?" Andrew asked. "On which side? Do you have a gun?"

Hugh's voice sobered into the searching, thoughtful one Anne remembered. "Yesterday John Elder, the minister of Conestoga, spoke on the courthouse steps. He listed all the grievances of the Westerners, said the same things Jim Glenn said ten years ago. Someone from the crowd yelled the question of how a man of God could defend the murdering Paxton Boys, and he said, 'All of us will bear the epitaphs of 'traitor,' 'murderer' before there is true liberty in our land.'"

"Listen! Is that the milk-cart bell? What did he mean?"

Hugh's reply was deliberate, filled with wonder. "Independence from England. Freeing ourselves—America—from the British Crown."

Anne burrowed under the quilt, curling her knees over her belly as far as she could. Andrew spoke her thoughts. "That's treason! You could be hung for saying that!"

"Yes."

Her brother had gone mad! War! Was that all men ever thought of? War! In the middle of one they plotted another.

The milkboy shouted, and Hugh and Andrew's clumsy male feet thumped down the stairs to the street. Anne wrapped the quilt about herself, rose to use the chamber pot, then dove back into the warm feather nest. She could hear a crowd gathering below in the street, voices raised in cries of bravado. She groaned and dozed; Ben Franklin's voice cracked her sleep, and when cries of "Coward! Wobblie!" rattled the windowpane, her eyes bounced open. Was the mob turning on Franklin?

Hugh and Andrew banged into the front room. "Yesterday," Hugh was saying, "our Benjie yelled, 'To arms against the rabble!' Today he's for taking an olive branch to 'our neighbors from the West.' Lord, what a man. Only he can get away with throwing chestnuts into the fire and pulling them out himself."

Andrew's head poked around the curtain into the room where Anne lay; a moustache of milk circled his mouth, and biscuits and buns sprouted from his pockets. "Ooch, wifie, look! The land of milk and honey." He plopped down on the mattress, and Anne sat up, clutching the quilt around her shoulders. Andrew collected his "smooches," then handed her the crock of milk and a huge, sticky bun. "I'm off to find my sisters," he announced around a mouthful of biscuit.

Surprise sprayed the milk from Anne's mouth. "What?"

"Ooo aye, they be my flesh and blood. I have to see how they're faring. And to tell them my news of marrying rich." At Anne's squawked "Rich!" he bit his lip, ducked his head, and mumbled words to cover his gaff. Before she could speak he had kissed her cheek again and was halfway to the door, where he affected a turn as though a sudden thought had struck him. "Oh, bye the bye, do you suppose that if I stopped at John Morton's house he could give me a wee bit of an advance on your dower to see me through the week?"

Anne shook her head to clear her ears. "The week!"

"Aye, I'm not sure where Margery and Geneva be now. It may take a while to track them down."

She sighed. "Ask Hugh to lend you some."

"I did. He hasn't got any."

"Don't be silly. Hugh!"

Hugh stepped around the curtain, the sparse winter light accenting his gaunt pallor; his eyes flickered like blue flames against a white ash log. When he tersely admitted his money was gone, Andrew, sensing a quarrel, bolted out into the Philadelphia streets like a colt let loose in home pasture.

Andrew MacMeans always had been a lad of the streets. It was there he felt at his best. Even before his mother died— and that had happened when he was three—he had had a deadly fear of being shut in a room, of being left alone with walls. And with good reason: He believed they were alive, as did his father. The Reverend Angus MacMeans, a man in perpetual motion away from reality, was an assistant pastor of the Netherbow Church on Edinburgh's Royal Mile, assigned, even in the prime of his life, to the duties usually given only to the inexperienced or the enfeebled. He had married late to a quiet, plain young woman whose uncle—her guardian—had died leaving her with debts and no means of support. Jane Magee was gifted in many ways: She sang in the choir that served the great cathedral of St. Giles; she knew long passages of poetry by heart; she kept, on meager funds, a loving home for Angus and their first daughter, Geneva. But when pregnant with Andrew, she unwittingly made the mistake of moving her family into rooms over an eating place on the Royal Mile. It was not the noise from below that disturbed their peace but the fact that two hundred years before, John Knox had lived on the other side of their parlor wall.

Angus, convinced that the words of the great Calvinist, the father of Presbyterianism, had become—as he thunderously practiced his sermons—imbedded in the plaster and wood wall, was determined to extract and record them for posterity. So Andrew from the time of his birth heard his father talking to the parlor wall, asking it questions, sometimes kneeling in prayer beside it, scribbling down answers. The little boy would place his own ear against the damp plaster just as his father did and when the old man would shout, "Ooo Johnny, how grand, how grand ye say it!" he was sure he heard the voice, too, a deep voice that bellowed about sin and hellfire and plucking out eyes. The closet in which he slept shared the same wall, and without any mouth it talked to him as he slept, and without any eyes watched him every minute. It had no hands and yet he would wake up feeling it touching him, pressing down on his chest, smothering him.

Jane died giving birth to little Margery, and Andrew knew her screams, which had gone on for days, also had entered into the wall. He knew because he heard them every night and sometimes even in the daylight. Now he had no doubts: Walls were alive and to be feared.

A widow from the Netherbow Church, a sour, grasping woman who squeezed all—vegetables, money, and people—that came within her reach, was hired to wet-nurse the motherless babe and never left. After a year Angus meekly submitted to marriage and thereafter spent his nights talking to the wall and his days dozing at the church. Six-year-old Geneva fought her stepmother at every turn, but the shrieking matches always ended with Geneva being exiled to the street, little Andrew with her.

Little by little Geneva expanded Andrew's world until by age four he knew every nook and cranny of the block and by five was earning coppers running errands. His father found out and put him in school. There Andrew sat in the middle of the room away from the walls and listened and watched as his sister had taught him to do. In four years he knew all the schoolmaster did and was dismissed. Angus, proud of his quick-witted son, enrolled him in the Academy, but Andrew stayed only one day—the class was small, the room was small, and the walls closed in and began talking to him. When his stepmother learned of his return to the streets, she apprenticed him out: first to a goldsmith, then to a carpenter, next to a mason, but Andrew was not clever with his hands and did not like being caned for his mistakes. He hid out with a pack of boys like himself who shucked oysters, unloaded wagons, sailed with fishermen, worked at any job that did not last longer than a few hours, a day at the most; his nickname from castle to bay was "Happy-Go-Luck."

The Reverend Angus MacMeans died as unobtrusively as he had lived, and even his wife, lying in bed beside him, had no notion that his timid heart had taken one final lurch and stopped. That morning, as usual, she went out to stand with the neighbors in the narrow street waiting for the bakery to open, so it was seventeen-year-old Geneva, slipping in to ask her father for money to buy cloth for a dress for Margery, who discovered that only a body, already growing chill, lay in her father's place. Years of matching wits with her stepmother had honed Geneva's mind to a very sharp edge; with only a quick sigh for her dead father, she dragged the wooden and brass strongbox from under the bed, snatched her mother's picture from the wall, and hurried to wake her brother and sister. By the time Mrs. MacMeans stormed back into the bedroom cursing her husband for a lazy, no-good slug a bed, the three children were on the dock and Geneva was handing the box to the captain of a vessel bound for America.

The big-boned girl with the mass of carrot-orange curls was not entirely sure if the captain was being kindly or penny-wise or both, but she took his advice when he said that the best path to success in America lay with giving the entire contents of the box to Andrew. "Dinna you ken, lassie? What's here would only pay passage for the three of you and you'd arrive in the New World penniless, without any kin and without any work. There'd be nobody to nurse you through the newcomers' diseases, and all you'd have to show for your troubles would be six feet of American soil heaped on top of your bones. But if you and the wee lass go as bond servants, you'll have someone to care for you while the laddie here uses the money for passage and to get set up in business. By the time your seven years are done he'll have a fine home for you and a dower so you can marry well."

The passage was calm and on the public dock of Philadelphia Geneva and Margery were auctioned off by the smooth tongue of John Cooperson, netting the captain twice what he would have charged for the passage. Andrew kissed his sisters good-bye and ran off down King Street to knock on the door of the first warehouse office he came to. The man behind the desk questioned him carefully, then said that their agent, Mr. Kenny in Pittsburgh, had been looking for a young man to learn the trading business and give lessons to his daughters. Andrew, showing the man he could do sums in his head, write out a bill of sale, and recite ten lines of Latin, was hired on the spot. As he turned to leave he thought to ask where Pittsburgh might be and was told that it lay to the west. "About like Glasgow lies to the west of Edinburgh?" he asked and the agent, knowing nothing of Scotland, nodded. Six weeks later a dazed and bewildered Andrew arrived at Fort Pitt, was immediately made town schoolmaster, and in a fortnight was speaking the words of the funeral service at Jim Glenn's graveside—still not quite sure where he was or how he would ever get out.

* * *

Andrew's search for his sisters lasted three days; at daybreak of the fourth he returned to Hugh's dark rooms with chapped cheeks and three loaves of bread, gotten on credit from the baker's shop below. As he tunneled his way through the loaves he reported that he had found Margery employed on the John Bartrum estate on the other side of the Schuylkill River. "Plump and happy as a mouse in a nest," he said, "and blooming under the attentions of a nephew of the family." Geneva was a different story. Andrew had had to wander about in the fogs of the West Jersey pine woods before he found her—tending vats in a turpentine camp. She had assuaged his fears for her by tossing her square jaw upward and saying that her master was easier to get around than their stepmother had been.

"My sister Geneva is a most powerful person," Andrew related with awe. "She didn't want to talk of herself at all. Her only anxiety was for how I had fared. She was," he said, puffing his chest, "impressed with my bravery at Fort Pitt and my good fortune in marrying well. That helped her over the shock of our father's savings being gone. I told her," he said, winking at Anne, "that your dower did not make me a rich man, but she seemed content on hearing that you are a strong bonnie woman with a doctor brother and a farm on the outside of town."

Hugh raised his head. For the three days Andrew had been gone Hugh had barely moved from his desk, where he was writing a paper to present to Ben Franklin's Political Club, the only society that he, as a philosopher, allowed himself. "What farm?"

"Octoraro," Anne said. "I've told Andrew how nice the summers can be out there."

Hugh growled. "He'll have no time for summering in the country if he's to make a success of business."

"Whoa back, Brother," Andrew said. "I don't see you bringing home a pot of gold every week. Besides, I didn't mention the farm meaning it for summer holidays."

"What then?" Hugh was angry. "Why mention it at all?"

"Well, it would seem that Annie is next in line to inherit if Bess and Zac and Tommy stay in the West."

"Ha!" Hugh jabbed the point of his quill toward Andrew. "You'd never last a week at farming. It's man's work." Andrew doubled his fists, Hugh rose. Andrew, a full head taller, his freshly cropped apricot hair tight to his skull, stretched his lanky body for a fight; Hugh raised his head like a haughty Greek god.

Anne hauled herself from her chair as quickly as she could—now was not the time to straighten out Andrew's misconceptions about her relationship to the Glenn family. Shoving her bulky body between them, she said, "There's a house for rent in Grey's Alley. If you boys can stop your squabbling long enough, I'd like to have you look at it before I sign the lease."

Hugh glared at his sister and shouted, "No! You can't live in Grey's Alley. It's near the canal. It's rough down there and it's getting rougher all the time. And a child—"

"I can't see," Anne said, hands on her hips, "that you have spent the past two days thinking up a better idea."

Andrew smirked at Hugh and put Anne's shawl around her shoulders. "It'll do for a time, luv. In six months I'll have the business flourishing and we can move over to Chestnut Street."

Halfway down the stairs Anne felt her insides drop. "Andrew, we'd better go by way of Front Street and see if Mrs. Held would be willing to come to work at once." She wiped perspiration from her hairline. "I think the baby's dropped. And as I remember, Mam said that means two or three weeks to birthing. I'd planned on six." Could the child be Jim's after all?

Andrew, his eyes muddy with worry, spoke firmly. "You wait right here and I'll fetch this dragon I've heard so much about. The three of us will go to Grey's Alley together."

As Andrew finished speaking he opened the door; light, warmth, and excitement smote their faces. The Paxton Boys had been allowed to present their petition of grievances to a committee of legislators and, in return for a promise not to harm the Indians the Quakers were sheltering for the winter, had been granted the freedom of the city. The square was filled with gawkers. Andrew dashed off into the back-slapping crowd saluting the buckskin-clad Lancaster men laden with purchases, leaping small boys who hunkered in awe gazing at tomahawks stuck in waist thongs, and bowing to young women draped in sashes of welcoming yellow.

Anne shook her head in wonder as she pulled her shawl about her. To think that these people had been on the verge of killing each other! Maybe Hugh is right. Maybe we do need to think up something better for America.

The square rippled with excitement; heads turned toward the courthouse. The Reverend John Elder, Ben Franklin, John Wharton, and the leaders of the Paxton Boys mounted the steps arm in arm. The crowd pressed forward, shouting, "Speech! Speech!" but the men waved and disappeared inside.

Anne lowered her eyes from the balcony; Robert Bailey, his back turned, his head tilted up toward the courthouse doors, stood in front of her. She backed quickly into the shadow of the hallway. The rich folds of his English wool cloak, the fine leather of his boots, his shiny brass spurs drew her like a magnet; she had to brace her hands against the doorframe. Annie! What are you thinking! You're a married woman! Married . . . The contrast between Andrew bounding off, his feet wrapped in deeskin, and this mannered, elegant man staggered her. She squinted, then shut her eyes and retreated as though the light had grown too bright.

Ever since she had knelt at the window of Glenturk seeing or dreaming—she had never understood which—the puff of smoke and the running braves, the center of her brain had remained dark; occasionally she even forgot who Andrew was or why her belly was so huge.

Robert Bailey turned to address his companion, and Anne stifled a gasp at the smooth clarity of his profile. The continual sight of the weather-carved faces of farmers or woodsmen with cracked pink lips buried in a brush of beard had made her forget that men could retain the beauty of boys. He kissed me once, she thought, more than once . . . how strange.

Feet clattered on the steps behind her and Hugh, shampooed, shaven, and dressed in respectable broadcloth, descended and stepped into the light. Robert Bailey never saw Anne as he called, "Good morning, Hugh! So the philosopher emerges from his cave!" Hugh brushed past Anne to take Bailey's outstretched, gray-gloved hand. "Well, MacKnight, I hear you're going to honor us with a paper Friday night."

Anne's eyebrows rose almost to her widow's peak. Hugh hobnobbed with people like Robert Bailey? Had she misjudged the importance of what he was doing? He looked back at her, his mouth open in the silent question, Do you want me to present you? No! Frantically Anne shook her head. No! The two men edged away through the fringes of the crowd.

When Andrew arrived with Mrs. Held, a ripple of childish fear caught Anne's throat, but the discovery that her own eyes were slightly higher than the housekeeper's flat black ones gave her courage.

Stepping back inside the hallway Anne took Hugh's walking stick from the corner. "Here, Mrs. Held. I think it would be best if I took your arm and you cleared a path for us with this."

Mrs. Held clamped her mouth shut and twitched her shoulders as though she would turn away; instead she hesitated then took the stick. "Life goes on. Don't it, Mrs. MacMeans?"

Anne bit her tongue to stop the smile. "Yes, Mrs. Held. Life goes on."

Arm in arm, accompanied by the sudden cries of those feeling the jab of the cane, they made their way to Grey's Alley.

April 1, 1765

Dear Bess,

Andrew did get glass in the windows on the first floor even though he broke two for each one he finished. Afternoon light filtered through putty streaks, is better than oiled paper filling the room with jaundice.

The baby is coming. The pains started while I was helping Mrs. Held with some scrubbing. Not bad yet, but Hugh will bring the mid-wife when he comes to supper. Right now I'd rather be alone just talking to you. I'd always heard that no girl wanted to birth a baby without her mother and now I understand. I feel closer to you than ever before—still like a daughter, but the miles between us makes me your grown-up daughter—two women involved in woman's business.

April 3, 1766

Dear Bess,

It seems like just yesterday I was pacing this floor waiting for Marybett—she is never called Mary Elizabeth, that is too dignified for the hellion that she is. Now here I am waiting for another and I'm almost as scared as I was the first time. Not about the birthing itself—Frau Gretchen says I do that "easy as soap sliding off the parson's rump"—but about having another child as angry as Marybett. Frau Gretchen claims she was marked by all I'd been through while carrying her. I'm inclined to think that being conceived in a moat must have had something to do with it, too. Any lingering doubts that she might be Jim's child disappeared instantly with the sight of her spiky carrot hair and face consumed by a black howling mouth.

April 4

Good morning Bess! Andrew has his son. And I have my good baby—James Alexander Glenn MacMeans. He's lying across my chest right now. Quiet and heavy with his blond hair—the softest thing I've ever felt in my life—brushing my chin. I feel I was visited by Jim as the Virgin

168

Mary was by the Archangel. He even has the broad Glenn cheeks and his eyes are so blue I know they'll never change. What a miracle! Bye, bye for now.

Chapter Thirteen

Hugh MacKnight swung wearily down from his dusty horse, and the news-hungry men in front of the livery gathered around him. "Tell us, Dr. MacKnight. What did the colonies decide in New York?"

Hugh, responding as Sam Adams of Boston had instructed him, raised his arms and shouted, "No taxation without representation! If no one pays the Stamp Tax, the Crown will be forced to abandon it."

Over the cheers Robert Bailey cried, "They all agreed?"

"For once they did." Hugh grinned as he rattled off the names of the colonies present.

"Say them slower," John Cooperson yelled, "and we'll drink to each one!"

"Give us the details, Hugh!" John Morton called.

Hugh wondered if he should keep his mouth shut until the stage that carried Franklin and the others arrived, but already hands were lifting him to a barrelhead. "Catch them at the height of their passion," Sam Adams had told him. "This is an issue that the most careful lawyer and loudmouthed mechanic is going to be in agreement about. No secret meetings anymore. Let everyone see and be intimidated by the force of your numbers. Philadelphia is your stage—lead them back and forth across it." A noggin of cider was thrust into Hugh's hand; he drank, then mopped the grit from his weather-lean face.

He named the colonies, allowing time for a cheer to follow each one: New York . . . New Jersey . . . Massachusetts . . . Rhode Island . . . Delaware . . . Connecticut . . . Maryland . . . South Carolina . . . Pennsylvania. The crowd had swelled to a hundred or more. "Tonight," he cried, "we'll meet at eight on the Public Dock! I'll read you John Adams' bills against the Stamp Act that the Massachusetts legislature has adopted! Pennsylvania can do no less!"

"Sons of Liberty!" a voice shouted, and Hugh never

hesitated. "Yes! Sons of Liberty! We are all Sons of Liberty now!"

The early dusk of October had yellowed the city by the time Hugh hurried across the Dock Street Bridge. Although his head pounded with excitement, he caught the sound of furtive footsteps behind him. He paused where the drawbridge met the street and bent as though to straighten a wrinkle in his boot; his right hand went to the small pistol in his cummerbund, his eyes to the high curve of the bridge. A stubby man with white hands dangling from long arms pretended to gaze at the canal below.

A British spy? Drop the dramatics, Hugh. He's probably no more than a pickpocket hoping wrestle your saddlebags from you. Collecting commissions by raising funds for the hospital had required Hugh to spend long hours on horseback, strengthening but not enlarging his physique.

He sprinted to the lighted corner of Walnut Street, then turned quickly just before entering Grey's Alley; the shadow was still with him. "Thanks for seeing me home!" he called and darted down the rutted path. One look at this place and he'll know we have nothing to steal. The tiny, weatherworn house sat forlornly in its neglected yard. Andrew had lost most of Anne's dower when his dry-goods store failed, and since then he had flitted from one job to another; his latest was acting as evening host for the Widow Robert at the Indian Queen, the income from which barely managed to pay the rent. Hugh's commissions supplied food and clothes, but for the past year there had been no money for Mrs. Held or repairs of any sort.

Hugh's "Hello!" brought cries of joy from Anne and eighteen-month-old Mary Elizabeth, who abandoned her efforts at dislodging her six-month-old brother from her mother's breast and dove for her uncle's legs.

Anne scurried about filling a basin for Hugh's feet and pouring whiskey for his thirst, jabbering about a letter from Bess and news of the town, but he, after a month in the drawing rooms of New York, could not control his frustration at the smell of soiled diapers, the smoke from the poorly drawing chimney, the window frame stuffed with rags. "I see Andrew hasn't fixed the window yet."

Anne reddened. "He's got the glass. Probably tomorrow."

Hugh touched the claw scratch on Marybett's cheek. "And how many tomorrows has he been promising to cut the door in half so every hog, dog, and cat off the street won't come wandering in every time we need to let this damn smoke out?" Anne, instead of flaming in anger, looked stricken. "Sorry," he muttered. "I'm tired." He stuck his feet in the steaming basin. "Ahhhhhh. Did Bess say anything about coming East?"

She shook her head. "No, her back—"

Hugh sighed. "Come sit by me, then I'll help you put the little ones to bed."

When the children were gone and the unkempt corners hidden in darkness, Anne and Hugh sat on the bench, their shoulders touching. "Are you with child again?"

"No." She paused. "Thank the Lord."

"You shouldn't have any more for a while. A year, maybe two. Your body has got to have a chance to catch up. Andrew will just have to mind his pullouts."

She looked at him from under her brows. "He won't like that."

"Do you want me to tell him? As a doctor, I mean."

She snorted softly as she placed a bowl of mush in his hands. "No. Now tell me all about New York. You look like you're burning inside."

He grinned. "I am. Both from the fires of liberty and the powders John Adams pressed on me for my bowels."

She chuckled. "Ah, Hughie. It's good to have you home. The evenings have been very long."

He twirled his spoon, letting the yellow blobs drop back in the bowl. "I have a lot to do, Annie. This Stamp Tax—it has to be repealed. There will be meetings. . . ."

Breath puffed from her lips. "The Sons of Liberty."

"Aye."

"Night meetings?"

"Aye. There's one tonight." She flipped the paddle into the kettle and paced, teeth clenched. "Perhaps," he said, "we could meet here."

"Here?" That mob here?"

He laughed. "That's what they call them in Boston—the mob indoors. No, I mean when a few of us get together to talk, lay plans. Just people you know—John Morton, Joe Cannon—"

"Hugh, soon it would be Franklin and people like that. This place is not fitting."

"We'll make it fitting." He stuffed his pistol into his waist and checked the one that lay in the niche by the door. "Annie, don't get it in your head to come to the dock. And even if the chimney smokes, keep the doors bolted. Tonight a man—Have you seen anyone lurking about?—a broad man with long arms. Bearded."

She laughed. "No doubt a British spy has followed the dangerous Hugh MacKnight home from New York. All right, I'll be careful, Hugh." She knew he was right; the closed frontier had confined new immigrants to the coast, and men had been pushed to earning their daily bread in strange ways.

They stepped onto the stoop. A torchlight parade glimmered down Front Street, feet marched to chants of "No taxation without representation!"

"My God, Annie! There's hundreds of them! What if Franklin isn't back yet?"

She gave his shoulders a little shove. "You'll love every minute of it."

The dark and the noise swallowed him; Marybett shrieked in a nightmare; Anne pulled in the latch string and bolted the door.

The advent of nightly political meetings in Anne's hearth room eased the melancholy routine of heavy household tasks, small children's needs and the social constraints of shabby clothes. The passing weeks and months now could be measured not only by Marybett's expanding willfullness and Jamie's mental quickness, but by the stimulation of twisting the British lion's tail in reaction to their enroachment on the colonies' freedom by enforcement of the Navigation Laws, imposition of the Townsend Duties and finally the landing of soldiers in Boston.

Chance meetings with Robert Bailey stirred Anne in a different way. Although by 1767 the population of Philadelphia had grown to forty thousand all activities still centered in an area four blocks long and two or three deep comprised of one old market and one new one, one hospital, one lending library, and one courthouse; and on Sabbath everyone—Quakers, Moravians, Papists, Presbyterians, Anglicans, and Anabaptists—brushed elbows on the thoroughfares. Whenever Anne's and Robert's paths crossed, he would stare at her with a curious intensity, and she would duck her head, pink flaring her high-boned cheeks; if she spotted him first she would scurry home like a chipmunk for its hole. Sometimes, trapped in a circle of mutual acquaintances, she would be forced to speak to him, to murmur words about the weather or children, but any questions she asked of him were redundant; she already knew through Hugh what he wore to the races and if a lady accompanied him, what he won at cards on Thursday nights, how he felt about nonimportation, how many ships he had, and where they sailed. She also knew something that made her skin tingle, for more than once Hugh had said, "Annie, that man is in love with you."

Although she occasionally daydreamed as she had as a girl, she was always careful to make the setting so preposterously romantic that her conscience could not prick her. She and Robert sailed away into cool New England breezes in summer, and in winter to the islands of the Caribbean; he dressed her tenderly in velvets and silks and brought her tea with his own hands; and in full moonlight with black water rippling, he kissed the palms of her hands and told her she was a woman of such beauty and goodness that he would give up his life for her favors. Then Anne would plunge her arms back into the tub of wash water, laughing at her foolishness.

The old market on Market Street had gradually enroached on the roadway until on busy Wednesdays and Saturdays a carriage could not squeeze between the stalls and the prison yard or the brick walls of the courthouse. Wares were shouted in a jangle of Scots, Swedish, German, English, and Dutch, and on hot August days makeshift roofs of blankets, tin, or boughs sheltered vegetables, seafood, and hanging fowl and game from the searing sun. Geese honked in pens, dogs barked, and red-faced women waved huge fans over piles of round cheese, baskets of blackberries, trays of wiggling eels. Through this dim, sweaty clamor Anne made her way, clutching her purse of pennies and inwardly scorning the wilting, worm-chewed corn and cabbage as better fit for the pig yard than her table. She pushed to Mrs. Englekraut's stall and dug through a barrel of cool green cabbage heads; then, as she lifted one aloft to heft its weight, a hand grabbed her wrist and Robert's voice said, "Please Annie, don't run."

She slumped against the barrel. In the two hours since she had squirmed out from underneath Andrew she had paddled Marybett twice, soothed Hugh when his foot went through a rotten floorboard and burned her arm on a kettle. Now this. "What do you want, Mr. Bailey?"

"To talk to you."

"Yoo-hooo! Robert!" From across the way Polly Wharton waved and began wending her way through the fish stalls toward them.

"The belle of Philadelphia is summoning you," Anne said, pulling her arm away and plopping the cabbage into her

173

basket. Polly, now in her late twenties but still enjoying suitors more than marrying, had been very willing to speak to Anne when Jim Glenn had been the talk of the town, but since Anne's return she had passed her on the street without a glimmer of recognition. Anne's hate was pure and shining. She pressed a half penny into Mrs. Englekraut's palm, and with Jamie clinging to one leg and Marybett glued against the other, started to move away.

Robert slid the basket from her arm with one hand and with the other on her back firmly guided her behind a line of farmers' wagons—out of Polly's sight. He whistled for a boy to carry the basket to Grey's Alley, then scooped Marybett up into his arms and gave her the rose from his buttonhole. She looked at him with coy green eyes, smelled, and shredded it to bits.

Robert's hand never left Anne's back as they padded through the odorous dust of Grey's Alley, up the rickety steps, and into the hearth room. Anne, embarrassed by the sight of unscraped bowls, nightclothes spread over benches, stockings lying like gasping fish on the hearthstones, and a horde of green flies drinking from an uncovered crock of buttermilk, muttered, "I'm sorry, Mr. Bailey, if you were expecting a butler to serve you British tea."

His fingers pressed her shoulder forcing her down on the bench. "It's too hot for tea." He turned to the children. "Go to your room and nap." When Marybett hesitated he lifted his hand and they scurried off.

Robert paced from hearth to window to door, his fist slapping into his palm; Anne sat stunned by his audacity.

He stopped pacing and glared at her. "Why don't you demand that your husband grow up and be a decent provider?"

"He tries."

"You need a housekeeper." Robert waved his hand in frustration. Marybett's singsong teasing and Jamie's whimpering cry of, "Give it back!" came from above. "And some help with those children."

The veins in Anne's temples beat white. "Andrew helps. He sees that the water barrel is filled. Two on washdays. And he milks mornings. Usually."

"How wonderful! Look at this place! Look at you. The handsomest woman in Philadelphia reduced to . . . What would Bess say?"

"Work never hurt anyone."

174

"Then why doesn't your husband try it?"

"He does try! He sells crockery!"

Robert's fist hit the table. "Why do you put up with it?"

"Because I married him!" Her own fist came down. "Because he's my husband!"

Robert walked out.

The next morning a boy came with a note. "Mrs. Mac-Means. I have need of a bookkeeper. Good wages. Robert Bailey."

Anne, her body suddenly springy as a colt's, built up the fire, and when the flatiron was hot, pressed her husband's best shirt. Andrew slouched in for noon dinner in a bad temper over the heat, over the clumsy job a farrier had done shoeing his horse, and over the word that his next shipment of crocks had not left Liverpool yet. Then, grinning with delight, Anne told him the news of the job.

Andrew exploded in a wild jig of joy, then yelled for Marybett to come stand on the shed roof and pour buckets of water over him. When he had dressed in his Sabbath britches and stiff linen shirt, he bussed Anne's cheek and set off down the alley, his tall frame bouncing with the disjointed energy of a fast-growing boy. Watching him, Anne smiled, catching her breath as a quick surge of caring shot through her. No matter what, she thought, he's still my Andy.

In twenty minutes Andrew returned, a puzzled frown on his face. "I could see Mr. Bailey," he said, "sitting at his big desk at the top of the stairs just as plain as could be. But his clerk insisted that he'd sailed for China."

Anne ground her teeth. How could he plot to embarrass her husband with a fake job offer? She clapped a bonnet on her head and tromped off to Front Street. Apron strings flipped from her waist and dust rose behind the swish of her skirt. Who did Robert Bailey think he was? Her cheeks blazed.

She stopped outside the huge brick warehouse, uncertain which way to enter. A wooden staircase reached to the second story, and Robert stood at the top. "The pay, Mrs. MacMeans, is a pound for five mornings a week."

"But . . ." Annie, it's you he wants! You! "You insulted my husband!"

"He's a strutting ass."

"He's the head of the family!" People had stopped to stare— she must sound like a fishwife.

"He may be the husband, madam, but you are the head of the family."

175

"Why are you mocking me? What have I done to you?"

He waved his arm. "Bah! That's no insult. Stop cowering before that boy. Will you take the position?" Anne, hands on hips, stared without answering. "I've sent a boy to Mrs. Held. She'll be at your house by nine tomorrow. She's agreed to work for a half pound a week."

She turned her back on him. A trick combination of haze and charcoal fires had turned the river green, almost as green as the Allegheny that had flowed past Glenturk. Jim, are you there? What should I do?

"I'll look for you at seven tomorrow, Mrs. MacMeans."

She walked away. Somehow she had to tell Andrew that it would be she, not he, earning their daily bread at Bailey's warehouse.

Mrs. Held had been unemployed, and the wage offered was princely. She arrived in Grey's Alley prepared to justify every penny's worth, and the chaos in the little house dissolved beneath the clomp of her heavy shoes. Jamie, whose love for everyone was unconditional, toddled after her wherever she went, and Marybett stood in absolute awe of the woman who had been so daring as to lose a hand someplace and never find it again.

Anne, in a revere unknown since Glenturk, woke to clear morning light on her quilt and the feel of fresh down about her; and even Andrew's butting and banging could be ignored by thinking about the work undone on her desk—and sometimes Robert Bailey himself. She would arrive at the breakfast table in her new chocolate dress, her hair brushed into a gleaming bun and, skirt swishing across a freshly sanded floor, take her place to be served her porridge and jam. Andrew, after the first shock was over, seemed proud of her position; with cautious eyes Hugh watched her bloom.

The autumn and winter proved dry and mild, and Anne seldom missed taking a long morning stroll through the waking, bell-filled streets where women swept stoops and where yellow cats padded home to sleep. At seven o'clock Front Street wore an easy face of yawning along-the-shore men, joking fishermen loading their dorys with stinking bait, and from the river the wrenching cry of an anchor chain, a mate's shout, and the whomp of canvas sails dropping from yardarms.

Her tread matching the solemn toll of the bell in the courthouse belfry, Anne would climb the twenty-one creaky steps, wish Campbell Jamison, the clerk, a good morning and take her seat on her high stool. Campbell, the son of Mr. Bailey's housekeeper and gardener, was newly arrived in America and so shy that in answer to her greeting would merely duck his straw-yellow head and nod. His hands, used to the plow, not the pen, labored long over his work, and it made Anne smile to think that Mr. Bailey's office was more a place of charity than efficiency—one good person could have taken both their places.

Robert sat on the other side of the partition, and if Anne paused by the half door she could watch him, a brown rock in the midst of a noisy, swirling empire of ships and packtrains, men and dreams, goods bought and sold, small fortunes lost and won on the whim of wave and weather. But as spring warmed into the summer of 1768, even his seemingly impervious personage was marred by a crease between his eyebrows, and more and more often his knuckles rapped his desk in exasperation. The embargo on British goods had spread from one port city to another, the rallying cry being that Boston should not bear the Lion's anger alone. Philadelphia merchants had straddled the fence longer than most, but now the Sons of Liberty, who had once forced the repeal of the Stamp Tax, ruled the streets again, swaggering with their cocky devil-take-the-hindmost bravado; their leader was Hugh MacKnight.

Sharp plans of action, not philosophy, dominated the meetings in Grey's Alley, and Andrew joined in with a vengeance; he had waited in vain for the shipment of crocks to leave Liverpool, and now all his hopes rested with the Dutch. In June Hugh dismissed the last of his patients with packets of huge pills and rode off to Rhode Island and Boston to coordinate the colonists in what he now publicly proclaimed as "resistance to the tyranny of the Crown." He was one of the few who dared name the king as culprit.

On a sticky July morning when the fog hung low and yellow from a thousand breakfast fires, Anne felt a new slackness in the air of Front Street. She paused, cocking her head, peering into shrouded silence. It's come, she thought, the port is closed to England. She sat at her slanted desk, hot and irritable from a poor night's sleep, idly staring at the columns of figures, wondering how long Mr. Bailey could afford to keep her on. How could they live if—

"Beg pardon, Mrs. MacMeans, you spoke?"

Anne gazed at Campbell's large boy-pink face. Already a blush covered his neck and cheeks and a glaze of worshipful blue his eyes. She had been very careful to keep their relations formal, fearing that any touch of intimacy would bring from him a declaration of devotion or a hasty exit out the door. She clipped her words, "Mr. Jamison, have you seen the bills of lading for the *Wanton Stover*?"

"Out of Maine? Aye. Still on Mr. Bailey's desk. Shall I—" He rose.

"No. No." In one motion she swung from her stool and through the half door into Mr. Bailey's room. There, perched on the corner of his desk, sat Polly Wharton, all ruffles and bustles and beehive hairdo.

"Well, dearie me," Polly said archly, "a lady clerk. You poor soul, have you been widowed long?"

Anne growled, and Robert hurried around his desk. "Polly, may I present Mrs. Anne MacKnight MacMeans. Mrs. MacMeans"—he ground out the words as he glowered at Polly—"used to keep the books for Mr. John Morton. She consented to help me out several mornings a week."

Polly raised one eyebrow and patted her great dome of hair. Anne, clamping her jaw, strode to the other side of Robert's desk. "I'm ready for the bills on the *Wanton Stover*."

Robert, keeping a wary eye on Polly, moved back behind his chair and began shuffling through papers. Polly spread her fan. "Your father—or somebody—supported those awful savages, the Paxton Boys, didn't he?"

Robert said quickly, "Her brother Hugh MacKnight is in politics."

The white feathers fluttered. "Oh, Hughie! Is he your baby brother? He is so divine when he gets all stirred up about Parliament. Cheeks all pink, tongue running on. You Scots—"

"Now, Polly." Robert, perspiring, ran his finger under the edge of his stock. "Boston has Sam and John Adams, Virginia has Patrick Henry, and Philadelphia has Hugh MacKnight. They're all Americans—"

"Troublemakers!" Polly spat. "King George should order them to London to stand trial for treason." She snapped her fingers. "And that would be that."

Anne folded her arms and said sternly, "The cornerstone of English justice is trial by one's peers. If American colonists were to be hauled on board ship—"

"Don't lecture me, Mrs. MacWhatever-Your-Name-Is! All those fancy words the rabble-rousers use—bah!" She turned her elegant profile toward Robert. "The poor always are so touchy about such things, aren't they?" The feathers of her fan flicked her chin.

"Polly, I must insist—"

Anne cut him off. "It's of no consequence, Mr. Bailey." Her shoulders squared, her chin went up. "We won't have to put up with her kind in America too much longer. As soon as trouble starts they'll race like mice back to the skirts of their bishops and the tender mercies of their mad German King Georgie. Good riddance, I say."

Polly leaped from the desk. "Scum with no breeding always—"

"Breeding?" Anne screamed. "You talk of breeding!" Her hands dove into the beehive of hair. Polly's fan cracked over her head. Anne pulled. Masses of hair came loose in her hands. Polly's fingernails lunged for her face. Anne knocked them aside with her arm and spit in Polly's eye. The screams of the disheveled belle reached the rafters; she rushed at Anne. Anne stepped to one side, raised her leg, and Polly sprawled on the floor, bustle high in the air, petticoats and pantaloons waving. Anne planted her foot firmly on Polly's back and uttered a whoop worth of Zac Glenn's best.

Then, ignoring Robert's limp-faced stare and the cheers from the men below, she marched off to her cubicle where Campbell stood, his cheeks sucked in, his white eyebrows raised, and his hands softly applauding. Anne stopped, stared, whirled back to see Robert bending over Polly Wharton; then she clapped both hands to her mouth. Annie, what have you done? She crawled onto her stool and buried her face in her arms. Her mind swirled. She heard Robert soothing Polly, Campbell saying, "Dinna greet, missus. 'Tis a fine way to begin a revolution." Her mind blanked, blackened.

Anne woke to silence. Her first thought was that Bailey and Sons had gone out of business and she was locked forgotten in an empty warehouse. She shivered, cold perspiration coating her flesh. No, it's dinnertime. She raised her head and saw the bills of lading from the *Wanton Stover*. She groaned, dizzy with shame and the humid, still heat. Robert had stood here as she slept. Slept at her desk after making a perfect fool of herself.

Unbinding her hair, she combed it with her fingers, then groaned again. Next you'll be joining the mobs in the streets, and applying tar to some merchant's rump. The outside steps creaked; Anne pulled at her clothes. Campbell? How could she face even him?

Robert Bailey opened the door. He held a tray with two kidney pies and a sweaty tin pitcher. "You're awake." He set the tray on Campbell's table. "Hungry?"

179

Anne turned her back and struggled with her hair; her fingers trembled.

She jabbed the pins into her hair and stood twisting her hands, her back still toward him.

"Anne . . ."

She didn't move.

His boots tapped on the floorboards, his fingers barely touched her shoulder. "Polly deserved what she got."

"That's no excuse." Drops of sweat tickled her sides, ran between her breasts. She could smell the musky warmth of him. Robert . . . Robert. Suddenly she was tired of holding him off with her eyes, of moving away when he stood next to her, of refusing rides in his carriage. Tired of—

His hand held her shoulder. "You had every right to do what you did."

She slumped, and her back rested against his chest. "Only a common fishwife—"

His grip and voice hardened. "You are no fishwife, Anne MacKnight."

Anne MacKnight. Was she really Anne MacKnight? Her head felt light; maybe she would faint again and he would catch her and . . . Her hips touched his belly. She barely managed to keep her hands clasped in front of her. He gently rubbed her upper arms, so close to her breasts, her nipples. His cheek stroked her hair. What was he saying? She put her head back, and he whispered in her ear. "Anne. My Annie. Listen to me. She's dead. My wife is dead. I'm free."

His arms came around her, and she turned in them. This time her lips found his. Starved. She must be starved. She gulped, trying to eat his mouth. His hands grasped her hips, pressing, squeezing. She clawed at his neck. Her body went out of her keeping.

His voice spoke from far away, on the other side of the blackness. She strained to hear, to clear her ears of the roaring in her body, but her tongue kept licking his. She was wet, wet everywhere. "Wait. Wait just a minute, Annie. I'll get the carriage. Here. Sit down here. Watch for me out the window. A minute. I'll only be a minute."

He was gone. She sat, her body doubled on itself, panting, sweating, trembling. She raised her head. The street was empty, wavy in the heat. Ready. I must be ready. She mopped her face on her petticoat, and reaching up, lifted her bonnet from its peg. Hurry! A carriage passed. It was not his. Ticks of thought sprang up here and there in her brain. She shut her eyes, willing blackness, willing his arms, his mouth, his hands on her breasts, her thighs. She was eighteen, lying in bed, dry-mouthed with lust, remembering his touch, touching herself. Robert!

Heavy, slow steps shook the stairs. Campbell. Campbell was coming back. Paralyzed, she bit her lip. He was naked, erect, his fair face above hers, his body so solid coming down . . . Dear God! No! Help me, God! She wrenched herself up, out of the chair. Seizing the iron latch, she flung open the door. Campbell was only halfway up. Before he could raise his head she turned away so the bonnet obscured her face. Clutching the railing, she tried to suck some of the wet wall of air into her lungs. She must not faint.

Slowly she started down. One. Two. Campbell flattened himself against the brick wall to let her pass. He thinks I'm upset about this morning. He won't say anything. He'll never know. I'll walk down the street, meet Robert on the next block. Eight. Nine.

"Can I be of help, Mrs. MacMeans?" His eyes were blue suns under the shade of his brows.

She put her hand over her mouth. "No. Thank you." Eleven. Twelve. The street was silent, heavy with noon. She passed Campbell, felt his eyes on her back. Eighteen. Nineteen. There, she was down. She lifted the front of her skirt over the puddles of dust. Campbell hadn't moved. She would have to turn up Spruce Street, wait for the carriage there in the shade.

But she didn't stop after turning the corner. She kept on walking and was almost to Second, almost home, when Robert's carriage rolled up beside her. He sat alone on the box. "Anne! Get in! Can you open the door yourself? I don't want to stop." His head swiveled up the street, then down.

Don't want to stop. A chill froze her spine. "No."

Robert's boots hit the road in a cloud of dust. The mare half reared, and he grabbed her head. With his other hand he reached toward her, but she was too far away. Words came hoarse on his panting breath. "Old Jamison was asleep. Too much rum. I had to harness up myself. Here, get in. Annie, get in!" The corners of his face dripped. "Please!" He tried to reach her again.

Anne shut her eyes, swaying in the sunburst blackness. The big house would be cool. The drapes drawn. Dark-paneled walls without eyes. Broad steps leading up . . .

"Annie, please. I love you. I've always loved you. We'll find a way."

Love. The word burned. They were climbing the stairs together, moving across the landing. She was leaning on him. His arm was strong. The last step. The long hall of open doors. Mrs. Jamison came out of one.

"No, Robert. It's wrong. It's wrong." She looked at him. He was no longer cool, but wild. If she moved just a little, he could touch her and she could go wild, too. Wild beyond reason, beyond sin. The way she had been in the cabin with Jim before . . . A black shadow fell over her; she stepped away. "No! It's wrong!"

Running behind the carriage, she entered the narrow mouth of Grey's Alley. She heard his cry, the crack of his whip. Turning, she watched the rumble of white dust disappear and wondered if she loved him.

That night she sat on the stoop and watched the palings of the neighbor's fence grow and march in the cream moonlight. The shadows still lay sharp on the eider dust of the road when the cocks began to crow. She rose and climbed the stairs to the heat of the garret and lay down beside Andrew. Stiffly at first, then when he moaned, rolled over, and fitted the length of his body to hers, she willed her flesh to soften, open. "Andrew," she said, "I want a child."

She sent a note to the Bailey warehouse saying that she could no longer accept employment there; she dismissed Mrs. Held.

Chapter Fourteen

At twenty-nine Anne took stock of her life. Children: two—five years had passed since Jamie's birth, and Andrew's daily morning flings had merely resulted in a series of miscarriages. Men: two—a brother who scorned money and marriage but whose passions were so attuned to Parliament and King George that at one twitch from either he would leap to the nearest barrelhead, or as in the present case, ride off to Boston; and a husband who enjoyed nothing more than sitting on his cart of crockery, joking with blowsy women who pressed pence into his hand.

Throughout the rainy winter of 1769 Anne wandered from room to room, musing about her options. Annie, you've had your taste of commerce and found yourself untrustworthy in the matter of disallowing the gentry from untying your bodice strings. Keeping a school? One shriek from Marybett and an answering howl from Jamie killed that notion. Quilting with the neighbors? Good deeds with the church ladies? She tossed her head and said with a snort, "Boring! I was never meant to be an ant. And surely not a saint." She decided to wait for God's call.

It came on a midsummer night as she returned from the necessary. Shooting stars showered the sky, filling her head with awe and her tongue with poetry. That's it, she breathed, and nightgowned and barefooted, sat on the stoop until dawn, planning a cloistered life as poet and playwright. After breakfast she enrolled Marybett in dame school and set off to purchase a desk. John Morton showed her one of cherry with curved Queen Anne legs, and she bought it on the spot.

On entering Grey's Alley Jamie cried, "Who's that?" Anne half expected to see the bearded "spy"—who still reportedly had made appearances there over the past four years. Instead, a gray-skirted bundle hunched on their stoop.

Anne approached cautiously and a tear-stained round face emerged from the plump, mousy figure. "Mrs. MacMeans? I'm Margery. Andrew's sister." Anne had no more than gotten her in the house before she added, "And I'm carrying the child of a nephew of the Bartrums who will have nothing to do with me."

When Andrew arrived home, recriminations blew in all directions. Finally he took the ferry to Jersey, hiked into the pine woods where Geneva toiled over the boiling vats of turpentine, forfeited the clothes and money due at the end of her denture, and brought her home.

Anne stood dumbstruck as MacMeans took over her house. Four days after Geneva's arrival, Mrs. Held—whom Anne had finally been able to pay for washing and ironing two days a week—stomped out the door, saying that she'd sooner chop off her other hand herself then take orders from "that flaming, ill-bred Scottish witch. No wonder her owner put an iron collar around her neck."

No sooner had Mrs. Held departed than Hugh arrived home from Boston. Opening the door to his office room he found two women, one weeping, one scrubbing the floor with lye soap; his possessions had been piled helter-skelter in a corner. He stormed into the hearth room and confronted Andrew. "I come home full of concern for the poor people of Boston who have British soldiers quartered on them and I find"—he swept his hand about the house—"that I have been invaded by Mac-Means!"

In the midst of the shouting match that ensued, Anne stormed out the door. Hugh followed, and the two of them walked to the top of the knoll overlooking the city.

Anne sniffed. "I just figured out that I would be a poet, and now with Andrew's sisters—oh, Hugh!"

"Well, I've got another use for your desk. I met John Adams' wife, Abigail. Both she and Mercy Otis Warren would like to correspond with you."

"Me? Hugh, don't be ridiculous! Their husbands are lawyers, important men. My Andrew—"

"And what," he demanded, "has that got to do with it? In Boston the women talk politics as much as the men. In fact, the Committees of Correspondence was Mercy's idea." He grinned and swaggered. "I'm to be a rider for them."

They bought milk and cheese from a goatherd and sat under an oak, talking of uniting the colonies, of an American Parliament, of war. . . . At last Anne rose and took his hand. "Time to go home, brother dear."

"Ah, yes. The crisis at home." Slowly Hugh got to his feet.

Anne laughed. "It's easier to plot revolution than to confront the problem of MacMeans in your house, isn't it?"

"Of course. Why do you think all wars are planned in taverns?"

In early September a huge shipment of Andrew's crockery arrived from Amsterdam. Hugh tapped a keg of Glenn whiskey, and Andrew raised his dram to announce that he was going to Pittsburgh to sell it. Jaws dropped. Pittsburgh? Andrew flapped his hands. "It's the chance of a lifetime. I'll make a fortune! I hear the lines at the land office stretch across town. And they'll all be willing to pay dear for crocks."

Anne sat stunned. Pittsburgh. Bess, Zac, Tommy. Andrew was going to Pittsburgh. Lines at the land office. Land to be had cheap. Good land like Glenturk. Land at the forks of the Yough, where the Glenns were. Waves of homesickness sloshed inside her.

"Watch out for Indians, laddie," Hugh said drily.

Andrew paled for a moment, then stuck out his chest. "Bouquet's got them pushed clear to the Wabash River in Illinois country."

A deep voice intoned, "I'm going with you." Heads jerked toward Geneva. "I'll help you sell your pots, brother, and then I'll see what's available for a husband. Nothing here seems to suit my fancy." She rubbed the white skin of her neck where her collar had been, then slung her arm across Andrew's shoulders. "When do we leave?"

Andrew had been watching Anne, who sat biting her knuckle. "Don't worry, luv," he said, "I'll not get snowed in. I'll be back in three months."

Anne released her fingers, but her jaw remained set. "I was thinking I might go along." Four tongues clicked. "I mean permanent. I mean to move there. To farm."

"Have you lost your wits?" Andrew shouted.

Above the clamor Anne yelled, "All right! All right! Leave me alone." She did not tell Andrew before he left that she suspected she was with child.

In January Anne received a letter from Andrew saying he had been caught by an early snowstorm at Fort Bedford and thought it likely he would return to Pittsburgh for the winter. He wrote nothing about her family or how he found them. Anne carried the letter with her all day, stopping to reread it whenever she passed a window; a heavy snowfall had darkened the house. That night she bent awkwardly around her huge belly and tucked the letter away at the bottom of her trunk.

"A massacre! A massacre in Boston!" A shouting man galloped past Anne, splattering her skirts with cold March puddles and rousing the early-morning streets, like a lumbering pond hit by a storm, into ripples, then waves of confusion. "What did he say?" "A massacre?" "Where?"

Frightened, Anne dodged into a doorway and crossed her arms over her unborn child; a gang of youths, arms beating the air, rushed by her crying, "War! War!" The door behind her opened, forcing her back into the walkway; a man pushed past, bellowing, "How many did they kill?"

She edged her way along the building as children, dogs, men on horseback, and girls waving broomsticks churned and sloshed against the bricks and shingles of Front Street. Anne stepped off into the gutter; the surging channel of shoulders, elbows, and small, butting heads swept her north.

On the high drawbridge over the Dock Street Canal she

grabbed the railing; Courthouse Square had become a dam, and the backwash of people was filling both entrances to Grey's Alley. Frantic, she tacked this way and that, running when she could, but the tide of a thousand, two thousand swallowed Front Street before her eyes. At Walnut a whirlpool of blindly shoving bodies sucked her into the vortex, then willy-nilly spewed her onto King Street.

As she stood panting, gagging, the crowd coalesced into a solid mass; men on horseback shouted and waved pistols, but their trapped mounts had turned to stone. Anne felt moisture on her thighs—urine? water breaking? blood? She grabbed the arm of a large woman. "Help me, please. I think—"

The woman's eyes were small like a pig's at butchering. She squealed, "My son's in Boston. Are they burning the town?"

Anne glimpsed a driverless wagon half loaded with flour sacks standing at the edge of Pemberton's wharf; she shoved her way to it, and clutching the side, tried to lift her foot onto the hub of the wheel. Hands grasped her waist from behind and eased her up into the wagonbed. Awkwardly she turned to thank whomever had helped her, but she saw only nameless faces, blurred and puffed with excitement, howling like a mindless hurricane.

A horse stood in the shafts, his reins about the whip post; Anne tightened the brake, then crawled to the middle of the wagon. Small boys wiggled like eels up over the side, playing "King of the Mountain" for possession of the driver's seat; the horse laid back his ears and stamped.

From far up Chestnut Street the great Liberty Bell began to toll; then others, lighter, quicker, filled the gaps between the sonorous bongs—Christ Church, the courthouse, First Presbyterian, Second Presbyterian. . . . The crowd grew hysterical.

Anne's stomach tightened. She touched the hardness. No, no! The contraction eased and she wiped sweat from her eyes. Then again the muscles pushed down. No, dear God, not here, not now, not here, please God, please, no, not my babe, I can't lose my babe. . . .

She rose to her knees and searched the crowd for a face she knew. There were some, but no name she could call out came to her tongue. Then at the spot where the whirlpool had frozen, a familiar copper head rose on a ladder of shoulders and the crowd shushed each other, crying, "Listen to Dr. MacKnight!"

"British soldiers fired on the people of Boston!" The sea of heads rippled as Hugh's words were shouted down Walnut Street, north and south on Front.

"American blood has been shed!" Angry cries rose like spray grabbed by the wind; he let the roar rise and fall. "In England the power-drunk Parliament crushed its own liberty-loving people on St. George's Field! Now they have massacred Americans in Boston! We can no longer fool ourselves with talk of negotiation! The evidence is plain! They mean to crush us, too! Where will they strike next? Charleston? New York? Baltimore? Philadelphia? Will this street—will our own King Street—run red with blood? Our citizens' blood?"

The tumult broke, inhuman, mad. The small boys leaped in a frenzy, the wagon rocked, foam flecked the horse's flanks. Anne cried, "Somebody get Dr. MacKnight! Please! My baby's coming! Get Hugh! Get Dr. MacKnight! He's my brother!"

A man turned to where Hugh swayed far above the crowd, took another look at Anne, and vaulted into the wagon. His long arms swung left and right, dropping boys like fleas over the side. He shifted the heavy sacks, made a nest for Anne, and lifted her into it. "Brace yourself. And hang on."

She grabbed his shirt. "Wait! I can wait a minute. Wait till it thins—"

The man grinned, his yellow teeth huge in the brown of his beard. "I'll get you out, lady. You just hang on."

He released the brake and stood grasping the reins, his knees wedged against the board seat. Cracking the whip over the heads of the mob, he shouted, "Stand clear! Stand clear!" People stumbled backward, and he whacked the reins on the horse's rump. "Giddyap!" The wagon began to move.

As another contraction blurred Anne's sight with pain she wondered why the man's back looked so familiar.

"Stand clear! Stand clear!" Whip singing, they inched into the intersection, angling south, away from Hugh and the thickest part of the crowd. The wheels screeched across the cobblestones. Rough hands banged the sides. The sea of people grew shallow, the man bellowed, the horse bolted free—blobs of spit flew from his mouth, his mane lashed the air, his hooves pounded into a gallop. Over the Dock Street Canal Bridge the wagon rattled and lurched; the flour bags shifted. Anne curled on her side, knees up, arms across her stomach. On and on they bounced until the wheels slowed in mud and the wagon stood shivering in the empty street.

"Where to, lady?" Anne raised her head; the man was grinning.

Her voice was tight as her belly. "Grey's Alley. Between Front and Second. But you'll never get through."

"We aren't staying here with me as midwife, lady."

She mopped her face with her sleeve. "There's a canal walkway, alleys that wind down from Third Street, but no wagon—"

He laughed. "I planned on carrying you."

Why was he laughing? What could possibly be funny? Anne felt the babe pushing, herself opening; her mind grayed. The wagon jolted, moved—back to the bells, shouts, the rumble of ten thousand voices. Hurry! Hurry! She cried in pain as she was lifted, carried. His arms were rocks under her, her own clasped around his neck. "Anybody home?" His thighs bounced up the steps. The hall was dark, Margery white-faced. The man roared, "Midwife, you fool!" and she ran. He laid Anne in Hugh's bed and tied her legs together.

When Frau Gretchen's round cheese breasts descended over her face, she felt her thighs spring free. Disconnected from time, from judgment, from everything except the need to get the baby out, she sobbed, sank into moans, dug her nails into flesh, prayed, and shouted for Hugh to come and save her baby. "Don't let it be like Willie's! Please, don't let it die like Willie's!" She screamed and screamed.

An apricot dawn slanted across the flat lands of Jersey. The breeze woke the island windmill arms, and creaking, stretching, pausing, gaining speed—whank, whank—they moved the ponderous stones against the grain. Masts swayed, gold-tipped, beside the gray, blunted fingers of the wharves; steeples wiped their dewy faces on the bluing sky. The newborn light sprawled down red-brick chimneys, across slanted roofs, squirmed past budding lilac boughs, and into rooms where embers slumbered beneath their ashy quilts, waiting for the bellows' breath.

In Grey's Alley, Frau Gretchen's snores rocked her chair across the bumps of the hearthstones; the tabby cat leaped from her lap onto the sunlit windowsill, where she licked her paw and scrubbed her ears. Across the hallway the sun's orange and yellow rays circled the bull's-eye of the window; the infant frowned, squirmed, nuzzled. Anne woke slowly, leaving the pains of birthing with her dreams; beside her was her babe. Yesterday, nothing; today, this. A miracle. Thank you, God, thank you. Tenderly, as if opening and examining a fragile gift, Anne touched the soft ridges of the miniature brow, the shaggy black hair, the sleep-puffed lips. She unfolded each wrinkled finger, unwound the blanket to gaze in awe at the perfection of delicate ribs, the rhythm of the beating heart, the smooth tummy, the tied cord, the private girl parts, the nubs of hips that moved the thin legs until both heels and toes were flat against each other.

Anne chuckled as she cradled and kissed the tiny feet, the narrow chest, the serious, owllike face, the half-curled fists. "My own. My own. Perfect. Just perfect." Both slept again.

When Anne woke for the second time, she studied the cameo face, asking in whispers, "Who are you? Where have you been? How did you come together just like you are? Did God take bits of everyone who's come before and make them up into you, your own sweet little self?"

The infant answered with yawns and chirps. "Ah. A bird. A dear, wee birdie. But such a serious one. Your uncle thought you'd be a fairy poet." The door clicked. "Ah. Now you shall meet him."

Hugh, combed, washed, dressed in his best waistcoat and britches, came smiling toward her. "Quite a start you gave us, Annie. You and your morning walks."

Anne raised her face for his kiss. "You and your revolutions!"

For a moment a cloud's shadow darkened Hugh's eyes, but they sparkled again as he knelt to look at his niece. "A special little girl. Do you know who she looks like?"

Anne shook her head, and Hugh brought the framed silhouette from the top of the chest and held it next to the baby's face. "It is! She looks just like Andrew's mother."

"Aye. Dainty. That's her Magee blood. It mixes well with the Black's black hair."

Anne laughed. "Well, let's hope her eyes won't be Willie's faraway blue. The Magees were kin to the MacIllwains, you know."

"But a little feyness, a little wood's poet won't hurt. In any case, she had her own spectacular beginning." Hugh settled his tidy body on the edge of the bed. "What were you doing out in the street?"

"Oh. I was restless. Feeling moody and shut in. The sun was shining and it smelled like spring, nobody was about. I stayed too long. But then if your war—"

"My war?" Hugh raised an eyebrow. "More the fault of your looking for greens down by the river, I'd guess. Well"—he touched the babe's cheek—"it turned out all right. From the looks of her she can't be more than a couple of weeks early. Do you have a name?"

"I guess it will have to be Jane, but she also makes noises like a bird."

"All right, then, Birdie Jane it is." He picked up the small bundle. "Come along and look at your world." He carried her to the window. "See, Birdie Jane. Philadelphia. That's the State House belfry. When I was a lad I went to hear a fine man, Jim Glenn, give a speech there. Will you come to hear mine, little elf?"

"How old will she be then?" Anne teased.

Hugh paused for a second, then went on walking and talking to the baby. Anne stiffened. Something was going on. Hugh was putting her off, working up the courage to tell her something. He turned from the east window and lifted the infant to his shoulder. Anne held her breath.

"I'm putting my name on the ballot this fall, but I may have to try more than once. We're forming a new party. Calling it the Patriots' Party. The mechanics will be the base. Once they get used to voting our way, we should have control. Two years, maybe." He paused, started to say more, then stopped.

Anne's stomach tightened, cramped. The strong morning sun shone on Hugh's left cheek, the baby's black head nestled against the right. Annie, you're going to lose him. She framed the picture of Birdie Jane and him in the sunlight so she would never forget. "Sissie, I'm going to Boston." Anne nodded. You're never going to see him again.

"You understand," he said, "if we don't stick together, they'll take us one by one. Boston. Portsmouth. Providence. Philadelphia. Baltimore. And we patriots will hang for treason one by one. You know that."

How odd. He holds the babe and yet "we" means his colonies, his patriots. She turned her face away, asking only, "Did you thank the man who brought me home yesterday? Give him some coins?"

Hugh's voice was flat. "He's been thanked. Sent on his way. Anne, don't—" He bit his lip.

She snuggled her shoulders under the covers. "I kept having this funny feeling that I knew him."

Hugh laid the infant beside Anne and kissed them both. "Annie—"

"You're going now!" She reached for his shirt, driving her fingernails through it, back into her own skin. "You're going now! You're leaving!"

"Annie, Annie. Shhhhh. Yes. I have to. I have a horse waiting. I . . ." He shut his eyes and laid his cheek next to

190

hers. The touch of his skin shot into her blood; she became drowsy, numb. Neither moved for a long time. "If I could wait," he whispered, "a week, even a day—I would. But I can't. It's like you with the babe coming. You couldn't wait. I can't, either. There are letters that must be delivered. Boston must know it's not alone." Anne held him with all the strength in her arms. "Andrew will be back soon. Maybe he'll bring Bess."

"No. I don't think he's coming back. Not now, anyway."

Hugh pulled away, gazing at her, then off into the bull's-eye of sunlight. "What will you do?"

Was he going to change his mind and stay? He mustn't do that. "I don't know yet. But I'll be all right."

"Do you want me to stop by and tell Reverend MacMillan? John Morton?"

"No! Please, no. Myles would want to lock me up—he has for years. And Mrs. Morton is such a busybody. No. I'll be all right. Really, Hugh. Don't worry."

"I'll leave all the money I can."

"Thank you."

"When that runs out—"

Her mouth twisted into a wry, tucked up smile. "God will provide."

"Annie." He bent and kissed her. "You're the most precious thing in my life. You and the children. You know that."

"No. First comes your revolution." She rubbed the tips of his fingers across her cheek. "Godspeed."

He kissed the infant's tiny brow. "I'll be back before you know it."

Then he was gone. The closed door was hard and blank. No, Annie, he won't be back for a long, long time. You're on your own. She lay staring at the door until she fell asleep.

The rest of the day Anne wandered in drowsiness, kneaded and stroked, bathed and warmed and fed by women's hands; men and war ran before her eyelids, beyond the shutters, singing in the streets, shouting, "Down with England!" In the night she woke screaming that everyone was dead—Mam, Pappie, Rebekah, Jim, Hugh, Andrew, her babe—everyone dead! They lay piled around her bed in the darkness.

Margery lit lamps and candles, made crosses in the sand on the floor; Frau Gretchen brewed a crock of the quieting tea. For three days Anne's body rested while her mind was away among butterflies and gaudy flowers. Her milk came and Birdie Jane sucked greedily. "She will live," Frau Gretchen announced. "The wee Bird has a strong will. She will live."

On the Sabbath Anne woke feeling, to her amazement, crisp as the ringing bells; Birdie Jane lay with her eyes—even the whites seemed blue—taking up the whole of her face. "Ah," Anne said, "your soul has come." She put her to her breast and told her about lambs, streams, sun, and moon, and she recited the genealogy of her people.

The door latch clicked and Marybett entered, proudly carrying tea and a raisin cake; behind came Jamie, shyly smiling, a red ribbon for his new sister clutched in his fist. While Anne sipped her tea and honey, Marybett peered in the baby's mouth and ears and examined the wrinkled soles of her feet; Jamie, curled on the other side of his mother, gawked in wonder.

Margery brought bowls of porridge with butter and cream, then stayed to rock and knit while the children marched their corncob dolls with acorn hats up and down the counterpane. Rich smells of Kingdom of Fife pie—rabbit, pickled pork, nutmeg—drifted in from the kitchen hearth; churchtime silence coated the streets.

As the noon bells spoke to each other across the heads of the houses, Margery leaped from her chair, patted the walnut braids circling her head, and shook out her skirts around her plump middle. Her miscarriage had not removed the fat of her pregnancy. Anne watched bemused as she slipped down a corner of the pillowcase she had hung over the mirror to keep the devil from stealing Birdie Jane's soul and pinched her cheeks until they flared pink. "Come, children," she wheedled, her eyes darting to the window and back. "Let your mother rest until it's time to serve the pie." The children ignored her.

"Let them stay," Anne said. "I've missed them, and really I'm fit as a fiddle."

Margery vacillated between the window and the bed, between reaching out to the children and flicking her skirts. Finally she stood dead center, biting her nails. She's still a child, Anne thought, going round and round trying to please her father, her stepmother, and Geneva. "Are you expecting someone?" she asked.

Margery jerked up on her toes. "Yes. No. Yes. I don't know. Yes, I guess I am."

Anne barely got the question "Who?" out of her mouth when a shadow passed the window.

"Please, Annie, please be nice." Margery's hands fairly hummed through the air as she dashed for the bedroom door. A quick, sharp rap came from outside. Marybett slid from the bed and ran into the hall; Jamie, clutching the dolls, hurried after her; Margery pulled the latchstring, shutting Anne's door. Through it she heard a man's voice and boots thudding into the hearth room.

"Who on earth?" Anne asked aloud, and a moment later the impatient knock sounded again, this time on her bedroom door. Fear, instant and inexplicable, twisted her innards. She grabbed off her wedding band and shoved it under her pillow; shifting Birdie Jane to her left arm, she took the cake knife from the tray and hid it under the covers by her right leg. The rap came again, more demanding, more insistent. Anne pulled the covers up to her chin; then resting her hand on the haft of the knife, she called, "Come in."

The man who had rescued her from the mob strutted in through the door. He stood, bulky and arrogant, at the foot of her bed, one squat hand around the bedpost. His long face, now shaven, resembled a coffin—square at the corners of his forehead, tapering to an overshot jaw and divided by a black wreath of eyebrows that stretched from temple to temple with barely a pause at the bridge of his nose. Eyes—pale, bleached stones—were embedded on either side of an insignificant nose; his mouth was a slashing stroke of India ink.

Anne forced her hand away from the knife out into the cool air of the room, toward the man who stood before her. "Thank you for your help," she said simply.

His hand, callused, matted with black hair, shook two of her fingers and returned to the post. "You were lucky." He paused. "Mrs. MacMeans."

She jabbed her own hand back under the sheet. Why was he staring at her like that? "I'm sorry to say I've forgotten your name."

"James Young."

Her heart pounded, her hand closed around the horn-knife handle. Why this awful sensation of danger?

"I didn't come for money." His voice was rough and loud. A plowman? Anne wondered. He stood silent, as though she should divine his thoughts. Slow-witted, perhaps? "Hugh MacKnight's your brother."

There's your answer, Annie. He's a distant relative needing

193

bed and board. She squinted at him. No, his air isn't that of a man who's come to ask, but to demand. Why had Margery let him in the house when they were alone? Where was she? Hiding the children? But she had acted so—

"Your husband is Margery MacMeans' brother."

"Yes." What did he want with Andrew? More money for helping his wife? Some sort of blackmail? She tried to remember if he had undressed her; the thought made her shudder. "You were very kind the other day, Mr. Young. Are you married? With children of your own?"

"I've buried two wives. With their babes." Anne's arm tightened around Birdie Jane. Galloping ghosts, Annie, is it Death himself standing before you? "I'm heading West. A Mr. Willson asked me to go to his settlement."

Her eyes widened. "At the Forks of the Yough?" He nodded. What a strange coincidence. "You're a Covenanter?" An odd smile glimmered on his lips. Covenanter or no, she wanted him out—now! "I wish you good fortune and God's blessing, Mr. Young. Please ask my sister-in-law to come in as you leave."

"Margery has consented to be my wife."

"What?" she screamed.

"Your husband's sister has consented to be my wife. Sister."

Anne leaned forward, trembling with rage. "Oh, no, Mr. Young! You can't force your way into this family like that! She is only seventeen and very innocent. Just because there are no men about at the moment doesn't mean we are an easy mark for any unscrupulous man who takes a fancy to—"

Yellow frost glittered on his opaque eyes. Her hand found the cake knife again. "We have lain together. I'm not the first. She consented to marry most readily."

"She knows nothing about you!" Anne shrieked, the cords in her neck bulging.

James Young folded his arms on his chest and leered. "All that she needs to."

Merciful God! What would Andrew say if he were here? What would Hugh do? Maybe her fear of this man was irrational, wrong . . . somehow connected to the mob and his strange, pale face. Maybe he was a hardworking, sober man who would make a good husband for a mouse like Margery. After all, he had rescued her. . . .

James Young shifted his feet and tightened his grip on the bedpost. "Lady, it's she that wants your blessing. Not me. I can do without it just dandy."

Anne wet her dry lips. "At the moment I hold the authority for this family and—" James Young snorted. She snapped her teeth and went on. "I hold the authority and will not give my permission until the Reverend Myles MacMillan clears your character." She raised her chin. "You'll find him at the First Presbyterian Church on Market Street."

The man swelled and shook his octopus arm at her. "Mind your manners, Mrs. MacMeans. Tomorrow I'll be the authority—as you so grandly put it—of this family."

She gurgled in rage as he thudded stiff-necked to the door; his thumb snapped the latch. "We'll wait, however, until your babe is big enough to travel."

"What? What are you talking about?" she shouted.

"Going West to join your husband." He walked out through her doorway and the front doorway, shutting neither.

She heard Jamie squeal, and she called to him. "It was him, Minnie!" He panted with fear. "The man who's always watching."

Ah! Of course. As she cuddled and comforted Jamie, the pieces fell into place. James Young was no spy, but one of those men who watched, waited for death or some mishap to allow him to step into a family where he could better his lot. "Probably proposed to his first two wives over their husband's caskets," she muttered. "But Myles will see through him. Myles will stop him." She stroked Jamie's hair. "Besides, what wealth is there in this family?"

Raw wind thick with the odor of rancid mud and the sound of boys freed from church, singing, "Yankee Doodle, keep it up, Yankee Doodle dandy . . ." swirled into the room. Revolution? Does he think a revolution will make Hugh rich? But West . . . why West? Does he see Hugh as a feudal lord handing him a hundred square miles on the Ohio?

The next noon James Young, with Margery trailing after, entered Anne's room and announced that Reverend MacMillan was ill and his assistant had just married them. "I think," James Young said, advancing toward her, "I'd better carry you upstairs so you can be with your children, where you can care for them."

Her head spun, but she whipped the knife from beneath the covers. "Lay one hand on me—"

He backed away, laughing. "Then go by yourself. Either that, or my woman and I will take the upstairs and your children can watch babies being made." He turned and caught Margery in his arms.

195

Fury gave Anne the strength to climb the stairs, dragging her bedclothes after her; then she lay dizzy, her eyes staring at the low, slanted ceiling. The dark timbers swelled rising like mountains against a whitewashed sky: the Allegheny Front, Tuscarora, the bluff above the Monongahela. She dozed; a sable furrow rolled from a plowshare, ravens cried, the odor of the earth's belly filled the room, her fist closed on rough seeds of corn. Bess. Tommy. Zac. Esther. And Andrew. She shut her eyes. God works in mysterious ways. Ho, Jim, she said softly, tell them I'm coming. I'm not to be a poet just yet.

Wilderness Revolutionist

Pittsburgh and West, 1770–83

Chapter Fifteen

Dear Hugh,

Yesterday I arrived at the Forks of the Yough—on Cinder, thanks to Dora bringing him up to Harris Ferry. What I have found here would break the heart of a saint! The family has collapsed into that despondency that is so common on the frontier. And to set you Easterners straight—it is not caused by some flaw in character but by exhaustion, fear, and loneliness, which shortens one's vision until like a savage one's existence is contained between sunrise and sunset.

Zac lives in wigwams more than with Tine, and she finds consolation with soldiers. Rhoda has gone full mad and her girls speak in grunts and shrieks and hide under the floorboards—Tommy accepts and struggles on. But Bess—oh, Hugh, she lives in a cave with a cow and a dog! When I first saw her I grabbed the children and ran. She does not complain about the dirt, the fleas, her goiter, or her jaundice, only that she had no one to talk to for seven years. Seven years! How could I have not realized that everyone around her was mute or mad or simple—except Zac, who was continually off hunting animals or Indians.

In a state of shock I rode off to find the grand house Andrew had described in his letters. I found the spot, all right—the great round hill with the stream at the bottom of the south slope, but Hugh, there is no house. No house at all! Just a huge stone chimney and a celler hole big enough to erect a mansion on. I haven't even seen Andrew yet—it seems he spends a great deal of time in Pittsburgh, which is seven miles down the Monongahela River—doing God knows what!

All this on top of having spent two months on the trail with that swaggering ape of a James Young! Are a woman's choices only in the various forms of her bondage? I shall live like a potato in this cellar, growing white sprouts and shriveling into brown wrinkles.

Your sister, Anne

November 1770

Dear Brother,

I did not become a potato, I got uppity instead. James Young started to boss everyone around saying what we would plant and sell. (He got a claim next to Tommy—where Geneva lives, taking care of Rhoda and the girls—and that made 1,000 acres in the family.) I railed against him, but nothing happened until Zac came home, called a family council, and made me head of the family! If you ever meet him you'll know that the respect of Zac Glenn is to be treasured like a rare jewel. When J. Young swore that no woman would tell him what to do, Zac thrashed him.

The crown, however, does not rest easy on my head. Are all families made up of Genevas, Tines, Zacs, and Andrews? I can hear you laughing and saying—are all nations made up of New Hampshires, New Yorks, and Virginias? If you will pray for my United Family, I will pray for your United Colonies.

Your loving Annie

P.S. Esther has returned. A beautiful, silent woman who scorns to marry either Indian or white.

P.S. A cellar is not so bad when you can walk from it to see a magnificent black stallion running, snow dashing up from his hooves, and hear the mighty silence of the forest and see the eagles soar. Write! Even if you must write of revolution—write!

Breakfast Hill Farm
April 1772

Dear Brother,

A birth announcement! I have "brought home"—as our minnie would have said—another son, Robert Hugh. It pleases me to have an excuse to say your name aloud many times a day. And he has a good house, not merely a cellar hole to live in. Birdie Jane flourishes like the grass of spring—as do I.

With love, your sister

April 1773

Hugh!

You are the uncle of healthy, lusty twins. John and Issac. In spite of their red hair, they remind me of no one so much as our caterwauling pappie. These live births make me wonder if the city air of Philadelphia had poisoned me so that I could not carry to full term there. It is something you men of medicine should look into.

Although many times the issue seemed in doubt, wee Rabbie has lived to see his first birthday. A long letter will follow when I have time to sit. However, that may not be soon, for there are rumors of Indian unrest, and we must fortify the house.

Anne

Boston Town
December 16, 1773

Dearest Sister and Friend,

Tonight the people of this town turned the harbor into a teapot! At last an act the British cannot ignore! About 7,000 gathered at South Church to again demand that Governor Hutchinson send the English tea ships home. He refused and Sam Adams' "Indians" (yours truly among them) boarded the three vessels lying at anchor. After smashing away with tomahawks we dumped the contents of 342 chests into the bay.

I am asking you, Anne, to act as correspondent in the West in this great cause. As you well know, Zac is a most unreliable writer and I trust your judgment as to which men should receive our news and how it should be presented to them. Whatever we might gain here on the coast will be for aught if the British and Indians become united in the West and sweep across the hills to raze our cities. Ideally we should extend our hold to the Mississippi, but who would lead such an army? And, indeed, who would follow him?

Plans are being laid for a Continental Congress to be held next year in Philadelphia (I have hopes of being a member!) Perhaps, Anne, you should be content with your family. The whole business of populating the wilderness has not evolved upon you!

Your loving brother, Hugh

Breakfast Hill Farm
April 15, 1774

Dearest Hugh,

You asked if I ever thought of returning East, and my answer is no. The coming of settlers is only one reason, another is the growing beauty of this farm and its prosperity, and the children now know this as home. Can you believe that Marybett and Jamie are now nine and ten? Marybett promises to be a tantalizing beauty of small stature and fiery will.

Jamie is so much like Jim I sometimes weep. Obviously we have a future scholar of stature on our hands, but like Jim he loves the land and bringing order to it; a crooked furrow makes him go into an absolute snit.

As to Birdie Jane, she is a darling and, as all four-year-olds are apt to be, curious and responsive to all about her. From the time she was a few months old anyone who talked baby-talk to her was set straight by a long, steady gaze from those dark blue eyes. (As to whether they have the faraway MacIllwain look we will have to wait a few more years to see.)

She knows her letters already—Bess keeps a school here in our house—and her favorite word is "why." Bess is going to start her on the fiddle at five.

As I read this over I saw that I had neglected the strongest reason why I feel that the Forks of the Yough will always be my home—the family ties. I now enjoy my role as "head" and would no more give up my position than George or Louis would lay down their crowns. What form of government do you plan for Pennsylvania? My guess is a republic. Will we wear togas and speak in Latin?

Anne

April 17

Rhoda is dead. She hung herself from the white oak that grows beside their house. She had borne a son—at last after all those girls, except for poor wee Tom—but he was badly deformed, and having no midwife to take care of it, she allowed him to nurse. Geneva, who has lived with them for the past two years, was absent when the birth occurred. (She, sharp trader that she is, handles most of the family's buying and selling in Pittsburgh.) When Geneva returned she tried to take the child from Rhoda but she would not let it go in spite of its monstrous appearance. When Tommy tried to talk to her about it, she turned on him, too. Yesterday, probably feeling that someone would steal the baby, she smothered him and hanged herself with him in her arms. We all tell ourselves it is for the best—her madness was a terrible burden on Tommy—but death is such a final thing. It closes the door on hope. And like Matt and Rebekah's going it severs one from their own childhood.

I believe I will always resent death. I know that this flies in the face of the belief that it expresses God's will, and yet I have come to a contrary position—I believe early death, or the madness that leads to it, is a signal that we as God's children are failing somewhere. I am certain God would rejoice if no child would die of hunger, no woman in childbirth, no man in war. Yes, I still live with the memory of Jim. When I am very tired or discouraged I go and plant an apple tree or tend the dozens already growing in his name, and I find him there ready to give me the quiet understanding to go on.

I know. I can hear you saying, "But some of us may have to die so that America may be kept for all—not just those favorites of king and gentry." And I suppose that if war comes to me I will fight as fiercely as any. Surely I would kill for my children and my land.

No newborn this April, Hugh. Perhaps you are right—six is enough. Rabbie is still frail, but Birdie Jane hovers over him while those rascally twins—who to spite me learned to walk at nine months!—keep me running thither and yon every minute. I am planting peas this afternoon.

Your loving sister, Anne.

Postscript. Yes, I received Mercy Warren's last letter. So gracious, so learned. I have been two months already trying to compose a suitable reply.

May 1, 1774

Just a line, Hugh. Tommy and Geneva are married. I believe she had this in mind from the first moment she set eyes on him. You never saw two happier people! Her fire and Tommy's gentleness make them a powerful team. We all continue well.

Anne

January 1775

Hugh! James Young has gone! For his part in Dunsmore's bloody little war he received land in Kentucky. May heaven rejoice! I feel as though a black pall has been lifted—hopefully forever!—from my life. Someday I will tell you the whole ugly story of our parting.

Sister Annie.

Philadelphia, America
April 1775

Dear Anne,

It has begun in earnest! At Concord Bridge in Massachusetts! The first shots were fired on April 19. I longed to ride over the mountains and bring Pittsburgh the news myself, but others have convinced me that I should not spend my strength that way. (I am still weak from winter pleurisy.) The official report of the battle is enclosed. Hoist your sidesaddle on Cinder and ride at once to Pittsburgh to deliver it.

In haste, Hugh.

Postscript. Eight thousand attended the Philadelphia rally. Citizens are mobilizing for war. Companies of militia of every creed and station are being formed. (Two companies are Quaker.) The only question we allow to be put to any recruit is: are you Patriot or Tory? God be with you.

HBMcK

Breakfast Hill
August 23, 1775

Dear Hugh,

Here is Zac's report from Pittsburgh: Training of the militia continues. Colonel John Procter's Westmoreland Battalion now carries a flag with a rattlesnake imprinted on it and the motto "Don't tread on me." The tax for ammunition is being collected, although not always peaceably. The resolution that was passed threatening dire consequences to any who dares to harm or insult an Indian has generally been observed. John Campbell's English tea was seized and burned beside the Liberty Pole. Although it is not yet settled whether the Forks of the Yough belong properly to Virginia or Pennsylvania, the issue is now submerged in the larger conflict. Are the reports from the West Augusta Committee of Correspondence adequate, or shall I continue personal accounts to you?

And I will add, Brother, that nowhere could the flame of liberty burn more brightly than it does here among these people who hold such vivid memories of suffering at the hands of the British in Scotland and Ireland. The harvest is abundant.

Your adoring Patriot, Anne.

P.S. I am so proud of you. Do you know you are being referred to as a "Founding Father of America"?

Philadelphia
July 6, 1776

Dear Sister Annie,

The Old Ticket in the Assembly continued their delaying tactics until we were forced to form a new Pennsylvania Provincial Congress in order to declare our commonwealth for independency. To think that they would have actually refused to commit this colony to something the people so ardently desire! When we get the chance to write a new one, the Constitution of Pennsylvania will read very differently—authority will rest with the PEOPLE! But no matter now, the glorious deed is done at last. "When in the Course of human Events it becomes necessary . . ." What magnificent prose Mr. Jefferson writes. New York has not yet signed, but they will.

Enclosed is your own copy written in my hand. I regret that neither the name of James Glenn nor Hugh Mac-Knight appears among the signatures, but surely our thoughts, our lives are there. I did not copy off the signatures. From Pennsylvania there were eight—our own dear John Morton; our Scottish friend James Wilson; Ben Rush (bless him!); Bess's friend James Smith—he helped write the first draft with Mr. Jefferson; George Ross, whom we elected in '68, remember? Benjamin Franklin and Robert Morris, and George Clymer were allowed to sign, too. Generous, eh?

Truly, Annie, we have founded a nation. We have cause to be proud and to rejoice, but in Mr. Jefferson's words we must "mutually pledge to each other our lives, our Fortunes, and our sacred Honor." Who knows what may be required of us in the coming months and years?

Your loving brother, Hugh

December 10, 1777

Dear Hugh,

The year of the three sevens has been disastrous. But why should I tell you that? You know better than I. At least the British have not driven me from my home as they have you, and I do not daily have to listen to the cries for help that come from the army at Valley Forge. It seems, however, that with the Shawnee and Iroquois against us (to say nothing of the British and Tories who lead them!) we will be hard put to hold this land. If only France . . . but for how many years have we sung that lament?

Zac survived his experience with the Eighth Pennsylvania Regiment, but returned saying he will never serve again under any officers but his own. Can Washington's record of defeat possibly be laid to his treatment of his soldiers? A hundred salted stripes for drunkenness! Good Lord, hasn't he learned that they are free, proud men even though they do not own plantations on the Potomac? But, as you know, it was disease, not bullets that wiped out the Eighth Pennsylvania. Zac tires of frontier patrols, however, and dreams of someone who will lead an army west and attack these Indians where THEY live.

So British officers drink their port with Robert Bailey in his drawing room? Well, I am shocked and yet I'm not. One thing I'll wager my life on is that the Jamisons are not serving it! All that seems so far away. I know I was tempted once, twice? But now I ask myself, by what? What as Mrs. Robert Bailey could have filled me with the sense of pride and great accomplishment that Breakfast Hill Farm does? Ease and luxury would have bored me. To close every day without sowing a field or touching breathing animals or smelling growing plants that will feed your children would have been a terrible fate for me. Love of the land was bred into my bones.

Andrew has his faults as a husband, but he is full of laughter and adores the children—the twins hold a special awe for him. His happy-go-lucky nature still sends him scurrying eastie-westie, and although he has become a passable farmer, most of the labor is done by hired hands.

Bess has a suitor. A certain Thomas White, who has the store at the Landing. She refers to herself as a creaky-jointed cow and tells Thomas, who is ten years her junior and never married, that he should go looking for someone who doesn't need rubbing with horse liniment three times daily, but he is devoted.

Esther left two months ago, and she may be gone for good. She is, after all, close to thirty now. She hugged me for a long time before she left and said something in Iroquois that I took to mean she was going off to find a brave to have babies with—she has never gotten over her fear of white men. I am glad for her and yet she is the only woman friend I have ever had—except Bess, who was always more a mother. Marybett and I still don't get on, but I sense that when Bird grows older we will be very close. Perhaps Geneva—yes, she would be a worthy friend; she carries Tommy's child.

Please!!! Do not let your friendship with Ben Rush persuade you that your place is with the army! He is a surgeon-general entitled to dry stockings and warm food; I fear you would enjoy no such comforts as a doctor at Valley Forge. Stay at York and plan a Constitution for the nation as fine as the one you gave Pennsylvania—where power truly lies with ALL men and the LEGISLATURE they elect. Two fat turkeys roast on the spit. I remain your sister Patriot in both despair and hope.

Anne.

York, Penna.
March 1778

Dear Sister,

France is with us! We are saved! Gates' victory at Saratoga turned the trick. Of course, Philadelphia gives the credit to B. Franklin, who has spent the war sipping claret in French salons. (I sound like one of the petty fault-finders that I rave against.) Our Congress will surely now reject the dominion status the British have offered and fight on for total independence.

Tell Zac that if he still desires to serve in the West, a Colonel George Rogers Clark will be recruiting there soon. He is a friend of Thomas Jefferson's—they even look alike, big, red-haired, imposing men. Although Clark is a Virginian he has none of the pretensions of the gentry and I'm sure will do well by any men under his command. I cannot reveal the nature of his objectives or British plans as we know them, but the future of the West, in fact, the nation, has settled on his young—I think he is twenty-six—shoulders.

I followed your advice and did not go with the army, but politics is discouraging. Sometimes I wonder if our people have the virtue to make a republic work. If they do not we will quickly fall into anarchy, with its attendant petty tyrants. There are those who say that we should appoint a benevolent monarch now and avoid long years of brutal civil strife. G. Washington's name is most often mentioned. King George. My God. I agree that to be legitimate a nation must name some Higher Power, but even though my philosophy is agnostic, I prefer God to George. He, God, does have a long-standing reputation for morality, and silence!—His rare appearances in burning bushes and the like can be interpreted rather freely. Of course, naming God opens another trap—theocracy. The rule of pope, bishop, or a zealot such as you say Z. Willson is could surely deprive us of public freedom and perhaps personal freedom as well. My hope lies in the plurality of religions that exist here—they will never unite, thank God! But perhaps they will agree to let each other alone.

Would that this land were backboned by the courage and ribbed by the common sense of thousands of Anne Aiken MacKnight Glenn MacMeans's! Perhaps it is. Perhaps they lurk in every nook and cranny, ready to burst forth if we men fail. "Lurk" is undoubtedly the wrong word—I have never seen you do anything but stand foursquare for what you wanted; maybe such unknown stalwarts hold every family together.

Your servant, ma'am, Hugh B. MacKnight

Breakfast Hill Farm
August 1778

Dear Hugh,

I know of no other way to say this than to simply write: Andrew has sold our farm. Sold Breakfast Hill Farm. To a Tory Quaker with a sack of gold who fled the wrath of his Patriot neighbors in Philadelphia. Why? Why? Why? He says we will go to the Carolinas. Is he God that he can so order our lives? I cannot speak to him, even look at him. My rage is cold and black.

Anne.

Philadelphia
October 1778

Dear Anne,

Where are you? Why haven't you written? Haven't you received my letters? You know you will always have a home with me. Please write.

With deepest concern, Hugh

Breakfast Hill Farm
November 1778

Dear Hugh,

Tommy is dead. His heart gave out while he was hauling a sledge up the hill from the river. I'm sure the trumpets played when he arrived in Heaven, for if there was ever a man who lived without thought for himself it was Tommy. Geneva in a rage of grief sold the farm and set out with their infant Alexander to find her sister Margery in Kentucky.

I have not written because there has been much sickness here. I will later. I promise. I hope you are well.

Your sister, Anne

Breakfast Hill
March 1779

Dear Patient Brother,

I am keeping my New Year's resolution to write. It is so difficult to compose a letter when things are going poorly. I kept putting it off, saying, "I'll write next week when things are better," and so it went week after week.

Just after Andrew sold the farm, the pox struck. Rabbie and Bird were immediately whisked off to Thomas White, but the twins, John and Isaac, lay close to death for weeks. Andrew and I never moved from their side during the days of crisis, and by some miracle they survived. If they had had one flaw of frailty in them they would surely have died, but their wills and their bodies would not let go of life. I watch them now, their hair flaming in the winter sun, their fair skin packed with freckles, running endlessly as six-year-olds do. (They are supposed to be helping Andrew with the tanning, but he is so easy with the children that they think nothing of running off to play for a while.) It seems impossible that they were almost consigned to the dark earth. How thin the line!

Andrew says it was my will, my hatred of death, that would not let them go, and when Bess heard him say that she shuddered as though I had made a pact with the devil. I think in those dark hours I would have. Nothing, nothing could be more precious than the life of a child. In fact, during the time we thought we might lose the twins, we conceived another.

I am listless. Perhaps due to being great with child or exhaustion—the pox was followed by summer fever, then measles. More likely, the dread of leaving Breakfast Hill has eaten into my soul. Only Marybett is excited about going; I believe she sees it in terms of a new stage upon which to practice her attention-getting arts.

Jamie causes me great concern. He is angry as only a fourteen-year-old boy can be and speaks to his father as little as possible. During those first days of my black rage against Andrew I enlisted him as my cohort, and that is bearing bitter fruit. He wanted to begin his studies for the ministry this year (Edinburgh is his dream), but, of course, Andrew could not pioneer new land alone, so he must go with us.

Zac is with Colonel Clark, the Great Long Knife, as he is known among the Indians, on the Upper Mississippi.

Anne

January 3

I am glad I have been unable to post this yet. Andrew returned from a trip to Pittsburgh last night to tell me that our 850 pounds—which is what the Quakers gave us for Breakfast Hill—is NOT ENOUGH to purchase Carolina lands. Your Continental presses have blasted any prospect of that! But we will have to go somewhere before planting time. I ran to Bess last night and cried on her bosom for hours. That is part of my agony, too—I had sworn I would never leave Bess again, but she could not stand a rough life in the wilderness, and Andrew absolutely refuses to even think of moving onto Zac's land. Suddenly he has taken to raving about not being beholden to the Glenns!

Anne

January 4

Andrew says we must go and take up cheap land in Kentucky. How can I ever consent to that? Take my babes into the heart of war and wilderness? No, surely God will not require that of me.

Anne

York, Pennsylvania
February 1, 1779

Dearest Sister,

Fortunately your letter arrived quickly. Under NO circumstances should you consider going to Kentucky! Live in Bess's old cave if you must, but do not set one foot in the Ohio country this summer. Col. Henry Hamilton has orders to bring his thousands of Indians slashing down from Detroit to Pittsburgh, then east.

As you know, Clark got only 100 volunteers from Pittsburgh instead of the 350 he wanted. One hundred men to hold a territory as vast as all the 13 colonies! How can we ask that of any man? In Kentucky there are 84 militia at Harrodsburg, 22 at Boonesborough, 15 at Logan's Station—that's all! If Clark folds, Kentucky cannot be held.

In haste, Hugh

Breakfast Hill Farm
February 25, 1779

Dearest Brother,

I have had no communication from you since your New Year's greeting. Are you ill? I pray you have not joined the army. Perhaps your letters are miscarrying—there are Tories everywhere. Soon they will even be living in my house, for we begin our journey down the Ohio as soon as the babe is born and the rivers are clear of ice.

We will join other settlers in Pittsburgh for the river trip and will no doubt stay on Corn Island at the Falls of the Ohio in Colonel Clark's fort until Andrew finds a claim in Kentucky. Send your letters there, although I cannot imagine them reaching me. Like Christopher Columbus's men I believe I am about to sail off the edge of the world.

Good-bye.
Annie

Chapter Sixteen

Andrew spent many days in Pittsburgh discussing the merits of *bateaux*, keelboats, flatboats, the nuances of tonnage, draws, footways, and cabin construction; his plans as usual were elaborate, the initial stages of building detailed and perfect. He and Jamie felled two dozen pine, trimmed and cut them into fifty-foot lengths, floated them to the calm cove at White's Landing, and nailed them together with studding to make a giant raft. Huge oaks were laid across pits and sawed into planking, which Andrew and Jamie then pegged to the studs and caulked with linen tow; the entire flatboat was enclosed with two-foot-high gunwales of poplar. Andrew showed off his plans for a cabin ten feet long with a fireplace chimney, a necessary open to the river below, two separate rooms, and a ceiling six feet high.

In late March Anne bore her child, a daughter named Annilea. She kept to her room searching for the strength, the will to begin tearing her roots from Breakfast Hill. If only there were some reason for it! She moaned and tossed on her bed, then walked the cold floor. Why? Dear God, why? I found my four hundred acres. I bore my seven children. I tended my husband. I planned and planted, hoed and reaped— Her fist hit the windowsill. Why? Just give me a reason why!

Mists sucked from the snowbanks blew against the window glass. Pictures formed. Blacks, Aikens, Watts, bundles on their backs marched across the small panes. Anne leaned forward. Where were you all going? Why?

Jamie Watt raised his sword and shouted, "No king! No bishop!"

Bartholomew Black MacKnight thundered in the face of Lord Hamilton, "No tithes! No rents!"

Hugh MacKnight shouted from the courthouse balcony, "No taxation without representation!"

Jim Glenn turned his back on his father's house and took her hand. "We'll go West, Annie."

She circled the room with his shoulder touching her. Jim said, "The Lord will not ask of you more than you can bear."

A poof of air escaped Anne's lips. Give me a more rousing slogan than that, Jim Glenn.

Call yourself liberty-mad. All your ancestors were.

All right. She straightened her shoulders. All right, I'm liberty-mad. A bit of Joan of Arc mixed with Mary, Queen of Scots—there, that ought to do it.

Word came from Pittsburgh that the Ohio was in full flood and the other Kentucky-bound families arriving. Andrew panicked; the cabin of the flatboat became a hasty five-by-ten, the interior walls hide hangings, the toilet a pot, the fireplace a box filled with sand. He paddled off to Pittsburgh and he returned the next day with a brawny youth, David Pegon, and a small black man, Joe Camp, to man the sweeps.

Horses and oxen were hitched to sledges, and everyone save Annilea began carrying and loading, puffing up hills and sliding down them; the boat sank lower and lower in the water. Barrels of seed, flour, cracked corn, cider, and whiskey were lashed to the gunwales; furniture was stacked and restacked in the lean-to; farm tools spilled over into the cabin; chests of clothes and mattresses filled the sleeping room; the plow and spare oxbow were strapped to the roof next to the towering mound of fodder. All this, and animals and people yet to come.

On the day set for sailing, Anne woke before first light. The entire family except she and Annilea had slept on the boat; Anne hadn't wanted to risk drowning a minute before she had to. She could not make herself believe that Andrew had built a boat that would float.

Swinging the Killyleagh kettle out over the embers, Anne bit her lip at the thought of drinking her last cup of tea at Breakfast Hill Farm.

She meandered through the bare, dawn-blushed rooms, touching windowsills and door latches, seeing children asleep in beds, hearing their feet run at the sound of Uncle Zac or Uncle Tommy's voice below. Memories of babies born, growing, being taught by Bess rolled as tears down her cheeks. Tomorrow another man's whistle would come from the barn, another woman's hands would swing the hearth chains, other childish eyes would peek through the rifle slits, playing Indian war games. Anne paused with her hand on Esther's big spinning wheel; she would never see her sister again. Her daughters would never be married from this house, her sons would never plow this land. . . .Anne jammed her fists against her cheeks. Nine years of toil for what? To leave it all behind and go to some lean-to in the wilderness? Bess's bonnet bobbed up the lane; Anne banked the coals and lifted the kettle for the last time.

The track up Breakfast Hill was slippery, and Bess's fingers clutched Anne's elbow as they steadied each other; Annilea hung, tied in the shawl, against her mother's chest. They climbed from shadow to sun and paused on the top, looking back on the hip of the barn roof, the great stone chimney that rose above the shadowed green curve of the hill. Anne stopped, overcome. "I can't leave you again, Bess. I can't." Then with a drop of spitefulness she said, "I'd feel easier about leaving you if you'd marry Mr. White."

Bess snorted. "What more would marriage give me? Tommy's girls and I have his house and free goods from the store already. What would I want to marry him for?"

"Bess don't you ever—"

"No."

"You don't even know what I was going to say."

"Yes, I do. And I determined when Reverend Blackwood

died that no man would ever claim the right to crawl into my bed again."

A wide smile overflowed Anne's lips. "So you took me as your child. And Hugh."

Bess patted the baby's bottom. "And all your children. I'm fulfilled, Annie." Hand in hand, they walked down the steep hill, past the ancient Indian fort, past the flapping canvas tent under which Rabbie, John and Issac and wee Annilea had been baptized, past the oak where Bird had carved her Uncle Hugh's name and the words "France is with us!," past the spot where Tommy fell, the strap of the heavy sledge across his chest, his pink cheek squashed against the grass.

The Landing swirled with joking men, giggling children, stocking-capped geese charging blindly about, well-wishers who came from the dark of the store with gifts in their hands—herbs, a pillow, a coon-skin cap, a sack of dried apples. A trestle table had been spread, and soon breakfast pie and whiskey dripped from jabbering chins. Andrew stepped aboard his flatboat, mounted the barrel behind the cabin, grasped the long rudder pole, and shouted, "All aboard!"

Anne hugged Tommy's pale girls, lost herself in the warmth of Bess's bosom one more time, waved her hand like a willow whip in the wind . . . good-bye, good-bye . . . while the sun lit her freckled cheeks. Bess swung her apron over her head and called, "Four hundred acres, Annie! Make sure you get four hundred!" Good-bye, Good-bye . . .

The mad spate of April had abated, but the river still was a dragon of swift-running humps. On the first bend Andrew lost control. The boat spun; Andrew tilted this way and that on his barrel trying to get the boat to level, to move ahead. Chests and chairs and children began sliding to the port side; the spin grew tighter, round and round, until the water leaped the top of the gunwales. "Throw it over!" Andrew shouted hysterically. "Throw everything on the port side overboard!"

The youth David raised the barrel packed with glass and pewter over his head.

Anne tackled his chest. "No! Move it to the other side! Balance it! Balance it!" They worked frantically, shifting, shoving, lashing; finally the boat ceased its lopsided spin. The men returned to the sweeps and Andrew cried, "Pull!"

They did, and the boat backed into the bank.

At last the men and Andrew coordinated their strokes, and the boat moved from shore into the rush of the channel. Faster, faster. "Slow down!" Anne screamed, pulling on the gunwale as though it were a brake. The men started to lower the sweeps. "No!" shouted Andrew. "We'll spin again. Just let me steer. We'll ride it." Anne looked about wildly. If only she could reach out and grab the shore, but it moved, too; everything moved. She waited to die, the breath sucked from her by the speeding wind.

Infant cries came from the cabin; Anne ran. The room was filled with smoke from a fire Marybett had built to warm the dinner stew. Bewildered, coughing, Anne scanned the ceiling—Andrew had forgotten to cut a smoke hole. "Pull the firebox out on deck!" she yelled to Marybett and grappled with the ropes that bound Annilea to the mattress. Seven-year-old Rabbie stood digging his fists into his tearing eyes. Anne shoved the baby into his arms. "Get outside with her. Wedge yourself into a corner somewhere." Anne, thick smoke swirling around her, tugged at the cowhide door covering; it would not come down. She got a stool and tried to stuff the covering between the frame and the ceiling. With a grinding, cracking lurch the boat hit a raft of jetsam; Anne pitched forward and slid the length of the deck. Coating her Sabbath clothes with muck. Andrew's frantic efforts to free them failed so they floated, ingloriously caught in the midst of the jam, to Pittsburgh.

The next morning the MacMeans floated around to Ohio Landing to join the other settlers. In contrast to their clumsy boats and wan children, the big flatboat with its lively, flamboyant-haired occupants appeared awesome, and the four families, by shouted acclamation, elected Andrew their captain. Andrew hid his surprise by drawing down his sandy brows and pursing his mouth as he walked wide, inspecting his fleet. Anne, horrified that her husband, who had almost drowned them on the first twenty familiar miles of river, had been chosen captain to guide them all five hundred miles into the unknown, nodded coolly to the ladies—"Mrs. Hunter," "Mrs. Smith," "Mrs. Illes," "Mrs. Ker"—and climbed the steps to top of the bank. Perched on a bundle of pelts, she cradled Annilea and watched the scene below in bewilderment. Captains were supposed to be men who foresaw danger, snapped out orders, stood firmly with eyes squinted in Godly wisdom, and yet there was Andrew—shambling about, slapping men and boys on the back while wives and sisters bleated like ewes at the approach of the shepherd.

Well, Annie, who did you expect? George Rogers Clark himself? She made a wry face. At least someone I could put a little faith in. Not a person who never confronts a problem until he's whacked over the head with it, who's always late with

215

the plowing, then wonders why the neighbors' corn stands taller than his.

Anne turned toward the town and put Annilea to her breast. The rampart walls had crumbled, the valley been sown with log homes and green kitchen gardens and the side of Grant's Hill furrowed by plows. So different from that summer of '63. She sighed. Sixteen years ago.

Cheers came from the landing; Anne turned. Andrew stood balanced on the gunwale looking almost the same as the fifteen-year-old she had married; no doubt Zac still could pick him up and drop him over a wall. His orange hair was tousled by the morning breeze as his arms swept away the people's fears with laughter. Ah, Andy, Andy. I suppose God meant you for me even if you do end up getting us scalped or drowned. She rose and started back down the steps; Marybett was painting *Captain Andy* in black tar on the bow. Anne murmured, "God keep us all" and climbed over the gunwale.

The fleet backed like water bugs into the river. On the *Captain Andy* Andrew held the rudder, Joe Camp and David Pegon manned the sweeps, and Jamie stood on the cabin roof and shouted out to his father what lay ahead. When in five minutes no crises had occurred, Anne uncurled her fingers from the gunwale. We're old hands, she thought as she gazed at the chaos on the other boats. Two of them were clumsy, keelless *bateaux*, one a poorly made flatboat, and the other a thirty-foot long dugout, burned and hollowed from a sycamore tree; the immigrant farmers and their sons—three of the families had come straight from the wharves of Philadelphia— had no idea how to control their awkward craft in the currents that surged between islands and the riffles that churned over shallows.

At twilight the fleet found itself at Beaver Creek, where the Ohio changed the direction of its flow from north to west. Although the current was swift, the river appeared clear of troublesome islands and jetsam rafts, and wearily the people settled themselves in the glare of a pink and lime sunset to lunch on cheeses and warm cow's milk. Andrew kept his captain's post on the barrelhead and ordered Jamie and the Hunter boy to take the Hunters' small dugout and gather rushes along the shore. Tied in bunches, smeared in grease, they were fixed fore and aft in each boat. Watchers were selected, and adults on each boat drew lots for three-hour shifts on the rudder.

The *Captain Andy* took the lead, and when the water turned inky, Andrew gave the order for the rushes to be lit, and a brave air of festivity sprang out of the darkness and lifted the people's spirits. But beyond the circles of light rose walls of menacing black, and only the smallest children slept; everyone else became listeners who, as the hours passed, learned how to hear and gauge the feel of shallows, islands, sandbars, jetsam, and shorelines that lay about them. They passed the word to the ruddermen, who now knowing port from starboard, kept their boats on an even keel.

At first light sleep felled the people, leaving them curled amid the disorder of cabin or deck. Boats slid, barely guided by drowsy hands, across sheets of pale water and through hushed mists; glowering clouds sank lower and joined hands with the river fog. A deluge of rain burst upon the boats. The MacMeans, like the others scrambled about in disarray. Cocoons of blinding gray wetness enveloped each boat; a corner of the Smiths' flatboat cracked into the Hunters' *bateau* and locked there.

The rain slackened, the other boats converged, and with ropes and poles the men worked to separate the two. Above their sodden grunts a Smith child shrilled, "Pappie! The fire got bumped out of the box! The mattress is burning!"

Andrew yelled, "Your powder, Smith! Where's your powder?"

Amos Smith stood plastered stiff with terror, then roaring, "Jump!" began pushing children and animals over the side. The Hunter family retreated to the far end of their *bateau* and lowered themselves into the water.

"The canoe, Jamie!" Andrew barked. "Pick them up in the canoe!" Then, cupping his hands, he shouted to the Kers and Illes, "Stand away! Stand away! She's liable to blow!" Smoke roiled about the stricken flatboat; stark fingers clutched its edges.

"Pappie!" Jamie stood with the towline in his hand. "I can't. Remember? The first day a log knocked a hole in it."

"You blethering loon! Anne, hold the rudder." Andrew leaped to the deck, ripped the line from Jamie's hand, stepped into the canoe, and paddled about, lifting white-faced children to safety. After depositing them on the deck of the *Captain Andy*, he advanced toward Jamie, his fists clenched.

"Look at me, boy! Did that canoe sink? No, there's not enough water in it to take a decent bath."

Jamie mumbled into his shirt, "How was I supposed to know?"

Andrew put his fist under his son's chin and jerked it up.

217

"You knew because I said so. I told you to get in it. That was an order. You obey orders. You don't argue. You do it!"

Jamie expecting a cuff, hunched his shoulders, but Andrew let his cocked fist fall to his side. "Straighten up! Stop acting like a whipped boy. You've run out of boy-time. It's man-time now, so damnit! act like one. What if those children had drowned while you were having your little display of I-know-better-than-my-old-man rot? What about that?" He poked Jamie's chest. "Now get in that canoe and see what you can do about pulling goods off that flatboat."

"The powder—"

Andrew flat-handed the side of his face, then seized his hair. "Look! See that keg floating in the water? That's your damned powder! Now, that is the last explanation of an order you're ever going to get from me. The next time you don't jump when I tell you to, you get whipped. Is that clear? Whipped!"

Andrew turned away, the corners of his eyes checking to see if everyone in the company had heard his words. Anne gawked and shook her head in wonder. Was that really her Andrew talking?

Possessions were hauled from the listing, smoldering flatboat. The eight Smiths were distributed among the rest of the boats; the three-foot hole in the *bateau* was stuffed with unwashed fleece.

Hands had just turned to morning chores when the lookouts bawled, "Rapids ahead!" and the four boats were swept like crumbs into the dark maw of the Allegheny Mountains, down a throat of whirling water into a black belly where both sky and river thunder—squeezed between thousand-foot cliffs—battered the people's skulls. Riffles made decks quiver, then rapids tossed them, tearing at their seams until water soaked the children sprawled full length upon them. Spray slapped the faces of those holding rudders and sweeps as they strained to ride the racing guts of the monster of noise and darkness. Rising, falling, mile after mile, past Mingo Junction, Buffalo Creek, Indian Short Creek . . . Tree roots as big as cabins lurched beside them, reaching for their gunwales with knotted claws and gnarled fingers. Mounds of fodder burst into the air as bows whopped into troughs; horses fell shrieking, kicking; a barrel loose on the deck of the Kers' rolling, keelless *bateau* crushed a toddler under its iron-rimmed staves. Death for all seemed seconds away, courage simply an instinct to live.

Above the roar they heard quiet, but disbelieved their ears until the boards under their feet grew steady and the boats, like bubbles of spit, circled in sudden calm. "Watch out for sandbars!" Andrew shouted, then raised his arm in triumph toward the eastern shore. "Martin's Ferry! Wheeling! We made it!"

Anne hitched her shoulders in pride. "Well, Mrs. Mac-Means, you outdid the sprites at their best, didn't you?"

The settlers remained in Wheeling three days, repairing their boats, burying the Ker child, discussing whether to walk back to Pittsburgh or continue on to Kentucky. They listened carefully to those who had been farther west. "Well, folks, I'll tell you how it is. The Frenchies call her La Belle Riviere, and there's truth to that. From here on she's a like a lazy serpent creature gliding south and west, a thousand miles of silver sunshine winding through green forests. Then like any beautiful woman she finds her mate and he forces her into his bed and bends her will to his. That, folks, is the Mississippi. Prideful, treacherous, powerful beyond believing, sweeping through jungle, across flatlands, swamps, and bayous, carrying enough silt and gravel to make a whole state where she spills into the Gulf of Mexico. A thousand miles of danger, that's what the Mississippi is.

"Indians? Well, the Shawnee hold the north bank of the Ohio. It's theirs by treaty right. A handful of whites occupy the south bank in Kentucky. The Spanish got the west side of the Mississippi and the Natchez pirates the east. Course, there's Indians all over, and there ain't none of them you can trust. Be with you one day, against you the next. Cherokee, Chickasaw, Natchez. But I'll be dead honest with you, folks, if it weren't for renegades like Simon Girty and James Colbert putting wild ideas in their heads, we might get along all right with them savages. And the Redcoats are going plumb out of their minds trying to get the Indians on their side. You got British officers painting their faces and leaping about war poles. Recruiting, Colonel Hamilton calls it. Personally, I agree with Colonel Clark—it should have stayed a war of the whites. Left the Indians out altogether. Did you know that Hamilton—he commands the British from Detroit—pays his Indians for white scalps? Hair-buyer Harry, we call him. Yep, it's plumb dangerous west of here. In fact, come summer it'll be dangerous right where you're standing now.

"What are your chances? I don't know, but a lot of folks are taking them. All kinds been coming past here—speculators, Tories, settlers like yourselves, lads that want to join Boone and Kenton and be Indian-fighters, even a few hoity-toity Europeans. Yep, all kinds. But let me say that it's a one-way trip. There ain't no way back from a bullet in the head, or drowning, or starvation. And the chances of surviving a walk north along the Natchez Trace or sailing around, getting through the storms of Hatteras and the British men-of-war, and landing on the East Coast are mighty slim. No, sir, you think real good now about if you want to go on. Once you leave Wheeling you've thrown your dice. And then there ain't nothing you can do but wait to see how they come up."

Men hunted early, then hunkered in the sun and talked; women doused their sniffling children with mullen tea, then stared at the river; a prayer meeting was held, with Andrew leading. Then the families spoke their minds: The Smiths would turn back, the rest would stick together and see each other through the first winter. A quarter moon hung in the west, and the east was flushed with the first streak of day when the MacMeans, Hunters, Illes, and Kers loaded up and the boats slipped onto the lavender river.

Andrew surveyed his fleet from a newly built platform rising high in the stern; Jamie stood beside him, holding the new rudder, a thirty-foot pole of ash with a huge whorl from the trunk of a maple nailed to the end; Joe Camp and David Pegon stood with their arms folded over the sweeps, ready for trouble. None came. "Six miles an hour," Andrew announced. "Corn Island in a fortnight." Anne cautiously pulled a rocking chair to the square bow.

Opening her shift, she held Annilea to her breast, and gradually her body melded with the tugs of pleasure, the orange sun on her shoulders, the rippling morning water colors, and the silence of people holding hope in their mouths. "Shhh," Bird whispered to the twins. "Don't run. The river is sleeping. We don't want it to wake up angry." They drifted around a wide bend, past a long island of quarreling crows. Anne began to rock—the deck stayed flat and smooth; she tipped further, back and forth to the ends of the rockers; Annilea gurgled. Bird served porridge from the Killyleagh kettle; Marybett marshaled the little boys, Rabbie, John, and Issac, to tend the animals: the milk cow and her calf, the sow and her piglets, the ewe and twin lambs, the three geese, Andrew's bay mare, the white ox, the collie and her pup, and Bird's black cat, Kitty-Midnight. Anne had left Cinder with Bess, out of danger. Andrew waved cheerily to his fleet and whistled "Maggie Lauder."

Anne twisted to watch him, his rake-thin body black against the white morning sky. Perhaps, Annie, his Calling is to be a river captain. It would satisfy his restlessness, his stopping dead in the middle of adzing a log or digging a ditch to trot off to White's Landing or Pittsburgh, excusing himself by saying, "I feel like I'm going to root if I stand still too long. The soles of my feet get all itchy. Besides, on a farm there's no one to talk to." She imagined him running a line of flatboats from Pittsburgh to New Orleans, setting off on exciting journeys while she waved from the stoop of Breakfast Hill, and the idea tickled her.

She rocked and hummed, and the river became swells of deep blue while along the shore trees minced on the tiptoes of their roots and the fallen ones lay indecently, their private undersides exposed. Next spring, she thought, the floods will carry them from the spot where they have lived for a hundred years or more, pushing them along with the rootless humans floating toward the sea. But traveling trees are dead, traveling humans are not. Anne squinted up at Andrew. Perhaps, Annie, getting himself untangled from Geneva, from Hugh, from Zac, and from Bess has given him a new birth of his own. Maybe . . .

For uninterrupted hours Anne sat watching the endless panorama of beauty unfold: islands humped with trees rising like castles out of the morning fog; gentle hills upon which sailed white clouds of sheep, bearded men, sphinxes, and elephants; long sunsets casting both a carpet and a canopy of gold, crimson, and purple. Fretting cares dissolved in wondering what lay around the next bend—buffalo grazing on top of high yellow banks, hundreds of thousands of birds flying overhead, the excitement of other humans waving from a boat moored along the shore, or merely the continuing fantasy of flowing acres of water at once male, female, parent, friend—and lover.

Obsessed, Anne left cooking, plucking of birds, fishing, scrubbing pots, tending beasts, and spinning wool to others and sat guiltless and idle, knowing that soon she would have to step onto the muddy, stinking bank while her perfect friend glided on without her. When she thought of the parting she understood why her mother had been seduced into trying to join the water kelpies forever.

Anne and the Ohio were not the only lovers; there were also Marybett and David. Seventeen, brawny, his neck and shoulders thick from years of labor on the docks of Cardiff, David looked on the American wilderness with stunned awe. He had never hunted or even touched a rifle before, didn't know how to milk or ride, had never seen an Indian, and never had been in love. In his ignorance he supposed all girls were like Marybett, flashes of red and green, of temper and wild merriment, and so instead of being driven to distraction, he courted her by standing silent with his bronze arms folded across his bare chest, an Indian loincloth covering his hard buttocks, and the sun glinting off the brown hair that curled along the muscles of his thighs and calves. It was Marybett who was being driven wild. When David went off with the other men to hunt, she would climb on the back of Andrew's mare and sit motionless watching for his return, even managing to ignore Bird who, tongue in cheek, hummed love songs as she spun on her niddy noddy.

Another river bond sprang up between Joe Camp and the little boys. Fascinated by his blackness, they never tired of rubbing his arms, trying to make the "soot" come off. He taught them to braid hemp, to fish, to whittle ravens and sparrows from bits of pine, and he told them tales of Africa, of his white masters, his wives, his forty-one children. "Small men's hearts are near their mouths," Anne would murmur as she listened to the magic of parable, of truth that rolled from his tongue by day and his fiddle by night.

Rabbie was Joe's favorite, and Rabbie never had been anyone's favorite before. Sickly the first year of his life, he never established himself as a person before the birth of the boisterous twins. They were the image of their father, while Rabbie was small and plain, with straight, sandy hair and eyes of indeterminate gray. Anne, determined neither to dote on him, bereaving herself if he should die, nor cripple him with suffocating concern if he should live, left him alone to make his own way. The boy clung to the edges of the family, his bed-wetting and thumb-sucking sending his father into fits of arm-waving despair. Joe Camp did not patronize Rabbie, but told him plainly that he preferred him to "those double-trouble, smart-alecky brothers of yours. You, boy, got the patience to be a fisherman, and that's what we're going to make of you." Soon everyone came to rely on Rabbie to provide fish for the noon meal, and Andrew suddenly realized he had a fourth son.

After the supper plates had been dipped in the river and turned to dry, Rabbie would hand Joe his fiddle, and Bird would take hers—a gift from her Uncle Hugh on her fifth birthday—from its velvet-lined case. She would cock her head while Joe played a new tune, joining in the second time around; in a week hardly a song had been written that they couldn't play together. The other three boats would row in close, and the hand-clapping would last until the sky was shattered with stars; then Anne would unleash her power as a teller of tales.

Each day the sun grew warmer, the river smaller and slower, the people more given to easy banter and long naps in the afternoon. On the thirteenth day of the voyage Bird woke from a snooze on the platform, clasped her freckled arms about her skirted knees, and tilted her long swan neck—that and the MacKnight squareness of jaw and the Black hair she inherited from her mother, the rest of her was Magee—up to gaze at her father. "Pappie, do you suppose I'll have a teacher in Kentucky who knows a lot? Will we be seeing Uncle James?"

"James Young?" Andrew stuck out his tongue. "Blah! That man knows nothing. Set a beggar on horseback and he'll ride to the devil."

"But he's in Kentucky and Auntie Margery and Auntie Geneva are with him, so we must see him sometime."

Andrew jumped from his stool, and the platform shook under his feet. "I'll see my sisters, but I'll have no truck with that man!"

Frightened, Bird slipped down the ladder and into the shade of the canvas where the animals stood.

"He tried to have his way with me." Anne uttered the words in the same murmuring tone as the river.

Instantly Andrew was at her side. "What? What did you say?"

Anne's eyes glazed. The house at Breakfast Hill was filled with New Year's gaiety. She stepped from the smells of suet, spices, bread, and buffalo into the smack of cold air and sunbright snow, up to the lacy fold of bare trees above barn, through the heavy door into the stone springhouse. The sun sparkled across the frosty floor as she ladled yellow cream into a pitcher. Footsteps crunched on the outside snow; James Young stood in the doorway, his crooked teeth stained like grubs in the rotting log of his beard. "I've come to say goodbye, Sister." His tongue was thick with whiskey.

"James Young," Anne said, "came to the springhouse the day before they left for Kentucky." Andrew's sharp face ran with sweat.

Anne heard boots crack on cobblestone, felt the hands, the mushy, mildewy hair of James Young's face covering her mouth and nose, and the shoving thighs. She heard, "I been waiting, bitch. Ever since I laid you on your birthing bed in Grey's Alley, I been waiting." His tongue ran around her teeth, her gums. He squeezed her against him with one arm and moved his other hand to the buttons on his breeks. "Just wait, Mrs.

223

MacMeans. Just wait till you feel the good-bye present James Young has for you."

Andrew's eyes were crazed marble. "What did he do?"

Anne grabbed James Young's hair in both hands and jerked his head forward, then back. His throat gurgled, his boots slipped. Anne wrenched herself free and he fell—flat on his back. His hands clawed at her ankles. She kicked, and clutching the edge of the door, stepped on his face. Out into the light. Free. She fled down the path, across the gray shadows, the cold burning her lungs.

"I got away," Anne said. She scooped a bubble from the river.

"Why didn't you tell me?" Andrew raged. "I'd have killed him!"

No, Anne thought, Zac would have killed him. "That's why I didn't tell. He was leaving. And if he was dead, who would feed Margery and all those children?"

That night Andrew paced the platform, black against the dark satin sky. "Annie, I owe him for so much more than that. Someday . . ." His fist cracked again and again into his palm; the stars in the river winced.

The four boats floated close to the lush Kentucky shore as far from the gathering Shawnee as they could; away from their campfires and howls, away from renegades trying to trick them into ambush, past Point Pleasant, Limestone, the Licking River, the Kentucky River, into the Falls of the Ohio, where low water already had tamed the rapids into riffles.

Once moored at Corn Island they found that the fort was being abandoned and a new town laid out on the southern shore on the rise above Beargrass Creek. Named Louisville for the King of France, the cleared area bustled with the construction of the new fort that Colonel Clark had ordered, and the MacMeans, Illes, Kers, and Hunters had barely adjusted their heads to the harsh movements and noise of what seemed to them like a horde of humans when John Campbell, a Tory who had been driven from Pittsburgh, approached. He slapped shoulders and kissed hands, saying he would show them which lots were for sale.

Anne's spine fused into a ramrod. "You own this land?"

His tongue slid like butter over and around their questions as he built golden images of the future Louisville as a great center of commerce. "Lots are half an acre and—"

"Stop right there," Anne said. "We're farmers, not city squatters. Now, who can show us a few hundred acres? About four hundred apiece would do it."

John Campbell's lip curled. "There is no land left in Kentucky, Mrs. MacMeans. Most of it has been promised twice over already."

Andrew stepped forward. "A man needs a long spoon to sup with the devil—or a Campbell, especially a Tory Campbell. We'll be looking elsewhere."

He led the group back to the boats, but before they obtained a temporary lease on forty partially cleared acres seven miles up Beargrass Creek, three weeks of plowing and planting time had been lost, and the Shawnee buzzed across Kentucky like hornets from a nest. The boats, grounded on the drying marsh grass, served as a fort until the men and boys had felled, hauled, and lifted timbers into a palisade.

On the last night on the *Captain Andy*, Anne, grubby and bent from a day of wrenching garden space from the stubborn bushes, sat with her *Commonplace Book* in her lap. With a tired sigh she dipped her quill and wrote:

"We descended the Ohio River to Kentucky."

Chapter Seventeen

To the Indian Tribes on the Wabash River from George Rogers Clark, Lt. Colonel, Army of America, Greetings: We desire you to leave a very wide path for us, as we are many in number and love to have room enough for our march: for in swinging our arms as we walk, we may chance to hurt some of your young people with our swords.

Captain Zac Glenn had a marvelous time with the army of George Rogers Clark. Their ragtag force of frontiersmen marched through the Illinois country offering the tribes either the war belt or the peace belt. "If," Clark told them, "your choice is war, then fight like men so that the Long Knives may not be ashamed when they fight you." Nations that accepted peace and kept to their wigwams while the white men fought would "flourish like the willow trees on the riverbank"; the others could "expect only the tomahawk and their women and children will be given to the dogs to eat." Tribe after tribe accepted peace. Moving to the Upper Mississippi, Clark used surprise and bluff to take four French towns without firing a shot, then spent his evenings dancing with the beautiful sister of the Spanish commandant of St. Louis, Thérèse de Layba.

The British governor of Detroit, Henry Hamilton, determined that his army of eight hundred be in a position to advance on Kentucky and Pittsburgh in the spring of 1779, marched and floated his men across six hundred miles of wilderness to retake Vincennes on the Wabash River. Clark wrote to Governor Patrick Henry, "I know the case is desperate, but sir, we must either quit the country or attack Mr. Hamilton. Great things have been effected by a few men well conducted."

On February 3, eighty Americans and a hundred French volunteers set out to cross two hundred miles of half-frozen plains; in two weeks they reached the flooded Embarrass River, ten miles from Vincennes. Forced to abandon their horses, their last source of food, too weak to walk without the support of water, the Frenchmen reached a state of mutiny. Clark blackened his face with powder, raised his rife over his head, and uttering a piercing war whoop, plunged into the shoulder-deep icy water.

Jamie MacMeans threw a bundle of dry cane stalks on the fire, and Zac Glenn's huge shadow climbed the palisade wall. "Well, Colonel Clark led us for a mile or so until the urge to desert had left the Frenchies' bones, and then we huddled on this wee bit of dry land for the night. We woke with ice cracking all over us and our beards were frozen to our shirts and our britches were frozen to the ground. There was no path to be found and nothing to be seen but the glare of the sun on the ice, and as we started out for the far bank of the Wabash, the water lapped the chins of the little men."

Zac told how—when they had reached dry land—they paraded in and out of the hillocks with banners flying, fooling the French of the town into believing a huge army had come; how the militia deserted Hamilton and during the night supplied Clark with barrels of dry powder and helped build breastworks under the range of the fort's cannon. The next morning, after their first meal in a week, the Americans settled down to peppering the fort with sharpshooter fire. A number of British regulars fell, but to Clark's demand of surrender Hamilton replied, "We refuse to be awed into any action unworthy of British subjects."

In the afternoon Clark ambushed a returning hunting party of French and Indians; some he let go, but he personally helped carve up four braves, dump them in the river, and then, all blood and sweat, walked over to parley with Hamilton and his officers on the parade ground.

Zac drank from a crock of malt, wiped his lips on the back of his hand, and resettled his floppy hat on his tangled black hair. "There was an old *bateau* with some rainwater in the bottom and the colonel washed himself right there in front of them Britishers while jabbering on about how much he enjoyed sinking a tomahawk into flesh every now and then. He kept on playing with them, saying he wasn't going to give them any terms at all because of the way they had stirred up the Indians to massacre the families of the men who were with him. When he had them shaking in their boots—except for Harry Hamilton, who stayed stiff as a ramrod—he said he'd consider letting them keep their arms and baggage.

"The next morning the Redcoats marched out and"—Zac paused, waiting for the cracks in his voice to dissolve—"the American flag was raised over Vincennes. Most of us had chewed the fringe off our shirts to keep down the hunger pangs and our feet were rotting inside our moccasins and the land we'd captured sure wasn't much to look at, being all under flood. But when Colonel Hamilton handed Clark his sword and me and Captain Bowman marched him off . . ." Zac wiped tears from his cheeks with the back of his hand and then simply sat down.

Long after the others had retired to the lean-tos that stretched like warted black leaves along the inside of the palisade walls, Anne and Zac sat by the fire. "This Henry Hamilton," she said, "where did he come from?"

"Ireland. His family lives in a big castle there."

Anne nodded. "On the hill above Killyleagh."

"He the one who drove you off your place?"

"Aye. Put my schoolmaster in the dungeon, chains on the door of the church. Broke my pappie's hunting sword on his knee and declared him an outlaw."

Zac cautiously touched her hand. "Well, he's the outlaw now, Annie. He'll rot in the Williamsburg jail until this is over."

"Thanks for catching him, Zac." Her eyes closed, her voice slurred. "A man like that shouldn't be loose in America."

He settled his arm around her. "You're tired, Annie. More tired than any woman ought to be."

"I feel about a hundred. Zac, the soil here is so heavy that our ox could drag the plow for only an hour or so in the cool of

227

the morning. Andrew had to lead hunting parties, so . . . Oh, Zac . . ." She leaned forward, resting her head on his hunkered knee.

"Go on, Annie."

"Zac, sometimes we women put harness straps across our chests and . . ."

"Dragged the plow," he finished bitterly.

"Aye." She rocked slowly back and forth. "My milk dried up. Annilea was fussy and sickly in the heat. We women planted gardens and as soon as a shoot appeared some animal would nip it off. It wasn't long before seed ran low and the bickering began. The Illes and Kers had brought nothing, but the agreement had been to share, so . . . Her fingers left soot streaks across her cheeks. "A mountain cat got Andrew's mare." Zac lifted her against his shoulder; tears limped down along her nose and into the corners of her mouth. "At night I'm asleep before I lie down. Sometimes I pray that there will be an Indian alarm so I can spend the day inside the palisade. Zac, have you ever been so tired that . . ."

Through a blur of sleep she heard Zac say, "I'm sure Colonel Clark will understand your not going to the victory ball. Pioneering new land doesn't leave much strength for dancing."

Her head snapped up. "What do you mean? What do you mean, 'not going to the victory ball'?"

"Well, Annie, from what you've been telling me—"

"Zac, why do you think I've been stitching lace on my blue gown? Of course I'm going."

Beargrass Creek was too low to float even a bark canoe, so the families strung out single-file along the path. Zac led followed by David, with Marybett clinging to him as though if she didn't inhale the same air as he she might fall dead; Bird trailed them, imitating her sister's sighs and simpers. Jamie had abstractly scorned the ball as "the devil's trap," although his fear of seduction by seventeen-year-old Nancy Hunter was very concrete. "You go, Bird," he'd said. "I'll take care of the little ones."

Anne carried her indigo dress over her arm and Andrew had a clean shirt and a velvet frock coat that Mr. Illes had grown too stout to wear draped around his neck. Andrew walked with many a backward glance and carried his rifle level in both hands so the powder wouldn't spill from the pan; Kentucky crawled with Shawnee.

All afternoon people poured into Louisville. Some men might have turned back when they found their way blocked by raiding parties, but the women raised their chins, pointed out detours, and on they came—from Harrodsburg, Boonesboro, stations on the Licking River, the Salt. Many of the women trudged barefoot carrying their only shoes, lifting their skirts above the dust, and men with toddlers like papooses on their backs wondered if a ball was worth their scalps. When they arrived, the enormous quantities of rum and sugar, the tables heaped with cooked game, the shock of emerging from isolation and fear into society made the parade ground a scene of near-hysteria. When the sun began its slide toward the river, the men retired to the north bastion, the women to the south, and all prepared for the formalities of the evening.

A full-length mirror sat in the middle of the south room, and when Anne had managed to work her way through sixty giggling, primping women to view herself, she was amazed at the transformation. The shadows of the lace cap softened her sun-scraped skin, her fairy green eyes flirted, her chin dimpled above a high lace collar that hid her work-wrinkled neck. Another woman stepped beside her and murmured, "In America it's the women who wear the dueling scars."

For a moment Anne couldn't think what she was talking about; then she saw what the other's large bonnet could not hide: a deep red slash that crooked the corner of her mouth and split her chin. She ran her finger down the white thread of her own scar. "Yours is new. It will fade. This summer?"

"Yes." The woman winked in the mirror at Anne. "But I'm alive. The Indian is not." She pulled her bodice aside to show Anne the small pistol hidden there then extended her hand. "I'm Molly, Captain Todd's wife."

"Anne MacMeans. Shall we scarred ladies storm the battlements of society together?"

Linking arms, they strolled across the parade ground, patting each other's ruffles and stray hairs into place; then before climbing the stairs to the hall above the east barracks, they pulled on long gloves that hid swollen knuckles, callus-imbedded with grime and the myriad scars of cooking burns.

The room, sweet with the clean tang of new wood and shimmering in the light of scores of candles, wore a ruffle of tentative early comers, white-chested women in silk and men in velvet britches and spotless hose. Anne said with a gasp, "Are you sure we're in Kentucky?"

Molly laughed. "For tonight let's pretend it's Versailles."

The shutters stood open, but without a breeze the August

heat remained inside, and the addition of more and more scantly bathed bodies caused the temperature to rise and noses to be covered with hankies. Anne took out her fan, an extravaganza of peacock feathers willed to her by Rebekah Glenn. Marybett appeared at her elbow. "Please, Minnie? Just for a few minutes?"

Anne handed her the fan and Marybett swept away, her green dress and orange hair flashing like a bird of paradise.

"Why," Molly asked, "give a beauty like that anything more?"

Anne frowned; she always had difficulty realizing that others saw Marybett as beautiful. "Oh. She's young. She's in love with a very handsome boy. It's a time when everything should be perfect."

Molly nodded. "You're right. In Kentucky a young woman may have only one night to wave a peacock fan."

Any man dressed in buckskin and anyone whose rum-sodden limbs gave way twice or more as they ascended the stairs was being turned away at the door; surrendered rifles, knives, pistols, and tomahawks filled a long plank table. In spite of the fair number of males being barred entrance, those present—the men who were there, self-consciously tugging on too-short sleeves and shifting awkwardly on legs bulging in silk hose—still outnumbered the women twenty to one, and clean-shaven young bloods, widowers, and bachelors stood hungrily eyeing every female who entered.

Although Marybett hung on David's arm, she glazed other men's eyes by smiling left and right. Bird had climbed on the bench and stood lips pressed tightly together, watching the scene with round eyes. "I'm glad my Bird is just nine," Anne said.

"Ha!" snorted a woman standing on the other side of Molly. "Nine or ninety, that won't matter tonight. Just you watch. Someone will ask her to dance sure as she's standing there."

"Well, those men of Clark's have been gone fourteen months. Say, where is the great man, anyway? Didn't see hide nor hair of him this afternoon." "The word is that he was detained over on Corn Island, but if you ask me, he's just waiting to make a grand entrance tonight." Molly laughed and added, "And just like a French town, he'll capture us all without firing a shot."

Anne bent close to Molly's ear. "Do you know him? What's he like?"

"Hang on to your heart, Mistress Anne, you're in for the treat of your life."

"Will he dance with us all?"

"Probably. He's so smitten with his raven-haired Spanish beauty that he won't know one of us from the other."

"Who?"

"Thérèse de Lebya, sister to the commandant of St. Louis. True love, they say." The scar twisted her mouth. "A new king and queen for the West."

Before Anne could question her, Clark's drummer boy, his round face shining, circled the room, playing little raps with his long sticks; then, taking his place on the dais beside a wigged violinist in French-cut britches and lace, he waggled his head and danced a jig. Clark's militiamen, remembering how he had floated on that same drum across the frigid waters of the Little Wabash, roared their approval; the Frenchman elevated his nose and sniffed.

A group of men entered and stood shuffling about the door, patting their hair and rubbing the toes of their shoes on the backs of their britches. The drummer beat a tattoo and called, "Captain Todd!" Josh strode in and winked at Molly. The boy's high-pitched voice announced them one by one, giving each a drum roll as they entered. "Captain Pickett! A small dandy of a man strutted in. "Captains Owen and Bowman, the heroes of Vincennes!" The crowd cheered. "Captain Glenn, the panther of Pittsburgh!" Zac wore the honorary tartan, kilt, and socks of a Black Watch Grenadier, and the bulk of him shook the floor as he walked; to the ohs and ahs of the ladies he returned a come-try-me smile. "Captain Marshall!" "Captain Craig!" "Captain Boone!" Daniel waved and moved from the crowd to join the officers. "Captain Shelby!" "Captain Cox!"

The assembled captains snapped to attention; the drummer's flourish rolled endlessly, then his shout pitched among the eaves, "Colonel George Rogers Clark! Commander of the Western Army of America!"

Colonel Clark did not pause but strode directly from the hall into the room; the effect was as though the archangel Gabriel had arrived for Sabbath services. Six-foot-four, arrow straight, his boot heels clicked, the fringe of his gold epaulets swung wide from his shoulders, the buttons of his deep blue cutaway coat caught the candlelight like a score of miniature suns. Piles of auburn hair foamed from the high sweep of his brow. His eyes, shadowed by broad cheeks, blazed like a fox's in the night; his long and straight nose commanded the lower part of his oval head and jutted into his smile; a spiraling tumult rocked the room. Stepping to the dais, he raised his long arms as though lifting a rifle over his head, and the resulting stomping and shouting would have broken the floor of a lesser room. As he stood absorbing the adulation with the natural grace of the powerful young, Anne caught a glimpse of what Zac had been trying to tell the people that night by the leaping fire of cane. All of Hugh's grand words—liberty, independence, a new nation—became flesh in the form of this one man. No wonder the Indians invested the Big Long Knife with magical powers; no wonder the French had given him the entire Northwest without a shot; no wonder bickering ceased when he spoke and women's hearts hung between beats.

Colonel Clark took a cup and raised it. "To America!" When every hand had grasped a vessel and raised it, he shouted again "To America!" and the entire population of Kentucky swallowed as one. For thirty minutes toasts and huzzahs to Clark, each captain, each victory, to France, to Spain, and finally to America again spilled through the boughs of the trees to the wandering river and the paths beyond, leaving the pores of the people clogged with excited sweat. The swooning began.

The fiddler raised his bow. Mr. and Mrs. James Herrod positioned themselves to lead off the minuet, and every eye followed Clark to see which lady he would choose. He strode through a forest of flutterings and bowed—to Bird. A hush fell over the room.

"Would you care to dance with me?"

She looked straight into his eyes. "I'm not this tall at all, Colonel Clark. I'm standing on a bench. I'm only nine years old."

He smiled. "Just right."

Her cheeks blushed the color of his hair. "I can't do the minuet. I never learned."

"I'll teach you. You'll be light on your feet as a bird."

Her eyes blued to a black in which stars twinkled. "That's my name. Bird." She curtsied, opened her mouth, shut it again, then stammed over the forbidden word. "Why . . . why . . . why are you asking me?"

The colonel extended his arm; ruffles curled like frosted etchings against the royal blue sleeve. "Because my Thérèse is not here. The color of your hair is like hers, and it makes me miss her less when I look at it."

"All right." Gravely she placed her small hand on his arm. "I was afraid you might me teasing me, Mr.—Colonel—Clark."

Tiny Bird MacMeans and the hero of Vincennes did far better dancing the elegant, stately minuet than most of the impatient, striding Westerners. Even Anne and Andrew, who often had practiced the precise, mincing steps in their hearth room at Grey's Alley, found it difficult to force their hard-muscled bodies to meld into the stilted ritual. Faces grew long and strained, and globes of perspiration stained underarms. The last squeak brought an exploding puff of relief. Heads were mopped, then turned expectantly toward the fiddler; toes tapped. The Frenchman adjusted his wig, tweaked his bow and plunged into—another minuet. The groan was universal, but the Kentucky captains gamely arched their arms to begin again, and most of the dancers followed suit. Soon mutterings could be heard, and a few folks heady with rum aped the effete stance of the violinist.

Colonel Clark stepped to the dais and whispered in the man's ear; the foolish fiddler yelled back, "Colonel, you cannot play a minuet fast! It is a dance for gentlemen. I play only for gentlemen!" He sawed into the minuet again, and this time the crowd around the punchbowls hooted. He stopped, and purple-faced, shouted, "Barbarians! American barbarians!," then launched into a French tirade. Captains Todd and Glenn saluted their commander. "With your permission, sir," and picking up the fiddler, they marched out of the hall. His screeches sounded down the stairs.

Over the laughter and applause Clark shouted, "Who knows another fiddler?"

"I do," Andrew cried, and shot off to find Joe Camp. Bird looked up at Colonel Clark. "I have my fiddle with me, and *s'il vous plaît*, I could entertain a bit. Just while we wait for Mr. Joe."

Bird stood on a chair on the dais, and the drummer boy gave her a wink and a roll; she tucked the fiddle under her chin, and looking like a yellow willow twig set in a pile of leaves—Bird had removed her shoes, and her green flounce spilled over the chair—she raised her bow and began the first song she had ever learned, "Auld Lang Syne." The drummer followed, tapping the tune, the people hummed along, the tightness left Bird's arm, and the bow began to glide; when they burst into singing, her lips pressed into a smile, and her cheeks bunched like a merry squirrel's under her eyes.

Anne clutched Molly Todd's arm, afraid she might faint with pride. The clapping subsided and Bird called firmly, "The Blue-Tailed Fly"; she raised her fiddle high, and the room exploded into bouncing, stomping jigging.

"Anne MacMeans!" a voice boomed. Anne turned to be

crushed in Geneva's embrace. Then Margery's fearful brown eyes swam before her. She shut her own. She didn't want to see, didn't want to know if James Young stood there. When she heard his sneered, "Good evening, Sister," she clamped her hands over her ears. He leaned closer. "I see you've pushed one of your brats to the front already."

Eyes closed, she panted, "Andrew—and Zac—will return in a minute." James Young's boots retreated, and seconds later, Margery squeaked. Anne looked. Andrew and Zac stood in the middle of the floor—Andrew a bumpkin in his ill-fitting frock coat, Zac a gray-bearded Highland general who thundered, "I'll pitch him out for you, laddie." Zac stepped toward James Young, the pleats of his kilt swishing from the mounds of his buttocks.

Good Lord! Andrew must have told him about the springhouse. Anne moved, but Andrew was Mercury himself, and before the startled James Young could raise his guard, the heel of Andrew's hand had smashed into the corner of the long white face. Then catching the boot that swung toward his crotch, Andrew jerked it up; James's head hit the floor with a powerful crack. Andrew, his face lit with a devil's grin, hammered shoes, elbows, knuckles into the whimpering, rolling body. Zac, who held the doorkeepers at bay, called, "Are you done yet, laddie?"

Andrew rocked back on his haunches. "Aye." Two sergeants carried the writhing James Young, but Andrew walked proudly between his guards.

Colonel Clark bowed to Anne. "Do you cause brawls wherever you go?"

Anne dipped a curtsy. "My first, Colonel—no, second. Didn't my husband do a tidy job on him?"

Joe's fiddle sang, and the candles impaled on nails along the long walls shook with cries of "Go it!" and the thunder of feet. George Clark leaned toward Anne and shouted, "Now that I have sent the competition to the dungeon, may I have this dance?"

Anne arched an eyebrow. "I don't know as I should steal my daughter's beau."

He turned to the front, where Bird stood on her chair, her elbow darting back and forth to match the blur of Joe's song. "The black-haired Bird is your daughter?" He studied Anne from the auburn curl pasted to the damp of her forehead to the dimple that starred the pressed edge of her smile. "And Zac Glenn is your brother?"

"In a manner of speaking."

"I fail to find any resemblance."

"There's a line of panthers in the family," she said drily. "Zac was fathered by one of them."

George Clark's throat swelled in a booming laugh and his eyes snapped up freckles from her cheeks; he extended his arm. "Shall we?"

They maneuvered to find open space. The grinning Joe Camp resembled a flea lunging through the air in time to the music, but the whites of his eyes remained stained with an ex-slave's sorrow. Whistles, yells of "Jig! Jig it!" bounded over the jack-in-the-box heads.

"Wait, Colonel!" Anne cried and bent to undo her shoes. Marybett whirled past, crying, "Go it, Annie!" and giving her mother a wink. Anne was on the stump at Bo Dickie's wedding, and Jim, a flash of love and broad, clapping hands, echoed, "Go it, Annie!" She tossed her shoes in the general direction of a corner and clasped her fingers around the tall man's neck. His teeth shone. "I don't have to stoop to watch your eyes."

"Well, keep watching them or you'll get so dizzy you'll end up flat on the floor. Scot-Irish women give no quarter when it comes to jigging. It's in our blood."

The heat of his hands circled her waist. "Ready?"

"Aye," she nodded, pushing her palms into the hairy sweat on the back of his neck. "But mind your boots."

He raised one shiny black leather one, then whooped and plunged as though leading the army into the swamp before Vincennes. Anne's bare toes hit the boards, and her wide mouth mimicked his cry.

Chapter Eighteen

The harvest was even smaller than the MacMeans had anticipated; Zac returned to the Forks of the Yough; winter descended with brutal cold. By mid-November Beargrass Creek shimmered under a wrinkled glaze of ice, by December travelers reported that no water in Kentucky flowed free—except over the Falls of the Ohio; in January ice on the Kentucky River was six inches thick, a foot on the lazy Salt.

Cold circled the trees, gripping them until their very sap froze and then the living things exploded, cracking the crystalline air and littering the forest with shattered limbs. The earth became iron. Small animals weakened and died; larger ones—buffalo and deer—came to the fort and ate the scant fodder spread for the cattle and horses. Birds froze and dropped from the trees; forests became tombs and the fort on Beargrass Creek as silent as the frozen plumes of woodsmoke.

The settlers huddled within their hasty walls while the chill of death fingered their backs; rations of journeycake were divided, subdivided, then nonexistent. The very old and the very young refused to leave their beds, and winter crept through the logs, reached into the coverings of skins and rugs, and slowed the beating of their hearts to death. Women numbly contemplated what sins they might have committed to be punished so, questioned why God had allowed them to believe that Kentucky was a mild land flowing with milk and honey, only to spring this trap of icy suffering.

Men used their strength to haul logs, then sat staring at the sunlight of their burning until their children's hungry cries sent them out into the wind again to search the hollow trees for sleeping bears, the thickets for frozen turkeys. Once a trader came, his packhorse laden with cornmeal. Blue-lipped, the settlers asked, "How much?"; the trader blew on his hands. "$175 a bushel." Andrew was one who laid his money on the barrelhead.

It was a hard winter in many ways. David Pegon went hunting and by nightfall had not returned. Anne's heart froze, and in the morning she dared not look at Marybett. To her the day of silence, of not hearing him shouting at the gate had the voice of nevermore. Marybett, however, was merely puzzled. Then she decided his hunt must have taken him to Louisville and once more whistled at her chores. After three days it occurred to her that he might be dallying with the girls at the fort, and she stomped about in anger, shouting that she hoped he never came back. On the sixth day she asked her father if he would look for him.

"I have been, Marybett. I even went out on that first night and listened for him calling." He shook his head. 'I haven't found one sign."

"Then he must be in Louisville!" She ground salty tears into her chapped cheeks.

Andrew's shoulders drooped under his bearskin wrap. "Yesterday I met a man who had just come from there." He reached for her hand. "He says nobody of David's description is in town."

Marybett tossed her head and sniffed. "I guess I'll have to go and roust him out." Despite her parents' pleas, she set off for Louisville; Andrew, rifle cradled in the crook of his arm, trailed behind.

A storm cut short their search. "Don't worry," Marybett told her mother. "He's lost his way and holed up somewhere till the weather breaks."

No trace of David Pegon was found. Perhaps his feet, numb with cold, had slipped and he had plunged into a ravine to lie with a broken leg until he froze; perhaps a lean mother bear had been aroused and in her winter madness torn him from limb to limb; perhaps he had gotten lost and wandered around until he lay down in the cold to sleep; perhaps an Indian hunter, hungry as he, had spotted the blood of his kill, had crept ahead to wait behind a tree until the white hunter passed, and then . . . How was David, a boy from the docks of Cardiff, to know about all these things?

Marybett drifted out of her mind.

In Louisville they hung Joe Camp. Word had come from the East that he had killed his last master with a pitchfork on the steps of his veranda as he stood receiving guests. When accused, Joe nodded. "That's what I did," he said. He was hung with his fiddle clamped under his arm. That same night the winter wind took up Joe's song, blew it from where he hung beside the east barracks down the solid, bubbled black of Beargrass Creek, then strained his bow's laughing cry through the chinks in the palisade, into the lean-to of the MacMeans; Rabbie woke with a horrible cry.

On the first day of February Jamie and Andrew, gaunt with cold, prodded the steaming ox into the forest and hitched her to a fallen tree, the girth of which equaled half Andrew's height. The cadence of their axes trimming limbs shattered the stiff silence; the sweat of Jamie's brow froze his coonskin cap, his mat of hair, and his eyebrows together in a clump. The glare of the sun on the ice of the creek, as the ponderous beast dragged the log groaning across it, made Jamie's eyes squint, and he put both hands to his forehead to loosen the pull of the frozen hairs on his skin. At that moment the ox slipped, the giant trunk lurched. Andrew cried, "Look out!" too late. Jamie had fallen, and his right hand was crushed under the log.

The surgeon in Louisville said it might heal straight, it might not. Anne had no camphor for a salve, no greens for poultices, so she wrapped the smashed thing in the bark of a slippery elm and prayed.

Ever so slowly the days lengthened and the sun sucked at the frosted earth; the snow wasted into fog and steam, and the rains came; Andrew left for Harrodsburg. The boughs of the lean-to roof sagged, and Anne rose in the night to drain off the puddles that caught in the hides that covered the children. Returning to her own mattress, she twisted with damp and cold without Andrew's warmth, then rising, her stomach jumping with worry, lit the wick of the bear grease lamp and took her *Commonplace Book* out of the trunk. Drops from the roof pinged and splattered as her shivering hand formed words.

April 10, 1780. We have found much confusion in rights of land in Kentucky and, having had fine proposals made to settle on Mississippi land, my husband has signed an engagement to that purpose. He has gone to Harrodsburg to transact business respecting it.

A friend promised to provide for our family, myself and the seven children, in his absence. I believe he has done his utmost, but as our provision depends on his success as a hunter in killing of buffaloe &c., we have not gotten sufficient to supply our wants. Although Andrew has written to me not to move until his return to us, I am under the necessity of doing the best I can for my children. They are beginning to suffer as I am getting only nine pounds of meat for eight of us to live on for three days.

A certain Capt. Pickett came today and told me several things: that, as my husband has stayed longer than he was expected to, his return is very uncertain; that my family is suffering; that all the Fort (we live in a Fort on account of Indians) are going down the river—except for two Tory families; and that I would endanger our lives if I stayed. All this I know to be true. Capt. Pickett said that if I will go along with the company to Mississippi, he will provide for us so that I will not want. He has promised to stay at the mouth of the Salt River for ten to fifteen days so that if my husband is alive he will surely have come before that time. We fear he has been killed by the Indians. So through mere necessity to relieve my children and stay their crying I have consented to go. When I did so, Capt. Pickett's wife came and brought us plenty of meat. I know no reason why he did not supply us before,

*unless it is fear that my husband would not go with him to
his intended settlement.*

The Betty lamp sputtered and Anne hurried to scoop more
grease into the bowl; without light she feared the apparition
would return. Too many nights she had woken hearing Andrew
cry, "Annie!," lain listening for his footsteps, then risen to lift
the hide doorhanging and gaze out into moon shadows,
imagining he was outside the palisade, calling for her to come
and unbar the gate.

Several times she had gone barefoot across the cold mire
and lifted down the heavy log. Sometimes the marsh grass had
rustled with footsteps; once she had seen the form of Andrew
staggering through the ice-rimmed creek, crying, "Anne! Help
me!," stretching out his arm, then falling, an Indian arrow in
his back. She had run to the bank, but the water was empty. Or
did red swirl through the black? That white—was it a patch of
snow or a tablecloth? Were those trees, or Zac and Tommy
catching up the ends of the shroud, lifting Jim's body to carry it
through the night to Fort Pitt? An owl called, or was it herself
raising her face to the fog of morning, crying, "Why? Why?
Why Jim?"

Anne, her bony frame rattling with cold and dread, took the
lamp and set it on the earth beside her mattress. She crawled
under the musty quilts, pulling the Bible out from where it lay
at the bottom, and settled Annilea—one year old that day—
against the curve of her chest and belly. Scratches of noise
tugged at her ears; she opened the book quickly and read
aloud. "'Therefore, because the king's commandment was
urgent, and the furnace exceeding hot, the flame of the fire
slew those men that took up Shadrach, Meshach, and Abed-
nego. And these three men, Shadrach, Meshach, and Abed-
nego, fell down bound into the midst of the burning, fiery
furnace. Then Nebuchadnezzar the king was astonished, and
rose up in haste, and spake, and said unto his counselors, 'Did
not we cast three men bound into the midst of the fire?' They
answered and said unto the king, 'True, O king.' He answered
and said, 'Lo, I see four men loose, walking in the midst of the
fire, and they have no hurt; and the form of the fourth is like
the Son of God.'"

Annilea whimpered, and Anne closed the book, locking her
arms about her daughter and whispering, ". . . and they have
no hurt; and the form of the fourth is like the Son of God." Her
eyes watered with cold and sorrow.

That afternoon, after Captain Pickett's visit, Marybett had screamed, "He's dead! He's dead! Just like David! Pappie's never coming back. You can watch all you want to. Sit all day and watch the gate, but he's not coming. Never! Never!" Flecks of spit had formed at the corners of her mouth as she described in grisly detail how the Shawnees had tortured and killed him. The victim's name sometimes was Pappie and sometimes Davie. She had run out of the palisade and shouted after the captain's canoe, "Give me a gun! Give me a gun and I'll kill them all! I'll kill every Indian in Mississippi!"

Jamie had accepted his father's disappearance with a stoical "It is God's will." Since his accident he had taken the role of Job chosen by God to be tested with pain, and his vision of being draped with the black robe of Geneva and standing with an open Bible before his congregation had shifted to that of a martyr in the wilderness; the Mississippi plans, he believed, confirmed his fate. He had taken over the responsibilities as man for the family as best he could—although his hand prevented him from hunting—and was tender with his mother and his little brothers and sisters. His eyes, however, never showed the least spark of hope or joy; if Kentucky could swallow David Pegon, hang Joe Camp, and kill his father, what hope was there for him? He had Bird sew a pocket on the inside of his doeskin shirt, over his heart; there he placed his New Testament and waited, confident of his impending removal to heaven.

Bird, however, whenever she noticed her mother sinking into melancholy would kiss her and say, "He's on his way, Minnie. He really is."

On the fifteenth of April Captain Sam Pickett—after escorting the Illes, Kers, and Hunters to Louisville, where the flotilla was assembling for the journey down the Ohio—returned in the *Captain Andy*, which Andrew had specifically taken downstream on the high spring water before he left. "Thought I would try her out," Picket told the open-mouthed Anne as he strutted about in his knee-high French boots.

Anne boarded; the shapes of her stored belongings jumbled time and place, and a hot knot began to smoulder at the base of her skull.

When Sam Pickett climbed on the platform and took the rudder, Anne suggested that Jamie knew the boat and could handle it better, "especially in fast water."

The captain put his hands on his hips. "Mrs. MacMeans, I'm in charge of getting this craft safely to the Ohio, and if Mr.

MacMeans doesn't show up—which appears most probable now—I'll be in charge of it all the way to the Mississippi." He added with a smirk over his shoulder, "When your son is man enough to feed your family, then he'll be man enough to take the rudder."

Anne's skull seemed to zip into flames; she ground her teeth and gripped the rail until the tendons and veins almost burst through the backs of her hands.

At eventide the *Captain Andy* was moored on the narrow floodplain where Beargrass Creek meets the Ohio and Pickett, announcing they would sail at sunrise, waded to the steep path that led up to Louisville. He was to return with his belongings and his two sons to man the sweeps.

And what will you do, Annie, if he brings Mrs. Pickett, too? Her hips sagged deeper into her rocker, her hands into the lap full of greased fleece. What can I do? He's fed us for two months and will for goodness knows how long in Mississippi. If only he wasn't such a pompous donkey. And he's to be the leader. Where's Colonel Clark? This is his expedition. We're settlers for his fort. Or where, dear God, is Andrew? Sweat prickled her face, and she knew that Captain Pickett had no intention of waiting for Andrew at the mouth of the Salt.

She sat motionless, a white line of pain slicing her brow. Small orange-bellied, lavender-backed clouds quilted the sky over the bastions of Louisville high on the bluff; Beargrass Creek shone like an orange mirror into which a giant had nailed whole trees, attaching the sky to the land. Horses' hoofbeats mixed with the pounding of the Falls of the Ohio; Anne did not raise her head.

She did not want to look at Sam Pickett, think of his snores filling her cabin, where she and Andrew . . . Without warning a cry, a long black snake of anguish uncoiled from her belly and spurted between her open teeth. "Andrew! Where are you? Please!" Her fingers ripped the oily fleece. "For God's sake, where are you? I need you! I can't do it alone! I can't!"

Her children's hands held her shoulders, but her forehead cracked on the rail of the gunwale. Help me, God, help—

"Pappie!" Bird yelled. "It's Pappie!"

Don't do that, Bird, she thought. Don't try to bring me back that way. It's cruel. Don't. Bird seized her head and lifted it. "Look! Look!"

Far down Beargrass Creek galloped a horse and rider, black and dun in the waning light. The man's ankles flapped below the horse's belly, one arm circled his head. Closer. Closer. "It's a demon!" Marybett shrieked. Against the gloaming the figure's hair and the horse's mane and tail whipped like flames of ebony, but no sound of hooves could be heard.

Wake up, Annie, wake up. Don't fall over the edge. Wake up. Bring yourself back. She strained, squinting toward the galloping apparition. A trick of the setting sun, a warning . . . "Behold a pale horse; and his name that sat on him was Death, and hell followed with him."

The horse plunged crazily into the floodwaters, his nostrils red, his neck lathered in foamy white. His knees churned the water, drove it into pink spray; above the laid-back ears, a face took shape, jutted white in the grayness. Andrew! "He's dead! He's dead!" Anne howled.

The horse floundered and sank, hands reached for the gunwale—Andrew's hands, the knuckles bony and crossed with scars; the hair wet, curled copper wires. Andrew hitched himself up on his elbows. "Hello, Annie." His freckled, wet cheeks rose in a grin. "I'm back."

While the possum he'd brought stewed in the Killyleagh kettle, Andrew told the story about his journey to Harrodsburg, which lay between the headwaters of the Salt and Kentucky rivers sixty miles southeast of Louisville. Anne had difficulty focusing on his words.

"I set about inquiring of Mississippi, and ooch! the tales I heard. Some came from the devil, some from God, and the truth was hard to find. Remember the party that was slaughtered by the Shawnees at the mouth of the Licking last fall? Well, the story is that the leader, David Rogers, and the thirteen who escaped went on to New Orleans. Not only to get ammunition, but to ask the Spanish governor for a loan for Virginia and"—Andrew's voice grew tight—"also for his support of Virginia's claim that her western boundary is the Mississippi."

Anne sputtered and he said, "Wait. It gets worse. They say Thomas Jefferson, who's succeeded Patrick Henry as governor of Virginia, and George Rogers Clark are conniving to cinch that claim by erecting a fort—at the juncture of the Mississippi and Ohio rivers."

"No!" Anne cried.

"Yes. And when this vast state of Virginia is established, Governor Jefferson surely will be named king of America."

"You mean," Jamie blurted, "our Fort Jefferson is going to help get everything for Virginia?"

"I don't know. Maybe Clark and Jefferson are thinking only

of protecting America, and their enemies have put out these stories. Probably it's a bit of both. But I guess, since you say the group's sailing tomorrow, that we may have no choice about going or staying."

Anne rose and stirred the broth so hard that grease splattered in the fire. "Now, wait," Andrew said, reaching out to touch her skirt, "before you go flying off. Let me tell you about the land we'd be settling in Mississippi. The grant is for a hundred and sixty-eight thousand acres. Five hundred and sixty for each settler and militiaman, and a hundred thousand for Clark."

Bird jumped and squeaked, "That's two hundred times more than for us!"

Andrew nodded and went on. "Remember how friendly Pickett told us the Chickasaws are? Folks in Harrodsburg sure hooted at that. And worse yet, they got no payment for their land. It went to their enemies the Cherokees. This isn't the first time the Cherokees have managed to get white men to pay them for land that's not theirs to sell in the first place."

"So," Jamie said, the Job-like droop returning to his shoulders, "the Chickasaws will attack us when we land."

"Ooch, laddie, I can paint the picture even blacker for you. I heard that, one"—he ticked off the points on his fingers—"the Spanish are only fair-weather allies and will seize the east bank of the Mississippi the first chance they get. Two, that the new Fort Jefferson will be squeezed between two British armies— Campbell's troop advancing from Florida to Louisiana, then up the Mississippi, and Sinclair's thousand men coming down from Michilimackiac. That catches us neat as bread in a goose's bill. Three, that we can expect no help from the East because General Henry Bird and his Shawnees are determined to wipe out Louisville and all Kentucky this summer. They may. With Clark at Fort Jefferson there is nothing to stop them."

He tapped his knuckles on his wife's knee. "That, Annie, is why I sent you a note not to move until I got back."

"Andy, we were starving. Mister Illes couldn't seem to—"

He put two fingers over her mouth. "Hush. Let me finish. I tried sixteen ways to Sunday to get clear title to Kentucky land. Impossible. The tomahawk claims of the first settlers are everywhere. The mess about a separate state of Vandalia still is not cleared up. No one knows what the new American government will do after the war. And to top it all off, Virginia has promised its soldiers more land than exists. I think they've given it out all the way to Mississippi already.

"After I heard that, I decided we'd better find militia moving East and go with them. The man I was staying with"—he lifted Issac on one knee, Johnny on the other, and hissed into their ears—"a man who chewed crocodile bones for breakfast, yelled at me, 'Militia just draw fire, boy! Look at the forty Monongahela men Simon Girty's redskins slaughtered. Light out on your own!' I told him I had a wife and seven children and that although my twins ate whole crocodiles for lunch I thought we might have a little trouble swallowing General Bird. 'Then stay put!' he roared. That's what I decided to do, and let the devil take Clark's contract. I hoisted my canoe on my shoulder and set off for the Salt."

As Andrew told his tale of wandering lost in the "melting bowl of Kentucky mush," Anne watched him stroke their children's heads, and her cheeks sucked against her tongue and her belly dropped. His hands silhouetted against the fire moved with quicksilver grace. Aye, Annie, he is Mercury running across the sky with wings on his heels, his face sharp in the wind. Suddenly his awkward feet, jiggling knee, hopper-flat hips, peeling nose, one crooked tooth, red stubble edging his shovel-shaped chin were not flaws but endearing parts to be kissed. Luv for him is on you, Annie. She nodded and caught Andrew gazing at her with wonder. True, Andy, it's come to this: I need you. She pressed her lips in a smile, and her bare toes curled in passion. After seventeen years of marriage, Andy, it's very strange to feel as though we'd just met. Joy spread his lips and desire lowered his eyelid in a wink. Anne laughed from the base of her throat, and the children gawked.

An incredulous Pickett family arrived and quickly left, casting threats of prison over their shoulders should Andrew not sail with them in the morning; stars trickled across the sky; the MacMeans dined on possum and turnips; the children rolled in their blankets.

The floodwaters swirled in creamy rings around Andrew's thighs as he carried Anne to the foot of the path that led up the hill. In a hollow filled with the dry dead leaves of oak and beech, he hung his wet britches on a tree while she spread a bearskin on the ground; another covered them as they lay talking, watching scraps of leaves pattern the face of the moon. Then their throats thickened, barring words, and Anne wiggled out of her clothes. She curled her hips into the nest of his lap; one of his arms cradled her head, the other fell across her breasts.

She felt the weight she had borne alone spread and enter

him, and the safety of darkness and warmth, of living skin, released a thousand sighs. His chest rose against her back, and his breath whistled on her shoulder. In spiraling rings the world collapsed into itself, into this hollow, this bearskin, this circle of flesh—into a memory of a boy's white crescent form and a dream of floating on a green river of peace. She turned her head and they tucked the corners of their mouths together, breathing into each other; their fingertips, tingling with a language unknown to the tongue, moved into dimples and creases and curves, giving greetings, asking, "How are you?" When all was known, they saw their own souls in the other's eyes. "Hello in there," she said. They laughed, and nuzzling into hair and chests and soft places, each became all for the other.

Safe in joy and in joy to come, they tumbled to the dark side of the moon, the center of the tides where madness was oneness, and they strove to shove the other, themselves, off the edge to speed like a comet through the space of night showering sparks of ecstasy.

She murmured against his cheek . . . I never knew . . . He said . . . I never felt . . . They said . . . I never dreamed. Endlessly they circled the white and black sphere of tenderness and passion; one ending was but another beginning. Sleep was and was not.

"Annie," he said and she opened her eyes; the trees had separated from the night. He shifted his body, tearing their skin as they moved apart; they could not settle into themselves, be separate again. Kissing softly, they dozed, woke again; he stirred, her arms pulled him back, then it was he who would not let her go. It was too hard, too hard to be alone again . . . too frightening.

They absorbed the fort's morning canon boom into their embrace, into their oneness as they lay, covers for each other. Not until the voices of the men at the latrine trench startled them with their nearness did Andrew raise his head, his eyes reflecting the wide blue green of the sunrise sky. They saw that they were two, not one, that they had left the womb of the other, been born into themselves again. Wordlessly their eyes relived the night, revealed their dread of letting go. He started to sink back into her and she said, "No. The children." "Aye," he said, lifting himself on his hands to stare down through the trees to the bits of pale water. "They've had enough worry. We should be there when they wake."

They rose. Dressed. Arms about each other, they followed the path down the hill to Beargrass Creek. Took their places on the boat. Stood, breakfast cakes of pemmican in their hands, damp and silent as the tree trunks reflected in the floodwaters.

Anne took out her *Commonplace Book* and wrote, "We appear to have no alternative but to descend the river. It is not, though, without fear of the issue."

Chapter Nineteen

Accordingly, in the month of April 1780, we sailed away to the Mississippi. Without any disaster, we landed 12 miles below the mouth of the Ohio, where we built a fort for our defense and called it Fort Jefferson.

Anne chose a clean page in her *Commonplace Book* for a letter to Hugh. Dipping her quill, she shifted her fingers around the black crow feathers and began.

Fort Jefferson
July 1780

Dear Hugh,

I have never been as hot, sticky, itchy, feverish in all my life—or was it this bad at Fort Pitt? No, it couldn't have been. The summer weight of Mississippi presses us down into the earth until we are all worms, blind dumb worms.

I didn't mean to start off my letter with complaints but the heat is so much a part of every breath that it takes precedence over Indians, disease, hard toil—everything.

A messenger is going East from here tomorrow. I don't know what word, if any, Congress has of our settlement here, but let me give you the true facts so you can inform them. (Assuming their city hearts are interested in anything that transpires in the savage hinterland.)

The land at the exact juncture of the Ohio and Mississippi rivers was so low and swampy that Clark had decided that there was no possibility of a settlement there. (If levees had been built, the Indians could have broken them and flooded us at will.) In truth, we would have floated past the confluence without seeing it—the Mississippi looks like just another tributary into the Ohio, which is fully a mile wide at this point—except for the drastic change in the character of the river. The sudden turbulences, whirlpools, and mysterious swells made some—the insufferable Capt. Pickett among them—believe we had gone too far and were actually approaching the ocean. Although all the families of our convoy had, since leaving Pittsburgh, floated for 1,000 miles on the Ohio, the twelve miles we spent on the Mississippi were our most fearful ones.

(I am marking this paragraph off as an aside, dear brother, for your enjoyment alone, not that of the Continental Congress. In my haste to be the first woman to step onto Mississippi soil—we all must be allowed our little vanities—I did not choose my spot carefully and sunk into muck up to my ankle bones. As I bent to retrieve my buried shoes, a huge swell of water, as brown as a new plowed furrow, splashed high against me. I straightened, turned—looking for all the world like a dirty, speckled sparrow—and came face to face with Colonel Clark, who stood in his shining uniform, ready to welcome his settlers to the Mississippi lands For a moment embarrassment tied my tongue then I uttered these historic words: "If I had known, Colonel, I would have worn my ball gown." He laughed as he bowed and his reply is even more worthy of historical note: "Is the advance guard of civilization ever tidy, ma'am?"

He and I have become friends in a manner of speaking, but it is always Bird that captures most of the great man's attention—much to Marybett's frustration. Her goal, it seems, is to make every man in the fort aware of her, lead them on, then scorn them. Perhaps she is afraid that if she loves them they will disappear like David Pegon, or perhaps she is practicing some twisted form of revenge: a punishment against men? against herself? against human affection?)

To return to the details of our condition here. The bluffs on which our fort sits are over 200 feet above the river, and our lookouts can see for miles to the north and south. The building itself is on a promontory of flat land which slopes gently south to Mayfield Creek (so named for the militiaman who drowned there) and on the north falls off sharply 70 feet into a ravine. The settlers (8 families of us) cultivate the bottom land along Mayfield Creek. The fort is protected by a ditch 80 feet long on each side, four feet deep and eight wide, and the dirt from it has been thrown up against a palisade of stout logs (about 9 feet high) that soon will be topped by a 10-foot wall of hewn timbers. We, both settler and soldier, cling like bugs to the interior walls in canvas or bough shelters—our only separation from the blazing sun and drenching rains of this climate.

The fort looks down on an island inhabited by Indians—at least it is at this season of the year—who must enjoy the cool breeze of the river, and their gardens look fertile. It makes an ideal place from which they can raid their favorite enemy the Cherokees. (Or perhaps we are their favorite now.) They are Chickasaws and for the men war is a way to prove their skill and courage, and the women have developed the art of torture to a high degree. When Clark suggested negotiations they replied, "We desire no friendship with you." We believe they are waiting for instructions from their chief James Colbert, a Scotsman who married into their tribe. They are cautious about offending the Big Long Knife (some are friendly and visit with us regularly), but they have made two raids in Clark's absence and done much damage to our crops.

Fortunately the land is very rich and we have made great proficiency in clearing it. We have planted a great deal of corn and it appears that our settlement will prosper; it is extremely unfortunate that Colonel Clark has had to absent himself from our defense. Shortly after our fort was completed messengers arrived saying that St. Louis was in grave danger from British and Indians moving down the Mississippi from Michilimakinac. Clark raced 100 miles up river to the defense of his Thérèse. He arrived 24 hours before the enemy, rallied the Spanish, and saved the town. From captives he learned that General Bird's force of 1,000 Indians, Frenchmen, and renagades like Girty and MacKee had come through the Illinois country and were almost at the Ohio. This time Clark didn't even wait for his army, but stopped here only long enough to paint his face like an Indian, then he ran the 300 miles back to Louisville through the forest. He thought that his mere presence there would make the Indians hesitate to attack; he was probably correct. In any case we have been left with only 30 militiamen under the command of a certain Captain George (Pickett, thank heaven, is with Clark); it is poor laboring for the world under the frown of God.

I feel, dear brother, as Jim once said of Zac and Tommy's position at Gists, like a pawn in a game of chess. We have been moved to a certain square as an obstruction to those who would conquer some more valuable piece— perhaps a bishop (Louisville) or a rook (Pittsburgh), considering, that is, that Boston and Philadelphia sit as queen and king. We MacMeans are a delaying tactic only, our square is expendable, we will neither be protected nor withdrawn. My husband, children, and I are to remain here, at this far point in the wilderness, as a diversion for thousands of Indians who are well aware of our weakness. If they choose to eliminate us they will do so.

Andrew has suffered more than the rest of us from the ague; I will go to fetch him for dinner and find him lying between hills of corn, shaking until his teeth rattle. The children are healthy and do not seem to mind the heat as much as we, and since they do not bear the full burden of adult toil they are actually quite gay. It is odd how children can view the prospect of death as but another incident in their lives. Annilea is a lively two and the darling of the fort. I fear she is being badly spoilt. Jamie tried to do too much with his hand before it had sufficiently healed and it is swollen and useless again. He accepts it with a stoic patience designed to drive lesser mortals like his mother and father to distraction. Bird writes faithfully in the journal Bess gave her so one day posterity will have a Bird's eye view of this venture. (I should write to you more often, Hugh—you bring my Puckishness to the surface even while I am mired in the Mississippi mud and heat.)

The man who will carry this letter, Wm. Ker, will be in Williamsburg for several weeks, and if you can get a reply back to him, he will carry it here when he returns. My spirit and love fly to you with this letter.

Your sister, Anne

On the day of William Ker's return from the East, every settler in the fort was kneeling in the cornfield beside Mayfield Creek, straightening stalks Indian boys had, in a fit of deviltry, trampled the night before. When the delivery packet was empty, Anne clutched a wrinkled letter from Hugh against her sweaty breasts and ducked up-river through a cobwebby little patch of woods. Wiping her muddy hands on the grass, she tenderly slit the sealing wax, flattened the paper, then held it close to her eyes.

Philadelphia, Penna.
July 30, 1780

Dearest Anne,

We here in the East are as heartily sick of war as you. The British sit in New York, and General Washington sits outside and watches them. Do you realize that our last major victory was at Trenton in 1776! Four years ago! The British have taken Charleston and overrun South Carolina and Georgia. General Gates is in the South, but he has to rely on untrained militia. All in all it appears as though the fire is going out under the cauldron of liberty, and sensing this, the British have begun to make overtures to Americans in high positions to desert the cause now and avoid hanging later. Probably many are tempted. Robert Bailey has already returned to England, leaving his business to his sons.

I wish I had more cheerful news to give you as you sit perched on the edge of our nation. Do not be too hard on Colonel Clark; he is holding the whole Northwest single-handed. Would that he could finish up there and come and do the same for us in the East. Somehow I believe he would find a way to dislodge Clinton from New York. Perhaps he would just smear gunpowder on his face, give a war whoop, stride into the city, and demand his sword. Bluff and courage are exactly what we need.

I do not blame you for feeling like a pawn, but the very fact that the American flag has been planted there will stengthen Franklin's hand in the negotiations to the extent that the British will have to accept the Mississippi as the boundary of our nation. (Assuming, of course, that we emerge victors from this stalemate.)

I read parts of your letter to Congress, and Fort Jefferson received three rousing cheers! God and America bless you all.

Your obedient and loving brother, in haste, Hugh

Anne leaned back against the thick, hot grass of the bank; the limp letter lay on her grimy skirt, and ants crawled across it. He had written of nothing but war. Not a word about his health. how he spent his days. If only there were peace. . . . She brushed mites from her damp arms and imagined a house on the rise between Mayfield Creek and the river—a big house with pillars, and lawns rolling to the water's edge. The rooms would have high ceilings, and shutters and blinds to keep out the heat. There would be clear water for bathing, sparkling cool water in sweaty pitchers to drink. Spiders, snakes, alligators would be far away, shut outside by thick walls. Brick. Yes, the walls would be brick like the house on Chestnut Street and so thick that the bellowing of the bull gators could not be heard inside. She'd change her clothes three or four times a day. A housekeeper would bring them and spread them on her white bed as she stepped from her copper tub. The children would be clean; there would be guests. . . . Hugh in white britches and a royal blue coat would walk in through the door and—

"Hi." Bird flopped down beside her.

Anne slipped out of her drowsy dream.

"That looks like fun," Bird said.

"What looks like fun?"

"The Indian children. They're swinging out over the river on a vine. The big boys are swinging halfway to our shore."

The narrow tip of the teardrop-shaped island lay opposite them: halfway was less than a third of a mile. "How old are they?" Anne asked. Bird had the sharpest eyes in the family.

"Not more than ten or twelve. But I think they see something upriver. Up past the bulge of their island. They keep swinging out and pointing."

"Probably Colonel Clark coming back."

"Ha. You wouldn't be lying there if you thought that. You'd be out there flapping your apron to beat old Harry."

"Don't talk rough, Bird."

Bird's body jerked forward. "Minnie"—her voice was low—"one of them just lit out, running for the village."

Anne sat up and shaded her eyes. They could see much farther up the river than the Indians could. Was there something black on the water—up past the tip of the island? She couldn't be sure; everything was brassy, shimmering in the torrid noon heat. The lookout cried from the bluff, and an answering "Hello!" came from the river. Maybe it was Clark coming back!

She and Bird clambered over the banks to the water's edge. Sun glinted off a rifle barrel; they ducked behind a fallen tree. "They're setting up an ambush on the island!" Bird cried.

"Upriver. What do you see upriver?" If the Indians had seen Clark or any militia, they wouldn't be preparing to attack—

they were too weak, their village too exposed. Perhaps a single boat of settlers? That would be a tempting target. Barrels of corn and maybe liquor, clothes, guns, powder—and scalps. They would gamble that the fort would not risk losing men in a retaliatory raid to avenge a few strangers. They feared only Clark, and he had been gone a long time now.

"A flatboat," Bird said. "One small flatboat."

A half dozen families had drifted into Fort Jefferson over the summer; only one, the Musics, had survived. The others, undone by disease or terror, had either died or continued on to Natchez, five hundred miles down the Mississippi.

Bird pressed her mother's knee. "Look there." A brave, a knife in his teeth, a spear tied on his back, crouched on the bank of the island. "He'll see our skirts."

For an instant the memory of Esther's red dress blinded her then she looked. Bird's dress was butternut. She blinked with the realization that no child of hers had ever worn red.

The brave waded into the water, peering upriver. He still couldn't see the flatboat, the women and children minding the sweeps, the lone unarmed man at the rudder.

Anne leaped around the roots of the tree, shouting, "Colonel Clark! Big Long Knife! Welcome!" Whipping off her apron, she waved it toward the landing. "There is room for all the soldiers you have brought! All the many, many Long Knives!"

The man leaned hard against the rudder; the boat swung across the channel. Something about the people seemed familiar. Bird jumped up and down, frantically waving her kerchief upriver. "Look! There he is! Big Long Knife himself! Colonel Clark's back! Hooray!"

The brave plunged into the channel, trying to see what else was coming; a shot from the landing turned him back. The flatboat swirled past Anne and Bird and grounded on a sandbar below the landing; militia and settlers swarmed toward it. The bushes on the island trembled; brown faces and long bows appeared.

"Chickasaws!" Anne squeaked. She gulped, then bellowed, "The island! An ambush!"

Arrows flew, powder flashed; the leaves on the island tore with the white man's bullets, and the willows swayed with running bodies. Anne and Bird scrambled over the two mudbanks and the high, grassy one; Anne collapsed, and her heart, making up for skipped beats, thundered in her ears.

"You all right, Minnie?"

"My ankle. I think—"

"I'll get someone." Bird disappeared into the woods.

Anne lay puddled with sweat. The shooting stopped; an excited clamor rose from the landing. Anne raised her head. "No! I don't believe it!"

The bushes parted, and there stood Geneva. "Annie! We've come!" Her wiry, orange hair poked out straight from the sides of her head, and her teeth were bared in a doggish grin.

Anne's body thudded back against the earth. James Young.

"There be Indians all over Kentucky, so we thought it best . . ."

She was going to have to live gizzard to gizzard with James Young again.

"We thought you might be pining for family."

Not you, not you. God got the signals mixed.

Chapter Twenty

Not all the Chickasaws hated the palefaced newcomers. Some were curious; some wanted to trade; some who were feuding within their own family or village crossed the channel to make friends with the Bostoni, as they called them; and some young men and women winked at those with different skins and longed to lie with them under the stars. Europeans had been traveling the Chickasaws' Great River since the time of their father's fathers; young men had won scalps fighting the Spanish, then again with the British against the French. War was the pleasure of the Chickasaw men, and the hair of Shawnees, Cherokees, Creeks, and Choctaws hung in the lodges on the island; their *mingo* and *tishmingo*, chief and war chief, were proud copper men; their great chief was a white man, James Colbert, who held a commission in the British army.

Alexander the son of James stepped onto the island of the Chickasaws one day in August, and the women murmured behind their hands. He had the straight, long body of his Indian mother and the fair skin and hair of his Scottish father; he came alone and unarmed. A feast of buffalo was prepared, and the clan chiefs sat down in the council house without walls and waited on him as an honored guest. They would not talk of serious matters, the mingo said, until the tishmingo returned from his raids down the Great River.

For two days and two nights their patient brown backs swayed as they reached for food or drink, passed the pipe, or felt the rhythm of the drums; but when Alexander spoke, they stiffened. His language was his mother's; the quick, hard thoughts his father's. He could not wait longer, he said, for the tishmingo. The council must hear his message. He rose, a war belt in his fist, and told them that the whites must be driven from the bluff. He warned that if these few blades of Bostoni were allowed to flourish on the banks of the Great River, scores, hundreds would follow and cover the land like the tall grass of Buffalo Plain.

"Since the planting moon," he said, "three hundred boats full of white men have landed at Clark's town by the Falls of the Ohio. "Where, if not on the land of the Chickasaws, will they build their houses and shoot their meat and sink their plows?"

The chiefs dipped bread in their broth and did not look at the women passing by to tend the fields of corn.

Alexander, impatient, spoke again. He urged an attack on the fort—a sudden surprise to gain the ditch, mount the walls with ladders. The chiefs murmured about the cannon, which would eat their young men. Alexander replied that a captive from the fort had confessed—on his second day of torture— that there were no balls for the cannon. "It is like the limp member of an old man," he said. The chiefs studied their thoughts; rich, throaty singing swirled from the fields.

A circle of sun fell through the smoke hole and glistened on the golden topknot of the great chief's son and on his eagle feather. "There is," he told them, "another way—fire-arrows at night to drive the Bostoni from behind their walls. Then you may hunt them like rabbits in the forest and there will be many fine bodies upon which your women may carve their signs. Many scalps for your belts, much honor among the clans of the Chickasaws and the tribes of your enemies."

The chiefs' eyes shone black in the shade of the roof of cane as they nodded and told one by one tales of enemies slain and hearts eaten. The women came bearing fresh-roasted corn and beans; the men ate and dozed.

The wind of late afternoon had dried the sweat on the backs of the chiefs when the mingo spoke. His old face was cracked with frowns and his voice growled like his belly as he reminded them of the magic of the Big Long Knife and his fury if he returned to find his people harmed. Alexander answered him quickly: Colonel Clark was gathering men to attack Detroit; he had no plans to return to Fort Jefferson. The chiefs questioned him, and Alexander's words grew in power. The Big Long Knife had eyes only for the glory of a great victory in the North, on the shores of the shining water.

For a long time the mingo swayed in thought, then told the chiefs to go among their braves and learn if their hearts leaped to do battle with the Bostoni.

On the fourth day the mingo, who wore the horns of his clan, the buffalo, spread his hands and told Alexander that very few of the braves wished to climb the hill and attack those who dwelled behind the stout walls of the Big Long Knife. "We are a small village," he said, "rich only in corn and children. If we attack and fail, the whites will wreak their vengeance on our fields and burn our houses of grass. The half-white chief can return to his woman far away, but all we possess is here on our island, where the cool breezes blow."

Alexander stretched his neck until his topknot touched the reeds of the roof; he folded his young arms across his chest of blond hair, his eyes blazed blue as bolts of heaven. "What if there were a thousand braves to link arms with you? A thousand fierce Chickasaw and Cherokee warriors to fight beside you?"

"How could that be?" the mingo asked.

"I can promise you a thousand warriors before the moon has waned," the son of the chief of the Chickasaws said.

The mingo called the others to sit in a ring around his blanket of feathers; at twilight he spoke again to Alexander. "My chiefs cannot agree among themselves. Some are angry that this plan has been made without us. It is our land, not Cherokee land, that the Bostoni sit upon, although"—and his eyes darted like snakes in the water—"it is said that they received the white man's gifts for it. Other of my chiefs counsel that our people should sit quietly and watch the white men kill each other. Some would choose your way."

He signaled for the women to light the fires and his pipe while Alexander thought on these things. When he had smoked he lifted his head of buffalo horns and spoke again. "Our tishmingo is not here to fasten our hearts on one course. It is unwise to fight with a divided heart. We will stay in our village and you must find another island where your guests may spread their blankets."

Alexander leaped to his feet and firelight blew on his face as he shook his fist. "My father, the great chief, wishes war. You will obey his wisdom. You will fight. You will help to drive the white man from this land before he devours you like a sea of crawling caterpillars devours the corn."

He whipped his tomahawk from the thong of his loincloth and raised the weapon high. "Warriors, who are not women, are already in their canoes, their faces painted for battle. They have grasped the war belt and are coming to help you destroy the enemy of all red men. You will receive them, and you will join with them."

The chief of the deer clan rose. "You forget under whose council roof you stand, Alexander Colbert. I, for one, will no longer listen to the forked tongue of the half-white boy who would place the Chickasaws on the same side of the wall as the Cherokees. His love is not for us but for the Redcoats; his hatred is not for our enemy but for the French and our neighbor the Bostoni, who have done us no harm." The chief of the deer clan picked up his blanket and shook the dust from it; the chiefs of the clan of the turtle and of the bear did the same.

The deer chief spoke again. "The Bostoni have truer hearts than those who call us 'red brother' and send our young braves to die that they may prosper." With straight backs the three chiefs walked from the council house without walls where the others sat clicking their teeth.

"Let them go and put on the skirts of white women," Alexander spat. "I will tell those of you who are men the promises of the Great White English Father across the sea."

By the time the remaining chiefs pulled their blankets to their chins, his promises covered the sky like stars of the Milky Way. At dawn the mingo took up his tomahawk, and walking to the middle of the village, drove it deep into the war post. He told the women to prepare for many guests and the braves to paint their faces.

Some young men, impatient to secure honor and scalps before the strangers arrived, attacked the cattle, the fields, the homes of the settlers who lived beyond the pale of the fort. They scalped Mrs. Music and her children, leaving them to burn with their lean-to; Mr. Music returned from hunting and found dogs tearing at their charred and roasted bodies. His mind snapped. No one ever saw him sleep again; he prowled the woods by day, the parameters of the bluff by night, looking for savages to kill.

Fort Jefferson's nine-foot-high ramparts of logs and dirt were to have been topped by hewn logs to a height of ten feet, but that task had not been completed. Malaria had so weakened the militiamen that of the remaining thirty, only ten could hold a rifle; hoisting timbers to that height was clearly beyond their strength. Many of the settlers, including Andrew, also suffered. Along the east side, into which the gate had been built, and the south side, where the land lay flat for fifty yards before sloping to Mayfield Creek, thick barked logs had been jammed upright in a palisade high enough to protect a tall man; on the west wall, which edged the two-thousand-foot-high concave river bluff, and on the north side, above the ravine, five-foot poles, poorly chinked with mud, provided some protection to those guarding the walls but none against assault.

The swivel gun sat on the rampart at the southeast corner, its empty mouth pointing over the grazing field and the approach to the gate. Diagonally across the dusty enclosure in the northwest corner, the lookout platform sat atop the high peak of Colonel Clark's two-story cabin, which now housed Captain George; Captain Owen; and young Billy Clark, the colonel's cousin. The militia and the nine settler families slept under the bough or canvas lean-tos that ringed the timbered rampart walls. In the center was a well, almost dry now and stinking of wastes; the enclosure, ankle deep in red dust, was one twelfth the size of Fort Pitt's acre parade ground—twenty strides to each side was the way Anne measured it when she paced to soothe her guilty fear that the sin of greed had placed them there.

In the young braves' raid, six oxen and three cows had been driven off; the remaining two milk cows were tethered inside the east wall, and children slipped out through the wicket gate, returning with arms of pea vines for their fodder. The older boys and girls formed a bucket line down the precipitous ravine to Swamp Creek and kept the two drinking barrels and four fire barrels filled. No one dared venture down the south slope to the bottom lands of Mayfield Creek, and the men did not go out to hunt but waited on the ramparts, rifles propped in chiseled slits between the logs.

On the day after the raid, three Indian families appeared in the field behind the east gate; the men wore the eagle feathers of clan chiefs, and their wives carried children and bundles; they raised their open palms in the sign of peace. Captain George crouched by the cannon opening, parleying with them, and Bird, who had learned some Chickasaw from her Indian girl friend, repeated to her family what the chiefs said:

A thousand Cherokee and Chickasaw braves are coming from the south and east to destroy the fort of the Bostoni. We are angry with the half-breed Alexander Colbert, who without our wisdom planned this war, and with our mingo, who has not waited for our tishmingo to advise what we should do. We three choose to fight on the side of the Big Long Knife.

The argument over whether or not to admit them to the fort ended when the women opened blankets full of corn and fresh buffalo meat. The men were disarmed as they stooped to enter the wicket gate, and the women and children were locked in an empty grain shed; Captain George announced in loud tones that they would be burned alive if their men turned out to be spies.

The chiefs sat down with Captains George and Owen and told them that the Indians would begin arriving within days and that Clark knew nothing of the planned attack. William Ker and his younger brothers Henry and Conrad volunteered to run to Louisville; they stained and painted their bodies, squeezed out between the palings on the north side, and pitched down the steep path into the steamy forest. Marybett flung herself on the dust and beat her fists; all three had been her suitors.

The next morning as the women squatted, pounding the Indians' corn into meal, the lookout shouted that there were war canoes on the river, some carrying as many as thirty men in black war paint. The thud of mortars on stone ceased, and the women's eyes grew glassy.

All week whoops from the Chickasaws' island welcomed boatloads of warriors; Cherokee and Chickasaw men spilled over the land. Supplies in the fort ran low, but the men did not risk hunting except at night, when the throb of drums from the island joined the chorus of cicadas and gators. Big game had fled long ago; a rabbit, a coon, a possum was now a triumph, and soon there were only rodents and snakes, green corn ears, and pumpkins so small their blossoms still clung to them.

On a night when clouds covered the moon, Joe Hunter and his sister Nancy, a girl as tall and strong as he was, crossed the Mississippi on a raft, returning in the fog of morning with two calves they had killed on Buffalo Plain. Joe had a Cherokee arrow lodged in his back, the head buried too deep to be cut out; the wound was packed with mud. The two calves, divided into sixty pieces, were gone by midday.

Anne made a strengthening broth of cracked bones and fat and was forcing spoonfuls between Andrew's clenched teeth when the drum rolled and she and Geneva were called to duty on the lookout platform. "Margery," she called, "would you finish here with Andrew?"

When the shrunken woman moved beyond the shadow of her lean-to, James Young threw a tankard hitting her back. "Get back here!" he bellowed. "God will take care of the MacMeans—if He chooses."

Jamie took the spoon and said, "Go along, Minnie." Gently he raised his father's head and held it against his chest.

Anne enjoyed sharing time on the lookout platform with strong, cheerful Geneva. In many ways their coming had been a blessing; their flour, cabbages, and herbs had kept her seven children as well as Geneva's and Tommy's Alex and the six Youngs—Moe, Sarah, Susan, Sally, Jo, and Daniel—the healthiest people in the fort. James Young, finding no one to bully, had spent his time rolling dice, drinking tafia with the militia, and hunting with the besotted Mr. Illes; Margery and the children wore the bruises of his frustrations. Geneva had confided to Anne that they had been forced from Kentucky by the collective hatred of their neighbors. "One husband in particular, who accused James of molesting his wife." Anne turned away, gagging on the memory of that mouth on her face.

"Is it the women's tongues here that keeps you backed off from them?"

Anne wiped tiny insects from her arms with her kerchief, shook it then stuck it back in her bosom. "Partly. Right from the beginning they labeled me snooty—Captain Andy's wife with her fine boat and furniture."

"Aye. When I heard you had left Breakfast Hill, I wondered if you weren't too much of a lady to get on well in the wilderness. I did, I wondered that."

Me, a lady? Too much a lady? Anne chuckled.

Bird climbed the ladder, holding a wailing Annilea in her arms.

"Have you seen that boat?"

Anne shaded her eyes. She could see nothing but brown water lazing around islands and between hills. "No."

Bird, puffed with importance, gave her mother and aunt a minute-by-minute report as the boat approached. "A war canoe." "Five paddlers on each side." "Cherokee paint." "Three men sitting in the bottom. One looks white. The other two are either Negroes or painted all over."

"I'll get the captain." Geneva disappeared down the ladder.

The boat was quite close now. Anne saw silver hair and pale arms clutching the gunwales. Dugouts shot like arrows from the bowed end of the island; voices sorted themselves into a singsong chant. "What are they saying, Bird?"

Bird took off her hat and pushed her pigtails away from her ears. "It's Cherokee. I don't know. Maybe "eagle." Maybe "He-Who-Sees-Beyond-Eagles"—something like that."

Captain George pounded up the ladder. "Is it James Colbert?" He held the spyglass to his eye. "No. Too thin. The two black men lifted the white man to their shoulders, above the flotilla of chanting braves; the hot, sullen air rocked with the Cherokee cries of welcome. "He must be a sage. Some religious figure. I wonder if they've been waiting for him to arrive and give the battle his blessing. A counterweight for the Cherokees against the Colberts. If so, they dance tonight and attack at dawn. Humph. He's a cripple."

Few slept that night—either on the island or in Fort Jefferson—and the full moon gave the illusion that it was not truly night, but another kind of day lit by a sun of yellow cheese. The shadows of the patrolling sentries oozed across the mulled dust; sick men moaned, Joe Hunter raved in delirium, children whimpered in dreams; those who would soon relieve the men on the walls shut their eyes and cursed sleep that would not come. Anne sat under the canvas of their lean-to with Annilea fixed like a leach on her chest and Rabbie's head in her lap; the moon-white faces of Johnny and Issac lay beside her. She tried to picture the attack, what she would do.

Shoot them, Annie? Shoot them and Bird? Jamie and Marybett, Andrew? A pistol to your own head would be easy compared to that. How could you kill them if any chance remained of their living? Hadn't Esther survived capture? But Meshach had wanted her, loved her. The Chickasaw women love torture. What if I don't kill them and have to sit bound, watching them be burned bit by bit? Hear them screaming for death when I can't help them?

Dizziness spun her head again. She waited until it passed. What would Bess say? "Be glad you have a pistol, not just a tomahawk"? Probably. Bess did not hate death the way she did. To her it was simply a passage to heaven. But then it had been she who had killed at Glenturk, who had pushed Tommy's infant into her arms and slapped her face, crying, "Run! Run!" Aye, Annie, Bess was the hero there, you the coward.

She moaned aloud and rocked Annilea. This time she could not hesitate. She had to decide so she would be ready. Sweat rolled down her sides. Play it through, Annie, imagine every detail, every feeling you'll have. By the time the moon rolled to the peak of the sky and left her in shadow, she knew she would not kill them. She would send them out between the poles on the north side to tumble into the ravine. Give them a chance. Maybe they could hide, build a raft. . . . Maybe she was being a coward again. She laid Rabbie's head next to Bird's, snuggled Annilea close to Andrew, then paced the enclosure until the sky stole the light from the moon.

Her children's eyes were still shut in sleep, lashes dark on their gray-tinted faces, when she touched the cheeks of Marybett and Jamie and whispered, "Time." Andrew seemed to be breathing easier—he or Bird could tend the little ones when they woke. The guard changed with passing grunts; Jamie squatted by the powder barrel; she and Marybett went to the rampart; Marybett would shoot, she would load. Occasionally a gray shape along the wall stretched, but no one spoke. The pulsing orange cap of sun gleamed above the black trees, and they braced themselves.

Up from Mayfield Creek warriors burst with howls and shots that thudded into logs, ripped between them, or whirred over the defenders' heads. As one wave charged across the field, another fired. Was there no end to them?

"Wait!" Captain George shouted. "Wait!"

The footfalls shook the earth. The faces slavered like mad dogs.

"Now. Fire!"

The point-blank volley ripped open heads and chests, and those who could, scrambled backward to the edge of the plateau. Those who could not were shot again—and again.

There were no more attacks en masse. Throughout the day the braves made feints here and there, harassing, hoping to find a weak spot; sharpshooters picked them off.

At twilight the Indians built fires on the south and east edges of the headland and from the shelter of the slope below emitted infrequent screeches or fired missles. One arrow lobbed over the palisade pinned Geneva's skirt to the earth as she—with little Alex by her side—dipped water from a barrel. Uttering a terrible oath, she broke the shaft over her knee, stormed to the wall and put a ball into the light of each of the dozen circling fires; the soldiers cheered as hunks of burning willow rained down upon their enemy.

261

When full dark had settled, Captain Owen duck-walked from one family to the next, whispering, "We're going to dig a tunnel under the northeast corner. We need a way to get water in and take out the dead."

"Who died?" Anne asked.

"Joe Hunter. And Private Roberts—malaria. And the Illes infant hasn't got long. For digging we'll need one member from each family."

"I'll go," Andrew said. "The least I can do is lie on my belly and scrape dirt. Besides"—he squeezed Anne's hand—"ever since the broth I've felt stronger."

"Can the tunnel be done in one night?"

"I doubt it. The earth is hard as rock, and we'll have to dig deep under the timbers. And it's got to be big enough for a man to crawl through. We can't send boys for water at night."

"It'll be a way to send out the children if—if it comes to that."

Andrew didn't answer. When she had told him her plan, he had said simply, "Whatever you feel is best." He crawled off; dust rose silver in the moonlight from the movements of his hands and knees and mingled with that from the feet of the Indian women already carrying loose dirt from the hole. The diggers talked loudly to cover the ring of their picks striking the iron earth and the scrape of their shovels; then a fiddle was tuned and the men sang. Anne couldn't remember sleep coming, but when she woke—Annilea glued to her chest with sweat—the sky above already had lightened with dawn.

That day was much the same as the day before, except those inside the fort were thirstier, hungerier, and more exhausted, the braves outside livelier and more daring. The whites ate dry journeycake and swallowed one mouthful of water; the redmen roasted buffalo. The children cried.

On the second night the tunnel was finished; the dead, whose smell had by then pervaded every corner of the fort, were buried under the north wall; enough water was carried up the dark, steep slope to fill the barrels and enough fodder gathered to still the lowing cows.

On the morning of the third day the Indians still encircled Fort Jefferson. Captain George called a council, and it was agreed that somehow they had to seize the initiative, throw some confusion into the Indians' siege plans. Two suggestions were accepted: that a cow be killed and a feast held, hopefully bluffing the Indians into believing that they had no concerns about food supplies; and that under cover of this revelry the cannon be loaded with every hard object that could be found— shoe buckles, buttons, rifle and musket shot, iron nails—and be dragged out the tunnel and buried with the muzzle pointing toward the area in front of the gate.

Boughs and poles from the lean-tos were burned, and over the pit of embers, slabs and haunches of beef were roasted; in spite of the heat the people hunkered close, mouths watering, unwilling to waste even the smell. When the sun had slid from its torrid zenith into hazy horizon clouds, the feast began. The men on the walls made a great show of casually tossing scraps to the dogs who roamed the ditch; children were encouraged to laugh and sing "London Bridge is falling down" as they marched through arched arms; men bellowed as though full of fight and tafia. Bird and Mrs. Ker took up their fiddles; boys and girls circled the walls with floppy hats on sticks, and women sat banging shoes on the earth calling, "Dance faster, Billy!" "Swing out, Captain!" "Jig! Jig!"

In the dark before moonrise, men rolled the loaded cannon down the ramp into the tunnel and out to the lip of the ditch overlooking the ravine, where it was buried with its muzzle pointing to the field in front of the gate. Into the now vacant opening on the southeast corner of the ramparts Marybett and Nancy Hunter placed a peeled log they had blackened with tar. At midnight everyone but the guards was curled ready for sleep with bellies full, mouths smirking at the thought of the cannon, and minds half convinced that the Ker boys had reached Louisville and Clark was on his way.

The following day—the fourth of the siege—the pressure by the Indians was relentless. The Kers' one remaining son took an arrow in the throat and died a few hours later; Mrs. Illes was killed by a ricocheting bullet; Emil Small, a militiaman, went mad, rushed out the wicket gate, and sped across the grazing field into the forest. That afternoon the Chickasaws displayed him, stripped, shaved, and blackened, ready for torture. Women danced about, pantomiming his fate: the gauntlet, the stake, the mutilations, the fire. Private Small, shocked out of his madness, trembled and wept; the woman whipped him across the field and down the slope. One by one Indian bands followed the sounds of feasting and dancing back to the island until the headland lay deserted.

Captain George, convinced that Emil Small's agonies had bought them a few hours of peace, ordered the guard reduced to one on each wall, water to be fetched, and the milk cow and her calf to be let out to browse. Cooling shadows crept across the promontory, and the unaccustomed silence weighted the eyelids of men and women; rags soaked in rum were placed in cranky children's mouths, and the fort dozed. "Captain George! Ho, Captain!" The shout of Alexander Colbert propelled the people headlong toward their posts. "I'm ready to offer terms. Terms too good to be true for men outnumbered more than a hundred to one."

Captain George, crying, "Stations!" ran bleary-eyed from Clark's cabin; militiamen tripped over small boys sprinting to water barrels; women, their minds still out of their bodies in dreams, fumbled heavy rifles as they made for the walls.

Anne, Marybett, and Nancy Hunter arranged themselves on the southeast corner, their skirts covering the opening through which the fake cannon might be glimpsed. Colbert—in Indian paint—stood under a huge live oak on the edge of the slope to Mayfield Creek; beside him knelt two Negroes, and between them the silver-haired sage. Anne studied the brambly white figure through a rifle slit. Was he responsible for the sudden offer of terms? Was he more knowledgeable, more skilled in trickery? Or could it be that the torture of Private Small had stirred his conscience? How white men could stomach—

"Come halfway, Captain George, and we'll talk like gentlemen."

The captain didn't answer at once; he was striding about the wall getting reports from the guards, who, although they had not seen one Indian, did, in fact, believe they ringed the fort even on the ravine and bluff sides.

Marybett whispered to Nancy. "The cow!" The animal grazed thirty yards from the gate; the calf nuzzled her udder.

Captain George, finished with his tour, shouted, "I don't see a flag of truce in your hand, Colbert!"

The young man stepped into a broad orange tail of the sunset and waved a white cloth. "Good God!" Anne gagged. "It's Emil Small's shirt!"

"Colbert's handsome!" Marybett whispered.

Nancy nodded. "They say his sister Susie is the most beautiful woman in America."

"Look at his body!" Marybett's eyes burned. Colbert had stained himself with walnut and painted his left nipple as an eye; the blond hair from his topknot fringed it like bangs; he stood wide-legged, his chest forward.

"He's leaner than your Davie was, but there's something about his stance . . . See?"

Captain George, halfway up the ladder to the platform, called, "You're a brave man, Alexander Colbert, to trust my men not to put a bullet through your renegade hide. I don't have that same faith in the redskins you've got hidden everywhere. Have your medicine man give a signal that if I show myself I won't get an arrow in my back."

The powerful black men made a seat with their hands and carried the cripple into the light beside Alexander; their bodies glistened against his dull-white skin. The sage took the eagle feather from his hair, waved it three times, and chanted a Cherokee song. Anne shuddered as she realized that the words to the Scot lullaby "Balow my Babe" would fit the tune he sang. How did white men come to desert their own? But Esther had . . .

"You're safe, Captain," Colbert called. "This man's medicine is very strong."

Captain George, a stocky, dark man, stood on the platform with the lanky, red-haired Billy Clark by his side and slowly raised the youth's hand. "William Clark, nephew to the Big Long Knife. His death would be avenged with a hundred times a hundred scalps."

Below her Anne heard the wicket gate creak open. Marybett shook a handful of broom straw through the opening and called, "Bossie, Bossie, come, come." The cow walked toward her, then stopped; the men beside Anne began to argue about the best way to bring her in.

Colbert and George sparred with boasts; then the chief's son dug his heels in the dust and began his speech, using first Chickasaw then English. He described the conditions within the fort with frightening accuracy: He named the militiamen too sick to fight, listed the meager food supplies, said the well was foul. Captain George's eyes flicked to the Indian chiefs, and he motioned for Captain Owen to train his pistol on them. No, Anne thought, you're wrong. It can't be them. They would have told him about the tunnel. It must have been Emil Small, throwing them off by pretending to confess everything.

The cow was grazing again, and one of the militiamen called down in a hoarse whisper to Marybett, "Why don't you just stick your pretty red head around the corner and ask young Alexander to please let you get your cow? I've never seen a man deny you a favor yet."

Nancy grabbed Marybett's arm. "Don't you dare! That no Indian could resist lifting your red scalp is closer to the truth."

Colbert raised his arms in the air; the hair under them

265

curled like carded gold fleece. "Before another sun sets your children will begin to wither and to die. Their murder will be on your soul, Captain George. Now listen to the offer He-Who-Sees-Beyond-Eagles has made. A generous offer that no one but a man of powerful medicine would dare put forth to Cherokee and Chickasaw warriors thirsting for blood." He paused dramatically, then continued. "When morning comes we will step back and leave a wide path for the settlers among you to march to your boats. We have not harmed them. They wait as you left them, safe on the creekbank. You may take whatever baggage you wish. No one will touch a hair on your heads or even speak loudly to frighten your children. You have our word of a safe journey to Natchez."

Anne snorted. Little Turtle had said the same thing at Fort Pitt. Safe passage—ha! She hoped Captain George was not foolish enough to believe him. Captain Owen climbed to the platform, and the three men held a conference; Anne breathed a sigh of relief at George's reply. "It is you, Mr. Colbert, who is in a hurry, not I. It is your warriors who are restless. It is they who left their squaws in the cornfields saying that they would return soon with presents of kettles and blankets, white women's clothes, and prisoners. They have been gone from their wigwams a long time, and still their hands are empty.

"You promised the young men scalps, you promised the warriors a chance to test their skill in battle and bring honor to their clans. And you have given them nothing.

"The Cherokee guests have eaten the corn of the island Chickasaws and there will be hunger in their village this winter, and who knows what terrible things may have happened in the far-off villages of the Cherokees while they have been away.

"No, Mr. Colbert, the clouds hang over you head, not mine. Do you hear children crying? Do you hear women wailing? Do you see men throwing down their guns? If you do, they are red people, not white ones."

Alexander sucked air into his lungs and raised his haughty nose. "My warriors are impatient not to return home, Captain George, but for me to unleash them so they may drive the Bostoni thieves from their land."

Captain George leaned over the platform rail. "You are mistaken. Their hearts beat fast to be gone before Colonel Clark returns. Perhaps it is already too late. Perhaps that is the noise of his army on the river now. He will bring cannon. Your braves know that the wrath of the Big Long Knife can shake the earth."

Colbert took one step and then another toward the fort. "You lie! Clark has deserted you. He cares only for the glory of taking Detroit. He has left you here to die on the vine like a rotten pumpkin."

"The sun has made the brains of Colbert run to mush. Colonel Clark would never desert the fort named for his friend, the Great Chief Jefferson, and he would never desert his kin, William Clark. If your people go home now, I will ask him to spare your villages. If you are still here when the sun rises, I cannot be responsible for his terrible vengeance, which will reach into the wigwam of every Chickasaw and Cherokee."

Colbert's voice cracked with a white man's anger. "Lower that traitor's flag tonight, Captain, or we'll wade in your blood to rip it down. By midday tomorrow the Union Jack will fly from those walls." He turned halfway, then stopped; the light from the edge of the sky fell full on his body, turning it to brass. He raised his arms to the Great Spirit of the western sky.

The wicket gate slammed open; Marybett and Nancy raced for the calf. Together they hoisted him, and Nancy put one arm under his rump and the other around his front legs; he struggled and bawled. Indian heads popped from the bushes; the girls raced for the gate, and the cow followed her calf. A bullet zipped through Marybett's skirt. They zigzagged. An arrow caught Nancy's sleeve, and another winged past Marybett's head—another and another until the air swarmed with them. Rifles cracked.

A great cry went up. Alexander Colbert lay writhing on the grass.

The three Chickasaw chiefs vaulted over the palisade and raced toward the fallen Colbert. Bullets from both the fort and the forest cut them down before they reached him. Marybett, Nancy, and the cow lunged safely inside the gate. Mr. Music danced a jig on the platform; madness swirled in the acrid powder smoke. Captains George and Owen bellowed, "Cease fire! Cease fire!"

The black men had not moved; the sage lifted his eagle feather, and the Indians lowered their bows and muskets. The braids of the white man's hair hung silver against his lean chest; his skeletal face watched the gate as though waiting for a vision to appear—or reappear. Four braves lifted the limp Colbert into a blanket; blood remained dark on the grass. The sage's eyes scanned the palisade; then he raised his hand, open-palmed; when it dropped onto a Negro's shoulder, he was borne away, his whiteness a light dipping into the darkness.

Anne stared at the spot where he had been, trying to re-create his image so she might study it, but only his magic remained. Slowly she unclenched her hands from the rifle she held, feeling in the sudden, dark silence as though she stood at the bottom of a well. Her back slid down the palisade logs and she sat with her arms clasping her legs. He-Who-Sees-Beyond-Eagles swirled about her, calling her Anne.

The others came down from the walls and stared into faces. Who had shot Colbert? The Chickasaw chiefs? Mr. Music? Everyone denied aiming at Alexander Colbert.

"Aheeeeeeeeeeeee!" Death wails shot skyward from the mouths of the Chickasaw women who knelt by the three chiefs.

Captain George cleared his throat. "One of the chiefs shot Colbert. Let it end there. It will go into the record that way. No more speculation. That is an order. Sergeant, lock the gate on those women."

"The children!" someone blurted.

"Put them out, too. Better that than starving in here." Captain George rubbed his chin. "The question is, what will they do now? Their leader was shot under a flag of truce. If he dies, will hundreds of them come storming up here at dawn and simply overrun us?"

"On the other hand," Captain Owen said, "they might feel it is a bad omen and just go home. That medicine man of the Cherokees sure seemed to take it calmly."

"Maybe he shot him," a voice offered, and everyone laughed.

"Well"—it seemed as though Captain George was trying to wear away the stubble on his chin with his fingers—"if he doesn't die, I'm sure we can expect something terrible. He'll whip them up with talk of revenge. Nothing those savages understand better than that. Let's prepare for the worst."

Anne, feeling that her legs would give way if she tried to stand, volunteered to keep watch from where she sat on the wall, saying that at night her keen ears made up for her faulty sight. Once greased against mosquitoes, she leaned against the fake cannon, stared at the bolted black doors of heaven, and asked herself, What makes you think you know that man? A crooked whip of lightning shattered the southern sky, then another and another. She shut her eyes, but the pain of the

268

light danced on her eyeballs. Faintly at first, then like a giant's ball rolling up the river, gathering speed, came the roar of thunder and wind. Anne held her hands over her ears, but the battering burst through her palms. The wind exploded up the slope, and hundred-foot trees bowed like reeds against the sickly, yellow-black sky; dust hit the walls with the force of hail. Jim roamed the forest, shouting, "Willie! Willie!" A shadow sat down next to Anne. "Our son is dead," she said.

Margery shrieked, "The devil is loose! The devil is loose!" Others cried that Colbert's ghost had come back for revenge; children howled as the palisade rocked in the blasting wind. The whole sky blinked with bursts of light, and the shadow rose to ride an eagle across the edges of the clouds. The tumult swept northward, leaving the fort shivering in a pool of lightning-charged calm. The stars shone; not a drop of rain had fallen. Andrew brought Anne a blanket and wrapped it around her; she made no sign that she knew he was there.

A grotesque, lopsided moon rose over the black forest, the bends of the great river, and spilled its lemon light across the field. Anne stirred and pricked her ears. Had she heard a rustling? No, it was the rising wind . . . wasn't it? Again . . . nearer . . .

A hundred flaming comets burst across the sky. Had judgment come? The arching balls of fire whooshed, twisted, plunged among the sleepers. Bullets whacked the logs. Anne rose to her knees. Indians do not attack at night! Swift shadows crossed the grass. "Attack!" she screamed. "Attack!"

Feet ran up the walls; a brave teetered on the pointed palisade, then jumped. He landed next to Mr. Music. The two men crouched in the light of the burning balls of pitch, circling, tomahawks in hand; then with a howl of glee, Mr. Music leaped in the air and in an arcing dive smashed down upon the youth. He hacked him to bits.

Two more blackened warriors hurtled from the walls; one Geneva split in two with an ax before he could gain his feet; the other fell from a blast of Captain Owen's pistol.

Andrew was beside Anne now, firing, passing her the hot, empty rifle to load; flashes of powder encircled the walls in a constant flickering stream. Although the fire-arrows lay scorching nothing but dust, boys raced to outdo each other in pouring water on them. Captain George shouted, "Put up those buckets! Now!" and a minute later, "Cease fire!"

Once more the night belonged to the moon. Anne heard Annilea's howls and walked stiffly down the ramp. The children launched themselves at her. "Where were you? We couldn't find you!"

The dead Indians were stacked in the corner and covered with canvas; journeycake and water were distributed.

An hour after the first attack, the sky burst into flames again; Anne pushed the children against the wall and drew her pistol. She measured the distance to the tunnel entrance; if they came over the wall again . . .

The enclosure burned like brimstone in the lake of hell; another round fell, and a child ran flaming, screaming; a woman tackled her and rolled her in the dirt. A militiaman, struck in the face, tore at his skin. No figures appeared on the walls, and after two more volleys, all was silent again. Men shoveled the burning arrows into the well; children scooped cornbread from the dirt and stuffed it into their mouths. When Marybett had milked the cow, they drank greedily. Captain George patted Captain Owen's back as he crawled into the tunnel with a sack of powder.

Another fire attack came at two, and this time the platform burned, but by lavishly pouring on water, the cabin was saved. Andrew, coughing with inhaled smoke, collapsed beside Anne. "Why didn't they let the damn thing burn? Water's more precious than the house of a commander who's deserted his people."

"Deserted! Andrew—"

"Wipe the hero-worship out of your eyes, Annie. Deserted is just what I mean." He curled on his side, his wasted body racked with coughs.

After the three-o'clock attack the wads of pitch were carelessly smothered with dirt by exhausted men; water was rationed to one sip apiece. Andrew, in a gesture of angry defiance, drew a bucket from the well and set it in front of his lean-to. "Try to take it away," he bellowed at the sergeant, "and I'll shoot you. Colbert was right. Clark has left us here to die while he wins more glory and more land at Detroit."

Captain George drew Anne to one side. "Your husband's delirious, isn't he?"

She nodded; for undermining morale and for charging his commander with desertion, Andrew could be shot. "He's very sick. I'll try to keep him quiet."

"Be certain that you do."

Anne sat rigid against the timbers; Andrew had fallen asleep, his head resting on her thigh. When the blue-black sky turned gray, she shook his arm. "Time, Andy." He sat up and rubbed his shoulders and neck. "Aye. To the walls. For the last time."

"Andy . . ." She looked for hope in his eyes, and finding none, bowed her head.

He bent and kissed her temple. "Luck, Annie."

"God keep you," she said. Then she called Marybett down from the wall, but when the soot-streaked girl hunkered before her, her words dried up.

"What is it, Minnie? Hurry. We have to get back. It's getting light."

Anne pressed the pistol into her hand. "Take the children over by the tunnel entrance. If the walls are breached, don't hesitate." She squeezed the bony shoulder. "Don't hesitate! Lead them down into the ravine and circle through the swamp to Mayfield Creek. I believe the Cherokee sage told the truth when he said the boats had not been destroyed. Choose the smallest one that will hold you all, and get onto the river. Stay on the river. If Indians capture you, demand that you be taken to He-Who-Sees-Beyond-Eagles. Call him . . . call him Willie Glenn."

"Who? What?"

"Hush. There's no time."

Marybett's eyes were flat. "Jamie?"

"No. I'll send him to take your place on the wall."

"You?"

"No. I must load for Andrew and Geneva."

"The people on the walls will be trapped."

"Yes."

"You want me to take Annilea, too?"

"Yes."

"Minnie, we won't all make it. The swamp—"

"Just try." She reached out to touch her daughter, but Marybett had turned her back.

Anne stood between Geneva and Andrew, a loaded rifle in her hand, a powder horn across her chest; her heart beat so hard her head trembled. It was light now. She could see the Indians draw their bows. Fire-arrows whooshed overhead; one volley, then another and another. A mass of brown men joined the archers; they whooped and screeched and jostled each other into a frenzy. Gradually the cries of the thousand voices lost their humanity and became like the sound of the storm—mindless, unstoppable. Anne glanced over her shoulder for a last look at her children; Bird saw her and waved. Anne turned back and rested her forehead against the smooth, yellow logs. "Our Father, Who art in heaven . . . Fire!"

The hammer of Andrew's gun hit the flint, the powder sparked in a roar. Anne handed him the loaded musket and took the smoking rifle. Drop a ball down the muzzle, stuff in wadding, ram it home, pour powder in the pan, hand it to Andrew, pick up Geneva's rifle, realize it's Tommy's . . . Jim, Jim, are you there . . . the ball is home, pour powder . . . take Andrew's . . .

From the east the earth erupted in unholy thunder—the Indians were rushing the gate. A hundred, two hundred men carrying a giant battering ram in their midst had burst from the woods and were racing across the grazing field toward the gate. A hump of dirt in the ditch moved; Captain Owen's head and back emerged. Flint struck steel; the short fuse sparked. Bare copper feet pounded on the hard earth, faces wore contorted, colored masks—

The explosion rocked the hilltop. The carnage was unimaginable.

The sun rose as red as the blood of the mangled corpses, as silent as the fort on the iron-red cliffs above the Mississippi. War canoes trailing widening wakes across the glassy water moved northward, southward. The wails of the women rose from the island of the Chickasaw.

Chapter Twenty-one

Anne steadied her right wrist with her left hand, then carefully wrote:

> *September 19, 1780. The Indians had attacked our fort twice during the summer without great injury, but the third time they appeared commissioned to destroy. Four persons were killed and one taken prisoner. All our corn was cut down, and very many of our cattle killed. Our Commander Capt. George had received from Illinois three barrels of flour and sixteen of corn, but this was all we could expect. Our prospects were now very gloomy; our men still durst not go out to hunt, and our little stock was constantly diminishing.*
>
> *God, in mercy, prevented the Indians from destroying our boats; we had seven left. In these, we settlers*

embarked on the Mississippi with all the property we could take. We design, if possible, to reach Natchez and from thence go round by sea to our old habitations. We have gotten enough of our new settlements.

Accordingly, on the thirteenth of September we set sail, agreeing to keep together for fear of the Indians. But the third morning after we set out, the others left our boat behind saying that as soon as they had killed some meat, they would wait for us. But the wind had risen very high and all in our boat were so sick that we could not sail on that day. We have seen the other six boats no more.

There are three families—MacMeans, Young and the Widow Glenn—consisting of nineteen persons in our boat, of whom only two are men. God has seen fit to continue, and increase, our affliction.

Anne held the pages of her *Commonplace Book* open to dry and stared through the cabin door at the river—the Mississippi was not a lover, but a wiley foe.

Mysterious swells, shifting channels, sandbars, whirlpools, snags, and sawyers were its weapons, and no one on the *Captain Andy* possessed the strength of wit or body to master her. With James Young and Geneva on the sweeps and Andrew at the rudder they blundered from their moorings each morning and floated from one disaster to another; then, barely able to stand, they made shore for the night.

The fourteen children huddled under the mildewed canvas that had once sheltered the MacMeans' fat and healthy beasts; they shivered, pressing their thin bodies together while rain poured in torrents upon the leaky roof and ran across the boards, soaking their skirts and britches. When after a week of deluge the sun shone again they sat like dazed, wild creatures listening to the cries of their sick mothers that issued from the cabin. In contrast to the lean, fair MacMeans, the Young children were dark, with huge, beseeching eyes, and their shorter limbs gave them the appearance of rag dolls from whom most of the stuffing had been lost. Alex Glenn was different from them all; his body promised to fulfill the height and strength of both his mother and father, but his face was pure Glenn—broad cheeks, slightly pouting lips, hair as yellow as young corn silk.

In the dark cabin amid the dark shapes of furniture that had once graced Breakfast Hill, Anne and Margery lay curled on their sides, knees drawn up to their chins, muttering gibberish while their fingers plucked endlessly at the bedclothes. Their guts roared with a fire that threatened to hemorrhage and flood their insides; their skin was burning paper. Anne had fantasies of finding the skinning knife, cutting open her belly, and pouring in water to put out the blaze, but ropes held her tightly to the mattress, and her twistings only brought new cries of pain from Margery.

From the beginning Anne had known the disease for what it was: typhoid. During her wanderings in Ulster she had seen whole families sicken and die, leaving perhaps one child to drift from house to house, begging to be taken in, but the doors always were slammed in their small, sad faces.

James Young would not enter the cabin despite Margery's endless piercing shrieks of "Husband! Husband!" Geneva and Andrew tended them, laying cooling cloths of river water on their heads, moistening their cracked lips, and shifting the ropes away from their raw flesh. Then, exhausted and ill themselves, they would curl on pallets of skins for the night. In the morning in the flat, flickering light reflected off the river, they would kneel beside the wasted bodies, wondering that they still lived.

On the third day after Anne's and Margery's collapse, Geneva wiped the rose-splotched chest of her sister, saying, "She was not meant for this, Andy. If our mother had lived she would have seen that wee Margery stayed behind the lace curtains, watching life from the window. She was not meant for this."

Andrew looked past the flap of deer hide to where James Young sat stuffing his face with flour cakes. "Surely not meant for a husband who only gave her one child after another without ever a word of kindness. If only—"

"None of us would be here if we could change it, but it isn't so bad for you and me, Andy. You had your Annie, me my Tommy. Who did she ever have but that monster bullying her about?"

"Wasn't she happy as a child? I remember us always taking a sweet home for the baby. You and me trudging hand in hand up the Royal Mile, stopping to pay the baker's boy a half pence for a butter scone."

"Aye. That's how it was Andy."

They dribbled water into Anne's and Margery's mouths and dipped cloths for their foreheads. "You think we will all die?" Andrew asked.

Anne's eyes opened, and she raised herself on one pointed elbow. "Don't let James Young near my children."

Andrew drew back in surprise. "Annie! You're awake! Are you better?"

Her eyes burned red in the dimness as she rasped, "If I die don't let James Young have my children. Get the children back to Bess."

Sweat broke out on Andrew's brow and drops poured down his face; he hid his shaking hands between his thighs. He swayed, almost tipping over. "I think it is you who will get them back home, Annie."

She collapsed back onto the mattress. "It is too far. If only"—her words were pants of bitterness—"the others hadn't deserted us. They could at least have taken the children."

James Young's boots banged the deck. "For Christ's sake, what are you doing in there? Let's get this tub afloat."

Anne watched Geneva's wide buttocks and Andrew's pinched ones crawl under the flap into the daylight. She wondered if she were about to die. She knew that people sometimes got clearheaded just before the end. It seemed easy. She would simply will her heart to stop before the pain returned and blotted out her mind, before Margery began screaming for James, before she started to worry about the children again. The blood pounded deep in her skull. What had Andrew said about her getting them back to Pittsburgh? As though it were up to her? She twisted the rope across her chest and found it slack. Margery was crawling out under the ragged deerskin. Don't, Margery, don't! Her cry never left her chest; she was slipping back. Flames leaped in front of her eyes, circled her forehead. She clenched her teeth. I can't die. I can't.

Margery crawled up behind James Young and wrapped her arms around his legs. He whirled, pushed on her bald head, and yelled, "Get away from me!"

Her skin and shift were translucent; her limbs a jumble of crooked sticks; she rose up and clutched at his chest. Her lips curled and her bloody gums worked, but no sound came out. He screeched, raised his knee, and kicked her chest. Then he jumped to the gunwale. "Keep away from me!"

She lunged at him and he stepped aside. For a moment she teetered there on her thighs, but instead of reaching back with her hands and clutching the rail, she stretched her arms forward, as though someone stood on the water. "I'm coming!" she cried.

She floated outward over the river and disappeared into the

dazzling glare of sun on waves. Like sparks from a fire, the gold flecks danced in agitation, then returned to their winking rhythm.

"She's gone," Andrew said, staggering against the rudder. "Margery's gone." Perspiration drenched him, and the world turned upside down. He hit the hard boards of the platform, clutching his belly. "Geneva! The rudder—"

Through swirls of fire Anne saw Andrew, black against the strong light, hitching his way through the doorway. His elbows would drag him a foot or so, then he would lay panting, the wind rattling in his throat. When he reached the mattress it took him a long time to get over the edge and work his way down into the deep nest of feathers where Anne's body lay; at last his elbow touched hers.

"Annie, luv." His voice was the wind in the pines, sighing and going on. "I wish I could have done better by you."

For a week they lay, untied in sickness as though in passion. The breath of one became the breath of the other, the sweat of one the sweat of the other; their hands fumbled trying to soothe; their bellies, crouched in agony beneath their knees, screamed in unison; and their weakened minds traveled together in and out of the light of day and the dark of night. Their breath, snores of wind in the backs of their mouths, linked them to this world, but their spirits hovered, tenuous.

God placed his hand on Andrew's heart. "Enough," He said, "be still." Anne woke when Andrew went. She felt his spirit brush by her cheek, saw him stand on the ramparts, heard him say, "It's meself. Andrew MacMeans."

The fever cooled in Anne's blood; she reached for the tin cup and found it empty. Chinks of sunlight speckled her blanket, and a broad stripe of it lay under the doorhanging. She crawled toward it. A crowd of children sat dumbly by the gunwale; some cried out in fear when they saw her. She reached the cup toward them and sprawled on the warm planks of the deck. I must tell them their father is dead, she thought.

When Anne became conscious again she found herself propped against the cabin, Jamie's arms around her. He held the cup to her lips. She wanted to gulp, but Bess was in her head, whispering, "Slowly, Annie. Wet your lips. Now your mouth. All right. Now swallow a little." It hit her chest like ice, and she gasped in pain. After a moment she asked, "Where are we?"

Jamie's eyes filled with tears. She frowned. He motioned to starboard. There was no water, only a dry riverbed. Far off, a blue stain ran beside a green island. They were stranded fifty, maybe a hundred yards from the river. She shut her eyes and put her head on Jamie's shoulder. I must still be asleep, she thought.

"She's dead," James Young said.

Anne struggled to open her eyelids; the sun was gone. "I am not dead." She had meant to shout, but she could barely hear her own voice.

Jamie stroked her cheek. "Not you, Minnie. He's talking about Aunt Geneva."

Anne shut her eyes again. The lids hurt. No. Not Geneva. Geneva isn't even sick. Margery is dead. Andrew is dead. But no, Geneva would see that they got home. She is strong. Like Zac. Nothing can touch Geneva.

"Can you take some broth?" Jamie asked. Bird knelt in front of her, a bowl in her hands.

Anne nodded. The taste was strong, salty. It rekindled the fire in her stomach. "No. No more." Her mind seemed to be sitting on top of an empty corn husk. She wondered if the sickness had left her paralyzed; she had no idea how to move her limbs.

"Please, Minnie." Bird's eyes were faraway blue over the full spoon.

Anne opened her mouth and swallowed again. "What happened?"

Jamie put his mouth close to her ear. "Uncle James shot a buffalo. By the time we got the boat to shore—Aunt Geneva was sick then, too—it was almost dark. We didn't know we had tied up over an old riverbank. By morning the water was five feet below us. Uncle James said we'd get the buffalo first, then tip the boat over the bank." His voice cracked, and he wiped tears from his cheeks. "I was worried, afraid we were in a channel that was going to dry up. But all the other grown people were sick, so I had to do what he said. We hunted for the buffalo all day and never found it. By the next morning the channel was ten yards farther away. Now . . ." He was crying.

"It's not your fault, dear." How were they ever going to get the boat to the river? To push it that far . . . "How long have we been here?"

"Seven days," Bird said, "and Uncle James won't hunt. He won't let Moe or Jamie hunt. He just sits and stares at the mud. Sometimes he laughs."

"Lay me down," Anne said. "I can't sit up anymore."

When she woke it was morning and the children were climbing back over the gunwale onto the deck. They were crying. Marybett and Jamie carried shovels. For a minute she didn't understand. Then she remembered. They must have buried Andrew. And Geneva. She saw their bodies in the ground, dirt on their faces . . . No! Not now! Annie, don't think about them now. They are gone. Their spirits are safe in heaven.

Bird brought broth and she forced herself to eat half a bowl; she drank water so greedily that the mud had no time to settle to the bottom of the cup. The older children were feeding the younger ones behind the cabin. She tried to picture them all. Moe a little younger than Bird. The twins Sarah and Susan about nine, then Sally, Jo, and little Daniel. Alex Glenn was only five. It would be hard. "Is James Young sick?" she asked Bird.

"With typhoid? Maybe a little." She shook her head. "He's strange, Minnie. He wouldn't even help bury Pappie and Aunt Geneva. And the ground was so hard. We wanted to do it right so that animals—"

"Fetch me Marybett."

Marybett's eyes were the color of tarnished copper, and before she could speak, Anne said, "We're going home."

Marybett turned her head so she could look at her mother from the corners of her eyes.

"I want you to take charge of unloading the boat."

"Everything?"

Anne nodded.

"Right now?"

Anne nodded again.

Every time a child said, "I can't," Marybett said, "You can." Her spirit snapped over them all like a whip.

It took fourteen days to move the boat across what seemed like a thousand miles. Each hummock was a mountain, each depression a canyon, every fallen tree and high bank a crisis that led to tears and collapse. When James Young saw they were making progress he cut larger logs to place under the

278

boat and used his strength on a pole as a lever. From moving one boat length a day they increased to two; the closer they got to the river the more demonic Anne became. "We're going home!" she would cry. "Home to Breakfast Hill Farm! To Uncle Zac and Aunt Bess! Push! Push! We'll get there! We will!"

When the first of the great logs, cut so long ago on the banks of the Monongahela, touched the Mississippi, Anne sat down on the crust of the bank and cried. Her head trembled with weakness, her hands and feet bled from deep cracks, her mind seemed to have no dimension beyond one moment ahead and one moment behind—but that had been sufficient.

They ate, rested, had a swallow of rum, pushed the *Captain Andy* onto the water, and slept with the rock of the waves; they woke smiling. The furniture and goods sat on the old bank stark in the morning sun, and the day was spent cheerfully lugging what they could to the river; the way seemed much shorter now.

Anne's mind went forward—five hundred miles to Natchez, five hundred miles to New Orleans, thousands by sea past Florida up the stormy coast to Philadelphia. The very thought made her weary and she recorded their ordeal as briefly as she could:

October 7. A few days after we had been left in this poor condition, all sick and no inhabitants near, Margery Young, my husband's sister, and wife of James Young died. At this time I was unable to help myself or others.

Shortly after Margery's death, as we were floating down the river, James Young shot a buffalo on the bank. We landed to get the meat, but the river was falling, and we were on a second bank, and did not know it till we were stuck fast. Little provision served us at this time, for very sore sickness continued. The seventh day after we landed here, my husband died, and the day following, his eldest sister departed, leaving her orphan child with his uncle, James Young. We lay here two weeks after this before we got the boat off, and then with great difficulty.

Chapter Twenty-two

High wind prevented them from leaving their mooring; purple clouds grabbed the sun from the sky; the deck pitched under Anne's feet.

"Minnie." Jamie spoke softly. "Bird and I gathered some ink berries. You can write now."

He helped her over the gunwale and led her to a bower under live oaks where she, with her hair whisping from the edge of her bonnet, a frown cutting her brow, lips tight, sat like a stiff winter weed. "People must know, Jamie. If they don't know they make up tales. A memory is all they have left. It's so little."

She opened her *Commonplace Book*.

November 20? By November our provision was done— all but one peck of flaxseed which we parched and beat into meal in a pot and made into a kind of soup. We had, also, six deer skins, one bear skin and one buffalo skin, all in the hair, and one elk skin in the parchment. These were all that the sixteen of us lived on for three weeks, except when we saw anything on the shore that we could eat, such as grapes, green brier berries, wild peas, tongue grass &c. Even these we got but seldom, at this season so that what little flesh we had left, after two months sickness, was lost remarkably fast. The danger of navigation at night always obliged us to land where we burned the hair of our skins and roasted them. It was the constant practice of the children to go up the bank in the evening in search of anything that they could eat. The evening of the fifth day of our present distress, my son of seven years, Robert Andrew, came back saying he could not get up the bank. I was sitting with my child of two years, Annilea, in my lap.

I divided my piece of roasted skin with him; he fretted. I told him to go to bed and he should have some grapes, if the rest got any. I gave him some after he was in bed, but he continued uneasy and fretful all that night. Next morning he arose and returned to bed without help, but mourned sore for something to eat. I gave him a piece of the elk skin that had boiled over night. This he strove to eat, but there was nothing that would quiet his poor heart, cutting for want of the supports of life. He continued striving to eat till the sun was about an hour high, and then he became delirious, lay quiet about two hours, and then departed. His eldest sister, Mary Elizabeth, and poor afflicted mother dug a grave in the sand and buried him. I returned to the boat expecting to see his sister Annilea also depart.

After some time I found about twelve grains of coffee, which I parched, beat fine and then boiled the powder in water. This I gave to my babe. She revived instantly, and was quite lively for two days. She could stand alone, and was sensible of sharp cutting hunger. The last day she screamed very bitterly after nightfall, as if pained at the very heart. She continued so till midnight, then became silent with little motion till about sunrise, and then silently departed from this world of pain, sin and affliction. Mary Elizabeth and I buried her also in the sand of the bank of the river, where the sun had cracked the mud to a great depth, almost wide enough for a grave.

Eagles quarreled in the blowing tops of the trees, and Anne imagined one screaming and fastening his talons on her shoulder. You failed in your trust. You took them from Breakfast Hill into a wilderness, where they died. Died of hunger. Died because you did not feed them. She rose, staggering under the weight of the bird.

Before each child was born she had divided her very being with it; her sustenance had been its sustenance. And after birth her milk, made of her body, had kept the infant alive, growing stronger and stronger. "A mother," she muttered, pushing her way through the boughs, "should die herself before her children die for want of food. I should have been able to keep them alive."

She lay on her mattress; sleep would not come, night would not come. Eyes—Rabbie's soft brown, Annilea's puddles of blue—begged for food, pleaded to be fed. "Minnie! Minnie!" they called, not believing she had let them die.

With darkness Johnny and Issac pushed close to her, but the empty places of Annilea and Rabbie were cold. Her eyes burst open. Cold! They lay in the ground! Alone! In the ground! Her babies! She must go to them! She rose, then flung her body

281

back, beating it against the feathers. "Twelve coffee beans, one cup of milk. They asked for so little. Why . . . why . . ."

Bird laid her tear-wet face on her back. "But Minnie, Rabbie and Annilea can't be hungry now. They're with Jesus."

Anne turned and held the bony bodies of Bird and the twins away from the eagle. Had God numbered all their days?

Not once had James Young raised his rifle to shoot the deer they could see on the shore, and he forbade anyone else to waste powder trying; he even mocked their clumsy efforts at fishing. Cowed by his blows and his madness, they put all their hope in moving downriver as fast as they could each day—surely they would find some human help soon, some white trader or settler or group of militia.

But war had emptied the Mississippi, and it flowed between banks of jungle fastness as though God had not yet thought to create human flesh or human spirit. The boat of angular, listless creatures drifted in an gray-green world that did not care when or how they might breathe their last. Their passing would be unremarked, unnoted, unsung, as though a tree sank into the ooze of a swamp, or a wormy fish floated belly up, or a bird lay with its feathers pressed against the forest floor, its yellow beak stretched wide in death.

Their human dimensions blurred into vague mists; will and words dissolved against the deaf forests, the blind river, the untouching sky. Sometimes Anne shook her fist at ancient hoary trees or the prehistoric ugliness of alligators and turtles; sometimes she turned to stone. Johnny and Issac sat quietly, tugging at their brittle hair, scattering its vivid orangeness on the deck. Jamie, gaunt, his neck loose like an old man's, moved his lips in prayer. Anne watched, remembering the plump, pink baby who, nuzzling her full breast, often had stopped to smile at her. Why, Annie, weren't you content with your blessings then? What goaded you? God? Pride? Greed? Her mind flicked away from any thought of Andrew.

Bird, she decided, would be the next to go. Veins showed blue through the delicate white of her face, and her eyes had the MacIllwain cast, as though she had already left them and gone around the bend into a beyond that only she could see. Marybett was a savage who snarled over scraps of cooked hide, bit other children's fingers, foraged alone, and brought nothing back to share. She crouched like a ferret, teeth bared, body curved, ready to strike, or at the smell of death—run.

James Young, shirt torn and flesh underneath slack and wrinkled, sprawled on the platform, the rudder loose in his hand. He muttered as he looked from one child to another, as though he counted them. Anne lowered her brows against the slant of the sun and studied him. No, it was more like he was choosing. He examined one body and then went on to another, dismissing some immediately, lingering over others, but always his gaze returned to Marybett. He licked his pink lips and the brown hairs that circled them.

Anne twitched as a spark of horror burst in her dry chest. Lust! Dear God! What is man? His cowardice is killing us, and he's looking for a place to put his member! His eyes swung to her, a smile touched his mouth; her bones rattled. He beckoned to her. She did not move. He motioned again. Still she hesitated. He pointed to the tomahawk in his belt. Her mind leaped. Had she misjudged him? Had he thought of some way to get food? Did he have a plan?

It took her a long time to gain her feet. The children, hearing her movements, turned to stare. The wind was raw, and they lay scattered in little clumps, each curled with a favorite partner: twins with twins; Sally Young with her little brother Daniel; Jo with Alex Glenn, who was five, the same as she; and Bird—now that Rabbie was gone—huddled with Jamie and Moe. Like cows or sheep who stop their grazing to watch the farmer pass, their expressions did not change, no thought brightened their eyes; some chewed their tongues. Marybett sat alone, her eyes glittering.

Anne picked her way among them, thinking, this isn't right, this isn't right. I must get the Bible out of the trunk. I wonder if Jamie can lift it. We'll take turns reading. We can't let go of our minds. Did I make a mark for today? It might be the Sabbath. I can't remember. Jim? Is it the Sabbath, Jim? By the time she reached the foot of the platform she had forgotten why she had walked in that direction; she looked stupidly up at James Young.

"There is only one way, Mrs. MacMeans." He took a drink from the cup beside him, and water dribbled into his beard.

She waited.

"The children."

She stared at him as he leaned his coffin face out over his knees, then shook her head—I don't understand.

"One of them would keep us all alive for days."

She caught at the gunwale. God is our refuge and our strength . . .

"I looked them over. Some are fatter than others."

. . . a very present help in trouble. . . .

283

"But perhaps it should be one of the frailer ones."

. . . Therefore we will not fear.

"It was stupid to bury those two of yours."

. . . the lord of hosts is with us.

". . . a lottery. We'll write the names and put them in a hat. There will be another hat, with all the slips blank except one. That one will have death written on it. The name of the child that comes just before the death slip . . ."

. . . the God of Jacob is our refuge.

"Of course, our names will be kept out."

"No."

"What do you mean, 'no'?"

"There will be only two names: yours and mine." She felt her cheeks grow warm with blood. Death had taken a human face.

"We have to care for the others."

"No. They are innocent. They did not ask to be brought here. If anyone is to die, it should be one of us."

"You're mad!"

"So be it." She walked off, leaving him kicking his heels against the side of the platform and cursing. In a voice that she did not recognize as her own, Anne gathered the children around her for worship. Afterward she cleaned them and brewed leaves for tea; then she ordered Marybett and Jamie to one sweep while she took the other. It seemed they made better progress, and that evening the children set their chins in bumps of determination as they climbed the bank to scavenge for food.

Anne found, however, that is was easier to control her body than her mind. Incapable of holding to a single resolve, it waved like a flag in crosswinds, occasionally hanging limp without a flutter. One moment she thought of plunging a knife into her own heart and letting her children feed off her body; the next she would decide to push James Young overboard and be rid of his evil forever. Then in the night she would remember the Bible story of women cooking and eating their children in starving times and wonder if perhaps he was right after all. Wasn't a lottery God's way? But whatever she concluded in darkness, in the morning she would look at the children and think, No, it can never be. Not the children.

For three days she continued her chores, willing herself to believe that help must be around the next bend. No? Well, then the next—or the next. Perhaps on the other side of that island. But her eyes could not avoid the sight of her own arms, scrawny and scaly as chicken legs, and the puffy bellies of the children, and she knew the point of no return was near.

She called Bird to her. "You knew when David Pegon died. You knew your father hadn't. Will you feel it when we—when we are past recovery?"

"I don't know." Bird rocked back and forth, chewing on the ends of her long black hair. "If I do, I'll tell you."

The air next morning was misty and cold, and Anne delayed leaving her warm nest with the twins and Bird. She procrastinated, wondering if anyone had gathered dry sticks the night before. Maybe it didn't matter, maybe . . .

"Minnie," Bird whispered. "Today."

"Today," Anne repeated.

"It feels like today is the last day. You asked me to tell you. I'm cold."

"Yes," Anne said. "Help me up."

Over breakfast tea James Young boasted about the lottery, saying that it would be soon, making sure the little ones knew that they, being of the least use, would be the first to be killed for food. No one looked at each other; no one spoke during the launching; they floated on the river as dumb as dead logs.

Jamie was holding the rudder when he spotted the bears on the island. Without a gesture or a word to anyone, he shifted the course of the boat and in a minute they bumped gently onto a long, very broad sand beach. "Haul her bow up, Moe!" Jamie called. "I saw bear right over there!" His cheeks cracked in a triumphant grin.

"Stay where you are, Moe!" James Young shouted. "I'm not using up my strength going after bear some crazy boy thinks he saw. Put this boat back in the channel."

Everyone stared in disbelief. Several voices repeated that Jamie had seen bear. Of course, he had to go after it. He was the only one strong enough to hold a rifle and track the animals, get close enough for a shot. The big man waved his arms in their gaping faces and shouted three times that he was not setting one foot off the boat.

Jamie got Andrew's rifle, powder horn, and shot bag. "Come on, Moe. We'll get one."

Moe reached for his father's gun, but James Young clamped his foot on it. "Please, Father," Moe begged.

James Young cuffed him across the side of the head, and he fell to the deck, too weak to rise. Jamie, his face splotched with anger, climbed over the gunwale and fixed the boat's tie line to a stump.

"Get back here, boy."

Jamie picked up his rifle. "I'm going after the bear."

His uncle rammed a wadded ball down the barrel of his gun and poured powder in the pan. "Go on. Start walking, boy. I want an excuse to shoot you. There's a lot of meat on your bones."

Jamie's lips quivered, and he looked at his mother. Anne stood as though in a trance, her face shrunken, her hands limp at her sides, thinking he was my hope, my Jim. Jamie straightened his shoulders and slowly and deliberately turned his back. James Young raised the rifle to his cheek. Jamie, his bare feet slewing in the sand, took one step and then another. Nothing happened. All the way across the rods of empty beach he walked alone, the weight of the gun pulling down his left side, his right hand hanging crooked, his feet leaving puddles of darkness across the bright sand.

James Young set his rifle against the gunwale and rubbed his fingers as though relieving a cramp; the others looked quickly away, squatted in twos, and began peeling dead skin from their hands or sucking their thumbs. Only Marybett kept staring, her eyes twin rocks of jade.

They hunkered, shivering when the pale November sun disappeared behind a cloud, expanding when it returned. Their ears, cocked for the sound of a rifle, heard only the ceaseless slap of the muddy river and the throaty rasp of ravens over the island trees. Their hope had blown like silky milk-weed seeds into the woods with Jamie while they remained—gray, twisted, empty pods.

James Young's boots thumped loudly on the oaken boards as he crossed to the cabin and threw aside the hanging; next came the scratch of a quill pen. In the strokes and pauses, those outside could hear what was being written: Daniel Young . . . Josephine Young . . . Alexander Glenn . . . John MacMeans . . . Issac MacMeans . . . DEATH. Then the sounds of folding, tearing, folding again. The twins, Sarah and Susan, sniffled and shook.

When James Young emerged, he held Andrew's floppy river hat in one hand, Margery's bonnet in the other; he set them down on the deck, and the squares of white that lay inside shimmered to life in the glare of the sun. The thin necks of the children held their heads at odd angles.

James Young pointed to Andrew's hat. "The names of the five youngest are in here. That's Daniel, Jo, Johnny, Issac, and Geneva's Alex. In the bonnet are four blank slips and one"—he chomped out the words—"with Death written on it." His eyes

286

made a circuit of the faces, stopping on the sobbing twins. "Hush your bawling and get over here. You'll do the drawing. Sit next to Aunt Anne. She'll be the one reading out the names." He strutted and fluffed the edges of his beard. Everyone lowered their eyes.

Sarah and Susan, their thin legs showing through their threadbare skirts, hunched themselves toward the center of the circle. James Young's foot nudged the hats until they sat in front of Anne; his boot tapped Sarah's rear. "Stop your sniveling and draw."

The bones of the child's hand were stark, the paper whiter yet; Anne's numb fingers dropped the thing in her lap. It lay there like an eye focused on her eyes; Anne's lips peeled back from her teeth. It fluttered, half opening itself. Pale horse, pale rider. What choice did she have? With heavy clumsiness she reached for the paper.

"Read it!" James Young roared.

"John MacMeans."

Johnny, lanky and disconnected as Andrew had been, got to his feet; his hair was an orange wire brush around his long, freckled, and solemn face; his eyes were green with dashes of blue. He stood quietly; only his right hand flinched when the second slip was drawn and passed to his mother. She turned it over and over.

"Blank. It's blank," she said.

Johnny sat down and put his arm around his brother. Issac laid his head against his shoulder, and tears ran from beneath his lashes. Anne's heart lurched. Issac! And Abraham bound Issac his son and laid him on the altar . . . and took his knife to slay his son. No!

The next paper was in her hand, and she read it with soot in her voice. "Alexander Glenn." Alex, the sturdiest, the fairest of all the children, stood facing her. Tommy, Tommy. How often he had sheltered her, protected her? Kill the only part that remained of him? Of Jim? She clenched her fist and raised her head; a movement far off by the edge of the woods caught her eye. Sun glinted off a rifle barrel. She peered, squinted. The small, distant figure of Jamie sat huddled on a log. Her fists dropped open. He had failed. There would be no meat. Nothing to eat. Her head felt light. Thy will be done. She opened the paper. "It's blank."

Her hand darted to grab the next slip from Sarah. "Josephine Young." Was that a noise? Again she raised her head. A sound from the forest? She strained, waiting. Nothing.

Jo knelt with the sun bouncing off the tilt of her tiny, peeled nose, her eyes brown and scared as her mother's had been. Anne opened the paper. "Death," she said quietly.

Jo looked about wildly, starting this way and that. She reached for her older sister Sally, but she stepped back. They all stepped back, and Jo was left alone in the middle of a circle of children. Farmer in the dell. Why don't they clap their hands and sing? Anne thought. The farmer in the dell, the farmer in the dell, hi ho the merry oh . . . the farmer in the dell. Farmer . . . wife . . . child . . . cat . . . rat . . . cheese. The cheese stands alone, hi ho the merry oh, the cheese stands alone. We all pound the cheese, we all pound the cheese . . .

Jo's right hand clutched her left, then her left hand her right as though they were two people comforting each other; her eyes had swelled to an enormous size.

James Young lifted the tomahawk out of his belt.

With the squealing cry of a frightened mouse, Jo dove head down between her sisters, scrabbled over the gunwale, and jumped for shore. Her tiny body splashed into the water; then she was up, wobbling across the sand. "Will you kill me, Father? Will you kill me?"

James Young swung one leg over the gunwale.

"No," Anne said. She got to her feet. "No, Mr. Young, you won't kill that child."

He turned, his eyes white stones under the jungly bush of his brows. "You've said 'no' to me for the last time, Sister."

"She's an innocent child!" Anne shook all over. "Kill her and we all are doomed!"

"You're mad!"

"You pretend it's God's will, but it's not!"

"So Anne MacMeans decides God's will, eh? Well, I would kill one. You would kill them all. Which do you think is the greater sin?"

Jo had crawled under the roots of a fallen tree and was digging her way into the sand.

James Young swung his other leg over the side. "You're weak. The weaker vessel. That's why God gave men rule over you. Men have the strength to do what must be done."

"No!" Anne lunged and grabbed his shirt; the cloth gave way in her hands. He raised his arm to strike her. "Wait. Wait. You don't understand. I hear noises in the woods." She babbled on, believing her lies, pleading for just one more day. "Help is very near. I feel it. Please wait."

He whirled away from Anne and drove his tomahawk into the sand. "Why did it have to be her? The scrawniest one of the lot. Why couldn't it have been the Glenn boy? He's got enough meat on him to last a week. We'll have another drawing in the morning." He scooped up his tomahawk and shook it at Jo. "And leave that one out of it. She isn't worth the strength it would take me to kill her."

Yanking Jo out from under the log, he held her by the back of the dress and shook her. "Whiny brat. Just like her mother. Always whining." Jo shrieked, and he threw her as far as he could. She landed with a soft plop, like a possum shot out of a tree. Moe ran to her and sat cradling her in his arms.

James Young leaned over the gunwale and grabbed Anne's shoulder. "And I don't want any more smart talk out of you. I'm in charge of doing what's best for everyone. Do you hear me?"

"You've never done anything except what was good for James Young!"

He laughed, and the rancid odor from his stomach rolled into her face. "You don't know the half of it, Sister. Remember Philadelphia? Remember you bleating like a sheep with a lamb stuck halfway out of your twat? You thought I took pity on you, didn't you? Well, you were wrong. I'd been watching for a long time, waiting my chance to bleed a little gold from Dr. MacKnight. That how I made my living, Mrs. MacMeans. Scandal, blackmailing the gentry." He punched her shoulder. "I got nearly a hundred pounds out of little Hugh MacKnight by writing him pleading letters in your name. Didn't know that either, did you? Always thought you were so smart, while it was me getting the better of you all the time. Bitch."

Anne raised her fist, and with every ounce of strength she had, whammed it across the side of his face.

"Stop it!" Marybett screamed. She stomped on the platform, her ragged green dress bouncing with fury. "Listen! Stop it! Listen!"

Everyone cocked their heads.

"I don't hear nothing!" James Young shouted.

"Wait! Wait! Listen! I heard a dog bark."

It came again: the deep-throated bay of a hunting dog. A rifle cracked and the echo of it spun across the water.

"It's Jamie!" Moe yelled. "He's got something."

They listened again. Two dogs barked, and a voice called to them. It was not Jamie. It was a man's voice—an Indian voice. Jamie lurched across the beach, the stock of Andrew's gun dragging behind him.

"Get ready to shove off!" James Young cried. "Jo, get your worthless self on this boat. Right now!"

Jamie leaned against the gunwale, panting. "It's an Indian hunting."

"Just one?" Anne asked.

"I don't know. Shall I call out?"

"Yes."

Jamie's "Hellooooooo" disappeared into the far willows that edged the broad slope of sand.

No one answered.

Marybett yelled, "Help! We need help! Food! Food!"

"Is anybody there?" Anne called.

The silence changed from emptiness to someone watching and not answering—a sham silence, perhaps a trick. They stared at each other, eyes darting in uneasiness.

"Shove off!" James Young cried, wrestling the rope from the stump. He and Jamie put their shoulders against the gunwale and pushed.

"Wait!" Anne cried. "Maybe—"

The blow from James Young's fist knocked her clear across the deck and into the side of the cabin.

Anne's spirit circled above her senseless body, then flew off to Breakfast Hill. Zac roared through the door, cried "Annie!," and tossed her above his head. She looked down into the face of her father; his voice boomed: "Yea, though I walk through the valley of the shadow of death I will fear no evil. . . . Thou preparest a table before me in the presence of mine enemies. . . ."

The white tablecloth sparkled in the sunlight, and Esther in her red dress brought greens from the field, and Tommy and Rhoda and all the girls waded across the creek. Laughter, the crackle of fire, the smell of dripping fat danced around their heads. Jesus stood by the table, scrubbing a red stain from the tablecloth between his knuckles, and the children frolicked with hunks of roasted meat in their hands. Jim shouted, "Ho, Annie!" His stride was long, his smile wide; she ran, and her feet left the ground; she floated upward. "No! Please let me stay!"

Elves and children danced on their toes. "Minnie! Minnie!" Meat juice streaked their small chins.

"Minnie! Minnie!"

"Leave me alone. I want to stay. Jim, help me!"

"Minnie, you're dreaming. Wake up."

She lay in the crook of Jamie's arm with something sweet pressed against her lips. She tested it with her tongue. Meat! Her eyes flew open. Jamie's face filled with light. She blinked. Jesus?

Gently his crooked fingers eased the piece of meat into her mouth. "Don't swallow. Suck the good out."

She coughed as the juice hit the back of her throat and Jamie held a cup to her lips. She gulped water, then leaned back, blissfully chewing and swallowing. Shutting her eyes again, she waited for heaven to unfold.

Jamie spoke; she tried hard to listen, but his voice kept breaking into trickles of laughter.

Johnny piped, "Let me tell. Let me tell." He put his small hands on either side of her face. "It was an Indian hunting on the island. With his wife and baby. He followed us in his canoe and brought us a whole quarter of a bear!" He snuggled his face into her neck, hugging her. "So Uncle James can't kill any of us now. We have bear meat instead."

Issac, chewing and dribbling blood, pushed himself under her other arm. "It's so good, isn't it, Minnie? And tomorrow he's going to get us more."

Johnny jumped up and pranced, the ragged edges of his britches flying about his knees. "He lifted me over his head with one arm."

Anne shook her head. Heaven was going to have to wait. Imagine—an Indian, an enemy . . . She sighed in wonder. Thou anointist my head with oil, my cup runneth over; Surely goodness and mercy . . . Jamie put another piece of meat in her mouth; her breastbone hurt from the strong hammer of her heart. "I want to thank the hunter."

"I'll get him!" Issac was off, his spindly legs weaving across the deck. A fire burned on the high bank, and a ring of shapes surrounded it. "Tell the children to eat slowly, Jamie. Very slowly, or they'll get sick and maybe die."

He laughed. "I tried, but it didn't do much good. The Indian's squaw made them listen, though." He added with awe, "She's beautiful, Minnie. So beautiful."

She, not the hunter, came and kneeled by Anne. Mahogany skin, flaring cheekbones, eyes of midsummer night, and a cap of black sheep's wool for hair. Childlike, Anne stroked the firm African-Cherokee flesh. The woman bathed her, bound her bruises in poultices, and washed a clean skirt and vest for her to wear; she untangled her hair, fed her broth, sang to her while her papoose nursed, and in the night she shared her breasts.

Before the mists of morning had blown away, the woman's round buttocks disappeared into her husband's canoe. When Anne cried out, the woman signaled that they were going to hunt and would wait for them downriver.

At noon the canoe emerged from the lee of an island and pulled alongside the flatboat; the woman leaned over the bow and motioned to Anne. Handing her a bear cub the size of a house cat, she said—in a mixture of English, Iroquois and Cherokee—"It was all we could find. The hunting is very poor. My husband says we must go back to our village."

Anne clutched the woman's arm. Take us! Please! The black, curly head shook sadly. Too many mouths. But—she leaned close to Anne's ear—wrapped in the leaves with the cub is a knife with a very long point. If the cannibal man makes trouble for you, strike upward here. She poked Anne just below her breastbone. A woman must know these things and be strong. She touched her forehead to Anne's. My heart will beat within you and give you courage. Anne thought of Molly Todd's pistol and kissed the soft, full cheek.

In the dark of the cabin Anne took the knife with the horn handle and the stiletto blade, wrapped it in a cloth, and placed it in her apron pouch; she hid the cub from James Young. That evening she cooked it, divided it into forty-two pieces, gave each person one, and locked the rest away in the drawer of her writing desk. Life was assured for three more days.

The day of feasting had sharpened their sensibilities. They woke with hurting bellies and irritated thoughts; quarrels broke out among the children, and James Young stomped about, cuffing and cursing. A driving rain forced them to land by midday, and Anne gathered the children under the canvas—they had no candles or oil to light the cabin—and tried to soothe tempers by reading Bible stories, but still they teased each other and pinched.

For three days, while the rain poured down and bits of bear cub simmered, Anne told stories as though she might never get another chance to share what she knew. Her tongue marched many forms across the soaked oak deck: strapping stark Celts with chalked hair; Druid priests; shining Romans on Hadrian's wall; stinging hornet ships of Norsemen and Danes; King Duncan and Macbeth; icy-hearted Normans who made Law the king; the golden Alexanders of Scotland; the hero William Wallace; the battle of Braxton Moor called Fodden, where ten thousand Scots, every noble, and King

James himself died at the hands of the English; and Mary, Queen of Scots. She told of Grannie Watt, Bartholomew Black MacKnight, the speech of Jim Glenn to the Pennsylvania Assembly, and the great bell's inscription.

Bird recited her Uncle Hugh's letters, Jamie the Declaration of Independence, Johnny and Issac the story of Uncle Zac at Vincennes. Moe began to speak of Fort Jefferson, but when he came to his mother's name, he stopped. On the platform above them James Young endlessly wiped his fingers around the inside of the Killyleagh kettle, sucked them, and belched.

"Someday," Anne said softly, "tales will be told about Fort Jefferson."

"Are we heroes, Minnie?" Issac piped.

A bark of a laugh jolted Anne's throat, and she stroked his head. "It's time someone told the tale of King Robert of Bruce and his spider."

The following morning Anne woke to the scritch, scritch of a whetstone on steel. Her teeth jangled, and the hairs rose on the back of her neck. She had slept on deck, preferring it to the mildewing feather mattress, and about her lay bundles of sleeping children, but James Young's platform was empty.

Marybett's sharp animal face appeared over the gunwale; quicker than the flash of a weasel, she was at Anne's side. "Uncle James is sharpening his tomahawk."

Anne stared dumbly at the dew and scratches that marked her daughter's temples and cheeks. How much does she find to eat? she wondered. Marybett shook her shoulder. "Wake up! He's planning on killing a child every three days. He told me he'd start right now if it weren't for soiling the bedclothes!"

Anne couldn't get her mind to focus; she asked Marybett for a cup of water, and after she had drunk, asked, "How will he choose?"

"He says he's just going to start with the fattest young one. 'The one most like a bear cub,' he said. He was laughing."

"That would be Alex Glenn."

"Mam, he wants to. He really wants to do it." Horror had twisted Marybett's features out of animal indifference back into human shape.

Anne dipped her fingers in the cup of water and wiped the overnight crust from her lips. Marybett was not a savage; savages kill for pleasure. Anne touched the dagger lying hard on her belly. Wisps of thought created a cloud picture; she could not see it clearly.

"Minnie! Don't just lie there. What are we going to do?" Anne sat up and showed Marybett the stiletto.

"Give it to me." Marybett put out her hand—slender, long, ribbed with bone and blue veins. Anne gaped; it could have been her own. Why had she never noticed the likeness before? "Give it to me," Marybett repeated. Anne hesitated. "He knows I'll use it on him. He'll think you're all bluff and just twist it out of your hand and throw it out into the river. Please, Minnie. He's afraid of me. I see him watching me, and he jumps when I move. He knows I'd rip him open and carve out his heart quick as a hungry . . ." She stopped, her chest rising and falling in shallow pants.

Anne got to her knees and then her feet. Marybett grabbed her wrist. "Give it to me! Look what happened when you slapped him. He knocked you clear across the deck, almost killed you."

Anne put the stiletto back in her apron pouch. "James Young is my responsibility." She wanted to pat that familiar hand, reassure her daughter, but instead she said, "Come with me, will you?"

Marybett threw up her head. "You haven't got the courage!"

How many times, Annie, did you call your own mother a coward? She wet her lips with her tongue. "Courage, my daughter, is merely fear that has said its prayers." The picture was very clear in her mind now.

James Young sat a few rods up the beach, his legs spread around a tiny fire, the whetstone and tomahawk in his hands. He looked up as they approached, and he said cheerfully, "No lottery this time, Mrs. MacMeans. We'll start with Alex Glenn. He's good for three days."

Anne walked deliberately toward him, stopping exactly an arm's length away. With one hand in her pouch she said, "You're a monster."

"Hey, Sister. What's got your back up? Need a little dunking in the river to make you talk more respectful?"

Anne spit in the triangle between his crotch and the fire.

Roaring in surprise, he clumsily started to rise. By the time he had his feet under him, Anne had the point of the knife in the soft flesh under his breastbone. "Don't move! One move and I ram this all the way through to your gullet."

His hands stayed spread like a baby bird's wings, his mouth open like a round, blind beak.

"There'll be no killing, James Young. No killing of anyone, except maybe me of you."

His eyes glanced down at his tomahawk. Marybett scooped it up and slid behind him. The underbrush of his brows settled low; he swallowed and deepened his voice. "You wouldn't kill me, Anne. I know you too well to believe that. Your tongue is all brag and no—"

She drove the knife in a full inch. He rose on his toes, and wind rattled in his throat.

"Don't move, don't move." Blood ran over her hand. "I have many reasons to kill you, and God would bless me for it. Remember the springhouse?"

His jaws moved under his beard, and his mouth opened and shut; beads of sweat popped yellow from his brow.

"I want you to swear that you will never harm one hair of anyone on this boat. And if you break your word, I will kill you the next time you shut your eyes."

"And what if I kill you?"

"Marybett will guard me."

Drool ran from the corners of his pink, cracked lips. "Please. Take the knife out."

"No. It's all I can do to keep from ramming it home. I want your oath." His blood dripped from her elbow. She moved her left hand to her right wrist, as though to carry out her threat.

"All right! All right! But you can't kill me. Who would man the rudder?"

"Better God than the devil." She nudged the knife upward. He screamed. "I swear! I swear! Now, please. Please."

Anne didn't move; her blood thumped from her heart to her skull, her limbs had the power of steel. "I hate you. I hate you. You're a curse on the earth."

The trembling began in his outstretched hands, moved to his head, his legs; he fluttered like an aspen leaf in the wind. She wanted to kill him; they could eat James Young. "Mrs. MacMeans. I swear. I swear by the soul of my dead mother, I will harm no one on this boat. No one. Now, please!"

The flesh of his belly pressed around her hand. Would he fall on her? She stepped back and pulled out the knife.

James Young fell to his knees.

Chapter Twenty-three

December 1 (?) 1781. Just as we were putting to land yester-evening, we spied some Indians on the other shore. We thought, as the lepers at the gate of Samaria had, that it was but death at any rate, and we, with much difficulty, got over to them. Though they were hostile Indians, they spared our lives and supplied us with plenty of fresh bear's meat. After night they brought us more, but then they took from us our clothes, both bed and body clothes—except what we had on—our pewter knives and forks, and whatever they chose. They went off and we saw no more of them.

This morning (after we might have sung of mercy and judgment) God gave us a singularly marvelous dispensation of goodness! We met with the friendly and generous Capt. Barber, who is navigating up the river and some of the tributary streams for trading. He could not take us along, not let us have one of his men to hunt for us and help us with the boat because he is heavy loaded and has far to go. Yet with a tender open heart he has bestowed on us a whole bushel of biscuit, half a bushel of hominy and twelve quarts of rice. May the blessing of God follow him and his descendents to the latest days!

Capt. Barber has urged us to make all possible speed down the river that we might overtake two families who are moving down and hunting, saying that they will probably relieve us or take us along.

December 3 (?) We can make little exertion, so we float along often in great danger of being stove. Though we now have provisions to prevent starvation, we do not have the quantity or quality to recover our lost flesh or strength. We are a disconsolate, heartless and helpless company drifting south, still 450 miles from Natchez.

December 5 (?) Water got in the bed of Daniel, a son of James Young's who is about five years old. I was unable to remove him, and his father let him remain in the water till he was past recovery. He died the next day after he was removed. I am so weak that I can not turn my head on the pillow, but do it with my hands. Yet when up, I can walk about.

Dec 14 ? Thus we have floated for fourteen days . . .

Everyone on board the *Captain Andy* had had their moment of crying out to a log that they mistook for a canoe, or waving to shapes in dappled shore shade who never responded, or waking from a slumped dream and calling, "Voices! I hear voices!" So when Bird called, "There they are!" eleven pairs of eyes stared into the chilly December mists more willing to disbelieve than to believe.

Even when James Young turned the rudder and the children crawled to the gunwales and hung their heads over, opening and shutting their small hands in gestures of hello, Anne was unconvinced. Only when she saw the expression of incredulous horror on the fat faces of the two women hurrying to the water's edge did she know it was true. But she also knew from the way they lifted the limp children from the boat and laid their feet to the fire that these plump strangers thought they would not last the night. Over and over Anne said, "We'll be all right now," but the women were too busy bustling about and casting their faces heavenward, imploring God in foreign tongue to pay her words any heed.

With strength gathered from hot rice broth, Anne beckoned to the returning hunters; the men explained that they were English brothers Peter and William Manchester, who had married Spanish sisters from Natchez. "If I do not live . . ." Anne passed them a note that read: Hugh MacKnight, Philadelphia, Pennsylvania. They nodded.

At twilight, Juan, the son of Peter and Gayla Manchester, passed among them, administering the last rites of the Popish faith. When he came to Anne she tried to push him away, but misunderstanding, he solemnly told her how he had studied with the priests in New Orleans and that God would approve his giving the sacrament. Anne hoarsely rasped that God had ordained only three sacraments—baptism, marriage, and burial. The lean, dark face, bearded as Jesus' had been, bent close and with a sweet smile he opened his missal and began the rite. As the black Latin poured over her, Anne shut her eyes, determined to close her mind and keep out the devil's words, but the singsong slipped in and soothed her to sleep.

Whatever the cause—the resistance of Presbyterian souls to dying under the sway of the Romanish Pope, or the insistence on life that swarmed from the women's brown hands, or God's decision that his fiery furnace had indeed driven all dross from their hearts—everyone survived until morning. Encouraged, the women doubled their efforts—feeding, bathing, combing, warming, applying salves to the many open sores—until Anne felt that to die would have been a most ungracious, even unconscionable, act.

Four days later, on the Sabbath, Juan, who had medical as well as priestly skills, pronounced them out of danger, and a feast of bear and pumpkin was prepared. The children were lively, Anne walked without help, James Young swaggered. While marvelous smells rather than the pallid odor of rice broth steamed from the great kettle, everyone gathered on the grassy bank for worship. The Convenanters lined out a ragged psalm; Juan led chants and responses; and Jamie, weak but determined, rose to give the closing prayer. The words "Let us pray" were no more out of his mouth, however, before James Young shouldered him aside, saying that he was the head and would offer the thanks for their survival.

Jamie slumped by his mother and sisters and Anne said, "No matter, son, no matter. God knows," but as James Young's haughty tones assailed her ears, Anne's fingers closed like a hawk's talons on Marybett's arm. "If I should die, take the knife from my skirt. Never let him get his hands on the children. Never." She paused and with a thin smile added, "Of course, God may have his own vengeance in mind."

James Young, clothed in Peter's outfit of furry bearskins, stood wide-legged, his face turned up to the dull winter sky. "Without my firm hand on the rudder, without my patience and faith in you, our gracious Father, without my constant care for the little ones . . ."

Anne gasped, then swayed against Jamie's shoulder. What was he saying! She saw William Manchester nod and the women follow suit. Annie, you should have told them, you should have told them.

"Ceaselessly I strove, Oh Lord, to keep Thy trust . . ."

He's building a story. A story he can tell again and again—in Natchez, in New Orleans, in Pittsburgh. He will be the hero, and if you dare say he had refused to hunt, preferring to kill and eat his children, it will be you who is dubbed mad, deluded, covering some weakness of your own with lies about the man who saved you.

With every sentence he uttered, James Young grew more pleased and puffed. "And you, Lord, saw fit to give me the strength to wrest from a savage Cherokee meat that kept us alive for days. In spite of the murderous knife his squaw held at my belly I stood my ground and won food for the widowed and fatherless whom heaven had placed in my care. The red heathen so respected my fearlessness that he brought more meat the next day and offered me his squaw to bed, which gave me occasion to lecture him on Christian morals."

"May God strike you dead for your lies!" The words blared from Anne's mouth as she half crouched, one hand on Jamie's shoulder, the other on Marybett's. Anne's bonnet had fallen back, and her bald skull and naked, high cheekbones glowed yellow in the pale light; her neck stretched forward like an ancient turtle's.

James Young drew back, then settled himself on his wide bare feet and looked at her with mock pity. "You see, Lord. That was another of my trials. The only adult left alive with me went daft." He nodded his head sadly. "A pity. She was once a bonnie woman." He shrugged. "The typhoid made them all mad. My wife cast herself into the river, although I clung to her pleading—"

Growls rose from Anne and the angry children, who leaned forward on their hands, teeth bared. James Young blurted, "Amen!," whirled, and drove his long skinning knife into the bubbling kettle. On its curved tip he raised a great hunk of meat over his head. Juice dripped into his open mouth, splattered his beard, his hair. Howling with glee, he lifted his whole face up into it; his mustard teeth tore and ripped at the red heart of the meat. His throat moved in animal gulps as he swallowed, and the air rushed whistling through his nose; his foot pawed the earth, and his hips thrust forward. With his left hand he stuffed a quarter pumpkin steaming from the kettle into his mouth. He vomited and wiped his face with the edge of the black bear shirt he wore.

In the crook of one arm he stacked as much pumpkin as he could carry, laid a haunch of bear in the other, and trailing grease and blood, quick-stepped down the bank to the river's edge. There, sprawled on his belly, he slurped muddy water, then buried his face in the mound of food, and twisting, growling, pounding his hips, he ate and ate.

Three days later Anne took up her *Commonplace Book* and wrote: "On the first Sabbath after we joined the families, James Young (this cruel man, as I cannot help but calling him) ate such a meal of bear's meat stewed with pumpkins, that in an hour afterwards he was speechless. He was carried to bed, and lay almost without motion till the Wednesday morning following, when he breathed his last."

With dry eyes they earthed James Young. Jamie read the burial scripture, and Anne added words for the commitment of wee Daniel's body, which his father simply had dropped over the side of the boat. The remaining Young children stared blankly at the sheet damp with drizzle and mud that contained their father, but when they once more sat in the shelter of boughs by a blazing fire they chattered like giddy magpies. Jo, snuggled in Anne's lap, looked up and said, "I'm so glad I didn't get et." Anne smoothed her brown hair. It was over, over at last.

It was decided that Moe, Susan, Sarah, Sally, Jo, and Alex would return to the Manchester plantation on Lake Chicot and that Gayla and Peter would load the trading furs and tobacco on the *Captain Andy* and take the MacMeans with them to Natchez. Anne gave her assent, but from then on took little heed of anything; in their deplorable condition it seemed unlikely that any of them would recover.

Natchez squatted in the heart of the Mississippi wilderness, 180 miles south of James Young's grave, 360 miles north of New Orleans. Twenty houses, some frame, most log, snuggled in the pine and cane under the red-brown bluff that rose 200 feet above the limpid curve of the river; the trading posts of Captain Barber; Captain Blomart, a half-pay British officer; James Willing, a Philadelphia adventurer; and Hanchett and Newman rimmed the landing. The sagging fort, which the French had built and named Roselie, now flew the gold and red flag of Spain. French, Spaniards, British (both loyalists and rebels), black slaves, Choctaws, Chickasaws, and the sun-worshiping Natchez Indians—a total population of several thousand—lived on the lands around Natchez, where in the rich black mold cane grew 20 to 40 feet tall, magnolia trees 100, and Spanish grandees had begun building mansions with the profits from tobacco and indigo.

Enormous live oaks topped the river bluff, and a long red road slashed diagonally down through the vines of green kudzu; near the bottom, houses sat cheek by jowl, their backs wedged against the bank, their pleasant front faces supported on necks of flat stones. Women sat by the bare, wide windows, gazing on the tranquil crescent of the silver-and gold-threaded river, waiting for whatever might appear; only on the dampest winter days were the blinds closed. The women spun by the windows, ate by the windows, and gossiped from them, always hoping to be the first to cry, "Boat coming!" and start heads popping up and down along the red-dirt road.

The river had remained empty in the fall of 1781, and the coming of the *Captain Andy* caused a tumult. Women clapped bonnets on their heads and shawls about their shoulders, clattered across their porches, across the wharf. Some cried out it was surely the Manchesters. But they had never come for winter trading in a flatboat before. And who were those children? More refugees from Fort Jefferson? After four months? Merciful God! They crossed themselves, muttered prayers, elbowed each other in their haste to scurry home to heat soup, stir up biscuits, grab quilts to cover those scarecrow bodies. By the time the *Captain Andy* docked, Natchez was ready to receive the orphans and then they discovered they were not orphans—not quite yet.

In a blanket Peter and Juan carried the still white frame of Anne MacMeans up the road, then off onto a winding, vine-choked path that led to the one-room house where Gayla and Maria Saitta had been born and raised. Squeezed into the bank and almost obscured by long-needled pines and drooping wisteria, the deserted house was raw with cold and thick with aged damp. A bevy of women laid a fire, banged open shutters that fell off rotten leather hinges, swept, warmed blankets to spread on the rope bed, and then when the emaciated woman was laid on them, surrounded her with warm stones and piled on buffalo furs. Like a general after a battle, Gayla dismissed her troops, saying that God had placed great trust in her by giving her this mother of five to restore to health. "You may all pray," she told them, "but the miracle of her living will go as a star in my heavenly crown. You may bring soup and bread and candles, but come quietly, and I will ask that your time in purgatory be shortened."

The women departed on tiptoes, Juan and Peter going with them. Anne stared through the frame of hastily torn honeysuckle vines at a strong blue sky that did not move, from a bed that did not roll with swells or pitch with wind or even drift. The children are safe, the children are safe. Go to sleep now, Anne. The voice sounded like her long-ago mother's. Was she going to die? It's all right, Annie, go to sleep. The voice faded and darkness closed about her until she lay like a child at night in a room where only the faint flicker of a candle shows under a door that is closed.

Gray winter rain fell on the gray river, pressed down the broad leaves of the trees, trailed tendrils of vines in gullies of mud. The north wind followed, freezing raindrops on oaken trunks, on crackling earth, on wooden roof shingles; it squeezed past the wattle-stick chimney and through the straw-stuffed chinks of the flimsy Saitta house and rattled Anne with shivers, shaking her into awareness of consciousness and unconsciousness. Going down she was a pebble tossed into water, weaving through shades of murk and green, then resting ever so lightly on a bed of silt; waking was a swell that raised the pebble to almost break the surface, almost see the sun, almost feel the air, almost know that Gayla prayed . . . Padre neustro que estás en los cielos, santificada sea tu nombre. Verga tu reino . . .

Spring burst from the ice in a cantilena of blossoms and songbirds, green growth, and human chattering as the people of Natchez shed their woolens and scraped their shovels. Anne's eyelids fluttered in the new warmth of the east sun. Rafters. Eaves. Honeysuckle. Sky. Gayla's black, caring eyes. The click of the beads. Water wetting her lips. The smell of breasts and tobacco. Anne struggled. We must get the boat to the river, tend the sweeps, cook the hides; Rabbie is crying and Annilea . . . She opened her mouth and spoke. "The children?"

"Each one fatter than the next."

"I must—"

"You must nothing. You are my excuse for a good long stay in my town. Lake Chicot has only swamp creatures and my bossy sister for company."

"But—"

"Hush. What is there for you to do, my dearie? There is not even a call for you to pray. My friends light candles, the English ring little bells." She shrugged. "God knows what the French do."

Anne listened. True. No children moaned with hunger, no boots raged on the cabin roof, no gators bellowed; the sheets that covered her chin smelled of sunshine. She spread and sagged, like a roped bundle whose knots are being undone, and finally loosed; her will escaped in a whistling sigh. There was no need to care.

Rosary beads resumed their click . . . Dios to salve, Maria llena de gracia . . . The first faint flush of color appeared in Anne's hands and feet.

Each day the sun's journey across the sky lengthened; Mississippi grew weighted and lush. Anne became sensible of hunger, the tickle of flies on her skin, the breath of Gayla's kiss, the drag of the bedclothes on her shins, but her mind remained a kaleidoscope of colored bits—even her children did not fit. They came and went: Marybett usually with Juan; the twins embarrassed and pushing each other; Jamie pale with pain; and Bird, who would plunk herself down on the edge of her mother's bed and say, "Auntie Gayla, best you hurry to the store. Fresh gossip has come in."

She would stroke her mother's hand while Gayla's wide hips squeezed out the doorway and then they would listen to the mockingbird and watch the April sun progress across the bedspread. Bird often read, but Anne could make no sense of the words. Gayla had said her heart was dead, and Anne believed it was true. God had not kept his word: He had given her more than she could bear, and she longed for the solitude of some desert place.

Beyond her window, revolution stirred.

In 1763 the French had surrendered Natchez to the British, then it had passed to Spain. For two years British settlers, the majority group in Natchez, had chafed under the rule of Captain de la Veillebeuvre and the seventy-six Spanish soldiers quartered at Fort Roselie. John Blomart, feeling certain that this summer of '82 would see the English forces from Pensacola crossing the Gulf of Mexico and coming up the Mississippi, organized a rebellion.

His anticipated quick coup failed—some Negroes warned de la Veillebeuvre of the coming attack—and Blomart was forced to set up a siege. The Widow Truly, who lived just below Gayla on the town road, reinforced her home as a blockhouse, and there Blomart's force of two hundred settlers, Indians, and *banditti* milled about in a holiday free-for-all. Twelve days later the Spaniards, convinced by a forged letter that the fort was mined, surrendered. Blomart's militia raised the Union Jack and marched the prisoners to the Widow Truly's yard; there they took their revenge.

Anne, rocking in the breeze on Gayla's vine-roofed porch, shrugged at the noise of beatings, whoops, laughter, and screams and continued counting the creaks of the rockers: one hundred forty one, one hundred forty two . . . That men were base and evil did not surprise her, and furthermore it did not concern her.

John Willing tromped up the path and with an arrogant,

rakish air cocked his elbows on the edge of the porch boards. One hundred fifty-one . . .

Gayla bumped her huge self through the doorway and, arms thrashing and face black with anger, smothered John in Spanish oaths. "Beasts! Only beasts would torture so!"

John grinned. "Turnabout is fair play, Mrs. Manchester."

"And Jesus, Mary, and Joseph help you when we get hold of the guns again."

"You won't."

"You are thinking you are so smart. One Spanish gunboat from New Orleans, and pow!" She threw her sweat-shined arms in the air. "Your rusty French cannon will fall like toys into the river. Splat! Splat! Splat!"

"You got it mixed up, Gayla. Blomart's the Tory looking south for Campbell and the British to come. I'm the American looking north for George Rogers Clark."

Anne's mind clicked another turn: Flaming arrows crossed the night sky, and Mr. Music hacked and hacked at the Indian youth; a child was on fire, running; a soldier was tearing at his face. Andrew lay crumpled beside her. "Deserted is just what I mean! Clark has left us here to die while he wins more glory and more land for himself at Detroit."

Anne opened her mouth. "Don't wait for him, Mister Willing. Don't ever wait for George Rogers Clark. He won't come. He never comes."

"What make you so sure, lady?"

She leaned forward to the tips of her rocker, and blood came to her face. "Because I waited for him. Me and all my family. We waited all summer, and he never came back." The skin of her hands tingled, and she shook them; a fine sweat wet her upper lip. "He told us to come to Mississippi with him." Her voice burned her throat. "Told us how friendly the Indians were, how well he would protect us." Her thin hips rode the edge of her rocker. "Promises! Empty promises! He didn't care one whit about us, only his precious Louisville, his wonderful, stinking Kentucky! Well, I say to hell with George Rogers Clark!"

Gayla jiggled with glee. "Annie, Annie, you are coming to life! Keep it up. Give it to him, Annie!"

John leaped to the porch and yelled in Anne's face, "He's the greatest hero in America!"

Anne pushed him away and rose. "Hero! After we saved his fort by holding off a thousand Indians, he sent a few barrels of corn. A few barrels of corn!"

John shouted back, Anne answered, and Gayla cheered every rise in Anne's voice. Finally John jumped back into the dust, whirled, and said, "I'll wager, lady, you were never anywhere near Fort Jefferson!"

Anne turned to Gayla. "I was. I know I was. It's the truth!"

Gayla wrapped her wet, fleshy arms around her. "It is the truth. Everything is as you say it is." She kissed Anne, then held her at arm's length. "The lock on your mind has been smashed," and crossing herself, added, "Now please God, the door will stay open and the breezes blow through."

Neither the American Colonel Clark nor the British Colonel Campbell ever arrived at Natchez; the Spanish retook the fort, and the town went to sleep in the summer sun. Anne, ghost white in the deep shade of the porch, rocked and fanned, turning her head only when her children came.

The nine-year-old twins, helpers on Polly Chamberlain's mail boat, told wild tales with the bounce and swagger of rivermen. Jamie folded his thin body against the house and sat with his Bible, his face pensive, handsome, old beyond his years. Bird boarded and worked at Captain Barber's store, but evenings she sat by the rocker, reading *Tom Jones* aloud until the light was gone, then helped her mother to bed and sang her to sleep.

The women in the windows would watch for the wistful slip of a girl in her gunnysack dress who trailed her bare toes in the twilight dust of the road and, holding out a fiddle, call for her to play. The first pull of the bow would carry Bird to the roof of the *Captain Andy*, where Joe Camp's fiddle flashed and her laughing father and handsome mother clasped hands, ready to jig by the light of the rushes. And her arm would slow and the women weep as notes of heartbreak, sweet, wild, and clear, soared above the cicada's clamor and pierced the river's blackness, seeking those who would never hear.

One breathless, jungly morning, when Gayla was off fishing for cray, Marybett arrived holding Juan's hand; they stood before Anne in the puffy dirt below the porch. Marybett said that they were going to be married and live on Lake Chicot. Anne blinked at the boneless young man with the swarthy skin and dark, dreamy eyes, at the gold cross on the black hairs of his chest.

"Where is David Pegon?" she asked, or perhaps she didn't, for no one replied.

Jamie handed her water; Anne sipped it and said, "You'll be a Papist."

"Yes, Mother."

Marybett's eyes slipped and quivered like clouds reflected in the river. Perhaps the girl had drowned.

"Do we have your blessing, Mother?" She moved her hand, fine-boned, blue-veined, to Juan's shoulder, and Anne heard Reverend MacMillan's voice. "Do you Anne Aiken Mac-Knight, take this man William MacIllwain Glenn . . ."

"Yes," Anne said. "Yes."

"Thank you, Mrs. MacMeans," Juan said. "There will be a child soon."

Anne nodded; the rocker creaked. The two walked away into the shimmer of the green kudzu. Jim took her hand.

The next morning Anne told Gayla she was going home.

"Home?" Gayla's mouth formed a well between the mounds of her brown, earthy cheeks.

Anne nodded. "Home. Where are my goods?"

"In the shed. But I don't think—"

Anne climbed stiffly off the porch, Gayla right behind her. She lifted the deerskin and reeled at the smell of rot.

"The mildew can be wiped off," Gayla began.

Anne turned away from broken hinges, water stains, and spreading joints. All the things they had so painfully lugged from the high bank to the boat . . . the writing desk with the Queen Anne legs . . . "The *Captain Andy?*" she asked.

"Sold for lumber."

"I'll see about passage," Anne said and started down the path.

"Wait! Wait!" Gayla called. "Your bonnet." Anne touched the fuzz on her head; it always bewildered her to remember that her hair was gone.

Gayla clapped Margery's old bonnet on her and tied the bow under her chin. "Don't worry about your hair, dearie. It is growing in white as the wool of a sheep. When it gets a little length you'll be the most beautiful woman in Natchez, and then we'll see about a husband for you."

Anne frowned and shook her head. "I'm going home."

"Oh, yes, I forgot," Gayla said putting her arm around her waist.

Anne had to stop and rest every few yards, and the sun was high by the time they reached Captain Barber's store.

"Light yourself here in the shade on the stoop and I will fetch Bird," Gayla bubbled. "She will be tickled to death to see her minnie in town." Her fat, damp hands fixed Anne's dry, thin ones in her lap, then settled her skirts over her rickety shoes.

Natchez dozed under a blanket of dust. Hogs lay on their sides, their bellies a naked pink; lop-eared dogs sniffed and shuffled; chickens banged their beaks against the boards of the porch; bees droned a soporific lullaby. Inside the store, voices rose and fell. Anne's head nodded in hazy sleep, then jerked up as a shout of laughter came from the wharf. Three men squatted in the shadow of a high-sided *bateau*, passing a jug, fanning themselves with floppy rivermen's hats, and sticking their knives into grasshoppers. Anne rose. They would know the price of the passage.

Her shoes tapped on the yellow pine boards of the wharf; the men turned, wiping their mouths with the back of their hairy hands. Anne heard her name whispered and then "typhoid" and "Fort Jefferson." Their eyes were rudely curious, as though a freak approached them. They chewed and spat.

"How-do." Her voice croaked; she coughed behind her hand and tried again. A man with a grizzled white chin tipped his hat, but none rose from his haunches. "I'd like to book passage to Pittsburgh."

The red-faced man hooted; the young one snickered and elbowed the oldest one, who asked, "Was you thinking of upriver or around by the eastern shore?"

"Whichever is quicker." Her voice was Philadelphia prim. "I reckon you're prepared to pay?"

Her chin shot up. "I am." The men ducked their smiles, and the young man made crazy circling motions beside his ear. Do they think me daft? she wondered. "What would be the cost for myself and . . . four children?"

"Ain't no trade upriver, so you can forget that route, lady. Unless you aim to walk the Natchez Trace." The red-faced one guffawed, and the others grinned.

Anne raised her chin higher. "Actually, I prefer to go by sea on a large ocean vessel. What would a sea captain charge?"

"Well, ma'am—the grizzled one scratched his chin—"first you got to get to New Orleans. That right there is almost 400 miles of whirlpools, snags, sinkers, and gators. That'll cost you something. And once in that city of ragin' sin"—he winked at his fellows—"you got to find a berth with some captain willin' to run the British blockade."

The drinker tilted the jug. "War's still on, lady."

307

"And the rebels is losing. General Cornwallis's tearing up the South for fair, and the whole East Coast is a blizzard of British sails. You can't drive a toothpick through."

"And," the youth added, "there's a passel of homegrown pirates waiting to call any ship Tory and confiscate the cargo."

"Yep. I heard tell that the Frenchies got a navy coming, too."

"Goddamned crowded, I'd say."

"Of course, most ships out of New Orleans go by way of Havana."

The old man spat, and tobacco juice pocked the pine. "Yellow-fever city, Havana is."

"Worse than typhoid." Again the looks and nudges were exchanged.

"That ain't no lie."

"So you see, missus, with all that to consider, any sea captain willin' to take on a sick lady and young 'uns would be a mighty rare find."

"Rare and crazier than a coot." The young man laughed and drove his knife through a grasshopper. More brown stained the wharf.

Anne held herself very straight. "I can pay."

The men looked at each other and nodded. "She can pay."

The red-faced man rose from his haunches. "Lady, I been tryin' to get myself out of Natchez for two years. And I'm a man what's able to work my way and who's willin' to sell a hundred acres to pay passage money. If I can't find a ship, how can you expect to?"

Anne's fingers fumbled in the pouch of her skirt, closing at last around her purse. She drew it out and opened it. "There!"

The men leaned forward, peering at the crumpled bills. The youth lifted one out, raised it, and let the breeze catch it. It dipped, fluttered, then floated among the river insects and garbage. "What are you doing?" Anne screeched. The men laughed. Tears began. "Why—"

"Lady," the old man said, "that paper ain't worth a holler in hell. There's new bills now. What you got is nothin'. Nothin' at all. Take my word for it, lady, you ain't never goin' to get out of Natchez."

Chapter Twenty-four

April 1782

I have been unable to leave Mississippi. Though I have some property left, it is so little compared to the expenses of a return voyage to Pennsylvania by sea, that when I speak of it, I am laughed to scorn.

After more than a year in Natchez, I recovered, and I and four of my children—Jamie, Bird, John and Issac—removed some distance into the country. Here I keep house for a man. We have been here about four months and this morning I felt an unusual anxiety to get a letter to my family, who, I suppose, still live in the Forks of the Youghiogheny River. I was preparing to go to town with my letter early, as I understood a boat was to set out which would take it. But I have been unavoidably detained till ten o'clock. I fear the opportunity is lost, however, I will proceed as soon as possible.

Anne, besplattered and weary, tottered on the crest of the bluff above the Mississippi. The dock was empty, the mail boat had gone. She sank onto a stump and held the letter to her cheek. Oh, Bess . . . She straightened, rubbed her eyes, and stared at the river. A *bateau* with the banner "Fort Pitt" nailed to its side approached the shore. Fort Pitt! She looked away, then back. It was still there. A stream of women spread onto the dock; their high-pitched cries of welcome and answers from the boat smashed Anne's disbelief, and gathering up her skirts, she plunged and slid down the red, mud-slick road.

Brushing aside the outstretched welcoming hands, she wedged her way toward the high-sided, sturdy *bateau;* a young farmer jumped onto the yellow pine boards to secure the lines. Anne rapped her hand on his back. "My name is MacMeans. Do you know the Glenns? Do you—"

"Whoa, lady," the youth said without turning. "Give me a chance at least to get the knots tied."

She pressed her fingers to her mouth, her heart banging, Fort Pitt, Fort Pitt. . . . These people were actually there just a few weeks ago! She rubbed her hand along the raw new wood of the boat, as though a bit of Bess might be clinging to it.

"Wally!" a man's voice above her called. "Don't snub her too tight! This river can rise a foot in an hour!"

Anne's nails dug into the wood. No, I'm pretending, wishing too hard. . . . Inch by inch she raised her eyes above the gunwale. Deerskin boots, neat linen breeches, thick middle . . . She stepped back, leaning against the edge of the crowd . . . snow-white beard, ruddy cheeks, bald head . . . Her knees buckled. Thomas White stood in the bow of the boat.

His blue eyes, cheerfully surveying the crowd, stopped on her and darkened. She opened her mouth, but his gaze moved on. She touched her bonnet, her neck cold with sweat. I do exist. I didn't die. I'm standing here. Me—Anne Glenn MacMeans. I'm not a ghost. I'm alive! "Thomas!"

The youth straightened. "You all right, ma'am?" He put out a hand to steady her.

"Call him," she whispered.

"Hey, Mr. White!"

The portly figure carefully descended to the dock and walked toward Anne. His smile was bland. He doesn't know me! Look, Thomas, look—it's me! Anne's hand clutched her throat.

He frowned. "Yes? Something I—"

"Thomas!" she yelled, pushing back her bonnet. His cheeks paled. "I've been sick; my hair's gone white. . . . Thomas, please!"

"Mericul God! Anne MacMeans!" His arms caught her, and she rocked in star bursts of blackness. "We heard . . . We thought . . . Zac went looking . . . He found some kin of the Kers who said all the Youngs and MacMeans had perished on the river. Said you'd died of the typhoid . . . Bess has grieved every day . . . sunk into the melancholies . . . wouldn't speak for weeks last winter."

"Andrew's dead." There, she had said it.

"Do you want back, Annie?"

"Yes! Yes!"

He squeezed her tighter. "I'll see to it. Even if it takes all my share of the flour money, I'll pay your passage round."

Then Anne swooned.

* * *

The mule that Thomas rented for Anne to ride to the Ferguson plantation was tall and stubborn, and for ten miles Anne banged her heels against his sides in a fruitless effort to hurry his plodding hooves. Thomas had said they must leave at sunrise, and it was already twilight when she slid to the ground beside the paddock gate.

As she bent, rubbing her cramped calves, the slave Bobbie took the halter rope and muttered, "The massa's in a powerful state about your leavin' for town without his say-so. I told him you waited till 'bout noon, but that didn't help none. He whipped a couple field hands, cursed out your Jamie, rode my Shirley, then stuck his head in the rum pitcher. You be careful, missus."

Anne straightened and grinned down at Bobbie. "It's over. I don't have to worry anymore. We're going home!" She swung up the rise toward the house—two cabins set on stilts connected by a roofed breezeway—and mounted the steps.

Sam Ferguson did not rise from the table where his ledgers were spread; his hounds lolled across his boots, his whip hung about his neck. "Beggars be riding noo, I see. Old shank's mare dinna be guid enough for you, eh? How much did the livery chisel oot of you for that son-of-an-ass?"

Anne ignored him, flipped her skirts, and called, "Children! We're going home!"

Jamie ran from the cookhouse; Bird, Johnny, and Issac, their cheeks pink, their mouths round with questions, tumbled onto the breezeway from the north cabin. Ferguson stamped his feet and roared, "You're what? How? You'll do no such thing, you—"

"Blah! Blah!" Anne stuck out her tongue at him.

Jamie caught the porch post. "Home?"

Anne lifted Bird and swung her. "Home! Home! Thomas White's come to town, and he's paying our passage round. Hurry now and get things together." She turned. "Mr. Ferguson, we'll be borrowing the cart." She was halfway to the door when his shout stopped her.

"Nobody's going anywhere! You're under contract to me for a year. You have served only four months of the twelve. In my book that's eight to go."

Anne's mouth dried. "What contract?"

Ferguson's shovel chin snapped. "It's common law hereabouts. The term of hiring is always a full year."

"No." Anne shook her head. "No one told me that. I never

agreed to that. We're leaving, Mr. Ferguson. We have no terms of contract. Children, gather your things."

"No contract, eh?" His lower lip jutted forward to touch the tip of his nose. "If that be the case, you're owing me board for these past four months."

"We've earned our food!" Jamie yelled. He spread the fingers of his good hand and began ticking off work done, but Sam Ferguson, his face tight as drawn purse strings, bent over his ledgers, then said, "I figure, Mrs. MacMeans, your bill to be sixty dollars new money or gold. You won't be setting one foot off this property until it's stacked here." He tapped the table.

"You claim to be a Christian!" Anne yelled.

"Sixty-four dollars!" Ferguson hung one hand on the butt of his whip. "Keep talking, Mrs. MacMeans, and we'll hit eighty."

Her hands curled into fists. "All right, Mr. Shylock, you'll get your pound of flesh, you'll get your pound of flesh."

By midnight Anne and the children had managed to sell almost everything they owned. They piled the neighbors' money before Sam Ferguson. His fingers moved like spider's legs as he counted the bills and coins. "Forty-six dollars and ninety-six pence, Mrs. MacMeans. Twenty-three dollars and four pence to go."

Anne snapped, "No one had enough ready cash to buy the Queen Anne desk, but—" Mr. Ferguson shook his head. Anne's palm slapped the table. "You know Jamie's fixed it good as new!" Ferguson sneered. "All right!" Anne shouted. "We'll leave everything! Everything but the clothes on our backs!"

Ferguson, his face wadded with drink, tilted back his chair. "I'm taking only cash tonight, Mrs. MacMeans."

Anne's hand dove for the stiletto in her apron pouch and closed on empty cloth. She looked wildly about the porch.

"This what you're missing?" In the palm of Ferguson's left hand lay her knife; his right held his pistol.

Tears of fury rushed to Anne's eyes; Ferguson's mouth arched downward in a triumphant curve. Play the mouse, Annie, keep crying. She slumped her shoulders; her voice dragged. "All right, Mr. Ferguson, you win. Come, children. Time for bed. Bird, bring the lantern, will you?"

"Leave the lantern here," Ferguson slurred.

The children's feet scuffed behind Anne's as they followed her into their cabin. Johnny slammed the door. "I hate—"

Anne put her hand over his mouth and said loudly, "Don't

bother lighting a candle, Jamie. It's late. Everyone just jump into their beds."

"With our clothes on?" Johnny was incredulous. "I'm all muddy."

"It doesn't matter," Anne said putting her hand on his shoulder to prevent him from pulling off his shirt. "I'm really too tired to care."

Out of the darkness came Jamie's formal, "Well, we did the best we could." Don't overdo it, son, Anne thought.

"He kept our money," Issac said with a whine.

Anne closed his lips with her fingers. "Don't worry. We'll get it tomorrow. Is everybody in?" Bed ropes squeaked. "Jamie, why don't you lead us in prayer?"

They repeated the Lord's Prayer in unison, and Jamie added a special request for a safe journey for Thomas White to New Orleans. Johnny and Issac, at last aware of the plot, smothered giggles. "Time for sleep," Anne said sternly.

Lamplight played cat and mouse with the dark under the door; the toenails of the hounds ticked the boards of the breezeway; the bottom of the pitcher scraped the table; Ferguson hoicked and spat. Jamie pretended to snore; the twins beside him tossed, making the bed ropes groan. Bird and Annie lay quietly side by side, their eyes wide, their minds planning in silent unison what they would take, how it could be carried, how they would get past the dogs and ease the mule out of the paddock. At last Sam Ferguson's chair rasped on the boards, and his voice muttered thickly, "Nigger, you there?"

"Yesser. Right here watching for weasels," Bobbie said.

"Well, watch for another kind of weasel tonight."

"Yesser."

Ferguson's footsteps dragged, and he cursed as the pitcher clattered on the floor. "Pick it up, nigger. And listen, if anyone be poking a head or hand out o' a window or door on that side o' the hoose, you come banging on my door. You hear?"

"Yesser. I'm to wake you if one of them white folks who works for you tries to run off in the night. Cuz they is your property just like us is."

Ferguson laughed. "Bring the lantern. Leave the rushes burning. You're bright, Bobbie. You know what happens to niggers who run. And what happens to those that pretends they don't see 'em goin'. You've seen a few hanging from the tree with their scroties cut open, ain't you?"

"Yesser, I surely have. Me and the dogs ain't goin' to shut our eyes all night long. Nosser."

When Jamie crawled through the window on the north side of the house, the night was black and thick as pitch. He caught the legs of the others and lifted them to the ground. A light rain pattered on the leaves, muffling the sounds of their footfalls as they moved cautiously down the slope toward the paddock. All five of them held pieces of dried meat in their hands, ready to quiet the dogs, but none appeared; the paddock gate did not creak, and the animals did not stir. The mule wheezed under the weight of the twins, bundles that held bedding, trenchers, cups, shoes, and the Killyleagh kettle heavy with cracked corn, the Bible, and the *Commonplace Book*. Anne had the feeling she had done this all before—many times.

The soft April earth absorbed the step of the mule's hooves and the people's bare feet. Anne held the halter and Bird on the opposite side the lead rope; Jamie walked behind, the mule's tail hairs laced in the bent fingers of his right hand, his father's rifle in his left. Once they had moved beyond the faint rush lights they might have been in the belly of Jonah's whale; Anne could barely see the white of her hand on the bridle, and her feet could not distinguish the ooze of the track from the ooze of the indigo field. If they blundered off . . . Maybe she should send Jamie down the lane to the slave cabins to see if anyone there had a light. No, that was asking too much. Ferguson would half kill any Negro who helped them.

Once past the tended fields the cart track narrowed and roughened; Anne stubbed her toe on a root, then lurched into a slippery puddle; a rock bruised her instep; Bird stumbled and grunted with pain.

"Stop," Anne said with a hiss over the shrill of the peeper frogs and the drum of rain on swamp water. "We've got to put on shoes."

John and Issac had trouble finding the right bundles, then more trouble telling which shoe belonged to whom. "Stockings, too," Anne whispered. Without them their feet would be raw in a mile. She leaned against the side of the mule to dress her feet. Water splashed, a gator bellowed. Would they slither up onto the track, grab their legs? "Hurry, children!"

"Quiet!" Jamie's voice clicked like the cock of his rifle.

They listened to the darkness, to peepers, rain, bullfrogs—then the slap of feet.

"Halt." Jamie's voice growled.

A lantern flared. "It's me. Bobbie." The light swayed gently toward them.

The long rifle barrel quivered, then steadied. "If that's you, Ferguson, I swear I'll shoot."

"No need, Massa Jamie." The glow from the tin-shielded lantern speckled Bobbie's grinning face. No one appeared from the blackness behind him.

Bobbie patted the flank of the mule. "Nice Jack, missus, but he be slow, mightly slow. You might miss your boat. He'd do better with a light out front showin' him he ain't about to step on a gator's tail."

"Thank you." Anne grasped the bail of the lantern.

"I'll carry it, missus."

"No. You go back. You'll be in trouble. You—"

Bobbie moved past her. "I be in deep trouble already. Best I walk you to the river and keep on goin'."

They arrived on the bluff above Natchez as an orange sun rose into a clearing sky; the black *bateau* tugged at her moorings, impatient to be gone on the wide, red river. Thomas White waved both arms above his head. Bobbie already had slipped north into the woods, and the MacMeans and the mule, grubby and swaying from lack of sleep, lurched down the red-dirt road.

As they passed the path to Gayla's house, Anne peered into the jungle of honeysuckle and kudzu and blinked in amazement when Gayla appeared. After hugs and kisses the two women walked close, arm in arm, and Anne, looking down on the top of Gayla's shiny black head, wondered if her friend had shrunk—she remembered her as three ax handles tall.

"I missed you yesterday cuz I was out tending my muskrat traps. I live here now. My sister Maria and I had a fallin' out." Gayla's pink lips pouted. "She wanted those Young ones and even Alex Glenn all to herself."

"But you had Juan and Marybett's baby."

Gayla stopped, her chocolate eyes round. "You don't know? You never got word?"

The hairs on the nape of Anne's neck prickled. "Word of what?"

Gayla's pout broadened. "My son took his wife and child to New Orleans to the mission."

"New Orleans! Why?"

"Marybett and I didn't get on." Her chins drooped.

Of course, Anne thought. Why didn't I realize that? Marybett and Gayla—tinder and powder. "The baby?"

"A little girl. They took my little girl away. And now all your family's going, too." She sniffed mightily.

Anne's mind leaped. New Orleans! I'll see Marybett in New Orleans, maybe. . . . Maybe she'll come, too!

Gayla sobbed. "She's all I have. She and my Juan. Your daughter's hard. I think she's maybe broken inside."

"But there's Peter—"

"My man and I have parted the ways."

"Oh, dear."

Gayla raised her round arms to the morning sun; teardrops jeweled the mounds of her cheeks and neck. "God cannot want that I stay with one man who never speaks, when the whole of Natchez longs for me."

Women bobbed "How-do" from their windows and emerged from their doors with baskets of biscuits, cakes, meal, and dried deer meat. "For our departing guests" Mrs. Barber bubbled as she hugged Bird. The gay procession swept the MacMeans to the dock; Anne took Thomas White's hand and stepped over the gunwale.

As the *bateau* slid onto the blueing river, Gayla's last call broke from the waving crowd, "There's sweets for our grand-baby in the basket!" "Our," Anne murmured. "How strange."

Thomas pointed to a pitcher of sweet milk, a plate of biscuits, and pallets laid on the sunny deck. "Rest," he said.

Anne, in the last minutes before sleep, watched the strong arms of the men of the sweeps and responded to Bird's question of "I'm a little afraid—are you afraid of the river, Minnie?" with a drowsy smile.

"No. The sprites had their chance, Birdie Jane. They'll not get us now." Her eyes closed, and she wondered why in the weeks when death had been so close she had never thought of water sprites at all.

"So that's how it is, Annie." Thomas pulled off his boots and sprawled in a chair. "There's only one boat in New Orleans that's bound for Philadelphia, and she's chockablock full. And nobody's saying when there'll be another." He mopped his bald head and dangled the damp kerchief out the window of the boardinghouse. "Look at the heat rising off those shingles. Godfry. If it's this hot in May, I'd hate to be in New Orleans in July."

Anne jumped from the edge of the bed. "It looks like I might be!" Her bare feet whapped the floorboards.

Thomas squirmed and poked his head out the window. "I don't know what to say, dear. I suppose you could look up Marybett and—"

"Don't be foolish!"

"Well . . ." As he pulled himself around to face her she saw his cheeks and hairless dome shine radish red. How would he ever stand the walk back the Natchez Trace? Maybe it would have been better for all of them if he had never come. At least at Sam Ferguson's she and the children had had food and a roof over their heads. She whirled away as he babbled about the war not lasting forever.

"Thomas! If my children and I have to board out here even six months, all our passage money will be gone and we'll never get out! Oh, I don't know. . . ." She banged herself down on the bed, cracking the back of her head against the wall.

"Dear, if there was anything I could do, anything . . ." He spread his hands helplessly.

"No wonder Bess won't marry you!" She bit her tongue. "I'm sorry."

He turned back to the window. "Don't fret about it."

Anne fanned herself with her hankie. "I thought the war was over. I thought Yorktown was the end of it. Why is there still a blockade? What's going on?"

The tiny chair creaked under Thomas's bulk. "Poker playing at the peace table. Everybody trying to get chips in front of them before they end it. I heard this morning that a hundred English ships are on their way down from New York to drive the French fleet out of Chesapeake Bay. Now, what captain wants to sail his ship into that hornet's nest?"

Anne bounced her rear against the bed ropes. "Apparently there's one who isn't afraid."

Thomas laughed. "Roger Greenwood is young, cocky, and very impatient to be rich."

Anne's green eyes narrowed to slits, and her brows rose tawny below her snow-white widow's peak. "Tell me about him."

Thomas wiped his palms on his knees. "He's just a lad. Nineteen, twenty. Been privateering all his life out of New Bedford with his pappie. A couple of months ago they captured this caravel and the boy set sail in it to New Orleans to sell the cargo. Now's he loading up with tobacco, and if he can get it to Boston, he'll be a rich man. And if manages to load on sugar in Havana, he'll never have to work another day of his life."

Anne hunched off the bed and took her bonnet from its peg. "I'll be back."

"Where are you going? It's one hundred degrees out there, dear."

"To see Captain Greenwood."

Thomas leaned down to pull on his boots. "You're as driving a woman as Bess."

"You don't need to go."

Thomas didn't look up. "Mrs. MacMeans, women do not walk the docks of New Orleans alone. It isn't safe."

"Safe!" Anne howled. "When in my life have I ever been safe? At Fort Pitt? In Kentucky? At Fort Jefferson? Alone on the Mississippi with a madman? At Ferguson's? Let me tell you something, Mr. White. The reason men have to protect women is because there are so many crazy men in the world. If there weren't any of you, we'd do just fine." She snapped the latch and opened the door. "New Orleans sounds like a Sabbath noon picnic after what men have put me through!"

Thomas leaned back, folding his big freckled hands over his paunch. "I don't know why I ever imagined that Indians, starving, typhoid, and family dying had softened you up, Annie. Go along. I'll sit here and fan myself till you get back."

To Anne the caravel looked small for an oceangoing boat, but it had a high stern, a broad bow, and a brave name, the *Jolly Roger*.

Captain Greenwood was very young, very tall, and affected the dress of a common sailor by wearing trousers that pinched his buttocks and billowed about his ankles. Ah, Marybett, Anne breathed, you should have waited for this one. You could have sailed the seven seas together and raised a dozen chidren on storm-tossed decks.

Roger bowed. "Your servant, ma'am." His hair bobbed in short brown curls.

Or if I were seventeen, Anne thought as she curtsied. His smiling mouth was as wide as her own, and she decided this youth could be won with frankness. "My name is Anne MacMeans. I hear you are not given to living by others' rules"—she winked—"but by the ample store of your own wit and courage." He raised one eyebrow, and his walnut eyes twinkled. "I have a tale to tell you."

He offered his arm, and they retired to the shade of his

cabin. Anne found herself making the story much longer than she had intended, but his exclamations of anger and sadness so completely matched her own feelings that they had finished a whole pot of tea before she fell silent.

He rose and called for his mate. In a long-voweled New Bedford twang Roger ordered him to inform the two gentlemen who had reserved the large cabin that they could either accept deck accommodations or wait for the next ship.

She asked the charge, then held her breath.

"You say your ten-year-olds have served on a ship before? All right. They will be my cabin boys, and there will be no charge for the passage. Can you provide your own food? We sail in two days."

Anne staggered into the brightness of the deck. It had gone too smoothly; there must be some trick, some new danger. "The British? Will they attack us?"

Roger Greenwood tilted his sailor's bonnet over one eye. "They surely will try."

"But—" To drown after all this . . .

"I promise you, Mrs. MacMeans, you will be in Philadelphia by September. I did not go to all the bother to capture this boat to have it taken from me." He tapped his hat forward even farther, and the twin navy ribbons fluttered. "Besides, the British will hang me from the nearest yardarm if they catch me. And I'm all for avoiding that."

Anne put out her hand and said, "Done." Then she went in search of Juan and Marybett.

The mission room was dim and earthen, and the babe's terra-cotta skin and dark eyes matched the patient, aged walls. Marybett matched neither her home nor the babe she held; she blazed like a wildflower, orange and white in a world of brown.

Anne bent over the child, her forehead brushing Marybett's hair as she searched in vain for a hint of herself or Andrew in the infant's features. "Don't you think," Marybett asked, "that there is a bit of Pappie in her mouth?"

Anne kissed the babe's cap of shaggy black hair. "She's Gayla through and through. Don't try to see what isn't there. It'll only make you both miserable."

Marybett's small dark teeth snapped. "No! She's not all Gayla. I won't have her be Gayla! Look, look here . . . see when she smiles."

Anne saw herself pushing her own firstborn squalling child

319

into the arms of the midwife, of Mrs. Held, of anyone who would take her. Had she hated Marybett because she was not Jim, or because she was herself? Anne sighed. Wisdom always comes so late. "One day you will have a son who looks like your father. I hope you will call him Andrew. But this one . . . Don't look at her and wish for someone else. Love her. Love her more."

"Ha!" Marybett snapped and her eyes glowed like a vixen's in the dark. "Like you loved me?"

Anne retreated to a corner and sat on a rug. After a while she said, "I was young, Marybett. I was frightened. The man I loved had been killed . . ." She stopped. The red eyes stared at her. Good Lord . . . it was Marybett's story, too. She bowed her head in her hands. The same, the same . . . is it always the same for a woman?

"You could have tried a little harder. Maybe even loved Jamie a little less."

Anne's hands plopped in her lap and she nodded. "With my mother is was Hugh."

As Anne left she hugged Marybett, but as always, her daughter stiffened. Too late. It's too late. But she said the words anyway. "Come with us. Come home to the Forks of the Yough. You and Juan and the babe."

Marybett backed out of her mother's grasp. "Present my brown, Papist child to Zacquill Willson to be baptized? I'm not crazy, Mother."

Marybett picked up a jug and they walked in silence to the well. The psalm of the seasons filled Anne's mind: For everything there is a season: a time to get, and a time to lose; a time to speak, a time to keep silent . . .

The water sloshed from the jug as Marybett filled a cup for her mother. Anne drank and took her daughter's hand. The small, cold bones squeezed hers once, very hard. Anne walked away.

Chapter Twenty-five

September 1782
*Some time near the beginning of June we sailed from
New Orleans, and had a prosperous voyage to Havanna.*

We were detained there two weeks, but health was preserved and the Captain's humane kindness never abated.

In the latter part of our voyage we have often been in danger from British vessels, it being the time of the Revolutionary War. The Captain, afraid to enter either the Chesapeake of Delaware Bay, has run the vessel into an inlet between the Chesapeake and Cape Henlopen.

All night the *Jolly Roger* lay at anchor, a silent black cat in a black night, twitching at ominous noises—a voice? a whomping of sails? the creak of anchor chains? Did British men-of-war, in fact, encircle them? The fog turned gray, the ship tiptoed to life. The Delaware shore, they believed, lay roughly five miles to the west.

The first dory of passengers, launched without a squeak or splat onto the brief, flat, gray pool of bay water, immediately disappeared. As the second dory was eased down on fat-greased pulleys, Anne stood, unwilling to let go of Jamie.

"Minnie, you must." His words were firm but his eyes, as always, yearned for answers beyond her ken.

Anne sighed, nodded her brow against his downy jaw, and then, eyes blurred with tears, lowered herself hand over hand into the running mists and took her place in the bow of the dory. Bird and the twins crouched in the stern, their small hands on the gunwales, their faces smeared by fog, the bundles bunched by their feet.

Lines tossed from the ship were silently caught and curled in the bottom. Joey and Billy, round-headed sailors out of New Bedford, then settled themselves on the center seat with their backs to the bow and fitted the long oars into locks muffled with rags. Billy pushed his oar against the black timbers of the *Jolly Roger,* and the dory began to glide.

Anne looked up at the faces lining the rail. Roger Greenwood winked and gave a thumbs up. Jamie raised his hand in a small salute. A boy, dear God, he's still a boy, seventeen. Her hand trembled more than waved. Please take care of him—he needs someone to lean on. Everything dissolved, and she shivered so violently she was afraid the British would hear the clacking of her bones. Jamie had waited until the last night to tell her he was not going with them, but sailing on to Boston, then Marseille. Captain Greenwood would allow him a sailor's wage in exchange for his passage.

"I'm going to Edinburgh to study for the ministry," he had said in a new, deep voice that rose from a chest broad with a summer of climbing rigging, hauling rope, and pumping bilge.

Anne had staggered against the rail, babbling 'buts,' saying there were good schools in America—at Princeton, Carlisle—

"No," Jamie had said, "I need to go back to some sort of beginning. Start over. Build whoever James Andrew Mac-Means was meant to be." His touch on her arm had matched the plea in his eyes. "Don't you see, Minnie, I feel as if I've been a failure at everything. Always tagging along behind Marybett and you and Pappie. I can be a good preacher, I know I can."

She had tried one last time. "But stay with us until Philadelphia. You'll find a ship—"

"No. My weakness is doing what other people want me to, then resenting it. Going on with you would be like going West with Pappie. A trap I'd never get myself out of." He had turned and looked into the night. "I hated him for that. For selling Breakfast Hill."

Anne had pulled back, stumbling against the anchor chain. Hate? Hate . . .

"Hsssst! Ma'am! Are you keeping watch?" The question from Second Mate Joey was a rebuke.

She cupped her hands around her eyes. Annie, we'll ram a ship before you see it. Why didn't they put Bird up here? There! What was that? That black on the water. She reached back and tapped both sailors' shoulders; their oars came up and hung poised, dripping, then dipped in easy backstrokes, holding the dory against the drift. The dark shapes coalesced into bills and tails—a raft of ducks. They floated in an undulating carpet as far as Anne could see.

She turned back; Joey pointed to the north and made sweeping motions with his hand. They would go around them—rising ducks surely would bring British cannon fire down upon them. She signaled that she understood.

Three times she tapped their shoulders and they swung west toward shore; each time they found their way blocked by more ducks and had to turn north again. Was the whole bay covered by them? Would they wander about until the sun burned off the fog and they found themselves sitting under the guns of an English frigate? Anne's shoulders ached, her stomach squatted in a hard, cramped ball. Had she made the wrong choice? Should they all have gone on to Boston?

Last night, stunned by Jamie's decision, she had fumbled her way to her cabin and huddled in bed moaning, "Don't hate, Jamie. We did our best. You always believed too much, had too much faith in us."

Bird squirmed to the top of the comforter. "He couldn't have meant hate really. You don't hate someone and then go clear across the ocean to their city. Pappie raised us on tales of Edinburgh. She touched her mother's cheek. "You didn't notice because getting things done was all you seemed to care about sometimes."

Knuckles rapped softly on the door, and Roger Greenwood stepped in. Turning so his body shielded the porthole from the light, he lit the lantern he carried. "Bird, why don't you run along to my cabin for a bit. If you keep the lamp low you can lie on the rug and read—not that there's a book in that case you haven't read a dozen times already." He winked. She screwed up her face and winked back.

Bird called the flirting betwen them "practicing," Roger called it "being nice to the child"; Anne smiled and called it "good for both of them." But she herself was stirred by it. She wanted Roger for one of her daughters, yet she wanted him for herself. She was old, she had white hair, she had a grandchild, but she wanted to lie with Roger Greenwood and feel his flesh as smooth as Andy MacMeans' had been in the moat of Fort Pitt. When the door shut behind Bird, goose bumps flecked Anne's arms and she blushed at the urge that rose from between her thighs. She gritted her teeth to keep from squirming. Her voice squeaked as she asked him, "Has there been a change in plans?"

"Jamie said you were upset by what he told you. I thought that if you were worried about making your way to Philadelphia without his help . . . well, that maybe you would decide on Boston after all."

She turned away so that the sight of his curls, his strong, young hands would not seduce her into saying yes.

"It's dangerous, Anne."

The sudden use of her first name almost undid her. "Let me think a minute, Roger." She imagined Boston: cold—no friends. Abigail Adams? No, she would never intrude as a refugee; besides, no letter had ever found her after those first few exchanges. She had no money. The road to Philadelphia was very long. Was New York still in enemy hands? "I'm too tired. I'd rather take the quick chance now. Get it over with."

He set the lantern on the stand by the bed, and the light gilded the line of his jaw, burned in his shadowed eyes; she held her tongue against the roof of her mouth.

"You're probably right." He sounded sad; she hoped he was. "Even if the British should capture your dory, they'd probably let you go." Then he grinned. "Unless, of course, you're related to General Washington."

"What do you mean?"

"Then they'd hold you for ransom—or treason."

"Oh, dear."

"You are?"

"Hugh MacKnight is my brother."

"The patroit? Well, then, you must lie like a sailor. However"—he paused, shifted his weight from one foot to the other, and cleared his throat—"it's only fair to warn you that the British probably would keep Issac and John to serve as cabin boys on their ship."

"They're only ten!"

"They look twelve or thirteen. In any case, believe me, they'd take them. Quicker than they would take one of my sailors. Do you understand?"

Anne stared, then clapped her hands to her cheeks. Oh, no! "What if—what if we dressed them as girls?"

Roger smothered a hoot. "Perfect! Perfect! A widow lady with three little girls. We'll do it! But make sure you hide Bird's prettiness under some ugly bonnet. Do you have enough skirts?"

Anne fingered the linsey-woolsey of the comforter. "We'll make do." She nodded. "You have Neptune keep the fog thick and the waters calm and I'll ask the brownies to help with the clothes."

He gave a thumbs-up sign, then picked up the lantern. At the door he turned back, suddenly a boy, nervous, wetting his lips. Anne caught the signal, and her heart pounded. He approached the bed, holding out his hand. "Mrs. MacMeans—Anne—I've never known a braver woman than you."

His warm fingers pressed her palm; quickly she stretched upward to kiss his cheek, a motherly kiss. He straightened, his lips curled inward, waiting. She touched his hand, which hovered uncertainly over the comforter. "And you, Roger, are a man any woman would be proud to have"—her breath caught in her chest—"for a son." A son! Fool! Fool! A lover is what you mean!

The latch clicked behind him.

Anne sighed. It seemed they had been rowing through fog for a very long time. She glanced to the stern of the dory, where John and Issac sprawled like fiery-headed, freckled rag dolls. Her gaze swept slowly along the port side, across the black ducks bobbing along the wall of fog; she shifted to face the bow and blinked, disbelieving her eyes. The gray hull was so sudden, so huge, so awful in its implication that she barely got her hand to the sailors' shoulders in time to stop them from rowing into it.

Joey quickly hauled in his oar; the children ducked as he stepped to the stern, and using the blade as a rudder, steered them carefully along the mammoth dark hulk of the British man-of-war. Once hidden under the great bowsprit, Billy grasped a dangling rope and held them steady. They didn't breathe as they waited for shouts or shots. None came. Nestled like a toy under the sweep of the prow, they were safe from eyes glancing out of the large windows of the captain's quarters and from the sight of sailors on deck, but fog-enhanced sounds—footfalls, a whispered "All's well"—gave the illusion that the British actually shared their boat. The contents of a chamber pot splashed a foot from the bow.

Capture had moved from possible to probable, and to Anne's frightened glance Bird still looked too attractive and the twins too much like boys. She raised her face to pray. She shut her eyes, shook her head, and looked again. If that was God, He had taken a most peculiar form. Large wooden breasts and red nipples dipped and rose above her.

She twisted, leaning her head back against the point of the dory's bow, and gawked up at the figure of a mermaid. Gaudy green and gold scales slithered up against the mammoth trunk of the bowsprit, breasts rose proud and flagrant, lips parted full and crimson, but the eyes were black, blank, and without soul.

Joey touched her knee and beckoned; she pushed back her bonnet and placed her ear on his lips. "Fog might thin any minute. Best shot is to row out under the bowsprit fast as we can." He pressd a compass into her hand. "Set a zigzag course westward. You all lie flat. Might be an officer with a pistol up there."

Anne's eyes rolled upward, and she nodded.

John, Issac, and Bird lay packed like little herrings in the stern, but Anne chose to lie face up. If there was going to be a bullet she did not want it thudding into her back; she studied the grain of the wood in the goddess' breasts while she waited. Oak, she guessed.

Joey and Billy raised their oars and leaned forward until their foreheads touched their knees. One, two, three! The blades sliced down and the boat leaped forward, a cat on soundless paws. Anne lay mesmerized by the girth and length of the bowsprit above, by ropes thicker than a man, by rigging that reached to a mast lost in the fog. Then everything vanished. No bullet sang, no one had even known they were there. How odd, she thought.

Turning over and crouching in the bottom of the bow, she studied the compass, then raised her eyes—she could not see! The world had turned yellow, like paper scorched by fire.

"The sun's burning through!" Joey said. "Take us straight in!"

Anne wiped her eyes and focused on the compass again. "Two strokes to port," she whispered. "One more. There. You've got it. Straight on."

The boat skimmed the waveless brass water. Anne could see nothing but clouds of swirling gold and white. She pushed her bonnet all the way back and turned her ear toward shore—if, indeed, shore still lay to the west.

Off to her right came the clean, quick crack of breakers. "Hard starboard," she called. "Sounds like a sand beach."

The dory swung about, and the men pulled in long, sweeping strokes; swells grabbed the keel and hurried them. Joey's voice was loud. "Get us on top of a big one, missus! We'll ride her in!"

In an explosion of light, the fog disappeared. Ahead lay sun-brilliant sand, green trees. "Pull to port!" she cried. "Now ahead!" Water piled up, rising before the bow. "Pull! Pull!" she cried.

The oars dug deep, the bow rose, the dory hurtled toward shore. Anne leaned forward; salt flicked her lips. She felt a kinship with the mermaid on the British man-of-war, and she raised her face to the breeze; then the bottom bumped sand and the backwater hissed. She jumped and held the bow; the children scrambled out with the bundles, and they all waded toward dry land.

By the time they looked back, the dory was diving through a breaker, heading for a white line of fog that sat on blue waves. "Godspeed," Anne murmured. "Godspeed . . . Roger . . . Jamie. . . ."

She touched Bird's shoulder and smiled. "Only fifty more miles. We'd better get started."

They saw no one until high noon, when they came to a small clearing where a woman was feeding what seemed like a quarter acre of geese; her house sat on stilts above a marshy piece of bay land. Anne called, "Hello!" The woman fled and the geese attacked.

Hooting with glee the twins battled the hissing, honking, flapping creatures.

"Stop! Where you from?" The woman's voice, heavily accented with Swedish, came from under the house.

Bird bent over. "New Orleans," she said proudly.

"We've had some trouble," Anne said quickly. "And we're looking for the road to Christiana, where we have acquaintances." There was no reply. Anne squatted and spoke into the shadows. "It's near New Castle. Up by the Delaware River."

A knotty grey head emerged into a strip of sunlight. "Marsh path." Her thumb jerked westward. "I never been."

"Is it far?"

The woman shrugged her pointed shoulders. "Father went. Mother and I never did. We stayed with the house. People go away and get lost."

They said good-bye, found the marsh path, and walked single file in the welcome brown shade; the restless twins soon skipped ahead. "Don't get lost," Anne called.

Bird giggled. "Lost is a funny word, isn't it Minnie? Of course, the person who is lost is not because they know where they are. I think I like the word 'separated' better. We've been separated from Uncle Hugh. We're separated from Philadelphia." She turned and skipped down the dappled path.

September 11. In this land of strangers God provided a wagon to carry us to Christiana and tomorrow we go from thence in a shallop to Philadelphia.

Chapter Twenty-six

September 12 had been named Victory Day. The previous September the citizens of Philadelphia had cheered the

327

American and French armies marching South to confront General Cornwallis in what had seemed a desperate last gamble. The news of their absurdly easy victory at Yorktown had touched off an orgy of celebration; now the soldiers were returning North, and the plans for Victory Day in the capitol city of America were formal and elaborate.

The parade would form on outer Chestnut Street where the French were bivouacked under guard—too many peasant soldiers had already disappeared into the lush, uncrowded countryside; then to the powerful cadence of the Liberty Bell they would march in review, row on row of blue and white, past General Washington, Count de Rochambeau, and the American Congress. As they moved from the State House down Chestnut Street, the many bells of the city would ring counterpoint to the thud of the victors' marching feet, the hoofbeats of officers' prancing horses, and the whip of flags in the wind.

Drummers and fifers would lead the thousand polished soldiers to the riverbank, north on Front Street, then up Market to the courthouse, where speeches would last from noon to three; at four a reception for the dignitaries, complete with chamber music, would be held at the estate of John Bartrum. Fifteen hundred invitations had been issued for the dinner at the French legation—an enormous pavilion built to celebrate the birth of their dauphin—and thirty French chefs had been hired to cook. At dark fireworks would burst across the sky, the tables would be removed from the marble floor, and the dance—expected to last until dawn—would begin.

Hugh MacKnight woke before the sun was up or a cock had crowed and lay silently mouthing the speeches he would deliver both at the courthouse and the dinner. People said his tongue was cast in silver, and Hugh had no intention of tarnishing its reputation.

He whistled a jaunty tune as he put on his perfectly tailored white britches, white silk hose, white linen shirt, and ruffled stock, then shrugged his broad shoulders into his powder blue coat.

Moving to the mirror, he brushed his thick blond hair into a queue and tied it with a wide black grosgrain ribbon. Since hearing from Zac a year and a half earlier that there was little doubt that the entire MacMeans family had perished of typhoid on the Mississippi, he had adopted the ribbon as a private badge of mourning; a black armband, he felt, would have snapped his thin thread of hope. He no longer drank to excess, as he had done for the first year, but his nights still were haunted by a boatload of corpses who rose to tell him tales of unbelievable horror.

Hugh leaned toward the mirror and examined the flesh around his eyes for signs of age; he found none—with maturity his jaw had assumed the proportions of his father's and stretched his skin into lean firmness. He gave himself a wink and a lopsided smile; his freckles were gone, but his eyes flicked with the lightness of a mischievous boy. Whenever matrimony entered the head of one of the many women he squired about town, he affected his consumptive cough— although he had been quite healthy for ten years—and with bowed head spoken quietly of his vow never to marry and leave orphans.

He tiptoed down the steps of the house in Grey's Alley and saddled his mare, Lady.

Philadelphia throbbed, bursting with flags and bunting, small racing boys and barking dogs, firecrackers and drums, people emerging in their Sabbath best to breakfast in coffeehouses and taverns. Hugh rode up one street and down another: Vine and Market, Walnut and Pine, Front and Second and Third and Fourth, inhaling his city with bursting pride. He passed the marks of the British occupation—fortifications and gaunt, burned chimneys surrounded by rubble—without rancor; it was over, America had won. Unwilling to leave the excitement of the streets for the staid company self-consciously assembling in front of the State House, he trotted across Fifth and down Market; men cried "Ho! Doctor MacKnight!" and belles wrapped in sashes of red, white, and blue blew him kisses from the balconies.

His heart pounded with the song of liberty his city sang. One day, he felt sure, it would surpass London and Paris in prosperity and culture and hopefully never be ringed as they were by a noose of desperate poor. True, the warehouses still stood empty, the wharves devoid of foreign flags, but the blockade could not last forever. Lady's hooves clattered on the boards of the public dock and he watched a sight that heartened him more than even a bevy of heavily laden merchant ships would have done—shallops and rowboats, sailboats and canoes filled with scores of country people plied toward shore. American flags fluttered from masts and from the arms of the great windmill; the ferry from Jersey was swathed in red, white, and blue; canons boomed downriver. Militia boys playing fifes and drums marched onto the dock. Lady high-stepped from the wharf and into the white and red-brick city gleaming under a crisp September sky. Church bells began to peel.

The captain of a shallop from Christiana, seeing boats tied six deep at the public dock, turned to tack toward a private one, and the passengers called gaily to other craft also crowding toward the welcoming wharves. Only Anne and her three children stood stiff and silent. A night on the open deck had left their limbs cramped, their clothes—the same ones they had worn escaping from Mr. Ferguson—wrinkled and damp, and their stomachs growling for food.

They had known that the boat on which they had begged passage had been booked as a Victory Day excursion, but since getting to Philadelphia had been the only thing on their minds, they had not even inquired as to the nature of the celebration. Consequently the wild excitement of hundreds of people in addition to the bulk of the buildings, the height of the spires, the width of the streets, and the magnificence of the carriages stunned them into dumbness.

Once on the dock they stood, a bewildered clump of tatters and bundles. Bird was near tears.

Anne lowered her head and pulled Margery's faded bonnet close to her cheeks. "Come along," she said stretching her arms to enclose them all.

They hugged the buildings on Front Street, Anne clutching the Killyleagh kettle in both hands, the children holding soiled clumps of blankets close to their chests. A small girl shrilled, "Mama, look at those poor people!" Although the dismayed mother shushed her child and hurried away, Bird and the twins hunched so close to Anne that she could barely walk. She tried to think of something brave to say, but the noise of hooves and wagon wheels on cobblestones, the shouts and slamming of doors, the blurs of jostling people had glued her tongue to the roof of her mouth. There was the sign "R. Bailey and Sons," the warehouse, the flight of wooden steps. How many had there been?

They look, Annie, as rickety as you. She imagined her young self with thick auburn hair and blushing white skin creeping down them past Campbell Jamison to meet her Robert. Another time, another life. Now you're an alien, an outlander, a Westerner, a backwoodswoman. Maybe you've been alone

330

with yourself too long, suffered too much to really come back . . . to mix in society again. Then her brain said, Annie, you haven't changed into something new, just gone back to what you were. Before Bess, before Jim . . .

Issac tugged on her sweaty hand. "I want to get inside. How far is the house, Minnie?"

"What," Bird asked, "if Uncle Hugh doesn't recognize us? What if he doesn't let us in?"

Anne stopped in her tracks. What if he didn't? What if he just stared, as Thomas White had? She leaned against a building, almost crushing Issac. What if he had married? She pictured his wife opening the door and gaping in horror. She would be beautiful like Polly Wharton, and Hugh would look over her shoulder and ask, "Who is it, dear?" And she would shut the door and say, "Nobody, dearest."

She barely recognized the entrance to Grey's Alley. The road had been paved with yellow bricks; white picket fences instead of trimmed sticks jammed in the mud surrounded neat, painted houses; the towers of a mansion rose on the far corner. They edged their way across Walnut; willow trees and sundials graced yards once filled with pigs and slop. The tiny house Anne had rented for herself and Andrew and Hugh almost twenty years earlier now had a wide veranda roofed with grape vines, and a neat stable had replaced the ramshackle shed. The door was new, paneled oak with a fan of glass across the top; there was a bell for ringing, and a brass nameplate.

Anne halted them in the middle of the road. "What does it say, Bird?"

"Dr. Hugh B. MacKnight."

Anne sighed with relief. Then she thought, No, he must have married! A woman must have seen to it that things were fixed up. But she did not want him married. She did not want to share him. She was alone, she needed—

The door opened; a boxy figure in rusty black emerged and turned to fasten the latch, her buttocks projected like the far end of a fiddle.

"Who's that?" Bird squeaked.

"Mrs. Held," Anne breathed.

The four of them stood in the delicate morning shadows, their clothes dark with dew, their faces weathered by tropical sun. Mrs. Held adjusted a market basket over her arm as she stepped off the stoop. At the bottom she looked up, and her limbs flew every which way as she yelled in fright, "Go away! Go away!" She flapped her stump at them.

They didn't move, merely stood like risen dead.

Mrs. Held reared back and folded her arms, stoutly guarding the entrance to the house. Anne shepherded the children slowly forward, and when they all stood in the sunlight, she said quietly, "Mrs. Held."

The woman lowered her head and peered out from under her bonnet. "Merciful heavens!" she shrieked. "The haints have come! It's haints!" Missus Held flung her basket at the little group.

Bird stepped out, pushing her sleeve above her elbow. "Feel! We're flesh. Not ghosts."

Mrs. Held stood her ground; her fingers wavered in the sunlight, then touched the bony arm.

"See, it's warm. I'm Birdie Jane."

Mrs. Held's large rear plopped onto the bricks of the road; she looked up at the faces looking down. A neighbor cried, "Are they harming you, missus? Shall I fire a warning shot?"

Johnny whirled and shouted his favorite sailor's oath, "You bloody gull! Do you want a belaying pin down your throat?"

Mrs. Held's jaw moved. "I supposed they called you Andy MacMeans."

"No," Issac said, "he's John. I'm Issac. My pappie is dead."

Anne and Bird helped Mrs. Held to her feet. "You all?" she asked. When Anne nodded, Mrs. Held turned and led the way up the stoop, into the house.

Inside, the smell of tobacco, books, and men, not babies, prevailed. Hugh's office was furnished with a high-back settee, a sideboard with a cut glass decanter and brandy snifters, and a huge brass-fitted desk littered with papers of state; the whitewashed walls were hidden behind sheets of paper flowers. A carpet from China lay by the small hearth, now enclosed with a marble mantel. Mrs. Held directed Anne to the settee, brought her tea in a china cup, then disappeared with the children to the hearth room. Anne drank deeply and almost passed out; the cup held Glenn whiskey lightly laced with tea and lemon. She blinked her tearing eyes—so Dora was still at it.

Hugh, according to Mrs. Held, had gone off early dressed for his day of "being important," but the mere possibility of his swinging in through the door kept Anne on the edge of the gold velvet cushion; there was no sign of a wife.

Mrs. Held clomped into the room. "I patched 'em." She had her hand on John's head, her stump on Issac's, and she twirled them around for Anne's inspection. They looked raw with scrubbing; John's sleeves were pinked off at the elbows, and both had new knee patches of royal blue velvet; their eyes glowed.

"We're going up to the State House," John said. "Uncle Hugh will be there, reviewing the soldiers. He's highfalutin'."

After they left, Anne explored a place both familiar and strange. The front room held the ghost of Geneva on her hands and knees scrubbing with lye soap, as well as the shadows of John Dickerson, Charles Thompson, and Joseph Cannon; Benjamin Franklin, Benjamin Rush, and the other Pennsylvania signers; and all the others waiting out the long, hot Philadelphia summers: John Adams, Thomas Jefferson, Henry Lee, perhaps on occasion General Washington. In the hearth room she pictured Mrs. Held brewing tea for the dignitaries in the new stone fireplace and also herself, a very young woman, rocking a suckling babe and talking to Bess in her head.

The attic roof had been raised to make two cheery bedrooms; new back stairs had been added; the neat garden was green with vines; and the orderly stable smelled of leather, horse, and whitewash. Just a few hours earlier, Hugh's hands had touched these boards as he led his horse into the sunlight; she wondered if his body still was tiny and taut, if he sprang like a cat into the saddle.

Gradually her bewilderment yielded to the reality of her senses—she was home in her brother's house. And Jim's voice came rich with peace: Well, Annie, I see you made it.

She wandered out to the far end of the alley and followed a new lane to Chestnut Street, but a thick wall of noisy townspeople awaiting the parade blocked her way. She retreated to the canal and from there to Walnut Street, which lay almost deserted in the noon sun.

Her stride grew lighter and faster and she was all the way up to Fifth Street before she realized it. As she turned in front of Sarah Franklin's house, a horse and carriage clattered to a stop, and Polly Wharton, in a blaring red silk dress, stepped from it. Anne drew back, immediately feeling once more like Mr. Ferguson's grimy housekeeper. Other women descended; Sarah Franklin bustled out to greet them; another carriage spilled out the Chew ladies, giggling and waving tiny American and French flags. Anne supposed that the dignitaries from the State House steps would join the ladies, and she imagined these women with powdered hair and elaborate feathers swarming like tropical birds about her Hugh.

333

She whirled on her heel, resentful and angry. What had they known of war? Maybe they had suffered with darns in their socks and without pins for their sewing, but she . . . The urge to spit in their faces, rip her hands into Polly Wharton's hair impelled her blindly into a lady emerging from a dressmaker's shop, a ball gown over her arm. Anne glared, furious that these city women, who probably had danced with the British, were tonight going to celebrate victory as though—

Before she knew what she was about, Anne stood beside the sparrow of a seamstress who was preparing to lock the door, asking if she had a gown in her shop. When the little woman shook her head, Anne blurted, "I'm Hugh MacKnight's sister."

The seamstress fidgeted, stammering, "I don't know . . ."

Anne's fingers found the purse she had stuck in her bosom for safekeeping. "Here is his purse with enough gold in it to buy you out lock, stock, and barrel!"

The tiny head bobbed. "I just remembered. Now I don't want you to take offense, Miss MacKnight, but if you need a dress so badly maybe—"

"Tell me."

The woman's head nodded faster. "One of the Frantz girls died. Her mother sent word that she wouldn't be needing the dress and to sell it if I could. I had planned on laying it away for a while but . . ."

"What did she die of?"

The woman's bird-like shoulders rose. "Oh, sort of drifted off, you know. Wasted away quite gently."

"Had she tried on the dress?"

"Oh, a long time ago she came for measurements, but—"

"Would it fit me?"

The bright eyes skimmed Anne's body. "Miss MacKnight has retained her slimness."

Anne snorted. "Yes. I managed that quite nicely. The color?"

"Emerald. Silk. With your eyes and lovely powdered hair . . ."

"The hair is real. I'll take it."

Hugh stood on the courthouse balcony with his head bowed, his shoulders pressed against the warm brick as the Reverend Whitherspoon ranted on in what was billed as the closing prayer. Hugh was tired; the speeches had been scheduled to end at three, and now it was four. The high-pitched voices of the ladies at the Franklin lunch had given him a headache. And tonight at the dance they would be excited, fluttering like hungry birds around him.

If only Ben Rush wasn't sitting there in his carriage waiting for him, he could slip home, pour a little whiskey down his dry throat, nap. He wondered if he could persuade Ben to stop by Grey's Alley for at least a minute. Unlikely. In all circumstances Ben was a very impatient man. But he did need a clean shirt.

He opened his eyes, sure Mrs. Held would be in the crowd somewhere; she hadn't missed one of his speeches since 1776. There was Ben, leaning out his carriage window, disgustedly rapping his fingers against the door. Hugh's eyes worked the crowd. Had she gone already? He began back at Ben's carriage again, and then leaned forward, squinting. Was that she? That woman bending down talking to a little black-haired girl? But Mrs. Held never talked to children. She classified children with the plague.

The edges of the restless crowd were crumbling as men hurried to seats in their favorite taverns. The woman Hugh thought might be Mrs. Held had straightened, but her back was to him. She appeared to be shepardling two redheaded boys as well as the girl through the packed square. Could she be minding them for a friend? Hugh shrugged. But she doesn't have any friends. Still, the square set of the shoulders beneath the black shawl certainly looked like hers.

When the Reverend Whitherspoon finally shouted, "Amen!" Hugh was down the steps like a shot. He had been seized by a wildly irrational need to catch up with his housekeeper—if, indeed, it was she—and those children. He twisted and slid past well-wishers, calling, "Mrs. Held! Mrs. Held!"

She stopped and turned to face him; the children turned, too. Hugh lurched and almost fell. Two more strides and he was on his knees in front of the girl with the oval face; the long, slender neck; the April blue of faraway eyes. "Birdie Jane?" he whispered.

"Hello, Uncle Hugh."

He didn't know what to do with himself. He took her hands and kissed them; he touched her cheek. "Birdie, Birdie . . ."

"I was hoping you'd recognize me."

He had to ask. He had to know. "Your mother?"

"Resting at your house."

He shut his eyes. Anne. Anne. Thank God. Thank God. "She's all right?"

"Well, she didn't get much sleep last night."

"But she's all right? I mean—"

Mrs. Held's voice boomed over Hugh's head. "She's suffered."

A hand tapped his shoulder. "Hello, Uncle Hugh. I'm John, and this is my brother Issac. We're twins, and that was an elegant speech."

Hugh stared at them. The twins. Of course. "Where's your father?"

Johnny bit his lip but kept his eyes level. "We're all that's left."

Hugh bowed his head into his hands. Ben Rush shook his shoulder. "What are you doing, man? Come on! We're late already."

Hugh didn't try to speak or rise. Ben put his arm around him and half-dragged him toward the carriage, but he refused to get in without his family.

At last the splendid carriage pulled by four matched grays and driven by a liveried coachman moved slowly up Market Street. Two grinning barefoot boys perched on the box, and inside, a stiff, smug, one-handed woman sat beside Dr. Rush, while on the other seat Dr. MacKnight stared into the face of his niece while tears streamed down his face.

The crowds thickened around the horses, and the driver called, "Members of Congress! Members of Congress! Give way! Give way!" The people good-naturedly stepped back and slapped the doors of the carriage as it passed. Then, recognizing who was inside, they burst into cheers, causing the barefoot boys in the patched clothes to jump up and down in delight.

The dress, undone from its dust covering, hung swaying and shimmering on the windowjamb in the hearth room; Anne crouched in the old wooden tub that once had bathed her babes. The color's not deep and solid enough for emerald, she decided, more the flickering green of the Allegheny flowing past Glenturk. She cocked her head. How fitting to have Allegheny green cover my rough elbows and leather-skinned arms, and its lacy foam the scarred backs of my hands, but—

and she looked down with pleasure—the fine, broad white beach of my chest will be bare. She had had the seamstress take out the hoops and wires at the waist, saying, "I've spent enough time looking like starved chicken to want to imitate one again," and once home she had chuckled, realizing that now the dress would sweep the floor, covering her moccasins, the only shoes she owned.

She soaked, scrubbed her hair with pine tar soap and lemon, rubbed off layers of old yellow skin, and ground away at her teeth with soda and salt, until by midafternoon she emerged white and pink. Like a lady at court, she retired up the stairs to nap naked between crisp linen and soft quilts.

Ribbons of rose sun slanted from the west window; the sound of a carriage and the children's voices woke her. She struggled to remember where she was and to uncurl the fingers of exhaustion that threatened to drag her back into sleep. Hugh! She sat up, cocking her head to listen. Hugh's bold and clear laugh knocked the breath from her lungs, and the sound of his boots in the hall raised tears that ran down the crumpled creases of her face.

Anne scrambled from bed, and grabbing Hugh's heavy black cloak from a peg, swaddled herself in it. The children's feet pattered, Hugh's stepped firmly on the edges of the treads. "Wait till you see mother's hair, Uncle Hugh," Johnny said. "It's new." Anne rubbed her eyes with the heels of her palms, but her tears only ran faster. The cloak, probably midcalf on Hugh, came to her knees, and she thought how strange her white legs and tan feet must look sticking out beneath it. But, she told herself, it's only Hugh coming. Only my baby brother Hughie. He opened the door and her heart burst.

For a moment they stood gulping in the sight of each other, then hugging, crying, babbling, they swayed in an exultation of resurrection; the years of suffering rolled from Anne's body like the old skin had peeled away into the water of her bath. The children, awed into silence, tiptoed from the doorway to surround them like slender, vertical shafts of a wider embrace. Sunset, wielding an artist's brush, tipped noses, tears, and lips with an ethereal light and flung a halo about their heads.

He put both palms on her cheeks. "Oh, Annie, if you only knew how—"

She touched his hair, saying softly, "I do. I do."

* * *

Hugh and Anne were late arriving at the dinner, and the noise of a fifteen hundred tongues and the glitter of two thousand lanterns greeted them as they drove from Walnut Street into the groomed grounds of the legation. Hugh helped Anne down from the carriage and laughed when he caught a glimpse of her moccasins. "We can't take all the pioneer out of you, can we?"

He stepped back, holding both her hands, gazing at the white curls piled on her head and wrapped with a simple green ribbon, at the embroidered silk that shimmered below the cleavage of her breasts and twinkled down her arms to lacy points. "No gloves, either," she said, wiggling her fingers. "Will Count de Rochambeau consent to eat at the same table with me?"

He kissed her cheek. "I don't think, Annie, he will even notice your hands. There is a glow about you that . . ." He shook his head. "I don't seem to be able to finish my sentences. I hope I will remember my speech."

Two full-dress sergeants-at-arms bowed to them. Hugh pressed a coin into the hand of one. "I want you to go to Mr. John Morton, who's seated at the head table and tell him that an extra place must be set beside Dr. MacKnight. Tell him the Widow—tell him Anne's come home."

"But sir"—the sergeant shook his head—"there's no women at the head table."

Hugh gripped the soldier's arm; temper flushed his cheeks and crusted his words. "Tell him a hero of Fort Jefferson will sit at my right."

The soldier clicked his heels and jogged up the hill of steps. Hugh offered his arm to Anne. "You're trembling."

"Aye. It's been so long. Not that I ever did know how to behave around gentry. I do better as Mr. Ferguson's housekeeper, outwitting dogs and hiding off into the night."

"Well, you don't look like somebody's housekeeper. You look like a queen at the court of Versailles." He kissed her cheek. "Annie, I'm so proud of you."

She laid her hand on his blue velvet arm. "Well, what do you think about me? I have a handsome brother who is a Father of His Country." Step by step, moccasin and shiny buckled shoe began the long ascent.

The French pavilion was a masterpiece of architecture: one hundred feet long with a colonnade forty feet high; the columns sat on marble slabs, and a hundred marble steps led up the west side and another fifty down to the floor of the hall. The east end of the vast room was closed by a wall on which was painted a picture of a rising sun surmounted by thirteen stars; to the left an Indian stood, apparently dazzled by its rays, and on the right another Indian scorned the sack of gold a woman clothed in the flag of Britain poured into his hands. Against that backdrop sat General Washington, Count de Rochambeau, and the members of the Continental Congress.

Anne and Hugh stood at the top between the great columns, Anne thankful that her myopia swirled the scene below into glittering waves of lights, powdered wigs, satin, silk, and velvet. She gripped the gold buttons of Hugh's sleeve as he, in an effort to still her trembling, murmured his speech in her ear. "Our nation is founded on diversity and balance, where all may strive for power, but none shall achieve dominion."

The majordomo rapped his staff and bellowed, "The Honorable Hugh MacKnight, member of Congress from Pennsylvania," then after Hugh whispered in his ear, added, "the Widow Anne MacKnight Glenn MacMeans, late of Mississippi."

Faces were raised; Anne and Hugh started down the long flight of wide steps—dark blue velvet, shimmering green silk, blond hair, white hair, short, tall, brother, sister, like, unlike, she inclining her head, he whispering, "In the great lands to the West live brave, free-spirited men and woman who have risked death and beyond death to secure those valleys and hills and rivers for America. It belongs to them, not to us. Not to Pennsylvania or Virginia or Massachusetts, but to the states they will form there."

Perspiration coated Anne's chest; she tried to breathe deeply, slowly. "It should be theirs to till, to govern, to reap its riches. Each one carving out their homestead free of rents and tithes. A land of living that they may will to the children who follow them."

She saw Glenturk, Breakfast Hill—gold grain, green corn, sheep on the lea, Cinder—and raised her head. They reached the bottom and walked the broad aisle between long tables gleaming in white damask linen, silver, and glass. She heard whispers run from mouth to mouth.

Hugh's voice was a plowshare edged with steel. "This is not a new struggle. It was a battle fought by my father in County Down, Ireland, by my sister beside the rivers of Pittsburgh and on to the farthermost ends of America—the forks of the Ohio and Mississippi, Fort Jefferson."

As they approached the head table John Morton rose, his glass lifted in a salute, his round eyes brimful of tears. Others followed suit—Ben Rush, Charlie Thompson, Joe Cannon; General Washington looked at the others, then stood himself and inclined his head. Someone began the applause that rippled along the table. Hugh squeezed Anne's hand, and her chin came up; she looked down her cheeks and smiled, and when they stood behind the table she saw among the guests the Reverend MacMillan, Robert Bailey's sons, Campbell Jamieson, Horace Jones—all with their glasses raised.

She picked up her own and whispered to Hugh, "To Jim and Andrew. Geneva and Margery. Rabbie and Annilea."

Hugh clicked goblets with her. "And to Jamie and Marybett, and the twins, and Bird—and you."

The next day the sleepy-eyed talk over the back fences and in the coffeehouses of Philadelphia was all of the great celebration. Of how they had been awakened at the edge of morning as the fancy guests from the French legation had poured into Chestnut Street singing "Yankee Doodle" at the top of their lungs. Of how the taverns and houses had emptied as common folk rushed to join the snaking line of velvet and silk. Of how when the fiddlers had struck up again in Market Street Square, Hugh MacKnight had been seen dancing with a tall woman who, talk had it, lifted her skirts high and jigged on the cobblestones—her feet stark naked bare.

Chapter Twenty-seven

While winter padded by on soft paws of slush and fog, Anne lived in the house in Grey's Alley, savoring all the tiny parts of living, glorying in the minutiae about her: the solid rafters above her bed, the coo of Philadelphia pigeons, the deliberate rasp of the coffee grinder—Mrs. Held counted her strokes— and downstairs the sight of Hugh and the twins, flushed and grinning, arm-wrestling across the breakfast table, the pop of bacon on the griddle, Bird's feathery kiss as she hurried off to dame school. Every detail was precious, and with them she patched the cracks of sadness that had allowed her heart to empty.

Dark days she spent beside the hearth, smelling kettles bubble while her mind lay fallow as a stubbled field under snow; but if the day were fair, she dawdled about the market, the shops of Chestnut Street, basking in things familiar, safe, trivial, aimless. With eyes both childlike and ancient she studied the angles of roofs, the shadows of wet weather vanes, the dusting of snow on sills, the reflections in puddled streets; she smiled at men who doffed their hats, joked with ruddy children, cocked her head at the gossip and bits of song that drifted from second-story windows where women shook bedding and left it draped in sun and cold. Then, delighting in every step she took, she walked home, repeating the word like a talisman: home.

For excitement she had Hugh. He bought her a cloak of black wool lined with red satin, a white rabbit muff for her hands, and a sapphire ring for her naked finger. Whatever she fancied—a vase of blown glass, a pastry, a fine cherry dresser with Queen Anne legs—were hers in a twinkling. She said a firm no to a carriage but an exultant yes to a bay mare, the twin of Hugh's. Side by side they trotted through the city streets and cantered about the winter-green countryside, taking dinner at the Red Lion Inn, calling on the Mortons, the Rushs, the Thompsons, where the sight and voices of old acquaintances pulled her life toward wholeness. On Sabbaths brother and sister shared a psalm book—with "Elizabeth Glenn Blackwood" stamped in gold on the cover—and chuckled behind their hands when the Reverend Myles MacMillan, at ninety-one, chided the new minister for putting on Popish airs.

In the early dusk of deep winter afternoons, when Hugh returned from the hospital—only the east wing of the grand design had been completed as yet—they read aloud over bowls of bread and milk. And in the shuttered, folded night—when the firelight had shrunk to embers on the green back log and Mrs. Held snored on her pallet—they spoke both in words and silences of where they had been for the last twelve years and where they might go now. They decided nothing, merely poured ideas back and forth as though they mixed a toddy to be set in the warm ash to mellow.

March winds blustered through the city, sweeping the debris of winter—dust and feathers and dry oak leaves—into the full black river and coaxing sprigs of last year's this and that to green the garden. Restlessness overcame Anne. She would hunker on the damp boards of the back stoop, watching cock robins dig worms, then stride off to market to paw through barrels of smooth, hard seed, sniffing handfuls while asking squint-eyed farmers how the lowlands were drying, the apple trees budding, the new lambs coming along.

When she showed Hugh her plan for the garden, he laughed. "Annie, that's a plan for forty acres, not forty square feet."

She pouted. "No, it isn't. You're not reading it right. See, this is only a corner of corn and this is a few rows of wheat."

"What good is that? A few rows of wheat, a few of oats, a few of flax? Why don't you stick to peas and herbs and flowers?"

She walked to the window. "I like to see grain grow. And even if we just fed it to the horses, it would be a treat for them."

Hugh leaned back, put his stockinged feet up on his desk, and raised an eyebrow.

Anne persisted. "You know how good corn smells when it's growing." She turned away, screwing her face into pensive lines. "Maybe we could get a few acres outside of town. Over by the Schuylkill?"

"Mmmmm," Hugh said. "Buy a few acres. Then buy a horse and plow, a harrow, hoes, scythes . . ."

"Think of how good it would be for the twins. Honestly, Hugh, if they don't get into farming soon I'm afraid they'll run away to sea."

"And who will teach them how to run the first furrow straight?"

"Well, you . . . or I . . ."

"Sissie, I don't want to have anything to do with plowing. I never did, that's why I'm a doctor. . . . You're getting restless, aren't you, Annie?"

"I just want to get my summer planned. If I don't have a garden I don't know what I'll do."

"You miss it, don't you?"

"What?"

"Breakfast Hill Farm. All the bustle of getting ready for spring planting. The lambs and calves, the puppies, gathering the first swamp greens, watching for strawberries."

"Ah ha! See, you do remember how it was."

Hugh nodded. "That's why I never left Philadelphia. I

342

remembered Killyleagh. I remembered the heaviness of everything—lugging milk buckets, pushing wagons out of mud, hauling sledges." The cleft in his chin deepened. "Lifting, carrying, pulling—always straining, always driving yourself beyond the point of tiredness. I would just fold inside and have to sit down. Sometimes I'd see even Pappie turn gray, and once I saw him collapse, just collapse. I knew that life would kill me, that one day I would simply not be able to get up. You were strong. You always found it in you to do the one last thing that needed doing; I couldn't. When my strength drained, that was it; there was no more."

Anne nodded. Farmers died from doing things that couldn't be done. "There were days on the Mississippi when taking one sip of water used an hour of my strength. Tired?" She shook her head. "I can't even imagine now how I did it."

"You could because you cared about saving the children. I couldn't ever care that much about farming." They sat quietly for a minute. Then he asked, "Are you still tired inside, Annie? Outside you look grand, but—"

"Lord no! Just the opposite. I never believed life began at forty. I thought that was just a sop they offered to old folks, but it's true. I'm bursting. My insides are just racing around. Now, take that look off your face, Hugh MacKnight. I am not looking for a husband."

He held up his hand. "All right, all right. Tell me, what would you be doing now if you were at Breakfast Hill?"

"I had a big map hanging in the corner of the hearth room— Jamie had drawn it for me. It showed all the thousand acres, what was woods, wetlands, and the slope of every field. I'd look at last year's dates for plowing and what had been planted where and then I'd write in the new year's plan. Of course, I would have talked to Zac and Tommy—we cooperated on our cash crops—and Andrew. And Bess. She had a good instinct for farming. She—"

They both stared at the fire; outside, sparrows cheeped. "What you're saying, Annie, is that you don't have enough to do here?"

"Well, nothing lasting. I don't seem to be happy unless I get a chance every day to do . . . well, something big. Like staying alive one more hour, or planting a field of flax, or getting a mare bred."

"What about business? I always thought if you had used your dower to set yourself up in trade, you'd have a fleet by now."

She shook her head. "No. Business . . . it's like a game. Not substantial like teaching, or raising children, or preaching—"

"Or politics or doctoring—"

"Or farming."

Hugh swung his feet from the desk to the floor with a thud. "I'll ask about wagons going West, Sis." He set his mouth and reached for his boots.

"But I don't want to leave you."

His eyes glistened like the grass that stood beyond the window, drinking the April rain. "You belong out there at the Forks, Annie. You're that kind of person. You came to America looking for four hundred acres, and you'll never be happy unless you're sitting on them."

She folded the garden sketch in small squares. "I guess I do want to go. But I've been so happy here this winter." She leaned forward and touched his hand. "Why do there have to be choices like this? I really don't want to leave you again."

"It's time."

"Time! Time for this, time for that." She whirled to the window. "I don't know who invented clocks and calendars, but I'm sure it was a man, and he must have had some of the devil in him."

"Why?"

"Measuring time off like that makes life seem all starts and stops. Remember how Mam used to say life was a stew? I always liked that idea better."

Hugh nodded. "If life is a stew, I guess that means nothing is ever lost; even the salt that seems to dissolve is really still there, flavoring it."

"Un-huh. And that's why children see things so clearly. There's not a lot of ingredients in their stew to mix things up. Clear broth."

"But old folks like us . . ."

"Yes. All mushy but full of flavor."

"Hmmm. And it would follow then that people do not ever leave your life."

"No. What's shared is in your pot forever. Like Jim. He never died for me. He's always been right there talking to me, loving me."

Hugh flipped the hourglass. "And a love affair is when the stew boils."

"And the pepper at forty surely spices it up."

344

Hugh rose quickly. "And it looks like your pot is bubbling, Annie. I think I best go look for a wagon heading over the Alleghenies before it boils over." Halfway to the door he stopped and looked back. "Would it have been different if Robert Bailey was still in town?"

Anne stiffened. "Why do you ask?"

"I ran into one of his sons the other day. He says Robert is in the West Indies and coming up to see how the business is. Campbell Jamison is thinking about going West with his father and mother, and that will leave them shorthanded."

"When is he coming?"

"Before fall."

"But he'll be going back to England."

Hugh shrugged. "I suppose."

Anne looked into the fire and lied. "I can't seem to remember what he looked like."

"After you left, he got stout and took to wearing a wig all the time."

"Not very appealing."

"Annie"—Hugh's voice was gentle—"there will never be another Jim. Or Andrew, either." She rubbed the edges of her teeth together. "Robert Bailey could give you a nice life."

"Hugh! Me in a London town house!"

"Well, how about a country estate?"

"Sounds boring."

"After what you've been through it should sound like heaven."

"I've always thought heaven will be very boring."

He fastened his cape. "I'll go look for an exciting wagon West."

A month later, however, Anne still had not left Philadelphia and Hugh teased her, saying she was dallying, waiting for the chance for Robert Bailey to ask for her hand in marriage so she could refuse him.

"Ha! The reason is those prick-me-dainties heading the wagon trains. They answer my first question glibly, the second with arrogance, the third with anger."

"That's what happens when you get old and know more than anyone else."

"There must be someone with more experience!"

In early May, one walked into the yard.

Anne, kneeling in the pea patch plumping up the soil around plants a raccoon had mauled the night before, didn't hear the picket gate open. Humming a little tune, she duck-walked from one plant to the next, not even feeling the eyes of the man who stood watching her.

"'Coons troubling your peas?"

She rocked back on her rump. The man dwarfed the garden, the yard, the house itself. She stared dumbly, then knowingly, but still unable to move.

He shifted his tobacco, spat, and folded his stained, fringed buckskin arms across the muzzle of his long rifle. His voice was much too loud for Grey's Alley. "Why don't you set a couple traps? 'Bout time Brother Hughie got hisself a coonskin cap."

She got to her feet slowly, her head reeling.

He put out his huge arms. "Hello, Annie."

"Zac. Zac."

He lifted her, swung her. Her feet left the ground. His hair smelled of bear grease, woodsmoke, and mountains. "I love you! I love you, Zac!" The warp and the woof were one.

"Too late, Sis!" He roared with laughter. "Me and Tine married up!"

For the next two days Zac, like a large, black, dutiful dog, followed Hugh and Anne about the city; he sniffed the river water, poked in the barrels at the docks, gawked at the buildings, peed in the alleys, and balked at riding in a carriage. The third morning, he set off along Front Street with a tall pile of pelts on his back and returned with four broad-backed Belgian horses and a stout wagon. "Get your gear together, Sissie. We're moving out."

"But—"

"You want to go, don't you?"

"I guess so. I . . . Yes." But her sigh was heavy.

"What's the matter? You got your eye on one of them gussied-up he-sheep? Gawd, I hope this one ain't fifteen, like the last one."

"No. No. The one I hate to leave is Hugh."

"Well, little brother made his choice a long time ago. But a woman like you hadn't ought to be in the city. It's wasteful."

"Ha! I know what you think women are for. Bedding and breeding and tending the fields that a man goes off and leaves because he thinks of more exciting things to do!"

He spat. "Some are."

"And me?"

His eyes were black and shiny. "Annie Glenn, there's nothing you can't do."

"Then why shouldn't I stay here? Maybe marry a merchant."

"And be like that Mrs. What's-Her-Name we visited yesterday? I can't see you spending yourself bossing a gaggle of servants who got nothing better to do than brush lint off a man's coat and straighten lace doilies. Get your gear and your young 'uns together, Annie. We can be outta here by midday."

"Don't boss me around, Zac Glenn! And who are you to tell me what I'd be bored with?"

"Because I was a man when you were a child, and I watched you grow. And I saw you manage the whole kit and caboodle of us for seven years at the Forks."

"Well, maybe that would bore me now."

Zac looked up at the sky. "You know them Quakers that bought Breakfast Hill?"

"What are you talking about?"

"Well, they didn't last too long. Land's been lying empty for two years."

"How long will the weather hold?"

"How long will it take you to get it all together?"

"Well, it's quite an undertaking . . ." She pretended deep thought. "Say, noon?"

He whomped her back. "That's my lass! Oh, you got money? Aunt Bess needs a pile of new books and the like. Lots of children at the Forks now."

"Hugh does."

"Good old Hughie. Well, skedaddle, then, Sissie. If I have to stay past tomorrow my lungs will be filled with chimney smoke, my skull split from the noise, and I'll have caught some disease from these paid ladies."

"Hugh!" Anne called. "Come out here and stand guard over your brother while I go shopping."

Hugh came onto the porch: white stock, white shirt, gold-buckled shoes. The brothers-in-law stared at each other. "What do you want me to do with him, Annie? I only come up to his armpits."

"Keep each other amused."

Zac shrugged. "What do you say, Hughie?"

Hugh shrugged. "I don't know. Indian Queen?"

The two men took a table by the window; Zac downed his ale in huge gulps; Hugh sipped his sherry.

Zac boomed, "You pleased with the peace treaty Johnny Adams and Benjie Franklin worked out with them bloody Britishers?"

347

Hugh, startled at being asked his opinion, drew back in his chair. "We got the Mississippi."

"Good thing, or we'd be going to war again."

"Be a long time before that land's all filled up."

"Don't be too sure about that."

They both drank in silence. Hugh asked, "You thinking of moving on?"

"If those pantywaists in that fancy State House down the road don't give us our state of Westsylvania, I will."

"They won't Zac. Every state is going to try to be just as big as it can. Pennsylvania will never give up Pittsburgh."

"I don't care for lace-gulleted Philadelphia lawyers telling me what I can and can't do."

"Neither did Jim. All you Glenns are alike."

"That's just it. We've been trying for twenty years to get along with you folks. Now we want our own government. You know that Pennsylvania should end at the mountains. Hell, you can have the mountains. Just give us west of Ligonier."

"The Assembly's looking at your petition."

"They damn well better be. If they turn us down, me and Tine are skitting out for the Ohio country." His fist hit the table; Hugh's glass shook. "Goddamn, Hughie, Philadelphia treats us worse than the British did. They think we're some colony of half-wits."

"Did you tell Anne?"

"About leaving? No, once she gets settled in, Breakfast Hill will take up her life. God, its a beautiful place, Hughie. And Tommy and Rhoda's girls are squatted all over the county. They got husbands, kids coming along every year. And, of course, Bess."

"Good old Bess. How old is she now?"

"She says she's seventy-five. Gawd, she looks like she could go another quarter century. The way she still cracks around that schoolroom—"

"Have you heard any more of Esther?"

"Yep. She's with the Delawares in Ohio. Mission village called Gnadenhutten. Them Moravians actually got the Indians farming. She's got a couple of nice-looking boys. Her man is real good to her. In fact, he's the village chief. She's happy."

"Does she talk?"

Zac shook his head. "Only Indian. But she smiles and sings at us. Maybe I can get Annie out to see her sometime. Be good for both of them."

They drank—Hugh working on his third sherry, Zac down to the dregs of his second pitcher. Hugh wiped his finger on the sweaty tin, then drew fancy swirls on the table. "I'm glad to hear Bess is good. I'd like to see her again."

"Well, come along."

Hugh drained his beaker; his voice was thicker. "I suppose I could."

"Good chance, Hughie. Nothing to be scared of when you're going West with Zac Glenn." He knuckled Hugh's arm.

"Summer in Philadelphia is never pleasant. And with the war over and Congress adjourned—"

"Be good for your health, laddie." Zac picked up a fresh pitcher and poured until the foam ran down the sides of his noggin, across the table, and into Hugh's lap. While Hugh stood hastily mopping at his broadcloth britches, Zac said, "I don't see why this place hasn't killed you long ago. And you were always a sickly one."

Hugh ordered a whiskey. "I wasn't supposed to see twenty."

"I know it!" Zac laughed, leaned across the table, and whacked Hugh on the back; his voice could be heard in the street. "But you turned out all right. In fact, I've heard tell you're pretty important. A Founding Father, they say." He tossed the empty tin pitcher in the general direction of the ale kegs. "I'm a Founding Father myself many times over, but none of the brats ever turned out to be a nation!" He howled with laughter and whapped Hugh on the back again.

Hugh downed his dram and grinned like a pixie. "I daresay there will always be more legends about Zac Glenn than about Hugh MacKnight. You should hear some of the things the Pittsburgh Panther is credited with doing."

Zac's roar of glee filled the room, and his fist crashed down on the table once more. "And I'll wager I've done 'em all!" He scooped foam off the new pitcher and rubbed it into Hugh's hair. "You're all right, Brother!"

Hugh sat for a moment, then with great dignity stood and poured his fresh dram of whiskey over Zac's head. "Damn right! We're Convenanters! No king! No bishop!"

Zac rose. The liquor trickled down his cheeks and ran in dark rivers across his leather shirt. Leaning forward, he flopped his hands over Hugh's velvet-coated back. "You should have been at Vincennes, laddie! 'Yankee Doodle, keep it up, Yankee Doodle dandy . . .'"

"You should have been at the victory ball. 'Mind the music and the step and with the girls be handy. . . .'"

Anne emerged from the stable as the two of them came singing, weaving down Grey's Alley. Mrs. Held was on the porch, her arms sternly akimbo across her chest. Hugh disentangled himself from Zac and draped himself around the square wooden figure; with great solemnity he slurred, "I'm going to see my Bess in Pittsburgh. Finest lady in all the world."

As it turned out, they did not leave for a week. Mrs. Held decided that she would not be left behind this time, and so the house had to be closed. Hugh, still riding high on a devil-may-care air, purchased a spanking new Conestoga wagon with a white canvas roof, a blue body, and red wheels; he put tassels and bells on the Belgians and had their thick fetlocks washed and brushed. He bought a traveling chest for his medicines and a new Pennsylvania rifle with plates of etched silver. He outfitted Mrs. Held in a new cloak and bonnet and told Anne to load the wagon with all the furniture she wanted from the house. When all this was added to the crates of books, Zac growled that the belly of the wagon would scrape the road, but he shoved in a dozen bolts of cloth for Aunt Bess and Tine, saying, "If they wear dresses cut from the same cloth, maybe they'll all get on better." He found a collie pup for the twins and a cat with kittens for Bird.

When Myles MacMillan heard they were going, he asked to ride along, saying that he had in mind to establish a school for preachers in Pittsburgh. "Ninety-one isn't old, Zaccheus. The Bible tells of men a lot older than I who conceived children." Zac sighed and said, "Well, you can come along, Reverend. But you'll have to find your own women."

Anne mailed a last letter to Jamie suggesting, that after a year or two in Edinburgh he could finish his degree at Reverend MacMillan's new log-house college. She also wrote to Marybett, saying, "I'll feel much closer to you when I'm back on the Monongahela." It didn't sadden her to see the shutters closed and the nails driven in—this time Hugh would be with her.

Rose shrieks of dawn fired the steeples as the red wagon wheels crunched and slid across the cobblestones of Chestnut Street. Zac held the reins, looking for all the world like a human copy of the powerful horses, and he shouted a great "Good morning!" to every Philadelphian who was up and about. The twins sat on either side of this beloved uncle—who ten years before had gotten totally drunk twice to celebrate their births—their boy chests stout with pride and their hands curled as though they, too, were holding in the clomping beasts; their young voices echoed his ringing hellos. Bird peered from the back of the wagon, her lap full of orange kittens, her eyes missing nothing, from the nightcapped heads that poked through the open shutters to watch them, to the way the dew of the stones gleamed pink in the morning light.

Anne rode beside Hugh—he astride, she sidesaddle, their horses' necks arched against their bits. They were dressed as though going to call on the president of Congress instead of setting off across the everlasting mountains to Pittsburgh, and when Bird called a teasing remark, Anne replied, "Well, Chester is hardly the wilderness, and we might as well look fitting the first day out."

Hugh muttered, "We'll be in itchy linsey-woolsey soon enough."

The Reverend MacMillan sat in a spring chair in the middle of the wagon, sipping his morning whiskey, dipping porridge from the Killyleagh kettle and warbling, "Praise God from whom all blessings flow." Children and dogs and the simple man herding cows to the common escorted them past Independence Hall and the mansion where Robert Bailey's sons lived; then alone the wagon swayed down the dewy road past the weed-covered British fortifications and through the governor's woods to the Schuylkill River. The triumphal arches erected when General Washington liberated the city still spanned the logs beside the ferry. The pulleys creaked and wagon, horses, and people moved smoothly across the morning blue water, and Mr. Grey refused to take any passage money from "such a fine member of our Congress as Dr. MacKnight."

Then they were on broad Darby Road, lined with blooming orchards, freshly plowed fields, and large stone houses.

Bird, skipping beside Anne's horse, looked up and asked, "Is this the road you took with me when I was a babe? I have the feeling I've been here before."

Anne nodded. "It wasn't much of a road then. And when I walked it the first time"—she paused and her eyes grew wide—"I was exactly your age!"

"I'll bet it was all gloomy and you were scared."

"That's true. And I had a rope around my neck."

"Aunt Bess is going to be surprised to see all of us."

Anne pictured Bess on top of Breakfast Hill, shading her eyes and looking east, her skirts whipping about her feet. Beside her Cinder would stomp impatiently and she'd stroke his ebony nose and say, "They're on their way. I feel it in my bones. Zac's found her and they're coming. They're coming."

Anne nodded. We're coming, Bess.

Although I had not written to my family and friends since I landed, not wishing to give them trouble, one of my brothers heard of my being in these parts. He found me in the month of May 1783 and brought me out over the mountains to the family and the haven which I so much desired.

Anne MacMeans Jamison
Pittsburgh, 1824

ABOUT THE AUTHOR

MARTHA BARRON BARRETT, who was born in Pittsburgh, Pennsylvania, graduated from the University of Maine, then raised a family and taught in the Philadelphia area. She now summers on the coast of Maine and goes south to New Hampshire for the winter, where she teaches adults at the University of New Hampshire. Her writing includes a weekly column and features for national magazines. GOD'S COUNTRY is her second novel. Her first novel, MAGGIE'S WAY, was published in 1981.

Heirs to a great dynasty, the Delaney brothers were united by blood, united by devotion to their rugged land . . . and known far and wide as

THE SHAMROCK TRINITY

Bantam's bestselling LOVESWEPT romance line built its reputation on quality and innovation. Now, a remarkable and unique event in romance publishing comes from the same source: THE SHAMROCK TRINITY, three daringly original novels written by three of the most successful women's romance writers today. Kay Hooper, Iris Johansen, and Fayrene Preston have created a trio of books that are dynamite love stories bursting with strong, fascinating male and female characters, deeply sensual love scenes, the humor for which LOVESWEPT is famous, and a deliciously fresh approach to romance writing.

THE SHAMROCK TRINITY—Burke, York, and Rafe: Powerful men . . . rakes and charmers . . . they needed only love to make their lives complete.

☐ *RAFE, THE MAVERICK by Kay Hooper*

Rafe Delaney was a heartbreaker whose ebony eyes held laughing devils and whose lilting voice could charm any lady—or any horse—until a stallion named Diablo left him in the dust. It took Maggie O'Riley to work her magic on the impossible horse . . . and on his bold owner. Maggie's grace and strength made Rafe yearn to share the raw beauty of his land with her, to teach her the exquisite pleasure of yielding to the heat inside her. Maggie was stirred by Rafe's passion, but would his reputation and her ambition keep their kindred spirits apart?   (21786 • $2.50)

 LOVESWEPT

☐ YORK, THE RENEGADE by Iris Johansen

Some men were made to fight dragons, Sierra Smith thought when she first met York Delaney. The rebel brother had roamed the world for years before calling the rough mining town of Hell's Bluff home. Now, the spirited young woman who'd penetrated this renegade's paradise had awakened a savage and tender possessiveness in York: something he never expected to find in himself. Sierra had known loneliness and isolation too—enough to realize that York's restlessness had only to do with finding a place to belong. Could she convince him that love was such a place, that the refuge he'd always sought was in her arms?

(21787 • $2.50)

☐ BURKE, THE KINGPIN by Fayrene Preston

Cara Winston appeared as a fantasy, racing on horseback to catch the day's last light—her silver hair glistening, her dress the color of the Arizona sunset . . . and Burke Delaney wanted her. She was on his horse, on his land: she would have to belong to him too. But Cara was quicksilver, impossible to hold, a wild creature whose scent was midnight flowers and sweet grass. Burke had always taken what he wanted, by willing it or fighting for it; Cara cherished her freedom and refused to believe his love would last. Could he make her see he'd captured her to have and hold forever?

(21788 • $2.50)

Special Offer
Buy a Bantam Book
for only 50¢.

Now you can have Bantam's catalog filled with hundreds of titles plus take advantage of our unique and exciting bonus book offer. A special offer which gives you the opportunity to purchase a Bantam book for only 50¢. Here's how!

By ordering any five books at the regular price per order, you can also choose any other single book listed (up to a $4.95 value) for just 50¢. Some restrictions do apply, but for further details why not send for Bantam's catalog of titles today!

Just send us your name and address and we will send you a catalog!